DEVOUR THE STARS

R Coots

Arts Eklektos

Cambridge, MN

Arts Eklektos
PO Box 70
Cambridge, MN 55008
https://www.artseklektos.com/

Publisher's Note: This is a work of fiction. Names, characters, places, and incidents are a product of the author's imagination. Locales and public names are sometimes used for atmospheric purposes. Any resemblance to actual people, living or dead, or to businesses, companies, events, institutions, or locales is completely coincidental.

Book Layout © 2017 BookDesignTemplates.com

Devour the Stars/R Coots. –1st ed.
978-1-7336359-1-2

First fruits to God

CONTENTS

Author's Note

Thank you for picking up this book! I hope you enjoy. At risk of making you run the other way, be warned that it is full of foul language, violence, and a lot more potentially disturbing topics. If that's not your cup of tea/bottle of whiskey, I get it.

If, at the end, you decide you want more, feel free to join my mailing list: https://www.artseklektos.com/ml-landingpage/ There'll be short stories to expand on the world, art, bits of world building, and the occasional rant about the math of space travel (math, ew).

Prologue -- Syrus

These creatures might look human. Might even talk and walk and sometimes act human. Make no mistake. They are nothing like humans. Forget that and next thing you know, you'll wake up in the Great Beyond, wondering how your life ended so fast.
-Professor Tolst, New Hopks College of Medicine

Syrus came back to himself sitting in a puddle of blood, groggy with a rage hangover, not sure where he was. Well, besides sitting in a puddle of blood. That didn't help much. He'd woken up like this so many times, it was difficult to tell if he was coming out of a drunken riot or if he'd had a particular reason for jumping the nav beacons and striking out for madness uncharted.

Fuck it all.

The lack of sniggering clued him in to the fact that this was a special case. Rissa always made herself known, whether in person or as self-appointed and absentee conscience.

Nothing.

He could count on one hand the number of times his rages silenced her.

The terror jumped up and kicked him in the face. With it came the memory of the last time he'd felt like this. Rissa screaming for help. He'd been so scared for her, he couldn't even pick a fight with her imaginary self. Hadn't stopped to listen to the comms. Hadn't checked his radar. Nothing at all to cover his trail. He'd just jumped in the closest ship and taken off.

She hadn't been there.

His head felt like it weighed a thousand pounds, but Syrus managed to look up and take stock of his surroundings. He was in a small infirmary. Their medunits looked different than the Navlad models. The display towers were thinner, more rounded around the edges, but the dials and readouts were the same in a general sort of way. A mangled arm hung over the edge of the far unit.

She was here after all. But only in body.

People stood around him, their dark armor blending in with the darker metal of the wall behind them. Splashes of blood decorated the floor, ceiling, and everything in between. Too much to have come out of Rissa.

Right. There'd been someone. Someone laughing at him. Saying something about death. And strength. Power, maybe?

A spacer-white face swam to the surface of his memory, topped by a shock of butter-blond hair and set with bright green eyes. With the image came the laugh. So full of smug pride that it felt like having a bucket of oil thrown in his face.

Syrus clenched his hand and met resistance. Soft, squishy resistance. He looked down. An eyeball sat in his palm, nerves and blood vessels trailing off to one side. He poked at it. The cornea gave, turning a little. Under the smears of blood, he could see a green iris, all the more bizarre for the burst blood vessels around it.

Who's laughing now, dick?

Blinking, Syrus looked up. Was that... It almost sounded like her. Was that someone else's body on the med unit table? Had the fucker lied about killing her?

That much he could remember, before the red haze of fury swallowed his short-term memory. The bastard had been describing... things. Things he'd done to Rissa. Rissa, who'd been so innocent and pure.

That was a definite snort of amusement. And it was definitely her voice talking to him. She may have been innocent at one point, but not since she'd met him. Pure? That wasn't very accurate, now was it?

"'F you're really dead, rather remember how you were." He didn't realize he'd spoken out loud until he heard the rasp of his voice in his ears. It was rough and broken, cracking in the middle of the words.

A fragment of someone screaming flitted through his brain. Himself, as he pounded muscle and bone to pulp.

Well, that explained it.

"Unfortunately, sir, she really is dead."

Syrus's head snapped up and he rocked back on his heels to look at the man who had stepped away from the pack lining the walls. Syrus wondered how he'd missed the man. He should have been able to tell someone was about to speak. Had an opinion. Something.

Fucked up people. Everyone on the ship was tainted. Between the poisoned air and the emotional muck, he felt like he'd been running up mountains with a full pack strapped to his back.

The man took another step forward and Syrus forced his eyes to focus. Spacer-pale skin, light enough to show blue veins underneath. Blue eyes shadowed by an ornate helmet that had no business in combat. Blood gleamed a bright, wet red where it covered his armor. Syrus wondered who it had come from. The dead man? Rissa?

Does it matter? What are you going to do about it?

Shut up, he told Rissa, glad he kept the words inside this time. *Unless you have something helpful to say.*

You're in trouble; how's that?

Syrus gritted his teeth and levered himself to his feet, dropping the squashed eyeball as he went. His clothes were so saturated with blood that he was literally sticking to things. He almost had to peel himself off the floor.

How long had he been sitting there?

Long enough.

Better question. Why hadn't anyone taken advantage of his vulnerability while he was down there? From what he'd seen of these people the last week or so, he shouldn't be alive right now.

"Sir? Your name please?"

They were calling him sir. The fuck?

"Shock," said a new voice. Female. A woman eeled her way up next to the man and watched Syrus with a critical eye. "Or the next thing to. If I didn't know better—" She scowled and leaned forward. "You are not a true Imperial."

Syrus scowled at the woman, trying to figure out what she meant. He sure as fuck wasn't one of the Edgelanders. Or from this floating freak show. What else did that leave? The Seps Coalition? They never left their sector.

You are a moron, Rissa told him, putting a phantasmal hand on his back. Right over the place where his maruste lived, displayed by the nanites that rode in the blood of anyone born in the Navlad Empire

Oh.

"I'm Savage," he told the woman. He waited for her to step back and look disgusted, but she only looked interested. Maybe a little irritated. Well, that was new.

He turned back to the man before she could come to her senses and realize how dangerous it was to be in arm's reach of him. "Who are you?" Syrus swallowed against the scratch in his throat and tried again. "The hell do you want?"

"I am Quinn, Second of the Kuchen Fleet Turan, temporary commander of the flagship *Edde Belo*, formerly under the care of Warlord Brander." The man's face soured slightly. "Which should be impenetrable to outFleet infiltrators."

Syrus coughed and spat a wad of blood to one side. One of his teeth felt loose. "Yeah, well, your air processors need some work."

Next to Quinn, the woman's blank face twitched. Some emotion buzzed in the air around her. From Quinn, nothing.

"Unfortunately, that is impossible," the man said. "As for what I want, that is currently... fluid." He tipped his head at the medunit table and the body under its hood. "What is done with her depends on you. She has already been promised."

"Promised?" So far he'd managed to keep from looking at the body in the medunit. That last comment though, it nearly made him lose his fight with his instincts.

No. Remember her as she was. Not as she is now.

"As a reward. For services rendered. The one who is to claim her has already been notified."

Suddenly, some of the things he'd seen and heard as he ghosted his way through the ship made a lot more sense.

He nearly lost his shit all over again. "What," he said through gritted teeth, "do you mean? Her body? To a *person!*?"

Neither of the people in front of him so much as batted an eye. Or let their emotions loose for him to feel.

No. Keep your head, you dumb fuck. Don't lose control again. Look at the mess you made in here. You think painting the whole ship red is going to help? Don't think. Don't feel. Don't turn back into the monster. There's no one around to tame you, remember? Have to do it yourself again. Like the Academy. These people are your enemies. You can't afford to let them see how weak you really are.

Somehow, though he'd never understand what made it possible, he managed to stuff it back inside. Tamp it down a hole and slam a lid on tight.

Even Rissa went quiet. He was alone in his head.

Just the way he needed it.

"There is one way to get her back. If . . ." Quinn trailed off and moved his face into a thoughtful expression. Something finally leaked through the mask. Something like triumph.

Syrus just looked at the man. Who knew what this bastard would do if he realized that not only could Syrus beat people to death, he could feel people's emotions and know when they were faking.

Fucker might decide to toss his guest out an airlock. Or worse, try to force the use of that talent in the mad crusade these people seemed to live for.

No, don't remember. Remembering is bad. Just pay attention, you moron.

Always so helpful, he told Rissa's ghost. *Except it didn't sound as much like her as before.*

"Warlord Brander was our strongest warrior," the man said. "Now that you've killed him, we are in need of a new one."

Syrus decided he was sticky and exhausted and in no mood to play games with a man who didn't have the decency to kill his prey. "Got a point in there?"

Around the room, the watchers shifted, armor and clothes scraping the walls softly. They sounded like a nest of snakes getting ready to attack. The woman next to Quinn went from impassive to irritated and back again so fast that Syrus nearly missed it.

Quinn bent down and scooped the battered helmet off the floor. He shook it sharply, flinging a spray of blood and other assorted tissue from the insides before holding it out to Syrus. "According to the laws of the Kuchen Fleet, you have won the Helm of the Warlord. And all the rights that go with it."

Syrus stared at it for a moment, wondering if his stolen translator had shorted.

The man kept holding the helmet out. The murmurs and rustling and clanks of armor around the room finally told Syrus he *had* heard right. This lunatic was serious.

"A question." A woman leaned forward from her place along the wall and touched Quinn's arm. "If I may?"

The man eyed her, then nodded. She looked at Syrus. Her brown eyes were dark, both literally and figuratively. Her mouth was small, lips thinned further by the frown pulling at their edges. She was spacer white, but her blondish hair had a smear of damp red in it. Probably from getting too close to the wall.

"Ask," Syrus muttered before she could open her mouth.

She narrowed her eyes at him and turned back to Quinn. "Why trust him? He is Imperial Navlad. We are killing his people."

Syrus laughed so hard he couldn't even tell what they were thinking. The ridiculousness of it was too much. He grabbed the feeling and used it to brace his shields. "You," he said, then coughed out another laugh and shook his head. "You just got done asking why I'm *not* Navlad. And now? Lady, you're the best laugh I've had in a month."

Probably the last you'll have in a long time, too.

That sobered him up real quick.

Syrus snatched the helmet, ridiculous thorny inlay and all, and tucked it under his arm. It was too dented to fit on his head, never mind the blood. "First order," he snarled. "Her body is mine."

The voices of the people lining the walls rose from a murmur to a shout. Syrus braced himself against the heat of their anger and watched Quinn, waiting. After a moment, the other man's eyes softened slightly and he bowed, sweeping an arm in the direction of the corpse in the medunit.

Then, still silent, he turned on his heel and headed for the door at the far end of the room. Syrus watched him go.

Rissa said nothing. Syrus decided he was ok with that. Whatever was keeping her quiet, at least he wouldn't be dealing with the constant internal monologue of a dead woman. Nothing his imagination cooked up ever compared with the real thing anyway. Now that she was gone—really gone this time—the fake was all he'd ever have.

She deserved a better memorial than that.

One -- Syrus

The only truth in life is strength.
Strength of arms and strength of will.
The man who has neither has no business wearing the Helm.
     -Kuchen proverb

The rard of the Ludesab star system hobbled down the ramp of a Fleet drop ship and fell to his knees at the foot of a makeshift throne, coughing weakly.

Syrus, sitting on the throne and wishing the day would just end already, looked down at the miserable, shaking piece of shit and curled a lip. "How did you manage a bunker in the middle of a fucking acid lake?"

The fear rolling off the broken rard stilled, electric prickles digging into Syrus's skin and turning to the crawling itch of disgust before slipping into the slimy ooze of a person who knows his superiority is bred into his bones.

Syrus leaned forward and kicked the rard in the face. Not hard enough to break anything, but enough to tip the man ass over end and send him rolling across the clearing in the middle of the rocky outcropping. He hit one of the granite boulders on the other side with a *whumph* of escaping air and a cry of pain. His son, still standing on the ramp of the ship, yelled and started fighting the Fleet soldiers who had him by the arms. They let him struggle, bracing their legs and planting themselves like they'd grown roots.

Around him, the slopes were a moving, shifting mass of people. Bloodied, bruised, and in some cases broken, they stood, knelt, or lay strapped to body boards propped up on the rocks. The Fleet soldiers had gathered up as many of the high-ranking prisoners as they could find and stripped their shirts to check the maruste on their backs for size and detail. Then the prisoners had all been herded through the inoculation process before getting dropped in this natural amphitheater to watch their lives be destroyed.

Now they coughed as a whole, trying to get rid of the smog of factory output clogging their lungs and draw in something better. Listening to the racket they made, Syrus would bet not a one had ever stepped outside the hab domes that covered this planet like blisters. The wind blew steadily, carrying particulate along to scrape at their eyes, their bodies, the landscape itself. Syrus could feel it scratch at his armor the way the crowd's emotions scratched at his mind.

This wasn't everyone. That wasn't possible or practical. But they'd be enough. Enough to send back into the system and tell the other Imperials how their new governor, or anined, took control. And how he would hold it.

Blood. It would involve a lot of blood.

The soldiers who had hold of the son of the rard decided they'd had enough of his temper tantrum. One of them cuffed the boy over the head. He slumped, stunned. The guards hauled him down the ramp and over to the edge of the clearing. While they tied him down with shackles and grav tethers, the guards in charge of the rard did the same. Once Syrus was sure there wouldn't be any sort of escape attempt, he ignored them and turned his attention to the men lining up in front of him. Ralenen—the highest unit commanders in the Fleet, barring himself and Quinn. He would have liked to kick these men across the clearing too, but it'd be harder. And it'd draw this little ceremony out far longer than he wanted. Breathing air that the Imperials couldn't might be an effective bit of intimidation, but that didn't mean it was comfortable.

Effective. Look at that word. How many credits you think you'd get paid if they knew you could say it in more than one language?

Syrus shoved the voice back down, to the corner of his brain where he kept everything else not needed for of surviving from day to day. He didn't have time to deal with his conscience, imaginary or not.

The ralenen stood looking at him, adding the slow drip of acid contempt and the heat of anger to the electric fear radiating off the watching prisoners. Fuckers. Whole fucking Fleet felt like this, damn it all. Even the ones who claimed to support his rule as Warlord did their best to bake him dry and corrode his brain.

So far he'd managed to hide his reaction to the constant state of near rebellion, but he knew if they ever figured out they could torture him just by standing in the same room as him, his ass was cooked. Too fucking bad his survival instinct outweighed the temptation to let them in on his secret. Three years and he was still paying the price for keeping Rissa's body from desecration.

Survival was a fucking bitch.

"Who wants this fucking shithole backwater?" Syrus snarled down at his men. "Step up."

Ten of the thirty men separated themselves from the rest and came to stand in front of him. Syrus nodded to the others, who stepped back to line the sides of what was now an arena. The ten challengers thumped their fists to their shoulders and bowed.

Syrus eyed them for a moment, then looked around for his second. He found Quinn standing in the hatch of the drop ship, almost completely hidden by the shadows of the interior. Syrus snorted. The man knew how to make an entrance when he wanted to.

"Quinn," he yelled. "You ready to get this thing started or what?"

If the man had a problem with the way his warlord handled the job of taking official ownership of a solar system, he'd never said anything one way or the other. He bowed, the bleak sunlight gleaming off the silver enamel of his helmet, and came down the ramp to stand in front of the candidates.

Syrus tuned out for the speech. He'd paid attention the first couple times he'd heard it, back when he was still learning this warlord shit and getting used to the fucked-up way the Fleet ran its business. But the words Quinn used didn't change much. So long as the trials went as planned, Syrus figured he didn't need to worry about them. He'd be gone by sunset and this backwater hole wouldn't be his problem to deal with. A few days in his quarters reminding his women that he still existed, a real bath, and he'd be off to stomp the next bunch of Imperial bastards into the ground.

Quinn shouted, and Syrus hauled his focus back to the arena. The ralenen were trying to kill each other. It was more organized than the free-for-all of battle, but since the pairs of fighters had all started at once, it wasn't tidy either.

Quinn moved through the combatants, judging. Watching. Every so often he'd put himself between an attacker and a downed body, hauling the winner off before the man could strike the killing blow. Feet churned the bloody sand to sticky mud. More than one man caught a glancing blow from a knife. Med-techs ran in under flailing limbs and slashing knives, loading one man after another onto floating stretchers.

Each time a wounded ralen rose, dripping, he snarled louder and swung harder. Some were more calculating. Some trusted brute force. They all puffed and blew, and Syrus knew it wasn't just because of the air quality. He could feel their emotions from here. He could barely keep a lid on the answering temper churning his insides. Lucky, his duties as Warlord didn't include keeping the ralenen in line during a Challenge.

Best he could figure, the reasoning was that they might turn on their warlord, knife him, and fuck up the leadership of the Fleet itself. Syrus didn't care about that. In his case, he'd be just as likely to lose his shit first and rip their throats out. Anything to make the pain stop.

The Challenge didn't last long. Quinn dragged the new anined off his last opponent and threw him at the feet of the throne. Then he planted a foot in the man's spine to keep him from going after the stretcher. Syrus raised an eyebrow at Quinn. For the third Campaign in a row, these two ralenen had found each other in the melee. And for the third time, the same man had been loaded on a stretcher and carried off. Well, their little pissing contest was over now. Syrus took a deep breath and braced himself against the emotions churning through the air around the anined. He still hadn't figured out how these people could be happy and angry at the same time.

"Milord."

Syrus looked up at Quinn as the man crunched his way up the hill to the throne. A killer's blue eyes watched him from under the man's helmet. The snakes that wrapped and twisted around the brambles lining its rim gleamed dully in the flat light. For one second, Syrus almost thought the snakes had turned to watch him, but it was just a trick of the light.

Fucking snakes. Why the hell did a space-going fleet have such an obsession with trees and snakes?

"Milord, are you ready?"

Syrus jerked out of his daydream of bashing that helmet to pieces and looked back at the ralen standing in front of him. "Yeah," he said. He waved at a cluster of soldiers standing just behind the throne and called out, "String him up."

The men obeyed, hauling long metal bars down the hill and dropping them in the middle of the little arena. More men brought equipment, while the rest started lifting and bracing things into place. In minutes, a framework had risen on the bloodied rocks and the soldiers started bolting on supports to brace it against the winds.

"Milord, if I may."

Syrus decided that if Quinn called him "milord" one more time, he was going to do something unacceptable and violent. His gloves creaked as he gripped the arms of his throne and waited, wondering if the man would say it again.

Nothing. Just expectant silence and the emptiness of feeling only this man could manage.

Syrus sighed. "What now?"

"Milord, we have a report in from the next system."

There were two possible exits from this shithole. One full of people to Conquer, the other *not* full of people. Of course Quinn was going to make him guess which one he was talking about. Syrus raised his eyebrows at the man.

Quinn coughed. "The unpopulated one."

Syrus took the slate Quinn handed him and propped it against his knee. He didn't crack it in half or twist it to pieces, or any of the other things he wanted to do. And he didn't order the soldiers to grab Quinn and drag him down to the torture rack. The rard was already in place anyway, dangling from the top spar and coughing quietly.

"We don't have a complete scan just yet. Long-range units are still sending back data on individual satellites. The mainframe of the *Edde Belo* is still parsing what geologic and astrological data there is. There is a planet in the habitable zone." Quinn stopped, frowning.

"The data, Quinn."

"It's the fourth planet from the sun," Syrus's second said. "Preliminary scan says it's uninhabited. But . . ." He looked down at his slate and seemed to make some sort of internal calculation before swiping his fingers across its surface. A batch of pix bloomed on Syrus's slate. "There are structures. They look Navlad."

So much for the data from the dummy-sat. Fucking thing had gone through, latched on to the Barbican framework on the other side, and told them nobody'd been through the gate since "ever." Right. Trust a sat labeled "dummy."

"It find any other keys coming in to that gate?" Syrus asked.

"No, my lord. Not yet."

Figured. It took the techs weeks to punch their way through the encryptions on the Barbs, forcing the keys to reveal themselves so the Fleet could move on to the next system. They started the moment Conquest began on the current system. Fuck, half the reason the Fleet didn't just Seed the planets as they went by was to give the techs time to break through to the next system.

This go around they'd been focusing on the populated system. The empty one was just a formality, a place to send green troops from the reserves on already-Conquered planets to season them up a bit. Now it looked like the techs would have to shift their focus. And fast.

The rard screamed and Syrus looked up from the slate. From the way the Imperial man strained against his restraints, the new anined had just made his first cut. The tethers between the shackles and their anchors snapped him back into place, a little tighter than before. Even odds he'd get his arms pulled off before the new anined was done skinning him.

The anined did something else out of sight, and the rard screamed again. The noise cut off halfway through as the man dissolved in broken coughs. But his fear didn't stop. Even up the hill, Syrus could feel it stabbing at his nerves.

He looked back down at the slate before he gave anything away. An empty system? Maybe a vacation planetside was what he needed. Go down, look around, not worry about how many men they'd lost in the latest push or if they had enough birds in the air to cover them all.

"Sure there aren't any people down there?" he asked. They'd been planning to use the next system to reorganize the ships in the Fleet. Bring up reserves from shipyards and planets further back in the chain of occupied systems. Then Seed the satellites so the Navlad couldn't use them, check for another Barb, and move on.

Quinn frowned and almost twitched. "Not so far as the sats can tell. No defenses in atmo or orbit, either."

Something in the quality of the other man's voice registered a bit clearer. This was about the buildings. Did he have some data he wasn't sharing? Something more than ruins that may or may not have been Imperial Navlad?

In the past few hundred years since the Navlad Empire started fracturing around the edges, any number of planets had been abandoned. Fuck, whole solar systems had packed up their colony ships, pulled all the solar panels around their respective stars, and taken off.

Some had headed for the Core of the Empire. Some had scattered to the Borders. Various conglomerates, federations, and even single-system holdouts like this one were scratching out a living just beyond the reach of the Imperial Armada. But not out of reach of the Kuchen Fleet. As far as Syrus knew, no one could keep the Fleet from forcing their way through any Barbican they found. Not with the security protocols this side of Hadra's Net so outdated.

Sometime in the past, there must have been a reason for a Barbican in this system to lead to the next. Structures meant people. Had they moved here, to *this* system? None of the histories he'd read mentioned anything about Barbicans being set without purpose. They were the gateways of the universe, the roads around the Galaxy. They made troop transport, freight, and even private travel possible. They shortened travel time from years to minutes.

Without the Barbicans, the rardog of the outer systems would have no way to back the capital. Agricultural Ajiri planets would have no way to ship their goods to the industrial Kovavek planets. They'd have no market outside their own systems. And without Ajiri planets, the Core and Kovavek planets would starve in short order. There were limits to how much of a population you could support when space was limited and your facility was dedicated to turning out battery components instead of food.

The Kuchen Fleet knew this. It was how they'd managed to penetrate so far into the Empire. It was why they'd started this mad quest to begin with. The Fleet ate away at the edges as the Empire crumbled from the outside in. And as they came, they absorbed the technologies of the conquered worlds and set the shipyards and manufacturing plants to building Kuchen designs instead.

"What aren't you telling me about this system, Quinn?"

"There seems to be a power source on the habitable planet." The look on Quinn's face would have been a scowl on anyone else.

Syrus raised an eyebrow, then laughed. "When was the last time we ran across an empty system? *Nothing* in it?"

"Before you joined us, My lord." The look on his face said: Don't ask questions if you already know the answer. Syrus made a rolling motion with his free hand. Quinn shut his mouth.

"You're paranoid," the warlord told his second. "That's good. But there's still a signal down there."

"My lord," Quinn almost blurted. "The risk."

"Of it being a trap?" Syrus tapped the edge of the slate. "That's true, but—"

The rard hadn't quit screaming since the anined first touched him. Until now, Syrus had shoved the happenings in the arena down into the deep parts of his brain, to be endured and ignored.

Fear blasted its way up the slope, through Syrus's exposed skin, and up his nervous system, frying the base of his brain. He snarled and nearly dropped the tablet. Stupid fucking bastard. Stupid relic of an obsolete—

He stopped. Set the slate on the arm of the throne and thought about what he was about to do. Could he do it? Could he manage it without blowing his cover?

How else was he going to find anything out? He could wait until they got through the Barbican. And maybe spring a trap before their sats could send them fresh data. Or he could find out what he could here and maybe avert disaster.

His only option in that direction lay with the rard. He couldn't send the techs back into the domes to see if any data centers had survived the last push his men had made through there. There wasn't time. Besides, he was only nominally in charge of the system. The new anined had just as much right as his warlord to say what would happen here. Once the rard was dead, the anined would have almost total control.

Syrus stood before he could talk himself in any more circles, then started down the slope to the clearing and its occupants.

"Milord?" Quinn asked.

Syrus ignored him and kept moving. A sort of rustling noise filtered through the air around him, the prisoners muttering to themselves as they watched his progress towards their ruler.

He stopped at the edge of the clearing and took a breath. If he'd thought it was painful when he was up on the throne, then being this close was hellish. He wanted to tear his armor off until he got to the nerves. Not only did he have some thousand odd people watching him like he was going to rip their leader's face off—now he had the anined giving him the stink eye. And putting out enough furious heat to make the dormant volcano they were standing on start spitting lava all over again.

Where was a winter lake when you needed one?

Syrus settled back on his heels and dropped his hands to the guns holstered on his hips. Deep breath. Feel the bad air burn the throat, and exhale. He could manage this. He'd managed worse. A voice screamed at him from the sinkhole in the back of his mind, telling him to get a grip and not give in. He ignored it. There was no one around to knock him on his ass or keep him from killing everyone in reach if he lost control. He'd have to manage the same way he always managed. Sheer force of will.

He snorted and curled a lip.

The new anined opened his mouth, probably to demand an answer as to why Syrus was interrupting the Transfer ritual. Syrus held up one gauntleted hand. "Just have some questions," he told the man.

The ralen growled—out loud, even—but stepped back and lowered the knife he'd been using to peel the maruste from the rard's back. Blood dripped on the gravel in small *pat pat pats*. The stones crunched under Syrus's feet as he circled the little clearing, moving closer to the scaffolding with each turn. The tension in the air climbed as he went, but he braced his shields as well as he could and kept moving.

By the time he came to a halt in front of the croaking rard, he could almost bear the pain. At least, enough to talk without losing his breath to agony. Syrus unclipped the hilt of a knife from his belt and used it to tip the rard's chin up. Bloodshot eyes met hard brown. Syrus waited, wondering if the rard would recognize what stood in front of him. But the only thing he saw in the man's eyes was panic.

"How many keys does your Barbican have?" he asked, slowly enough to disguise the rasp at the back of his throat. Just the air. That was all. Just the tainted air.

The rard's face fell. So, he'd hoped for some sort of salvation.

Syrus jabbed the rard in the throat with the business end of the hilt. "How many?"

"Two," the man croaked, trying to pull away from the knife hilt and failing.

A flare of heat at Syrus's back made him turn to look at the ralen. The man stopped, halfway into a step that would have brought him within punching range of his warlord.

"You stay fucking put," Syrus snarled.

The rard twitched against the weapon Syrus still had against his skin. Something surfaced and roiled under the fear, but it wasn't strong enough to make out clearly.

Syrus looked back at the prisoner. "Just the two? We found three."

The rard's Adam's apple bobbled against the hilt. "No! No! There are only the two. Please! The one, Antesab, the—the one you came from; and the next one in the chain! Erlkonsab! There isn't a third, I swear it!"

"Then why the fuck did we find three?" Syrus roared as he shoved the man back. The rard rebounded against the limits of the grav tethers attached to the frame of the scaffold and wobbled in midair as the shackles and their anchors readjusted themselves for the movement.

Too late, Syrus realized he'd activated the knife. The rard sagged in his restraints. Blood leaked out his throat around the living metal of the blade, which had grown through his windpipe and probably his spine too.

Syrus snarled and pulled the weapon free. Fucking perfect. Just what he needed.

"You! You ruined it!"

Something hit him from the side. Syrus went down under the weight of the enraged anined and the heat of his fury. In the background, the crowd shouted. He forced the noise from his mind. There was just the enemy, a knife he *shouldn't* use again, and the knowledge that unless he could get this man off him, it wouldn't matter if he had any sanity left at all.

Syrus dropped the knife, scooped up a handful of dirt and rock, and scrubbed it in the man's face. The man yelled and clawed at his eyes. Syrus lunged up. His armored fist hit the anined under the chin and sent him falling backward. Syrus followed, scrabbling to his knees, and then to his feet so he could loom over the man. Stupid fuck kept trying to get up, eyes screwed shut and roaring at the top of his lungs.

Syrus planted a knee in the man's stomach. Then he sank his fist into the man's jaw again. Something crunched, and the mandible shifted sideways by at least an inch or so.

The man found enough breath to shout, and then to scream as the pain hit. One flailing hand caught Syrus in the shoulder, the other upside the head. Stars and sparklers went off behind his eyes and he snarled. Fucking bastard. Think he was going to take out his warlord? Think he could take down the man who'd been holding the Helm for three fucking years? Against the whole *Fleet*?

Syrus pulled his fist back and took aim.

And found himself caught, arms pinned in a grip he couldn't break. No amount of straining or thrashing or well-used elbows could get him loose. Whoever it was lifted him to his feet and hauled him away from the fallen ralen. Syrus tried to throw his weight forward and then back, to overbalance whoever had hold of him. No good. He went for his captor's instep. No luck.

Milord! Milord, calm down!

Syrus stopped lunge. He knew that voice. That voice never called him "milord."

"Milord?"

That was the right voice. Not the woman who'd just been yelling in his ear, dead three years at least. What the hell?

He looked down. Two of the beaten man's aides were helping their superior up. Around him, he heard shouts. Screams. And weapons firing. He caught his balance as Quinn let him have his feet back, then turned to scan the crowd. They were trying to riot. The Fleet soldiers mowed them down like so much dead grass. Now that Syrus wasn't so surprised, he could feel the electric fear and acid hate they were giving off.

Or was that coming from inside?

He shook himself hard to resettle the armor on his body, then looked at Quinn—who was as calm and collected as if he were always dragging his warlord off some victim or another. As if he felt nothing at all. How the hell did the man do it?

Quinn would never tell. So instead of asking, Syrus said, "Well, that was interesting."

"Not quite the word I would use, milord."

Syrus snorted. So long as no one was screaming at him in a dead woman's voice, he didn't much care what they thought. He checked his thoughts, just to be sure, but she seemed to have dropped back into the sinkhole where he'd been keeping her. Along with all the combustible emotions he'd shoved down there with her. He stomped on the metaphorical lid, wedging it in a bit tighter, and sighed. It would figure that Quinn had come to lock his warlord down. Deciding who would take the Warlord's Helm while the Fleet was still under Campaign law would have been a bitch.

"Yargh!"

"Sir, please, hold still!"

"Yooar!"

Syrus turned around. The anined, jaw still hanging oddly, had gotten free of his keepers and was coming back for round two. Syrus grabbed one of the man's outstretched arms, yanked, twisted his hip, and let the man fly. Right into Quinn's armored body. Quinn braced himself and the anined hit the gravel with another yell.

"Well fuck," Syrus muttered. He grabbed the man by the hair and planted one knee in his back. "You want to give this up already?" he asked. "Cause the guy you thrashed to win this place is still alive. We can always give it to him."

The anined groaned. Syrus thought he felt heat blisters forming under his gauntlets. "Yeah, yeah. I killed your toy. Guess what?" He slewed the man's head around in the direction of the drop ship. The guards hadn't forgotten their duty. They had the rard's son on his knees, hands pinned behind his back and guns to the back of his head. "Now that his dad's dead, that little shit gets the job. And you get to finish your ritual. Ok?"

The anined growled.

Syrus forced the man's head up and down in a mockery of a nod, then let go and stood. "Ok. Quinn, tell the pilot to spin up the drives. He can finish without us."

"But milord."

Syrus glared at his second. "It's a formality anyway. We all know it. We're going to go get some real work done. Soon as we hit orbit around that planet, we'll take an atmo down."

Quinn's lips thinned, but he said nothing. Which was enough of an answer in itself. No. He didn't want his warlord running off for a side trip. He wanted to get on with finding a *populated* planet to bomb down to dust. Because mass murder was how he got his rocks off. Or something like it. As long as Syrus did what Quinn wanted, they were golden. But the minute his warlord got the bit in his teeth, this motherfucker decided life wasn't so good anymore.

Syrus gave his second a flat stare and waited. After another moment or two, Quinn gave him a half bow and started speaking into his comm unit.

Turning, Syrus climbed the short slope to where his throne perched on the rocks. He grabbed his helm, gold inlay and all, off the spike where he'd left it and slammed it over his head. Clean air filtered through the breathers built into the helmet and filled his lungs. His mind cleared slightly. Calm. Quiet. Just him and his demons.

Syrus took another breath, just because he could, and headed for the dropship. The crowds kept trying to riot, but the soldiers had them fairly well subdued. Syrus shook his head. He should have this fucking bucket welded to his skull, like a crown. Maybe then he could be free of people messing with his emotions.

But that wouldn't work. Someone would try to take the damn thing away from him soon enough. Now that the Campaign was over, the fuckers had free rein to throw as many Challenges at him as they could before the next Campaign. And if he welded the Helm on, well. They'd just hollow out his skull and wear that instead.

He smiled where none of them could see. They'd try.

TWO -- SYRUS

Some say they are searching. Looking for a place to settle. Those people are sentimental fools. If they are looking for a home, there are plenty of empty planets free for the taking. No. What they want is to swallow the Galaxy whole.
      -unnamed survivor, Vakunesab

Syrus cursed as he narrowly missed stepping in the blood on his way out of bed. One of the women still buried in blankets muttered sleepily and rolled over. He eased around the mess, wincing as the gash along his flank flared with pain.

Three fucking weeks since they'd left Ludaf, and only two Challengers. Two men from so far down the ranks that killing them had been more like getting rid of sick animals. Instead of Challengers who could actually put up a fight, he was getting assassins.

Syrus rubbed at the skin around the clumsy stitches set in by one of the concubines and scowled as the bandage came loose. Fuck. He didn't get these things cut out in the next day or so, they'd grow over and he'd have to slice himself open all over again to keep them from festering. He sure as fuck wasn't letting any of the med-techs near him again. Well, maybe Iira. But she'd be bitchy enough about the fact that he'd killed her Chief of Surgery. For all he knew, she might just finish the job the other woman had started. Syrus twisted his arm so he could look at the wound, but the skin pulled and pain flared a warning. He gave up. By the end of the day, he should be ok. He'd have to live with that.

A few grav-tethered seats and tables took up space in the bottom of the onion-shaped bulb of the main room, surfaces shifting with patterns of light from the starscape that covered the ceiling and walls.

Out of the corner of his eye, he saw a light blinking. He turned. The alert along the edge of the table he used for troop deployments was silent, but bright enough to reach all the way to the ceiling. Well, now he knew why he was awake at—he checked the chrono in the wall next to his bed—way too fucking early. Why the fuck?

Syrus padded over and thumbed in the receiver for the message. Too late, he slapped at the volume. "Milord," said Quinn's voice. "You wished to be notified when preparations for the drop were complete."

Behind him, someone rolled over and yelped as they fell out of bed. Surprise popped through the air and burst against his skin. Not enough to hurt though. Five more sleepy voices asked if the luckless woman was ok. Syrus shook his head and turned back to Quinn's message. The table rattled off the squad details and the hangar they'd be leaving from. In ten minutes, if their leader would be so kind. Syrus checked the hangar again and growled. Someone was fucking with him. Down three decks to starboard and almost a mile forward. Like fuck he'd get there in ten minutes. "You." He snapped his fingers at the women behind him. "Let's get armored up."

A woman came trotting over. Her shoulders and back were a lattice of old scars, partly covered by the honey-gold hair falling loose over her shoulders. Dark blood coated the side of her face and shone dully in the light from the table. Must have been the one who'd fallen off, then. Before Syrus could tell her to go clean up instead, she had his armor out of the repair box and was laying it out on a different table. "Milord," she said quietly. He braced himself against the desire dripping off her like syrup and resigned himself to grabbing the slipsuit that went under his armor. Together they managed to get him encased in the breastplate, bracers, and other bits of metal. It wasn't quick. With each piece, they had to wait for the edges to seal before they could let go. Why the Fleet didn't make armor entirely out of living metal, he didn't know. And except for when it came to putting the stuff on and off, he didn't much care. As the last edge oozed into the decorative thorns of its companion piece, he caught the woman by the chin. A breath in, full of lust and anticipation. A breath out, to keep from acting on them. "Get that look off your face," he growled at her.

Her expression fell. What, she thought he'd fuck her now that he'd gotten all locked in? "And make sure the rest of the place gets cleaned too."

He let go and she staggered for balance. Her frustration picked at the exposed skin of his face with tiny hooks. He grabbed his helm off the table and turned to go. "Spotless," he called over his shoulder. "Top to bottom."

There. That should be impossible enough to make her happy.

Syrus beat Quinn and the recon team to the drop ship. It wasn't by much, but every victory counted for something. The second swung into the cockpit and landed in his chair behind the pilot just as Syrus buckled in. The pilot, who'd only been edgy with her warlord parked in the copilot seat, went on high alert as Quinn got situated.

Syrus threw up whatever shields he could manage and checked his side of the controls, just in case. Satisfied that his station was active and ready for use, he leaned over to the woman. "Remember. You fuck this up, I won't have to punish you. Not interested in being debris in atmo or smearing my guts all over a mountaintop. Got it?"

Wide eyes in a white face turned towards him. She blinked.

He glowered. "You're part of the Fleet. Act like it."

It was like he'd stuffed a metal rod up her ass. She went ramrod straight, indignation sizzling out to blanket the fear. Then she went blank. Sucked it all back in, set her jaw, and turned back to look out the forward viewpane. It was translucent right now. They didn't need to know what the inside of the launch bays looked like. The material wouldn't go clear until they were in space proper.

Ten standard minutes later, they cleared the bay doors, flight control's clearance still echoing in their ears. Syrus kept one eye on the heads-up display over the pilot's chair and tapped his way through the data on his slate with the other half of his attention. The planet was a fair example of an Ajiri planet. Atmosphere breathable. Lots of carbon. Some silica. Respectable oceans. Enough fresh water on the continents to keep a decent-size population alive.

He flipped through the pix. Flatland, mountains, desert, swamps. Coastlines pocked with bays and harbors. Rivers flattening out into deltas that merged into oceans. One sat had caught a pic of some tropical island. The water around it was clear enough to show bright pink and orange glimpses of coral.

And here and there, about where you'd expect them to be, were settlements. Well, the remains of settlements. Larger along rivers. Larger still along the coast. Some were only a few houses clustered together on mountainsides. Other scans showed hollows in desert cliffs, too regular and closely set for animals. He flipped further. A day to the nearest body of water. Whoever left those particular ruins must have been well supported by tech or self-supported, in the highest sense of the word. He shrugged.

All the buildings were worn. Falling in on themselves. How long did it take for silcrete and synthstone to degrade? Would it ever? Why had everyone left? If anyone had actively managed the plant life, the native vegetation had long since erased any signs of it. No industrial activity that he could see.

No surprise there. Ajiri, or agricultural, planets like this were rare. A catastrophe, like losing their Barbican or solar collector, would have to happen before anyone so much as thought about starting a mineral operation. The solar collectors that powered the local Barb were still in orbit around the star. So why had everyone left?

He kept flipping. Saw something. Stopped. Had to wait for the slate to catch up, then started skipping backwards. Overshot. Repeated the process. Fucking slate. They could fold space and anchor it in a Barbican, but no one could make a user interface that didn't drive a person nuts.

Sometimes he missed the days when all he had to worry about was where his next meal would come from. That and killing the first person who tried to take it from him.

Finally, he found the image again. It looked like the top of a bunker built into the side of a mountain. Fallen trees leaned against it, obscuring the outline. But bunkers only came in so many shapes. A lifetime ago, he'd spent a lot of time figuring out how to crack them open. He zoomed out. Ah. There it was.

The pix to either side of the bunker were clearer.

Dens. Game trails. He zoomed out again. They disappeared completely where the mountainside gave way to snow and crevassed glaciers. Downhill of the bunker, they were hard to find under all the tree cover. But here and there he could see a beaten-down patch of dirt. These were old. Very old, considering.

He handed the slate back to Quinn. "Tell me what you see."

The man took it and frowned, then started flipping the pix and frowned harder. While he waited, Syrus went back to watching the pilot work. She had a surprisingly easy hand on the yoke. These drop ships were designed to punch through all the gaseous layers over a planet and land a squad of Fleet troops on a target city in the middle of heavy enemy fire. They had the reaction time of a dead duck in flight and control yokes that needed more muscle than finesse to get moving. All the hull plating, he supposed.

He didn't know what planet the Fleet got the design from. It wasn't Imperial, but whoever it was had probably expected men to be flying them. The fact that Fleet women had the same excess strength as their men, relative to body size, probably went a long way to helping them handle the flying bricks. The pilots also routinely fiddled with the drive collars and steerage jets, trying to make things work a little better. Mech-heads. Landbound, airborne, or space jockeys. He'd never met one who didn't tinker.

"Evidence of animal movement, milord." Quinn interrupted Syrus's train of thought as he handed the slate back. "What of them?"

Syrus pushed the pic up onto the hull on his side of the cockpit, then tapped into the tracking monitor. "See the signal?" He tipped the slate so Quinn could see it. It was weak. A barely there pulse of manufactured energy.

"Yes. Sir?"

Syrus opened his mouth to explain. The g-forces hit, pushing him back into his seat. He snarled at the pilot and reached for his harness. Bitch. Just had to hit atmo at nearly the worst possible angle. No warning either. He hated sitting in the passenger seat with someone else flying.

But her face was white and rigid. Her fear hit him hard enough that he nearly lost his breath. Accident, he realized. Muttering to himself, Syrus leaned forward, flipping the copilot HUD on and freeing the yoke from its latch against the console. Surprise and alarm lashed at him from the pilot's side of the cockpit. He ignored it. She needed a second set of hands to manage all the alarms and finicky bits; he might as well do his part to keep them all from dying.

>>><<<

The ship overshot the continent they'd been aiming for before Syrus and the pilot got the ship back in line. Syrus powered down his HUD and latched the yoke back in place, then unclipped his harness so he could turn to look at the pilot. Her hands were slack on the controls. The expression on her face hovered somewhere between awe and fear. The thrum of the first mixed with the acid of the second felt even more bizarre than it looked.

He reached over, squeezed a hand around hers on the yoke, then pushed her jaw shut with one finger. Standing, he looked down at her. "You see you're going to come in wrong, you ask for help. The second seat is there for a reason. Overconfidence gets everyone killed. Quinn, let's go."

They made it out of the cockpit before her indignation and shame drowned him, but it was a close thing.

Out in the jump bay, the soldiers were just unhooking their harnesses. Someone at the aft end had lost his lunch. His fellow soldiers laughed among themselves as he tried to scoop the mess into a disposal pan. One of the men in the forward seats saw the two standing in the hatch and jumped to his feet, barking, "Warlord!"

Syrus tried not to wince. This man had a voice for parade grounds and flight decks, not small enclosed spaces.

There was a general scramble as the rest of the men came to attention. Or tried to, depending on how tangled they were in the harnesses. The man cleaning up vomit got to his feet, slipped, and went straight back down again. Syrus decided he'd found the man who'd stay behind and guard the landing zone.

"As you were," he said. "All starboard."

The men moved over. Curiosity was thickest in the air, but he still felt the ever-present undercurrent of resentment and anger.

"Here's where we're headed." Syrus tapped the slate to wake it, then pushed the static image of the energy signature up onto the portside hull. Neither side of the hull had windows, but port didn't have an exterior hatch, so that was the side with the display matting.

He let them take a good look at the image, then shrank it slightly and threw the next pic up. This was the one of the dens. Incomplete on its own. Stitched together with the ones that came before and after, it spread out further than the image of the beacon. "See those?" He lit up the dens.

The men leaned forward. Behind him, Quinn's flattened-out bundle of emotions shifted slightly. Syrus let himself smile. They saw it.

"Could be a few different things using the dens." Syrus pulled the large pic off to the side and brought up the one of the bunker. "Best bet is on packs of jenmal."

They looked blank. That didn't surprise him. The Fleet usually focused on population centers and high profile military targets when they invaded a planet. Once they were done killing and enslaving all the people they could round up in the first strikes, they Seeded the atmosphere with poison. Anyone stuck out in the rural areas was fucked. The military outposts probably held out a little longer, but no air-processing system lasted forever. Neither did food or water. Nothing went untainted by the Seed. The only way to stay alive on a planet after it was Seeded was to bow, scrape, give your women to the invaders, and hope the anined of the planet doled out antidote faster than the Seed killed you.

"Jenmal," Syrus continued. "Genetically engineered animals bred for the Navlad Karukap." He stopped and rephrased it in Fleet. " Their military. Who put them here doesn't matter. It's why. This." He tapped the ping of the power signal. "This is the why. They will guard it. It's in their programming. They were given the DNA of the person or people allowed to get in that bunker when they were installed. That person is probably dead."

To top that off, he laid down the next bit of bad news. "The Empire as a whole stopped using jenmal about two hundred years ago. Right around the time arguments over the Imperial throne went from bitchy slap fights at the dinner table to some of the more remote Border systems breaking off and declaring independence. Course, you can still find them here and there on the black market."

More confusion behind those impassive faces. Mixed with frustration now. Syrus shook his head. "Back hall."

Understanding dawned.

Syrus kept going. "By the age of the dens, whoever introduced the jenmal put them there when they were still easy to come by. Either this is an old military outpost, or someone had contacts." He waited until the shifting and muttering stopped.

Not that they were ever far from a fight, but the rank and file first-gen recruits tended to need some sort of direction before getting shoved out the ship. Otherwise they'd just rampage over anything in their way. Sometimes they rampaged anyway, no matter what the orders were. That was why they got stuck out in front. They had to prove they could hold their temper and survive to move up the ranks. Or they'd die and solve a bunch of problems instead.

He wondered if they knew they were just fodder for surface-to-air missiles.

"We'll have to fight our way in," he told them.

Which, of course, got them back on task and made them pretty happy in the bargain. To be honest, he wasn't disappointed either. For months now, he'd been wasting his time with practice bouts and formal Challenges. During Campaigns, he had to worry about strategy and tactics. He hadn't really cut loose since... well, since he'd killed Brander.

That had been more cathartic than fun. He didn't remember most of it anyway.

Pulling the stylus free of the slate, he started running lines through the dens, crossing them over the bunker like spokes in a space-station hub. He was probably getting them wrong, but this was more for a visual picture than accuracy.

"General layout for this sort of defense puts the oldest den closest to whatever needs protecting. The babies grow up, they go build themselves a different place out along the perimeter. Further in we get, the more of them we'll find. The more willing they'll be to cross into each other's territory."

"Sir," said the man who'd announced him to the rest. "Why not set down up mountain?"

Syrus raised an eyebrow. At least *one* of them was trying to think. Just not very well. "How much you weigh?" he asked instead.

The man looked confused. "Ten roid, sir."

"And your armor is another ten. Even if she just dropped us instead of setting down, you know what would happen trying to hike off the glacier? You see all those crevasses?" He pointed at the deep blue cracks around the edges of the ice. "That's not counting the risk of avalanche. The noise this thing makes could shake all the snow off the peaks. She'll find a place to leave us down mountain. The terrain is more predictable. Besides, fewer dens up mountain means there are probably more traps in that direction. Can you survive walking over a landmine?"

The man shook his head.

"Ok then." Syrus pulled all the images back onto his slate, then headed towards the cockpit as the engines changed pitch. "Suit up. No heavy artillery. We're taking a look, not occupying the place."

THREE -- SYRUS

Distance from primary star: ~1 Ayeu
Eccentricity:.0254
Orbital period: 298 d, 11 hr
Rotation: 30 hr
Axial tilt: 28.223
Population: 0
    -preliminary report, Geo-Tech Uura Janiu

The only place to land the ship without sucking a tree branch into the engines was a clearing halfway down the side of the mountain. They'd have to walk fast if they wanted to get done with this before nightfall.

The wind coming from up mountain shook the ship, turning the ground below into a gold-and-bronze lake of rippling grass. Bushes clung to the edges of the clearing, purplish-black leaves flipping up to show silvery undersides. Whippy little deciduous trees reached out between the blue-green needles of evergreens like the bony hands of the old women Syrus'd snuck food from as a child.

Fresh air. That was another thing he missed. Untainted. Clear. He could almost taste it. Smell it. He couldn't wait. But first . . .

"Drop us and move down into the foothills." The pilot didn't look at Syrus when he stuck his head back into the cockpit, but he knew she'd heard him. "We'll send up a beacon for evac. Till then, you land, button up, and don't let anything chew on the propulsion. Got me?"

"Sir."

She was still pissed at him for having helped her get through atmo. He snorted and went back into the jump bay. So long as she did her job and came back for them when they called, she could burn him in effigy for all he cared. It wouldn't be the first time.

The first squad was already out. The four techs, who'd stayed at the back of the group during his little lecture, were up next. Syrus was too hyped on anticipation to get a clear read off them, but one look at their faces told him all he needed to know. His men were looking forward to this. *He* was looking forward to this. The women? They were spooked, but determined. If he'd needed proof that Fleet women were just as crazy as their men, he had it.

Tell them the biggest, baddest animals on this mountain would be actively hunting them, and they'd jump out of an Atmo class ship with only an eight-pulse handgun as protection. They had armor, yes, but it would slow them down if things came to a fight. They wore the stuff because that was what any Fleet person did when they dropped planetside, not because they had combat experience.

How the fuck had he ended up in charge of this insane excuse for a nation? Oh. Yeah.

They were out, all four clipping their jump harnesses to the drop lines and sliding down to the men waiting to catch them. He hoped everybody kept their hands where they belonged. He didn't have time to deal with any of that shit.

His turn. Quinn was half a breath behind him. They dropped the forty feet between ship and ground to land on soft knees, weapons drawn. The first squad was already setting up the perimeter, beating down trails in the waist-high grass as they took up station and scanned the tree line for the enemy. Syrus unclipped from the drop line and moved off to give the next squad more room.

A minute later, the second squad was down and moving to cover the gaps in the first squad's line. Syrus shielded his eyes as the pilot banked the ship and took off. They were on their own.

"One other thing." Syrus flipped the faceplate of his helmet into place and brought up the squads and their techs on the display. "Whatever's down here is gonna come check out the noise. Let's make as much time as we can before they find us."

>>><<<

It didn't take long.

The sun was high in the sky, beating them down with a uniform heat. Through the trees, shafts of light struck the ground in bursts of bright green. Moss, probably. Here and there, through the gaps in the tree branches, clumps of some tall plant with heart-shaped leaves all but glowed when the light hit the fine fuzz of gold on their woody stalks. The rest of the undergrowth was covered in thickets of hip-high bushes with deep purple leaves.

Something snapped off to his left. Turning his head, Syrus focused the various sensors in his helmet. Sure enough, the jenmal were here. The shapes on his HUD were heavy bodied, but their centers of mass were higher than he'd anticipated. Shoulders high, broad heads down in the classic stalking pose. They registered hot on the heat vision. Mammalian then. But not human smart. The things should have waited until further up mountain, where the slope and the close-packed trees would make defense that much harder. Apparently, whatever these things were, they weren't supposed to let strangers anywhere *near* the bunker. Not even if it gave them tactical advantage.

He looked again, scanning the trees around him. The critters had he and his soldiers surrounded. Pack hunters. So, whatever scientist had cooked them up must have added wolf. Or something like a wolf.

"Circle up," he told the men. "Techs in the center. Set a shield."

One of the women started to protest. He glared at her. "Set a shield and get inside. Or I'll cut you up and leave you for bait instead."

She pulled the grounding stakes from a pouch at her hip and crouched to start setting the shield bubble.

Stepping back until he met Quinn, Syrus nodded out at the circling pack. "Draw them in. As many as we can."

The other man nodded. The squad pulled the circle in tighter. If they'd been fighting humans on Campaign, one of them would have put up a siren set to the universal emergency frequency. Civilians came looking for help. Soldiers came to help civilians. They all died or got caught, depending on who showed up first. Not this time. This time, all they needed to do was wait.

Whatever was coming for them just barely showed above the branches. Dark fur. No help there.

The bushes rustled, and a broad head striped in white slid into view, followed by a huge spadelike paw.

A bajbar.

"Fuck!" Syrus spun and lunged for the shield. Teach him to make assumptions. "Pull the stake," he shouted at the nearest tech.

She stared at him through the haze of the shield bubble.

The ground under his feet trembled. Inside the bubble, a set of claws broke through the earth, followed by a dirt-covered head. The bajbar swung around, clamped its yellowed teeth around the leg of the nearest tech without opening its eyes, and started pulling. The earth around it crumbled, caving into the tunnel below. The woman shrieked and scrabbled for her belt. The creature let go, lunged again, and snagged its teeth on the join between the armor of her thigh and her groin. Blood spurted.

"Pull the stake!"

This time, the tech obeyed. The hum of the shield stuttered as she yanked the stake out of the ground. Around him soldiers fired, the animals roared, and Quinn shouted orders in a voice that would do justice to any parade ground. Syrus ignored them. He grabbed the nearest woman by the shoulder and threw her out of the way. The other two scrabbled for the other side of the circle. Good. That just left the bajbar and its victim.

Too close for his rifle. Instead, he pulled the hilt of a knife from his belt, flipped it on, and sank the blade into the thing's spine before the living metal had a chance to take its proper shape. The animal shuddered, stiffened, and died.

As he checked the tech's leg to see if the armor's med system had managed to activate in time, a yell pulled his attention back to the fight. He turned and saw a soldier go down beneath the weight of another bajbar. Half the man's face was missing. Syrus unslung his rifle and went to go plug the gap.

Another yell. Another man down. Leg crushed as he was dragged out of the circle. One animal took him by the throat—where the armor was weakest—shook hard, and then he was dead. The animals left him, turning back to the ring of defenders, and went down in a hail of rifle fire.

But there were too many. For each one killed at a distance, another got that much closer. The soldiers were left with a choice. Focus on the bajbar close enough to use claws and teeth? Or try to pick them off further out and end up easy targets for the ones popping out of the ground?

"Alternate," Syrus barked through the comms. "Every other. Start with Quinn. Half distance, half near in. You." He turned to the remaining techs. They huddled together, eyes wide and staring at the corpse of their sister. "Get her free of that thing."

They took a collective half step away instead.

Another rustle behind him. He spun, put a shot through the head of a bajbar mid-charge, then reached for the nearest woman, ignoring the electric jolt of terror that lanced through his armor and sizzled up his arm. "I said, get her free of it. Now!" She landed on her knees next to the body, yelped as she got a face full of monster fur, and crab-walked backwards. The other two went to help her up. Syrus turned his attention back to the fight.

This wasn't going as well as he would have liked.

More and more creatures were popping out of the ground. The alternating fields of fire helped, sort of. The half of the squad taking on the nearest bajbar had plenty of targets. Quinn's half took the distant targets, but there weren't as many as before. Not near enough bodies, either.

Something was wrong.

A manic yell, the clatter of a weapon hitting the ground, and the sound of running footsteps announced the fact that one of the soldiers had just lost his own private war with the Frenzy. The man ran out to meet the advancing tide of animals with a knife in each hand, screaming curses. The animals changed course to meet him.

Syrus snarled and shifted to fill the gap the man had left. "Either of you so much as *thinks* of following him," he told the soldiers to either side of him, "I'll kneecap you." Out in front of them, the Frenzied soldier had gone under, his weapons sending fur and blood flying everywhere as the bajbar put jaws and digging claws to work.

Syrus figured he should be happy the man hadn't turned rapist, like some Frenzied soldiers. The bajbar were further away than the women. And much more capable of taking down two hundred pounds of violent lunatic. The little popguns the women carried wouldn't have even fazed him.

The soldier had maybe thirty seconds, a minute at the outside, before one of the creatures either crushed his armor or punched through the living metal seals and hooked an artery through one of the expansion gaps. Another fifteen to twenty seconds of breathing room for the defenders while the animals sorted themselves out and realized their main target hadn't gone anywhere.

"Focus on these ones," he told the men. They didn't usually need to be told. But he'd seen too many squads get caught up in one man's Frenzy and lose all sense of strategy.

The Frenzied soldier had lost his momentum. Fewer bajbar showed fresh damage. Just in time. The dirt under his feet vibrated slightly.

"You got her loose yet?" he asked the women behind him as he sighted on an animal just breaking through the trees. It went down in a tangle of paws and pulped brain matter.

"Trying, Warlord." The scorn in her voice was clear. Good. She'd need it to get through this.

"All right then." Slinging his gun back over his shoulder, he toggled the comms. "On the signal, fall in. Dropping a sewer seeker."

A chorus of "Aye Warlord" answered him.

"Outta my way. Leave her."

The women left off trying to pull the fallen tech free of the pit and scattered. Syrus grabbed the body by the collar and hauled it out of the way, then reached for the bajbar. For one insane moment, he thought the thing looked at him. But it was just the head lolling loose on its broken neck. He hoped. It had been a long time since he'd gone up against this particular menace. Maybe they'd been made different back when they were put on this planet.

Paranoia gave him an extra edge of strength as he heaved. First came the paws. Then he hooked his hands under the thing's shoulders and around its back. His eyes watered at the reek of musk and some half-rotten carcass the thing must have rolled in. Bears, he remembered. They'd crossbred bears and badgers and hyenas, of all things. Fucking scientists, playing with things they had no business messing with.

If rumors are true, that includes people, an unwelcome little voice reminded him. *Good thing, or you wouldn't be able to do this.* He kicked the voice back into its mental hole and shut the lid—then sealed it. Now wasn't the time for memories.

People yelled at each other over the comm systems, soldiers to soldiers and techs to techs. Syrus didn't have time to worry about any of it. He'd have to trust his men to hold the circle and the women to stay out of the way until he could get this thing out of the ground. Bracing himself, Syrus heaved again. The carcass popped loose with a shower of dirt, and he nearly went over backwards under the weight of the thing.

He managed to change the direction of the animal's fall at the last moment, pushing it to one side. One of the women yipped when it landed, but so long as they weren't screaming in pain, he didn't much care. Dropping to his knees, he pulled the hand light off his belt and pointed it at the hole.

Huge teeth and gleaming brown eyes lit up in the dark. A snarling roar blasted his ears through the helm's speakers. A huge paw just barely missed his hand as the animal swiped at him. Syrus lurched back and fell on his ass. Fucking hell! How many of them were there?

The animal broke out of the hole, clawing stones and clods of dirt out of the way. Another snap of teeth took a chunk out of Syrus's boot sole as he jerked his foot away. Its claws caught the inside of his leg and raked down the metal of his armor with an earsplitting screech before they snagged on his boot top.

That did it.

He'd clipped his knife back to his belt without bothering to collapse the blade. Now he grabbed for it. Half a heartbeat to dodge the next attack. Skip the next. A *th-thump* of panic as the animal slipped back on the loose dirt in the tunnel and started to take his leg with it. He let the motion pull him forward and met the thing as it caught its footing and made another try for open air.

His blade skidded off the bone of the creature's forehead. He adjusted, dodged the teeth, and tried again. The knife hit home, driving in through the eye with a squelch. But it wasn't enough. The thing kept coming.

What did they do, armor plate its brain?

At least it was pissed off enough that it let go of his boot. The animal slid back, gathering itself for another attack. Syrus scrambled backwards, yanking his rifle around from where it hung loose on the strap over his shoulder.

If the discharge had gone off two inches to the left, he would have been serving cooked warlord on a platter. Instead, rocks and dirt and chunks of half-burned meat rained. The back half of the body thudded back into the tunnel. A couple of the techs screamed.

No time to breathe. He could feel the ground under him rumbling. He'd been too slow moving the bodies. The animals had made themselves new exits. They'd be coming up all over if he didn't get this taken care of. Fuck. He hated bajbarog.

In the second it took him to get back on his feet, the earth buckled in three more places. No time. Just had to hope to hell this would work.

He popped a sewer seeker off his belt. "Scatter," he roared into the comms. "Seeker away."

Then he dropped it on the body of the dead bajbar.

He had barely enough time to grab for the abandoned shield stake and roll towards the cluster of techs. Jamming the stake in the ground, he made himself as small as he could under the quarter shield the thing put up.

The world turned to noise and flying dirt mixed with charred chunks of jenmal. Something hit him in the shoulder, but he didn't look to see what it was. Any second now.

A second explosion, not three feet from the first. At least one of the women had huddled up behind him, hoping his larger frame would shield her from the mayhem.

Dumb idea on her part. They needed to move.

Twisting around, he grabbed her by the arm and all but threw her at the spot where the women had first tried to shelter. It was nothing but bloody mud now. But it was safer than where they were.

"Fall in," Syrus shouted, more because he couldn't hear himself over the ringing in his ears than because they needed to be told. Fucking helmets and their fucked up dampening systems. If they weren't saving his hearing, they were ruining it. He'd leave the damn thing off if it didn't mean the laws of the universe would cave his skull in for him.

Syrus figured his time was up. He yanked the stake again, nearly collided with Quinn as the second made a dive for the pile of soldiers, and jammed the stake back in the ground. It hummed to life, connecting with the other three stakes to form the full bubble. A soldier hit the barrier, stuck outside.

And then the man was gone in a wash of dirt and fire. Syrus sank past his ankles in the bloody soil as the shock of the explosion rippled through the ground.

Then another.

And another.

He crouched, watching the balls of fire climb the mountainside as seeker after seeker blew, scattered nanites to the wind, found another target with matching DNA, blew again, and repeated the process. On and on and on, all the way up the mountain.

Four -- Syrus

- - - wipe the drives soon. Don't even know
why I'm entering this. We've lost - - -
Just have to keep moving. Draw them off.
Not going to make - - - Miss her already
- - - [muffled crying]
    -recovered log files, Skatasi op Essi

Syrus decided he was doubly glad for the sai shielding in his armor. It was always helpful during battle, but in the aftermath of a disaster like that, he figured whoever invented the stuff should be up for veneration. Without it, he'd be well and truly cooked. Even without his sai, he knew he was surrounded by people who would happily knife him in the back if they thought they could get away with it. Well, if he hadn't done what he had, they'd *all* be dead right now.

Hell, even after nearly dying to hordes of bajbar, he was having a better time than he'd had in at least a month. It was one thing to be commanding during a Campaign, keeping track of an entire army. Another entirely to be out in the middle of nowhere, pretty much on his own.

Snorting, he decided it was stupid to think he'd missed this. At the end of the day, he'd be back in space and on his way to another planet. Hopefully one attached to the Navlad Empire. And it would be back to business as usual.

Maybe the next planet would even be a challenge. Overturning backwaters was getting to be so boring.

Someone behind him stumbled and cursed. He ignored it, saving his attention so he could avoid the same issue. The mountain, not especially steep, was giving them problems in the form of churned earth and loose stones. The bajbarog had been here long enough to build themselves a fucking warren. The sewer seeker had torn the whole mountainside to hell and gone.

In a city, where the things were meant to be used, they didn't usually do this. The explosions were generally contained by whatever paving and construction had been laid over the waste and subterranean transport systems. In dirt, though? Well. The bomblets were small, and the nanites only triggered an explosion on contact with the targeted DNA, but they were strong enough to damage anything in range of the blast. All the science in the universe hadn't worked out a way to prevent internal injuries. Or armor from cooking a man inside it before he could get out.

Which was why he had four bloody ident tags and a dented collar wrapped around his wrist, and the rest of his people were plotting his death where they thought he couldn't see. Dying on Campaign they understood. Dying in a Challenge was expected. Dying because their so-called warlord had decided to talk a walk dirtside was much harder to stomach.

Well, he'd either find something to give them a reason for all this, or he'd be getting back on the drop ship by himself. Maybe with Quinn. Maybe not. Hell, for all he knew the man was in on the—

He stopped. Looked. Turned around, ignoring the sullen glares and set lines of his soldiers' faces. Looked forward again. Checked left and right, just to be sure.

The difference couldn't have been more obvious.

Syrus and his people stood on churned-up dirt and fallen vegetation. Five feet away was a meadow, disturbed only by a few clods of earth and some branches that must have achieved flight before giving in to gravity. A bunker rose out of the grass on the other side, a single story of metal overgrown by the natural world. Deadfall trees leaned against the pitted metal of the building. Even through the streamers of hanging moss and masses of ferns around its base, he could see it clearly enough to tell what it was. The squared off lines and oblique angles the Navlad Empire built with were like a slap in the face after the sinuous curves and hooked edges of the Fleet.

"You two. Five and seven o'clock." Where that particular system came from, he didn't know. But it seemed to be universal. The two soldiers he'd pointed at moved out, testing the ground every other step or so. He didn't blame them. They'd already had to dig one of the techs out of a collapsed tunnel and nearly lost one of the men to the covered over mouth of a den.

"Quinn, see if the rest of you can get the roof cleared off. *Without* caving it in. If we can, we'll evac from here. Keep an eye out. There were those dens up mountain. Doubt we got them all."

The second saluted, gathered up the troops, and headed off at an angle. Syrus thought about telling him to stay in the clearing, but figured the man was smart enough to do that on his own. Instead, he snagged the shoulder of a woman with the markings of a computer-tech on her collar and pointed at the door. "Can you get it open?"

Her expression would have etched metal. Syrus thought he might actually be getting blisters on his hand through the armor. Growling, he shook her, just a little. "Then don't sit here wasting time. Get us in."

Spine straight, she limped off as fast as she could. Resisting the urge to rub at his hand, Syrus followed her. The last two techs trailed him like a pair of ducklings.

They ground to a halt in front of the doors. A thicket of berry bushes, straight out of some of the sappiest children's stories he could think of, stood between them and their goal. The computer-tech looked at the bushes, looked at Syrus, and raised an eyebrow.

He glared back. "You're a woman of the Fleet. Fucking deal with it already. You two, still got your readers?" When they nodded, he pointed at the clearing. "Get to it. Whatever you can find. And then tell me if Seeding will take." If the air filters in his helmet hadn't kicked in by now, there was no reason why it shouldn't, but not every atmosphere answered to Seed in the same way. Even if the Fleet never settled anyone here, it was smarter to have it under Fleet control than to leave it open for the Empire.

While the women got to work, Syrus crouched down and started poking through the bushes. None of the leaves on the trees looked like they'd started turning yet, but the air smelled more of high summer than spring. If his guess was right, and the animals were blocked from the clearing, there should be something the birds hadn't gotten to.

He was rewarded with a handful of small black berries that squirted purple juice when he misjudged his armor's grip and tried to pull too many at once. The reader on his slate spat out an EDIBLE result, so he ate them, took a swallow of water from his hip flask, and got to work.

Fifteen minutes later he'd filled two belt pouches and was working on a third when the computer-tech came wading through the bushes. "The door will open, milord," she said sharply. Syrus didn't need to be a Feel to know what she thought of him picking berries while the rest of them worked. He stood up, shedding plant matter left and right, and followed her through the bushes to the lock panel set into the side of the door.

Her slate was hooked in, green lights all around. Toggling the comm, he warned Quinn and his men in case anything on the roof decided to start moving, then nodded at the tech. She punched in the last of the code and slapped the button on the panel itself.

For a second, he thought it hadn't worked. Then something deep in the bunker groaned, something else clunked, and the hum of machinery filled the air. Another minute, and the doors moved apart.

They squealed and shrieked, the dirt-crusted tracks showering dust like fine rain. Stale air blew out the gap in the door. The stench made it through the filters of his helmet and Syrus loosened his jaw so he could breathe through his mouth. Next to him, the tech wrinkled her nose.

With one last groan of resistance, the doors stuck. Halfway open, at least. Wide enough for them to get in. Safety lights flickered to life inside, probably activated by whatever the tech had done to get the doors open. Syrus leaned through them. All he saw was hallway.

Dropping one of the full pouches of berries on the tech's slate, he clapped her on the shoulder. "Good. Now see if you can't get some more systems online."

>>><<<

He filled the third pouch with berries, retrieved the empty from an embarrassed computer-tech, and had that one almost full before she came stomping back over and told him she'd done everything she could from here. Her mouth was rimmed in purple, but he decided not to let her know. He needed something to laugh about. Whistling for the other two techs, Syrus let Quinn know he was going inside, unslung his rifle, and nodded at the women. "K then. Let's go."

They nodded. Clearing an enemy building with techs was always the same. Soldiers first, then the women. Their little hand weapons were a last resort, nothing more. Seven charges for attackers, the eighth for themselves, to avoid capture.

He doubted they'd need their weapons, but he didn't feel like taking any more chances today. Single file, they eased through the doors, one of the men from outside kneeling in the open door to cover the guard still at the perimeter.

The tech had managed to activate the normal overhead lights, but not all of them had survived. Patches of shadow lit by dim red safety lights turned the corridor into a patchwork of light and dark. Syrus checked them all before moving forward.

Nothing.

Nothing but old equipment in rooms off the hall. Nothing but stale air and dust in the whole place. Two levels accessible by stairs. A common room. A small kitchen. Three rooms with metal frames for beds set one atop the other, nearly to the ceiling. No mattresses. Not even the remains of mattresses. No signs of food or supplies.

Empty.

They found the control room on the second level, right up against the back wall of the bunker. He waved the computer-tech forward. She was wilting visibly, hair falling out of the knot at her neck and every inch of skin smudged with dirt. Her limp was getting worse by the step. "Anything else," he asked, "to account for the power signature?"

She was too tired to even get angry with him. She just unclipped her slate from her belt, went over to the console controls, and started hunting for a place to plug in. Soft green light lit the room as she found the correct buttons and got to work.

Less than a minute later, he had his answer. "Here," she said, pointing at the diagram hovering in the air in front of her. "The end of the hall has a door. Looks like they put an accessory generator in the mountain itself and routed most of the power away from the rest of the complex. Whatever's here, it's buried behind the bunker."

"K then, get it open."

"I tried. It's unlocked. We should have heard machinery moving. The door opening. Something. Whoever set this up, they disconnected it manually."

He raised an eyebrow at her. For a moment her eyes flared, but she unplugged her slate and limped for the door. He didn't try to hurry her. She'd probably punch him. Punishing her would make the whole process take even longer. So he walked behind her and to one side, trying not to make it obvious that he could catch her if her legs gave out. She made it to the door, very clearly *not* leaning against the wall as she pried open the service hatch and started fiddling with wires.

Syrus watched over her shoulder, but the space was cramped and her hands filled most of his field of view. From what he could tell, at least half the wires were decoys, stuffed in and attached to more decoys. Probably running through this whole wall. Finally, the woman grunted, reached far inside the opening, and pulled out a small handful. The cut edges shone bright in the light of overheads. Syrus stomped on the urge to take them from her and start testing them himself. She knew what she was doing.

On the third wire, something inside the wall gave a grinding noise, then a clunk. The metal panel of the hidden door slid an inch to the side. And stuck. Syrus looked down at the tech, who shrugged. "Old machinery, my lord?"

"Right then." He nudged her out of the way and stepped up to take a look. Nothing. No light coming through, no noise. Nothing. Grumbling, he wedged his fingers into the gap, wincing as the armor of his gauntlets screeched against the metal of the panel. Then he braced his feet and pulled. And pulled. And pulled some more. With another grinding noise and the squeal of unoiled bearings, the hidden door moved. He kept pulling, afraid that if he stopped to get a better grip, the thing would seize up on him again.

The tech leaned against the jam, easing further and further into the opening as he created space. He paused when she muttered a quiet "By the root," but kept hauling on the door. She might fit through. He didn't have a chance, not in armor. Finally, Syrus figured he'd gotten the door as open as it was going to go. He straightened, stepping up behind the tech to see what she was looking at, and felt his jaw sag in horror.

Five -- Syrus

The benefits of a strong sai making a bond must be weighed against the possible damages. If the body is left in cold storage for too long, the systems may not be recovered.
   -"Advantages and Disadvantages of Cryo in the Management of Unbonded Sai" Professor Rusithe, New Hopks College of Medicine

"Fuck," Syrus whispered. "The fucking hell?"

There wasn't much else he could say. It was too much to take in at once. What madman would have even thought this up? Worse, who would actually put it together?

Generator, hell. There was enough machinery stuffed into this room to fill a whole other bunker. Bundles of cords, tubes, and who knew what else covered the floor and climbed the walls. Banks of what looked like processing units were stacked five high in the back of the room, blips of light blinking here and there. An old-fashioned spin lock dogged shut a hatch set in the back wall. The muted thrum of something big and electrical meant that the generator powering this nightmare was probably in the room beyond.

And smack in the middle of the room were two huge boxes. Their lids were made of synthglass. It looked like at least half the cords and tubes in the room ran into the bases. More blinking lights, ranging from green to orange, lined the edges.

"What is it?" The computer-tech leaned around him to peer at the room. She hadn't been able to turn on more than a quarter of the overhead lights. The rest of the illumination came from safety lights set into the walls near the floor.

He'd walked into a nightmare.

Syrus shifted to the side and gestured at the room. "That," he told the woman, "is what it looks like when a fucking nutcase sticks two people in cryo in a facility that was never meant to house them."

She blinked at him, questions clear on her face. Probably wondering if her translator chip was working. Or if he'd actually used all the words she thought he had. His expression must have been enough to discourage her. He'd given her an incredible amount of leeway in the past few hours, but there were some lines you didn't cross with the warlord. That was a sure way to get yourself killed if you were a soldier, or sent back to scutwork if you were a tech or another of the women. They'd all learned that if he said he knew something, then he knew something.

"Get in there," he told her. Once he was sure she wasn't going to trip and break her neck, he turned back to the other techs. He had atmospheric and geologic left. He pointed at the atmospheric one. "Get up to the surface. Send Quinn down here. Tell him I want a status on the evac." She nodded and took off.

The other woman watched him from under her lashes, sullen exhaustion seeping from every pore. He watched her back for a moment, trying to decide what to do with her so he could get the feeling of jellified acid off his exposed skin. Finally, he shrugged and pointed back to the control room. "You able to use the equipment in there?"

She nodded, jaw set.

"Then hook in. Get everything you can. I want to know who put this here and why. And then I want to know who repurposed it. Got me?"

She nodded again, spun on her heel, and stalked off. He watched her go for a minute, as much because she filled out her uniform perfectly as to be sure she'd actually do what she'd been told. Then he looked back at the Room of Hell. It deserved the capital letters. He hadn't run across many long-term cryo facilities in his life, but he knew what a properly set-up one should look like. He almost wished he had one of his old Academy instructors here, just so he could watch the man have an apoplectic fit.

Picking his way through the clear spots on the floor, he headed for the computer-tech. "Well?"

"The system's been in sleep mode for years. Decades, maybe." She tapped a few more things on her slate and turned it to show him. "Whoever put them here wanted to make sure they would stay in the caskets, even if they were found. And that nobody could so much as start the wake process without the right passcodes." She frowned, slid a bar to the side, and pointed at the scrambled mess of Imperial block letters mixed with Fleet script. "It doesn't make sense. Short-term cryo is easier to set up. If you plan to come back in your lifetime, why lock them down like this?"

He didn't bother looking for patterns on the slate. The Fleet didn't dick around with training its people. Some of the computer techs were as good as any Imperial Crack. This woman might even be one of the prodigies. He'd stick to things he knew how to run. "Can you get through it? We can wake'm up, might be able to answer your questions."

She took the slate back, irritation and bad humor fizzing over her skin like diluted acid. "Opening the caskets will be easier than making the system start the drips."

Syrus snorted, but kept his mouth shut. She wasn't a med-tech. She was just as unqualified to make guesses about cryo as he was. The Navlad Empire still used cryo to send out long-range scouts for new Barbicans or to deal with criminals and renegade sai when the legal system couldn't cope. In the past three or so years, he'd never heard of the Fleet using the tech. "Milord?"

He looked up to see Quinn standing in the doorway, squinting at the light and the mess of the room. Clapping the computer-tech on the shoulder, Syrus told her to do what she could about the caskets and waded over to the other man. "Status up top?"

Quinn nodded his head in a shortened bow. "As you said, there are more of the creatures. They are sitting on the edge of the clearing. Watching."

Syrus hooked his thumbs in his belt. "Good thing we're doing evac from the roof then. How's that going?"

Quinn gave a half shrug. "It is as clear as it can be, milord. We could not remove the trees from the sides of the bunker, but they have been trimmed so as to leave the roof open. It will be a tight fit for the ship, but it should be manageable."

Syrus tipped his head to one side and gave the man a look. He was as muted as ever, but something in the set of his jaw...

After a moment, the second gave in. "The men are displeased."

"Tell me something new," Syrus replied. Of course the men were displeased. They usually were, unless they were pounding a planet to dust.

Quinn shook his head. "All but one of a squad dead. The others wounded. The tech—" His eyes flickered down, to where the tags of the soldiers and the woman's collar were wrapped around Syrus's wrist. "If we knew it would be dangerous, we should have left the techs behind. Or brought more men."

"Or maybe you people should give your women better armor when they go planetside. And something other than a popgun to defend themselves with."

A solar flare of rage erupted from the second. Then it was gone. The expression on the man's face stayed as blank as ever. Syrus had to hand it to him. Quinn knew how to hide what he was feeling. Which meant that checking his face for blisters would raise far too many questions. Instead, he grinned and leaned back against the door frame. "You got a problem with the orders I've been giving, Quinn?"

"You are the warlord," he replied, bowing his head. Which meant jack shit if the man ever decided to stop playing puppeteer behind the throne. The tightrope the two of them had been walking the last three years felt a little wobbly. The longer Syrus stayed with the Fleet, the more he figured out and the less influence Quinn had over his decisions.

But the man kept following orders, including the ones that'd landed them in this room. Looked like he wasn't *quite* ready to stick a knife in his warlord's back. So Syrus decided to take Quinn at face value for now and look back at the room instead.

The tech was still standing next to one of the caskets with her slate propped up on its edge, typing furiously and muttering curses under her breath. Syrus laughed to himself. The Fleet women liked to put up a front of unflappable competence. She must have felt safe enough to vent now that he wasn't standing next to her.

So long as she got it out somehow, he didn't care if she tried to hide it from him or not. People who tried to keep their emotions hidden didn't usually do a very good job of it. Being around them was like being wrapped in wet wool. Itchy and extremely annoying. Eventually he started prodding them, just so they'd blow up and give him a bit of peace.

"There is one thing, milord."

Syrus looked back at his current wet blanket and sighed. Prodding the man would likely end them all up in pieces. Syrus wasn't sure even *he* would survive the fallout if the man ever did let loose. "What now, Quinn? Riots up in the Fleet? Someone trying to take over? Make it interesting, please."

"The pilot forwarded this. Likely to you as well." Quinn held out his slate.

"What am I looking at?" Syrus turned the slate sideways, trying to make sense of the data. It looked familiar. "A dummy-sat? What, did the thing malfunction?"

Quinn shook his head. "No milord. It's another Fleet sat. It came through the Barbican behind us."

Syrus raised his eyebrows. "I thought we came through the only address on the gate."

Quinn's eyelids lowered. "It was the only key techs could find in the last system, but—"

Syrus waved at him with the hand not holding the tablet. "Yeah. Doesn't mean the Barb here had that address." Syrus flipped through the data. The Fleet put dummy-sats through Barbicans so they could latch on to the housing on the other side. They had two functions. One, to keep the gateway between systems open. Sometimes a Barbican was coded to reset the locks, even after the key had been given. Unless a ship transmitted the key just as it breached the grav shield that contained the Barbican's wormhole, they slapped up against the laws of physics and lost. The dummy-sats also acted as a relay for whatever sats the Fleet sent to scount the system ahead after the Barb was unlocked. Basic system data, for the most part. Astronomical information, traffic, so on.

Syrus had sent out at least five splinter Fleets since he'd put on the Helm. The records said there were more out there, older, pushing through their sections of the Barbican network. But this was the first he'd heard of a Branch meeting back up with the main Fleet.

"We sure this is Fleet? Empire hasn't gotten hold of the dummies? Copied them?" As far as Syrus knew, the Empire never used dummy-sats, but it was always a possibility. He wasn't interested in hailing a Branch of the Fleet just to find he'd really let the Navlad Karukap know where they were. The Fleet was good, but it wasn't equipped to deal with a full space battle. Not after the system they'd just taken.

"See here." Quinn flicked the screen of the slate a couple times, then tapped. A line of code resolved into a thorny bush growing out the top of a human skull, complete with unfurling leaves and a hinged jaw. The sigil of the Kuchen Fleet.

Syrus fought the urge to curl his lip.

If Quinn noticed, he didn't say anything, just kept the information coming. "Even when the Empire has found the dummies, it's not been able to fake the code that encrypts the seal. They've tried, yes. As of yet they've only produced poor imitations. So far, this system hasn't noticed that their gate has been infiltrated." He tapped the screen again. The eye sockets lit from inside, and the slender branches on the main trunk of the gnarled digital bramble grew slightly, more leaves budding out. A tiny neon-green snake slithered down the warped wood as it emerged from the skull's nasal passage and disappeared into the tangle of roots anchored somewhere behind the jaw. Syrus ignored the tone of the man's voice, which told him he'd have known the seal was intact if he'd been Fleet and not an outsider, and handed the slate back. Privately he was of the opinion that the closer they got to the Core of the Empire, the more likely it was that Imperial loyalists would find a Crack who could break the coding on the seal and duplicate it. If they could do that, they wouldn't be dumb enough to let the Fleet know they'd noticed someone cracking open their Barbican. Hopefully he'd be long dead before that happened. There were a lot of solar systems to Conquer before the Fleet made it to the capital.

"Check with the stat-sats sent into the next system. Get a scout over to the last Barbican and have them send a message to the Branch Fleet. Let them know who we are. I'm not having a bitch fight over who gets first rights to any system while there are two branches of the Fleet in spitting distance."

Quinn's lips thinned. Every so often, the fucker forgot Syrus had been surviving as Warlord with this bunch of testosterone-hyped freaks for more than a while now. Instead, he looked at his warlord and saw an outFleet invader. And then they wound up having a little discussion. Like this one.

Syrus leaned in so he could see the hard eyes under the helmet. "What Branch of the Fleet do I lead, Quinn?"

"You don't lead a Branch." The man's words were clipped and hard. "You are Warlord of the Turan. Main trunk of all the Fleets together."

"Then whichever warmonger complains, that's what you tell him. You fuckers put me in charge. I didn't ask for it. But I won't fucking sit on my thumb and let you people tell me how to run *my* Fleet. He has a different key to try from his end, that's fine. He can use it from here. *After* he checks in. He doesn't like how I do things, he can Challenge me."

Quinn saluted, turned on his heel, and walked off.

Grumbling about bastards and pissants, Syrus went back to the tech and the caskets. "Well?" he snapped at her. "You made any progress?"

"Yes and no, milord. I was about to come get you. I've unlocked the seals. You'll have to open them yourself."

Finally. He started with the closest casket. When the tech made as if to help him, he waved her off. Fleet born or not, she didn't have the muscle to manage it. Carefully, first one end and then the other, he inched the cover off the edge of the casket. Gravity took a while to realize that he was moving something and could use a hand, but once he'd pulled enough of the lid away from the box, all he had to do was keep it from getting out of control and knocking him over.

The tech had disconnected as many of the wires and tubes as she could, so there wasn't much left to get tangled when he caught the thing with the toe of his boot. Not the smartest thing he'd done today, but not the dumbest either. At least the boot was armored, so he was only dealing with bruises, not broken bones. Getting his foot out from under the lid was less fun. A few muttered curses and a punch to the top edge of the lid and he was free. He only tripped over a cable once on his way to the other box. The lid for that one came off just as easily.

Now, without the fogged synthglass in the way, he could see who was inside.

She would have been beautiful if she hadn't been so close to death.

Her pale skin was yellowed and chalky. A clear breathing mask covered the bottom half of her face, its curved lines distorting the shape of her lips, which should have been full and red but were a dusty sort of mulberry instead. Red hair peeked out the edges of the skullcap covering her head. Nobody had figured out how to make hair stop growing in cryo. The net built into the neck of the suit was full and then some, billowing around her head like some sort of amorphous creature from the oceans. He revised the estimate of years and put his guess firmly in the Decades column.

Trying to ignore the march of memories through his mind and the medicinal smell in his nose, Syrus pulled off his gauntlets and reached in, gritting his teeth against the feel of the gel that half-filled the casket. It was meant to cushion the body. Help keep the temperature down, too. That it hadn't dried and turned to rubbery plastic was good. Meant the seal had never been damaged. At least not till he and his people showed up. That also meant it was cold as a frozen zone planet and he was going to lose his fingers if he left them in there too long.

The slipsuits were designed to let the gel through. Something about hydration and keeping friction down. He'd listened to the lecture once, but it was one thing to hear about it, another to see—

There. A pulse. Faint, but still there. The suit was looser than it should be. When he cupped the back of her head and started to lift, the skullcap nearly came off. Grumbling, he stuck his other hand in and eased her up. Malnourishment at the very least. From the fine lines in her skin, dehydration too. And whatever current had been run through the suit to keep her muscles stimulated, she'd been in here too long for it to counter the atrophy. He needed a med-tech to look her over to be sure of the damage, but it looked like she was on her last legs.

The computer-tech made a small noise over on her side of the room. Lowering the woman back into the box and making sure the breathing mask hadn't shifted, Syrus shook cryo gel off his hands and went to check on the tech. She stared down into the other casket with a look of horrified fascination, hands outstretched and trembling. Hitching himself over the lid on his side of the unit, he propped a hip on the edge and looked down.

And got blasted by a wave of condensed anguish that would have put a neutron star to shame. He nearly fell off the box, saved only by grabbing for the edge. "What the fuck?" he gasped, once he could breathe again.

"I know milord," the tech said, completely misunderstanding his reaction. "If she'd stayed in here another year. Another month, even!"

She was skeletal. There was no other way to put it. The slipsuit lay in wrinkles and folds over her body where it should have been tight and smooth. The bones of her cheeks were sharp, even with the oxygen mask in the way. And her skin . . .

Once, in another life, Syrus'd been dragged over to a tanner's booth in the market and made to stand while piece after piece of animal hide was held up to his arm. Straight tanned hide would never work. It was too pale. Eventually they'd found a warm brown dye called, of all things, saddle. It had only been slightly darker than his skin. The logic had been that if people mistook his shirt for his skin, they'd just think his family was too poor to afford activating his maruste in the first place. Not much better, but enough to keep storekeepers from booting him out the door anytime he was sent to run errands. Nobody wanted someone with *his* glyph anywhere near their oh-so-precious merchandise.

This woman, though—she was darker than him. Dusky-brown skin that wasn't quite ebony, but didn't match any of the lighter woods either. The yellow cast looked to be the same jaundice as other woman. The light was bad, and he was blocking most of it, but that didn't keep him from seeing the finely webbed lines and high relief of the cracks that said she hadn't been properly hydrated in a long time. The woman in the first coffin was in bad shape. This one was worse.

"Get up to the surface," he told the tech. "Get Quinn back here. Or one of the others, if he's still talking to the pilot."

She took one look at him, anger long gone, and ran for the door. He heard her stumble once, but didn't look to see if she was ok. His attention was all for the women in the caskets. He needed to get the various IV lines and sensors unhooked from the slip suits before Quinn showed up and asked why he was doing this.

If he left them here like this, well. His little-used conscience would have something to say about *that* on his deathbed.

>>><<<

Quinn took one look at Syrus, arms full of stick-thin woman and covered in cryo gel, and headed straight for the other casket to fish out the other woman. Together they picked their way back across the floor, collected the computer-tech at the door, called the geo-tech out of the control room, and headed for the surface.

The setting sun smacked Syrus right in the eyes. He winced as he crouched to lay the woman down on the silcrete in front of the bunker. The gel had dried into a tight rubbery layer over his armor, and his hands had gone numb long before they made it up to the ground level. By the time he got the cap off her head and the mass of hair pulled out of every bit of the suit it had grown into, he had most of his eyesight back. The soldier standing guard stared at him.

Syrus ignored him, gathering the stiff cloud of black hair up in one hand and pulling it out so he could take a guess at its length. He made the judgement that it was too long, pulled the still-active spacer's knife from his belt, and wadded the whole mass up in his fist. A few seconds later, he'd cut it off somewhere around her shoulders and deactivated the blade.

It wasn't until he kicked the pile of hair to the side and picked the woman up again that he noticed the growling.

Sure enough. The bajbarog were back. Well, not back. But there were more of them. Probably from up mountain, where digging warrens wasn't possible but denning was. They stood at the edge of the clearing, shifting from foot to foot, heads low and growls rippling like low thunder through the air.

"They been like this the whole time?" he asked the soldier next to him.

"No milord," the man replied. "They were quiet until you came out."

Syrus looked at the creatures, then down at his baggage. "Quinn," he said quietly. "Toss some of that hair out there."

When the bundle, held together with a phase-net, landed just past edge of the meadow, the line of bajbarog shifted. And drew back.

Syrus nodded, hitched the woman in his arms a little to resettle her, and started for the downed tree his men had obviously been using as the path to the roof. "Thought so."

"The genetic tag," Quinn said as he caught up. He'd been a little more liberal in the hair he'd left the woman he was carrying, letting it hang past her shoulder blades. The sun lit her head like a bonfire.

Syrus nodded and started up the tree. "Good thing we're leaving from here. If I made the men wrap themselves in hair to get out of here unhurt, they might lynch me."

Not that they'd have succeeded. But it was a fun image, even if it didn't get much of a reaction from Quinn.

Twenty minutes later, standing in the forward hatch of the ship as it lifted off, he looked down and watched the bajbarog swarm the bunker. None of them attacked. In fact, he thought they looked a little lost. The thing they'd been set to guard was gone. No more reason to exist now.

He knew the feeling. The only difference was, he lived with it every day. As far as he knew, the animals didn't have the self-awareness to know how unwanted they really were.

Six -- Syrus

The Head of the Fleet is not the Heart of the Fleet.
Just as the Fleet is not the whole of the Kuchen
nation. But as a head directs the movements of the
body, so too does the Head command its many
branches.
      -Hierarchy of Rank, Fleet Training Manual

Syrus nearly tripped coming into his rooms. Catching himself on the edge of the door, he glared down at the woman kneeling in front of him. "What the hell are you doing?" he growled.

The surge of arousal that hit him in the face told him exactly who he'd knocked over. The woman pulled herself upright, rubbing at her jaw where it'd hit the floor, and held up a cleaning unit by way of explanation. "The blood, milord," she said, voice low and husky. "Milord, you told us to clean. Top to bottom."

Now he remembered. This was what he got for banning the cleaning crews from his quarters. Women underfoot everywhere he turned. Usually he didn't mind. Right now, the urge to plant a boot in her ass and send her halfway across the room was almost overwhelming. He could hear movement further back in his rooms, where the women stayed when he didn't want them in his bed. This one should be back with the others, not lagging here by the door.

"Move." He stepped away from her reaching hand. "You're going to get run over."

She blinked at him, and then at the small parade standing in the hall. Something dark passed over her face. Scrambling backwards, she put herself out of the path of incoming traffic. He noticed she managed to spread her legs and lose the shoulder of the short tunic she was wearing in the process. It was a good view, but he had other things on his mind at the moment.

Like the woman standing quietly against the far wall, her emotions so locked down that if he hadn't seen her, he wouldn't have known she was in the room. The only thing she had in common with the woman on the floor was that her hair was pinned up at the back of her head. Everything else, from the steady gray eyes to the knee length dress to the collar around her throat—every inch of her was the picture of a perfect Fleet woman. Except for the spectacular bruise forming around one eye, complete with medical tape holding the split in her eyebrow closed.

She moved aside when he approached, allowing access to the door panel she'd been blocking.

"Nice shiner, Iira," he said, pulling off a gauntlet. He grabbed a knife hilt from his belt and carefully nicked his thumb. After letting the blood well for a moment, he smeared it across the scanner on the lock panel. She wasn't anything like a sai, but she was too fucking observant. He didn't want her watching him crack open a door he'd kept locked for almost three standard years. Fuck. He should have thought ahead when he'd pulled the women out of the caskets to start with. Or else told everyone to wait for him in the hall while he got this over with. Making them leave now would just paint a giant target all over his weakness. Why the fuck hadn't he thought of the fact that he'd have to open up the infirmary?

The better question was: where else *could* he put them? Nowhere. That was where. Fuck.

Iira didn't reply, just bowed and moved further out of the way as the door melted open behind her. Syrus waved the med-techs and their burdens through, then thought of something. "You." He snapped at the woman over by the main door. "You 'bout done in here?"

"Yes, milord." She was back on her knees and cleaning again. He got a decent view down the open neck of her tunic when she looked up at him. "This is the last of it, milord."

He raised an eyebrow. The floor all but shone. Hell, she'd probably been scrubbing that same spot in front of the door since morning, just so she'd be in the way when he came back. Well, mission accomplished. Except he wasn't interested in playing evil Warlord for her right now. And he didn't need her slipping out the door and finding one of the men to latch on to instead. "Go see if the others need help," he told her.

He didn't wait to see if she listened. The med-techs and the gurneys had made it into the other room. He followed them in, Iira and Quinn on his heels. The pair of them radiated disapproval like a faulty reactor.

The door had shut behind them. "Out with it," he ordered.

"Milord," said Quinn. "It is the prerogative of the lesser to—"

"Take the leavings of the strong. I know." Syrus crossed his arms and glared at his second in command. "Except it wasn't a concubine that died. Run a tally of my women. They're all here. Instead of jumping all over me like one of your rapist freaks of nature, why don't you ask Iira where her Chief of Surgery went? When I saw her last night, she was more interested in cutting my heart out than stitching me up."

The man's face went flat, and he looked over at his wife. She nodded. Just barely.

Quinn looked back at his warlord. Syrus allowed himself a smile, just a slight baring of his teeth. "And before you get all snippy about the body, I already sent her down to reclamation. Her husband wants to say one last goodbye, he can join her down there." He leaned forward as Quinn opened his mouth. "My Fleet, my rules, remember?"

Fleet or outFleet, a body was a body after the person in it died. They all got sent down to reclamation eventually—but Syrus had seen what female corpses looked like after the rank and file got ahold of them. He knew of a few people who needed that sort of treatment, but he'd rather they were alive to know what was happening to them.

He took that mental image and stuffed it down a hole. Quinn didn't seem to have noticed his mental wandering. He just stood there, watching his warlord with a blank face.

"So," Syrus said. "I make the rules. And rules say dead bodies don't leave my quarters by the front door. You want to change that? You know how." How many times was he going to have to make this point?

Quinn's jaw clenched. Behind him, Syrus could feel Iira's emotional wall crack, but he couldn't get a clear read before she locked herself back down.

"No? Then worry about your own women. Your wife here managed to run into another door frame."

That, finally, was enough to pull the man's attention. Syrus went over to where the med-techs were rearranging the two foundlings and setting up the medunits, complete with tubing, needles, and more sensor pads than he'd ever realized could be stuck on and into a human body. They worked fast, but everything had to be tested and checked before they could start poking, prodding, and stabbing. He probably should have had someone in here every so often to make sure things were working, but the only thing he'd cared about was that the lock worked. Stitches and splints were enough to fix the injuries he'd received since taking the Helm.

He kicked the next thought into his mental hole and locked it down. No. Not fucking going there.

Behind him, he could hear Quinn asking Iira what had happened, and her even quieter voice telling him... something. Syrus couldn't make it out, and he wasn't too interested in eavesdropping.

"Iira," he said when the muttering had died down. "What can you tell me?"

"Not much, milord." She stepped around him and started checking leads and needle sticks. "They are in sad condition, as you well know. The data you forwarded confirms your thoughts. Dehydrated, malnourished. Liver and kidneys under a great deal of strain. Electro-stims kept their muscle mass up, but atrophy was starting to take hold." She shook her head. "It is not unexpected, in long-term cryo. The images of the units imply they were set up for it, but they had been working on reserve power for a significant number of years. How many, I cannot say until the computer-tech can parse the data. A minimum of two hundred years."

Two hundred? So much for decades. Syrus followed her around the end of the table that held the red head. He watched as one of the assistants removed the temporary oxygen mask they'd used on the flight up and replaced it with one hooked into the medunit. "Fits," he said. "Longer than I'd guessed, but bajbar take a while to dig in. For there to be as many as there were . . ." He shrugged and let her fill in the blanks. "What about waking them up? Getting them innocked?"

"First they need to stabilize. The drugs in their system will filter out in time, and that will only happen by replacing their fluids as we support their organs." She held up a hand to stop the question he was about to ask. "I cannot simply inject them with the wake drugs or the inoculation. For one, I am not sure what particular combination of meds was used. Considering the fact that it was a freestanding cryo unit you found them in, not a ship, it would have been a different blend than the ones I have encountered in the past. For another, there is a very real chance that forcing consciousness would do more harm than good. As long as we have them on secondary oxygen that hasn't been touched by the Seed, the inoculation doesn't matter as much. In fact, it could very well kill them as they are now. The best thing to do is—"

"Where is he? I know you're in there, *milord*! Get the fuck out of my way, bitch."

Someone in the other room cried out as they hit the floor. Quinn beat Syrus to the door, and the warlord had to stop to let his second through. Behind him, the med-techs went into a rush of motion. He didn't look to see what they were doing. The inferno of anger standing in the middle of the main room was too much of a draw.

The man standing over the crumpled form of a woman turned and caught sight of his audience. "You," he roared, and lunged forward. Quinn caught him around the shoulders. "You took her down there to die!"

Well. That answered the question of what the dead tech's husband would think. Interesting. Syrus crossed his arms and tilted his head as he watched the letten try and get past Quinn. The first rank of officer to command more than a squad or two, lettens were fresh out of Command training. They were also the first to be allowed to choose wives, instead of just taking leave time on the Breeder ships or conquered planets. It was like mixing several varieties of explosive and hoping nothing set it off. More lettens died from bad decisions in battle than ever made it to the higher ranks. And more letten wives got passed around the barracks as trophies than ever lived long enough to produce sons.

"What am I supposed to do with my daughter now?" the man yelled, still trying to get to his warlord.

Syrus decided his first opinion of the man needed some changing.

"You took her down to the surface and now she's dead and I'm saddled with a useless bag of flesh to care for. She's not old enough to *train*, much less marry off!"

The blade of the knife sank into the man's unprotected eye and Syrus rode him all the way to the floor. The bastard didn't even have time to scream. Growling to himself, Syrus pulled the knife out of the eye socket, tugging to free it from the bone. He did it slowly, moving carefully as he stood. The thing inside him was starting to buck free again. Letting himself off the chain now would just make a mess. One he didn't want to deal with. Assuming Quinn didn't shut *him* down the way he'd just done this moron.

"Very impressive, Milord Turan."

Syrus grabbed the edges of his temper and hauled them back under control. Fuck it all, what now? He'd just barely gotten his shit straightened out.

Syrus looked up and saw a man in full armor standing in his doorway, silver spiked crown of a Branch warlord built into his helmet. Now that the letten was dead, Syrus could feel something other than the pyre of emotion the man had turned himself into. And what he felt just on the exposed skin of his face made him wish he'd killed the stranger instead.

He'd never heard of a word that could describe the emotion this man gave off. But he knew what it was. One of the first feelings he'd ever learned to identify from a distance. Guarding against it was even harder than naming it. It went beyond hate. Beyond anger and rage, or any of the other emotions of the moment. It took the long view, calculated, and prompted decisions meant to hurt as much as possible. This wasn't an emotion. This was such a lack of true feeling that it was almost anti-feeling.

Syrus stood and clipped the knife back on his belt. "And you would be?"

"Forgive me. I'd thought you knew that I would precede my Fleet. I am Warlord Kizen, of the *Ataorl Banso*." And then he smirked, like he was waiting for this outFleet man to ask what the words meant.

"I am Syrus. Warlord of the Turan, and by extension, the entire Kuchen Fleet. I've been busy. Your alert must have gone astray." And now someone owed him cash for all those extra syllables. Beside him, Quinn's emotional lockdown cracked slightly. Syrus ignored it. It was clear that Kizen was insane. The main thing to do now was to keep damage to a minimum and get him *out* of the private quarters.

"Syrus." Kizen smiled a little. "An outFleet name, yes?"

"Was he your guide?" Syrus toed the body at his feet. "Quinn led me to understand that most ships of Kuchen design have the same layout. I'm sorry you needed someone to help you find your way." Asking him if his flagship had gotten destroyed and he'd had to make do with a scavenged Imperial ship wouldn't help. But it was tempting.

Something in the warlord's eyes shifted, and the bundle of not-emotion twitched. A heartbeat later, the man settled back on his heels and hooked his thumbs in his belt. "Indeed. My apologies. I was in a hurry to make my obeisance. I see I was mistaken in my choice of companion. He seemed to need directions, and I was trying to oblige. But it looks as though you have your people well in hand. If it's all the same to you, I shall go and request some rooms from the steward, providing he can be found. Then perhaps we will be able to plan the next Campaign." The man bowed and was out the door before Syrus could unclench his jaw to reply.

Seven -- Syrus

The maruste are our lives, child. Our lives writ in the only thing that matters.
Our blood.
      -nurse of the lis Chuis isk Fuerrus, to Delfi

The starscape stretched over the ceiling and portside wall, its glittering array like the panicked host of a fleeing enemy, to quote a Fleet saying. The nanoprojectors embedded into the metal walls of Syrus's quarters were keyed to the feeds from the cams in the outer hull of the *Edde Belo*, giving him a fair picture of the system as they moved through it. He could activate the floor too, if he really needed to know what was going on out there. He could also turn the display off if he wanted, but the glow of the planet's third moon was a distraction from the keypads on the doors. The one leading to the infirmary was locked, but that meant less than it had this morning. He couldn't sleep, so he thought instead.

Kizen would try to get Syrus to make the first move. He had to, or the whole Fleet would turn on him. The fact that Kizen had come ahead of his Fleet meant he'd hoped to provoke a Challenge before Syrus declared Campaign and the ban on Challenges took effect. He'd been too late

When it came to moving up the chain of command, Challenges happened from the bottom up. Syrus had checked the records against those brought over by Kizen. The other warlord had worn his

Helm longer than Syrus. The laws of rank were the same for warlords as for letten or ralen. The Fleet rated people according to chronology when officers were otherwise equally ranked. Only the fact that Syrus held the Trunk Fleet, not a Branch, kept him in authority now. The fact that the whole Fleet would turn on Kizen if he called Challenge on Syrus was small comfort. They lived by their own rules or died for breaking them. By the same token, if Syrus were to snap and attack Kizen, they'd greet the winner the same way Quinn had greeted Syrus. With an empty helm and bent knees.

Kizen was counting on it.

The stars on the ceiling shifted slightly as the ship made a course correction. His head almost echoed with the silence of the room. This fucking mess was screwing with his sleep, damn it all. *Kizen* was screwing with his sleep. Fucker just wasn't worth it, so how was he managing it?

Breathe. Calm down. He *could* deal with Kizen as a subordinate. Which was technically true. But until the man did something so insane that making an example of him was the only thing left to do, the footing was less than solid. And Kizen would keep trying, pushing until he made Syrus lose his temper. If he'd known how close he'd gotten today, they might have had a bloodbath right there.

Syrus growled and rubbed at his eyes with the heel of one hand. He wished he'd been able to just let go. Problem was, killing Kizen during Campaign would leave his second in charge instead of transferring command. And if Kizen managed to kill Syrus, the same would happen to him. Quinn would take over until they were done with the next system. Stalemate.

Did the man realize Syrus knew all this? If Kizen hadn't when he came on board, he did now. Syrus had sent Quinn to make sure the other warlord didn't get "lost" on his way to find the chief steward. And to make sure Kizen didn't start any shit when he realized the steward was a woman. Bastard seemed like the type. Somewhere in all that, Quinn would make sure the warlord knew Syrus's record.

If not, the history of Campaigns was right there on the Fleet network. Anyone could log in and see the chain of victories reaching back, unbroken for hundreds of years, with the commanding warlord's name listed for each. And a respectable number of those were tagged with Syrus's code.

Syrus snorted to himself, untangled his fingers from the hair of the woman using his shoulder as a pillow, and eased himself out of bed. Most of the women were in their cubbies tonight. By the time the women in the infirmary were straightened out and he'd gotten rid of the second dead body to grace his quarters in as many days, even screwing the concubines' brains out didn't sound like any fun.

The women were glad enough to be left alone. This one hadn't offered anything more than the knowledge that there was another body to take up some of the yawning space in the huge bed. Even that wasn't helping. A sleep-tousled head poked out from behind her curtain as he padded across the floor. He put a finger to his lips and waved her back. She vanished.

He grabbed a hilt from the rack and sliced his thumb open again, right over the barely healed cut from this afternoon. Teeth clenched at the pain, he smeared the blood over the lock and stepped in. The lights in the infirmary were on their dimmest setting, but he didn't bother to turn them up. He could see well enough as it was.

The women looked worse than they had in the caskets, if the wires and tubes and various blinking lights on towers at the head of each unit were anything to go by. Iira must have decided that getting clothes on them wasn't worth the effort, because they were both naked. They looked small under the sheets, swallowed by the drape and folds of the fine fabric.

Muttering to himself about technology and medicine and the unholy mix they made, he looked for a way to get the darker one upright without pulling everything loose. Turning her over was a guarantee of yanking half the leads out of her skin. Fucking hell. Why hadn't he thought of checking their maruste before they'd been turned back into evil science experiments?

He had her halfway to sitting up before he realized there was an extra light source in the room.

Her head hit the table with a thump. He stared at his hands. At the woman. Touched a finger to her forehead. A muted orange glow filtered through the cloth beneath her, rimming her body in light.

He hadn't felt so much like the bottom had dropped out of his world in years. Not since he'd walked into this room for the first time.

Fists clenched, he picked his way around the equipment and over to the other table. Another finger to the forehead. Another orange glow. Brighter this time. Probably because of her skin color. Maybe. Who knew?

He backed away, ran into the tower of the medunit, adjusted course, and kept going. It wasn't until he hit the wall that he looked down at his hands. They shook. What the fuck? What. The. Fuck? How was this possible?

"Milord? What are you doing?"

He nearly gave himself whiplash as he jerked his head up. Iira stood in the doorway. Her hair was a mess, the bruise around her eye looked even worse than before, and she'd clearly thrown on a sleeping robe without bothering to make sure it was fastened all the way. He caught a flash of skin before she pulled it shut and tied the cord.

In contrast to her clothes, the look on her face was cold and professional. Eyes steady, a slate and an IV bag in either hand. She watched him with all the passion of an ice queen.

Then he remembered that she'd taken one of the cubbies in the main room, so she could be on hand if something went wrong in the infirmary.

"What—" His voice broke. He coughed and tried again. "What woke you?"

She gestured at the medunit. "You set off the alert."

He looked at the blinking lights that covered the unit and wondered how in the cosmos she could tell one light from another. "Hmph. Well. They're alive. You can go back to sleep."

"On the contrary." She set her slate down on the corner of the nearest unit and the IV bag on the end of one table before bending to look at the readouts. "You have not told me what you are doing here, milord. If you intend to use these women, I will have to unhook them. Is that what you wish?"

If she'd been in arm's reach, he would have snapped her neck. As it was, his foot caught on a length of cable before he made it two steps. By the time he found his balance, he had himself under control. Bitch. When would everyone stop assuming he was going to follow in Brander's footsteps?

Why was he still surprised that they were so ready to help him down that road? Did they think he'd finally caved now that he'd opened up the infirmary? Did they all take it as some sort of sign that he was acting more like a "proper" Fleet soldier should? None of them had lifted a finger when Riss—when that bastard was alive. Plenty of young outFleet children acted more and more like Fleet soldiers the longer they were on board. They were all probably waiting for him to go native.

Well, he wasn't some green boy, brainwashed and drugged into forgetting where he'd come from. He'd show them just what happened when they tried to make him into something he wasn't. Why he'd—

Iira laid one hand on his arm, interrupting his vision of sending the whole Fleet into the nearest star. He caught himself just before his fist made contact with her jaw.

"Hell, woman," he snarled at her. "The fuck you think you're doing?"

"Attempting to gain your attention, milord." She left her hand on his arm. Even with the contact, she was just a shimmer of feeling to his sai, not enough to understand. What was this woman made of? Stone?

"Well, you've got it."

"Milord, I'll ask again. What were you doing?"

He made the decision before he could talk himself out of it. "I need you to look at something."

Iira had to disconnect about half the leads before they could move the woman with the dark skin. The glow lit up again as soon as he slipped his hands under her thin arms. Dull brown patterning on her back turned the orange of amber lit from within, getting brighter and brighter the longer he touched her. By the time he got her upright and half draped over his shoulder, the light was so bright he was almost blind.

How long had it been since he'd seen a maruste light up? None of the women in his quarters ever offered to show theirs off. Now that he thought of it, he wasn't sure they all had marks to start with. The further away from the Core, the less people worried about getting their maruste activated—if they had the nanites in their bloodstream at all.

When his sight cleared, he looked through the glow of floating glyphs and met Iira's eyes. "Well?"

She shook her head, shading her face with one hand as she leaned back and squinted. "You would know what they mean better than I, milord. We have not made a catalog of the markings of the Navlad." The unspoken ending to that went: because we're trying to wipe them out.

"Hold her, then."

Once the transfer was made, he backed up enough to see the glyphs in full. They tracked a glowing line down her spine, pulsing slightly, like a heartbeat. There at the top was her family. Nobody he recognized. Planet of birth, some place in the Core he'd only heard of in the news vids. The usual flourishes and loops that came with money. Skill set.

He frowned. "Hold still."

There was a spot. It varied from person to person and with age, but it was usually over the sixth cervical vertebra. He brushed some stray hair out of the way and traced his thumb down her neck, counting the bumps in her spine. There. The glyphs flickered. He twisted his finger and pushed.

And nearly lost his eyesight again as the maruste virtually exploded into light. Lines and curves shifted from solid to broken in the space of a breath. Letters and glyphs crawled across her shoulders and wrapped around her ribs, then dripped down her back nearly to her hips. The light of the glyphs broke out and up, painting the expanded story of her life on the walls and ceiling.

Iira made a noise and Syrus reached out blindly to steady her. When she stiffened under his hand, he backed up, knuckled his eyes open, and stared.

"What is it, milord?" she asked, eyes still shut against the glare.

"Let's check the other one."

He didn't bother trying to pick the redhead up. Iira detached her from the medunit, then stopped and looked at him. He couldn't feel a thing from her in the way of emotions. If she knew what he knew, looking at these glyphs, she would be terrified at the very least. "Milord? A question?"

She'd stand there all night if he didn't let her ask. "What?"

"They did not light up when you brought them in, milord."

"Not a question."

"Why did this phenomenon not occur earlier?"

Syrus looked at the young woman on the table. She didn't look much better than she had when he'd opened the casket, but something Iira hit her with must have started working.

His Chief Med-Tech just stood there. Waiting. The lack of emotion was worse than silence.

"They had slipsuits on," he said after listening to his heart beat in his ears for another minute or so. "You need skin contact. Even if I'd touched them, they were too far gone. I don't know if the cold storage had something to do with it. But once a body's far enough along the road to death, it just doesn't have the juice. The nanites in the blood need power. If a person has one foot over the edge anyway . . ." He looked up and shrugged. "No lights. Now, you going to help me?"

Iira nodded and moved forward. In one easy motion, she pulled the girl upright, sweeping the twisting coils of red hair over one bare shoulder.

He looked for the right vertebra on the sleeping woman. A flicker of light, a twist, and the bright orange light painted the insides of his eyelids with glyphs.

"Is that—" Iira spat out a mouthful of red hair. "Is that the seal of—"

"No." He cut her off and took his hand off the redhead's skin. The light blinked out. "It's not. Get them hooked up again. Go tell Oona to get the Fleet to the next Barb. Then go wake your husband. I'm declaring Campaign. As soon as Kizen's Fleet makes it through the first Barbican, get the ralenen over here. We'll meet him on the other side."

He left her there, stalking out into the main room and pulling on his pants and boots before heading to his command center. Then he collapsed into the throne, pulled up the data for the next system on the table floating in the center of the room, and sat there, watching his hands shake.

The Empire had found him again. It had gone back in time, laid a trap, and waited until his pride and restlessness made him stumble into it. How the hell had he ended up owning the contract on a pair of random women who'd been in cryo for at least two hundred years? It had to be a blood tie. No other explanation. Indentures didn't answer from the top down. Maruste only lit up when the person who owned the bond touched the bonded.

He knew. He remembered the pain as the priest activated the fresh nannites with their indenture glyph. And again, when it was broken so a new one could be entered below it. The only three things that belonged on his back. Two broken indentures and the loopy curves of He'la marking him as the lowest of the low, there for anyone to see. No Open Blossom. No matter what he did to mask them, blood would tell.

He clenched his fists and watched his knuckles turn white. Fucking Empire. One way or another, it always came up to bite him in the ass. Now his chances of staying hidden in the Fleet were even worse than before. As if hiding his reactions to being baked, electrocuted and drowned was *easy*. If they found out. If the Fleet figured out he had a blood connection to two women with the crest of the Imperial family in their blood. That it took a certain sort of person to activate an Open Bloom..

Death was one thing. That would come one way or another. Once lira told Quinn that the foundlings had something *like* the Imperial Seal on their skin, he'd go digging. He'd have to. And once he found the differences between the Navlad Imperial Seal and the family crest of its ruling house, he'd make the connection. At which point Syrus's freedom to range planetside would be gone. Quinn would lock his warlord up and run things in Syrus's name until they hit the capital of the Empire. No more fighting. No more killing. No more destroying the people who'd made this little adventure possible.

An honest death was better than being a two-bit chit in a bad game of War and Crosses. He had to keep hiding. Same as always. Eventually he'd die in battle and his true lineage would surface on his skin. By then they wouldn't be able to do anything about it.

He just had to hold out. Do his best to sidetrack Quinn. And take as many Navlad Imperials with him as he could when then time came.

EIGHT -- JOSSA

Check the wine! Bad grapes have been added to even worse fruit!
-first prophecy of the Delfi Oracle, literal translation

Everything hurt. Her bones hurt. Her muscles hurt. Her head hurt. Pain tingled up her arms, ran in streams down her legs, and curled into a hard ball inside her ribcage. The light was dim, and then it was gone, and then it was bright. Something thudded in her ears, hard and fast. Her heartbeat? She couldn't tell. She didn't know. All she knew was that it hurt.

But her heart hurt most of all.

Aching. Empty. Straining around the agony of loss and despair. And somewhere in the middle of it, a hole. Was she missing something, or had that always been there? What went in the hole? Was that the place for more feelings? It kept trying to fill itself, and then it drained right out again. Like an air leak in the hull.

Consciousness came slowly. The lights steadied. The blur resolved. Metal panels. Curved lines over her head; organic, almost alive.

Something beeped quietly.

Her head turned when she told it to. At least that part of her still worked. But all she saw were clear tubes hooked to a tall machine with lines and buttons and blinking lights in various colors. A bag of something hooked to the side of the... whatever it was. There was a word on the tip of her tongue, but she couldn't remember it.

Had they gone to sleep yet? Had Goris put them under?

There was something past the forest of tubes and... wires. That's what those things were. Something red and soft around the edges, but not far away.

Her arms gave fresh shrieks of pain when she tried to lever herself up. And then more as she caught her hand in one of the... things attached to her. And then *everything* hurt all over again as she lost her balance and fell back against the bed. Table? She couldn't tell and couldn't remember, and something about that red blur was too familiar to make her worry about it for long.

She made it up on the second try. Muscles screamed. The thudding in her head grew worse, and the beeping noises sped up. But she was sitting. Not lying down. That was progress, wasn't it?

She nearly fell again as she tried to rub her eyes, and all the things stuck to and in her skin pulled and dragged at her. It took a moment to realize that her hands were taped down. Another few minutes to get her fingers to stop fumbling with the sticky stuff and actually take hold and pull. She lost her grip twice before she managed to yank it loose. Then the needle. Yes. Needle. That was the word for it.

It was cold in this room. She shivered, swallowed, and jumped when she heard a mewl. Was that her? It sounded like her. And it had come when everything in her throat rebelled at being made to move.

Even her insides hated her.

Finally, she managed to free herself of the tubes and needles and odd little circle things that weren't tape, but weren't needles either. The whole mass of it hung around her, and she tried very hard not to get wrapped up in it as she eased her legs over the edge of the table. Table? It was too high for a bed. Beds let you touch the floor. Yes. Table.

Feet to floor now. Lose the balance and clutch at the edge of the mattress. Falling on one's face was never pleasant, and the fuerrus did not like his women to have visible bruises. Other places, maybe. But never their faces. Or their backs. Or any other bit of skin routinely on display. His ornaments must be perfect in every way.

Something about that didn't feel right. Ornaments? No. Not just ornaments.

She swayed as she shook her head, trying to clear the fog from her brain and make things work properly. There was an order to things, wasn't there? And she'd broken it? Or had she? This was so familiar. She knew she should know this. Should know how to get herself back online.

Or was she? Should she? Someone helped her last time. Someone was always supposed to help her. Help them. Come for them?

Pick up the foot. Come on. You can do it. Up. Forward. Down.

Pain ripped through her body. She hit the other mattress with a thud and hung from the edge by her fingertips, shaking and swallowing against the feeling in her stomach. Then she mewled again at the pain in her throat and tried not to lose her grip on the only thing keeping her from hitting the floor and never getting up. It was a miserable thought. If she fell, she'd have no way to catch herself. Nothing to cling to.

Did she even want to see what this was? The hole in her heart kept growing. Tendrils of anguish crept out of it, threading along her veins like water in a newborn stream she'd once watched grow during a rainstorm. Sitting under the shelter of the ship, nestled up against... against someone. Someone large and warm and smelling of grease and soap and the wine he'd stolen for her. Their picnic had been interrupted, so they'd had to move.

Who?

Hope. That was the name for the fluttery feeling. Hope. Maybe it was him! Maybe he'd have answers!

Inch by inch, she pulled herself upright, hooking her elbows over the edge of the mattress to steady herself. Then she stood fully, trying to find a place to put her hands that wasn't covered in trailing tubes and wires. And finally, finally, she got to see who the table held.

She nearly fell again. She *did* wobble dangerously as her knees buckled and firmed.

"Delfi," she breathed.

No response. Nothing. Not even when she reached, somehow, with that part of her that always knew where her sousi was.

Hand shaking, she managed to find fingers, pale and dry against her own, among the needles and sensor pads. Was that what they were? Oh well. There were more important things to worry about now. Such as the fact that the other half of her existence was lying on a table. Asleep. More than asleep. If she were only sleeping, there would be something leaching through the contact. Nothing. Even skin to skin was a failure.

Now she remembered. Goris must have put them in the caskets. The pain. The weakness. She was waking from cold storage.

Waking first.

So where was Goris? Where were Bajak and Sender and Adan? Where was Denz? He wouldn't have left Delfi here alone.

Where was Rui?

She reached out again. Nothing. Not even flickers. Was the problem with her? Was she being blocked from the outside? Or was she really alone? Someone had to have taken them out of the caskets. Someone *must* have given them the wake drugs.

Patting Del's hand carefully, she turned her attention to the walls. They were curved, fluid even. Sinuous lines drew patterns among the spiked metal brambles as they wound their way from floor to ceiling. Rooms had doors. People did not just materialize in places. So, where was the door for this room?

There. Not so far. And so far. Light years away.

She tried again to find someone nearby. She couldn't even place Del. Just the sucking, aching hole of agony, growing wider by the second. If she didn't find someone soon, if she couldn't find Rui soon, it was going to swallow her.

And then she'd be back in the dark place.

No. No. She could do this. Even if Del was asleep, the sousi bond should still be working. It had worked through cryo before. It had to keep her sane now. Rui had probably just gone to find some food. Or relieve himself. He couldn't be far.

She lurched from the safety of the table to the wall over an arm's length away and fetched up next to what must be the door frame. The metal was cool on her skin, and she could feel the engraved vines with their hidden snakes waiting to bite at her. None of the buttons on the panel looked familiar; but one was bigger than the others, so she tried that one.

And then she *did* fall, as the wall under her hand warped, twisted, and melted into the edges of the door frame. Pain blossomed through her whole body as she landed. Then the agony in her nose took precedence and she lost herself to another whimper.

The floor was cool and smooth under her skin. Not the fine latticework of a ship's deck plates. Maybe she'd just lie here for a bit. Until the crew came back and found her. Then she'd have help. They'd all hug and cry, and Rui would hold her, and together they'd wake up Del and they'd all be safe. No more running. No more danger.

Safe.

But as she reveled in the bliss of cold metal on too-warm skin, she started to feel again. Arousal permeated the room. Anguish too. A pain all outside what was going on in her heart beat at her. She tried to shield, but her concentration could not hold beneath the weight of all that emotion. Fear seeped in. She couldn't tell if it came from within herself or elsewhere.

The smell made it worse. Musk of a particular sort, spicy and warm. Perfumes of varying strengths.

She craned her head around, rolling to her side with a hiss of pain.

The lights were down. It was hard to see clearly from this angle. But the size and shape hadn't changed much in the centuries since mankind left the Home Planet. She doubted someone would have made many innovations to the construction of a bed.

Except if she was seeing this properly, it was a *huge* bed. Far larger than the one in her first passenger cabin. Larger even than the one she shared with Rui.

There was only one answer.

No.

No. No. No.

Tears burned their way out of her eyes and down her cheeks. The hole in her heart turned to a gaping maw, a Barbican in full decay. It couldn't be. It was supposed to have *worked*. They were supposed to go to sleep and then Rui was going to come back for them and—

She choked on a sob, and desperation gave her the strength to get her arms under her and push herself up. Fear energized her, got her on her feet and moving towards a door in the wall opposite the one she'd just come through.

No. This was never supposed to happen. How could they have failed? How had they been found?

She scrabbled at the panel next to the door. Portal? She didn't care. It was an opening. And if she wasn't locked in she should be able to—to what? To do something. Find help?

Foolish, foolish little bittehek. She knew better.

She still had to try.

Something finally answered to her hand. The wall moved, melting back into hiding and revealing a hall. Or at least, she assumed it was a hall. The lights were brighter here. She blinked against them for a few seconds. And reached again.

There. People. They should have been stationed at either side of the door. They weren't. At the end of the hall? She peered around the edge of the door and looked. Nothing there, just a niche with a helmet of some sort in it.

Other direction? She nearly fell through the door as she craned her head around.

Yes. A person's shape. Shaped like a person in her mind, too. She couldn't get a clear read on them. But it wasn't the flat dullness of the guards in the Palace.

Maybe the fuerrus hadn't found her. Maybe Rui had found a new place to hide instead. Maybe they were going along their back trail. They'd done that a few times. It never lasted long, taking cover in places people never expected them to try; but now that they were "dead," maybe he'd decided to risk it again.

"Rui?" She eased through the door, braced herself against the wall, and started inching her way towards the person at the end of the hall. "Denz? Is that you?" They were certainly large enough to be Denz, mobile mountain that he was.

She still couldn't get much of a read off whoever it was. Maybe it was Goris, checking on something the room wasn't equipped to tell her. The medic was never very forthcoming with either thought or emotion. But Jossa hadn't wanted to invade the other woman's privacy by doing a full scan. Surface skimming had never yielded much, but manners required limits. Now those limits were coming up to bite her in the achek.

Hope started to flutter again. Even though that room behind her felt like the bedroom of the fuerrus himself, nothing else about this place compared to his quarters. Nothing seemed like it belonged *anywhere* in the Empire.

Then the person at the end of the hall was in front of her. And her heart stopped in horror.

Lust. Greed. Triumph. Most of all, rage. He was made of it. Whatever other emotions the man held in his soul, rage was the framework. The foundation. The engine that pushed him forward.

She whimpered and tried to curl in on herself. Tried to back away. Tried to fight through the morass that was the being in front of her. She couldn't make her feet move. She had to move, to run. Run! Rui didn't come for you. He failed. He failed. Just as we all knew he would. Suicide run. Gone. Forever and gone. Run!

A hand on her breast, squeezing and pulling and sending the contact burn of the sick, sick soul in front of her right down to the core of her being. Someone laughed, but the sound echoed in her ears.

They had failed.

Her wail of agony and anguish rang from the walls around her as she collapsed. The fall of her hair shut out the world as she clung to the floor and wept.

And wept.

NINE -- SYRUS

Predominantly female, Feels, or empaths, were among the earliest of the psych abilities developed, but by no means the most common. Some only received the outside emotions. Others, rarely, could project as well.
  -"History of the Sai: A Scientific Overview"

Women and children. Push came to shove, Syrus always found himself stuck in a room full of terrified women and children. Every base the Fleet took, noncombatants squirreled themselves away in the vain hope of survival. He could have told them that even if you lived through a Fleet assault, you didn't actually survive. Not that any of them would listen.

A base like this had hundreds of nooks and crannies an adult could hide in. Hundreds more where only a child would fit. Some had life support separate from the rest of the base. Some just had a tank of air and a bucket to shit in. No matter the size or resources, each little rat hole was a place where people breathed shallow and prayed to their Ancestors for deliverance that would never come. The smart ones killed themselves instead. They knew the Ancestors would do fuck all to help.

What it boiled down to was that every time the Fleet gassed a base with concentrated Seed, sweeps crews had to go in while the place was still toxic and look for signs of life. No innocks against the Seed. No leniency from the invaders.

The men were shot on sight. The male children were rounded up and sent to the Training ships, so they could help take over and colonize other systems and bases in the future. Any female past puberty got slapped with a set of grav-shackles and sent off to one of the Breeder ships at the back of the Fleet. There was a reason these fucks had that rule about Challenging each other while on Campaign. They'd all be so busy stabbing each other in the dick over the newest piece of ass, they'd never make it past the first trading post in a system.

Nobody was likely to fight over the woman on the table next to him. His nerves already felt like they'd been doused in acid, what with all the fear in the room. It drove him fucking nuts, but it was a comforting sort of nuts. A way to keep from being infected by that easiest of diseases to succumb to.

Rage.

The woman on the table wasn't afraid. She was pissed as fuck. And thanks to Fleet custom, he had to keep his helmet off so the fresh meat knew the face of her oppressor.

He would've fucking killed her if it didn't mean he'd have to explain his reasoning. That he hadn't lost his temper for no reason anyone could see. Well, he could just keep on killing people once he offed the woman. Then he wouldn't have to justify anything, and all the fear and rage around him would be gone. He'd finally be alone in his head. And Quinn would be proud to see his outFleet warlord becoming more and more like the Fleet born.

Syrus sighed and rubbed his nose. Habit. That was his problem. A lifetime of hiding was hard to break. That and the fact that wearing a sai-blocking bucket on his head night and day would only give people a reason to wonder what he had to hide.

The woman on the table made a muffled snarling noise and he frowned at her. "You wouldn't be in this position if you hadn't decided to stick foreign objects up your cunt."

She glared at him.

He raised an eyebrow, then stepped down to the foot of the table. "Status," he asked Iira.

"This would be easier, milord, if you had let me sedate her." The med-tech didn't look at him. She had forceps and a probe in either hand and was poking around like, well, like a med-tech looking for something in someone's innards. "Or at least approve power to this sector so I can use imaging to find out how far up this thing is."

Syrus snorted. "You going to sit there and gripe or you gonna get that dick-eating *thing* out of her sometime this week?"

The look Iira gave him was pure venom. A fresh flare of anger broiled his face as the captive woman jerked against the straps and shackles that held her to the table. Iira muttered something to the effect of "outFleet cunt" and went back to prodding at the woman's, well... cunt.

Syrus decided to leave her to it. The prisoner was trussed up like a bird for roasting. The other captives were getting a lesson in what *not* to do where the Fleet was concerned, and he didn't know the first thing about pulling inorganic objects out of a vagina. For all he knew, she'd had it fused to her muscles before the Fleet dug her out of that little cupboard.

"Milord?"

He looked around to see a com-tech at his elbow, slate in either hand.

"Give," he said.

She handed him one of the slates, then held the other where he could see the display. "Milord, preliminary reports are in."

He looked. The last few safe holds in the base had been found, but the people in them had either killed themselves or suffocated before the Fleet troops could crack things open. Standard lifeform scans had been done, just to rule out anyone hiding in a mechanical maintenance room or the ductwork. He shook his head and kept reading. That last was just stupid. But protocol was protocol, and it had been around longer than he'd been alive.

Syrus gave the slate in his hand a thumbprint for verification and reached for the other one. "Warlord Kizen checked in yet?" he asked the tech as charts and data readouts spun on the new slate.

"His second sends his compliments, sir. Three quarters of their Branch has made it through the Barbican. They are on their way. He says they have sent strike-sats out to block the in-system communications relays."

"Tell him to pull them back. We've already got people on it." Which was guaranteed to piss Kizen off even more—but wasting people on a job already done was just as smart as running out ahead of his command and trying to take over the Trunk of the Fleet without backup. Man deserved it. Same as he deserved to park his ass in the Barbican Customs base while he waited for the rest of his ships. Bastard.

"The girls still in the market?" He gave the screen another thumbprint and brought up the next set of numbers. Lines crawled and Kuchen script flew across the slate.

The tech curled her lip, but she nodded. "Letten Uytalaa has them well contained, milord."

The *hiss-pop* of scorn up told him all he needed to know about the tech's opinion of that little arrangement. Syrus took a tighter grip on the slate to keep from shaking his hand out and grinned down at the woman. "You married . . ." He trailed off, waiting for her name.

"Tech-Ataoch Anaoa," she said stiffly.

The numbers on his slate settled. Some red. Some green. A few dark orange. He frowned. "Me neither." He pinched and dragged at the numbers. "But something I've noticed about women is that they don't like wearing rags. I destroy a fuck-ton of their clothes. If I didn't let them out every so often to go 'shopping,' they might actually try to murder me in my sleep." He looked up at the frowning tech. "Be a shame to have to kill them when I can just—" He stopped as the slate dinged at him. "We got a system map yet?"

"Partial, milord."

The woman on the table thrashed again and cried out. Syrus stiffened and snarled as fear and anger lashed at him. The tech next to him gave off her own small burst of terror. She tapped faster on the surface of the slate. "Got it," she breathed.

Syrus took it from her, compared the readout to the one full of numbers, and growled. "Where the fuck are those ships going?"

"I don't know, milord," the tech replied. "Survey drones didn't—"

Grief came from everywhere and nowhere at once. Just like a gut wound, death wasn't instantaneous. But it was coming, sure as could be. After a few heartbeats, Syrus wished it would hurry up and finish him off. He wanted to grab a blade and do the job himself, if only he could make his hands move. Just get rid of that unending agony.

If it weren't for the fact that half the room had collapsed in the same moment, he would have been done hiding. Syrus caught himself on the edge of the table and looked around. The tech was on the floor by his feet, tearing at her hair and keening like a dying animal. The soldiers in full armor hadn't been hit as bad. Not that they weren't doubled over, clutching at their chests, but neither were they crying and aiming weapons at their heads.

A whimper at his elbow cut through the emotional overload. The woman on the table writhed against her bonds, gulping out sobs as tears streamed down her face. He wasn't worried about her. She could swallow her tongue for all he cared.

Iira on the other hand. She'd drawn the little gun she kept strapped to her hip when she had to go off ship. And she had the barrel right up under her chin.

"It's all wrong," she whispered when she saw him looking at her. "I gave it up. Gave it all up. Should have never given it up. What have we become? How could we have fallen so far? I'll never—" She choked and wobbled. How could someone shake that hard and not be a piece of machinery?

"I'll never be enough. Never be able to help him fix it. Useless! Worthless! Don't need med-techs. It's all about strength, don't you see? I just—I can't!" She choked again, gulped, and put her finger to the trigger.

Syrus leaned over the captive woman's leg and slapped the gun out of Iira's hands.

"My thanks, milord."

A pinpoint of calm in the ocean of heartrending horror. Syrus turned his head to see Quinn, face as impassive as ever.

What the fuck?

"The fuck?" When you can't come up with anything coherent, turn off the brain-mouth filter.

"Oona has closed off the bridge. They are safe there. But she reports that... something... has caused every unarmored person still in the ship—and about half of the base—to collapse. And many of the armored as well. If we do not find the cause—"

Syrus levered himself back upright, coughed to clear the tightness in his throat, and tried to throw up a shield or two. Shit. He was so out of practice that it was like using wet cellulose to guard against artillery fire. How was Quinn doing it?

"Armored?" he asked through the haze.

Quinn gave him a look that would have withered grass. "Yes milord. Armored."

Oh. Yeah. Now he remembered. Funny how having all your failures and losses ripped out of hiding and dumped on your heart could drive everything else of your head. He looked closer at the man's helmet. Not his usual ceremonial getup. An actual combat piece. That made more sense.

"Well come on then," Syrus said, reaching for his discarded helmet. "I have a feeling I know who's causing this. Might as well bring her." He waved a hand at Iira. "We'll probably need her."

Quinn didn't argue—just pulled his sobbing, apologizing wife to her feet, placed a hand in the small of her back, and pushed her forward. Syrus slapped his helmet on, tightened up his shields for good measure, and followed his second out of the room.

>>><<<

The halls didn't quite run with blood, but only because the guards on the *Edde Belo* were stretched thin. That there was blood at all could be laid at the feet of custom. Being Fleet meant having an insane belief in your own indestructibility. Heavy armor was only for when you were getting actively shot at. On board, you compromised by wearing light duty gear of cloth composite. And no helmets.

Syrus stepped over the body of a man who'd jammed a knife up through the soft palate of his mouth and made a mental note to have the whole Fleet wear full armor while on Campaign. Even off duty. Women included.

It wouldn't be a complete fix. Nothing short of wrapping everyone in a cocoon of shielding would keep them from being affected. Armor had joints and gaps, and most of the anti-sai shielding was in the helmet. But it was much, much better than nothing at all. He'd made Iira take his helmet when they reached the first of the bodies, and right now all Syrus wanted to do was sit down on the floor, bury his face in his hands, and cry. He couldn't remember the last time he'd cried.

But he sure as hell wanted to. His mental shields had collapsed before he even made it out of the base infirmary. The only thing keeping him in control of his wits was fear of what would happen if he lost it.

His breath dragged in his throat as he sucked in gulps of air and seriously contemplated swallowing his own tongue.

Then, just as he was thinking he might actually follow through with that plan, the pain stopped. Like taking a step and finding a cliff, he went from grief and agony to numb deafness. He nearly tripped over his own feet in shock.

"Milord?" Quinn's voice was eerily calm.

Syrus took a breath, then another just to be sure he hadn't died, and shook his head. "It's gone. Take off the helmet and see."

The man looked at his wife. Bastard.

With shaking hands, Iira pulled the borrowed helmet off her head. For a moment she cradled it against her chest, shoulders hunched and head bowed. Then, slowly, she straightened. Her eyes were red, her face blotchy and tear streaked, but there was joy there like nothing he'd ever seen in *any* Fleet woman. Huh. Syrus raised an eyebrow but decided not to comment. Now that the grieving was gone, his head felt like someone had been using it for target practice. He didn't want to reach out with his sai until he was sure he wasn't going to get blasted again.

"Right then," he said. "Let's go see what happened."

>>><<<

Two crumpled heaps lay at the mouth of the corridor leading to his quarters. One was a guard. Next to him was one of the foundling women. Twenty feet to port from where Syrus stood, another body lay in front of the lift that led up to the bridge. Female, clothed. The stun gun on the floor next to her answered the question of how she'd gotten the foundling to turn off the fireworks. The flight pilot's helmet on her head answered the question of how she'd made it down here in the first place. The etched silver collar around her neck was enough to tell him who the woman was. Quinn's second wife. Oona.

Syrus thumbed his comm unit and dialed in the bridge. The tech who answered sounded worried, but relatively calm.

"Report," Syrus said.

"Bridge secure," the tech replied. "No casualties."

For a second he wondered how they'd managed to stay sane when Oona left. Then he remembered. She would have used the airlocks on her way out.

"Rest of the ship?"

She took a little longer answering that one. Just as he started to ask again, she spoke. "Engineering reports minimal casualties. Flight decks secure. The rest have not checked in yet, milord."

Which meant they were probably dead or dying. Great. Kizen was going to take this whole mess and practically wallow in it. Just what they needed.

Nothing he could do about that now.

"Keep trying," Syrus growled at the woman, then shut down the link. Kneeling, he scooped up Oona's gun and clipped it to his belt, thinking hard. One way or another, he was going to have to touch the foundling. He couldn't make Quinn take her, not with Oona to handle. Iira was in no shape to carry the woman. It would be stupid to make her try in the first place.

Brushing a tangle of near-black hair away from the too-thin cheek, Syrus touched his fingers to the foundling's neck. The air lit with the amber-orange glow of her maruste. Fully activated. He hadn't remembered to turn the fucking thing off the night before. Shit. Now he was really fucked up the ass.

Something hit the floor with a soft thud. He looked up. Quinn had dropped Oona. Not far. He was still kneeling. And she was still wearing the helmet. But his second didn't seem to notice that he wasn't holding his wife anymore. "Milord," he breathed.

Syrus decided he'd ignore the fact that the other man was actually showing emotion. "Don't ask me how or why or what," he said, hoping Quinn wouldn't push. Satisfied that there was still a heartbeat in there somewhere, he shifted, scooped the woman up in his arms, and stood. The light was even worse like this. Would it be this bad when he finally got around to screwing her?

He'd have to figure out what to do with her in the long term. She might be worth keeping in his quarters, if she ever woke up again. And managed to put on a little weight. But if he wasn't even going to be able to *touch* her without getting his eyeballs seared out of his skull, he'd have to figure out something else.

A tidbit of information, half remembered, flitted through his head. Some old proverb about the marriage night and orgasms and blinding light. Fucking hell. He was going to have to talk to her about this. Hopefully she knew which of her glyphs he needed to cut open to get the thing to stop the light show.

"Come on," he said once he'd managed to open an eye against the glow. "Let's get her put away and this mess cleaned up. Still got a planet to Conquer, and it ain't gonna wait."

Ten -- Syrus

Syrus had met some stubborn people in his life, but every so often Quinn reminded him of the difference between stubborn and single-minded.

The man was fairly subtle about it. He could afford to be. With Oona sitting there glaring daggers, all but demanding Syrus drop his two strays out an airlock, Quinn could sit back and make comments. Little hints as to what would happen if the rest of the Fleet found out what had happened earlier in the day.

"I'm saying no," Syrus growled at Oona where she lay in the infirmary bed. "I need them alive."

"In the meantime, you want me to lie to my crew," the woman replied. Frustration rolled off her like heat waves in a desert, pricking and bursting like needle-filled bubbles. "And tell them what exactly?"

"That the Navlad military managed to hide a sai on the Customs base. The scanner crews missed a compartment before they cleared the base for entry."

"Are you implying that my—"

Quinn cut his wife off with a hand over her mouth. Syrus raised an eyebrow. That was new. His second wasn't exactly restraining Oona, but it was as close as no nevermind. Interesting. This shitstorm with the sai woman must have rattled him more than he'd let on.

"Hush, wife," Quinn said. His voice was quiet, but the order was still there. "This is your warlord. Remember that."

Nice to know he'd been downgraded from person to thing. Syrus snorted and propped a hip up on the bed next to Oona. "You going to be civil now?"

She glared at him over her husband's hand, then nodded.

Syrus waited another moment before picking up the slate he'd set aside and waving at his captain. "Now. Let's sort out these deployments, hmm?"

Quinn took his hand off Oona's mouth. She took the slate and sighed, and Syrus headed for the nearest med-tech station to grab a stool so he wouldn't have to sit on Oona's bed while she argued with him about how they were going to cover all the missing posts. He'd brought the stool over to Oona's medunit and was just relinking it to a grav tether when the door at the far end of the infirmary melted open. Kizen came charging through like a one-man stampede. A med-tech ran over to intercept him, asking what she could do for him. Kizen grabbed her and threw her against a nearby medunit.

The rest of the techs got out of the line of fire, running back to their duties with heads down and shoulders hunched. That left the way clear for the warlord to come charging up the aisle.

"What the fuck is going on here?" the man roared as he ground to a halt.

Syrus didn't take his hand off the knife hilt clipped to his belt.

"You!" Kizen headed around the end of the bed towards Quinn. "What do you think you're doing, coddling this woman? We've got a system to conquer and a fucking cunt just flattened half your fighting forces without laying a *hand* on them. The hell do you think you're doing in here?"

If it hadn't been for the small sun of fury the man was giving off, Syrus might have laughed. Kizen thought he could intimidate Quinn. The other warlord's emotions aside, Syrus *still* would've let the tantrum play out. Except Kizen had blown past Syrus like he didn't exist. Acting like he was the ranking officer here. As if Quinn was supposed to obey him without question.

If Syrus didn't cut this off at the knees, the rest of the Campaign was going to be a shitstorm of squabbles and power plays. He had enough to worry about without inter-Fleet politics fucking things up.

So he set his slate on the bed and stood. "Talking to the wrong person," he said. "You want to bitch at someone, bitch at the person who gives the orders."

Kizen spun. "You," he spat. "OutFleet cur. You're not even fit to lick my boots. Why should I give two creds what you think? Whatever lip service this eunuch of a second here gives your title of Warlord, *I* know very well that you are merely the figurehead. Fuck, he probably *helped* you take down your predecessor—just so he'd have a tame body under the Helm while he runs this fleet into a star!"

Syrus couldn't tell what Quinn felt, if anything, eclipsed as he was by Kizen. But the man's face settled into lines that Syrus had only seen once before. When he'd held out the Helm of the Fleet, still full of Brander's blood, for Syrus to take.

Kizen was baiting them. Trying to see how far he could push the outFleet warlord and his crew. It didn't matter if he was doing it on purpose or not. Question was, how to shut the man down without turning this into an all-out brawl?

Quinn solved the problem for him. "The strong rise; the weak fall. If you have not yet synced records with our database, then you should do so. The vid of his fight for the Helm has been made available to all. OutFleet he may be, but he has kept to the tenets of the Fleet."

"Fah. Coddling your women." Kizen waved a hand in Oona's direction. "Is this in keeping with the tenets of the Fleet?"

"Getting a captain back to her post is," Syrus said before Quinn could do anything. "Until she's back on the bridge, we need to work from here. Now, if you have something *useful* to input, you're welcome to stay. Otherwise, I'm sure—"

"A woman! As Captain? How long have you been out of touch with the rest of the Fleets? Women don't belong in *any* sort of position. You stuff them on a Breeder ship or drop them planetside and mount as many men as you can on them until they birth enough squalling infants to make up for the men killed to take the damn system in the first place! You don't give them any more responsibility than that!"

Oona went from emotional stonewalling to supernova between one heartbeat and the next. Syrus fought the urge to slap at the invisible fires incinerating his skin. Instead, he fisted a hand in the bedsheets, gritted his teeth, and tried to throw up shields. He fucking sucked at shields. The more time he spent on this damned ship, the more he wished he'd actually learned how to use them.

But he'd always been so much better at enduring.

Satisfaction rippled through the air, cool and oily. It was almost unnoticeable, but it gave him something else to focus on. He took a full breath, unclenched his jaw, and narrowed his eyes at Kizen. "What did you really come for?"

Even a Numb would know that he'd surprised Kizen. He just had no control over his emotions. Or his face. But the emotion faded fast. "Where's the bitch?" the warlord snarled.

There it was. Syrus grinned and crossed his arms. "Your branch of the Fleet has been ignoring the 'strength of mind' half of the creed for a long time, eh Kizen?"

The man's face turned an even deeper shade of purple.

"I'll save you the trouble of the argument. Yes, she's in my quarters. No, I won't bring her out. She's got information. I want that information."

"She killed half your forces! Without ever laying a hand on them!"

Repetition could tell someone a lot. Kizen was stuck in a loop on this whole sai issue. The man was terrified.

"She didn't take out half the forces. Not even close." Syrus picked up the slate, still open to the figures he'd been looking over. "Only a quarter of the men. A sixth of the women were off ship, going over the base. A third of the women were at their stations in shielded sections of the ship.

"The rest, well." He shrugged and set the slate down. "We're stalled for a bit, true. Our support ships are intact. We can cycle the recruits about to graduate, train them up early and supplement with reserves from settled systems. It'll take a few standard days to get them shuffled through the Barbs. By the time we go our separate ways in the next jump through the Barbican, I should be at full strength. Good thing we ran into you. Wouldn't have had the backup in place otherwise."

Kizen looked like he didn't know if he should gloat or not. On one hand, he'd just been told his forces would have the honor of carrying the weight of the Campaign for the next week or so. On the other hand, he'd just been told that his forces would be responsible for the brunt of the losses in the Campaign for the next week or so. It was a risk, leaving an opening like that, but Syrus figured it would be worth it if he could get the man off the topic of the two women.

"What information could she possibly have that makes it worth keeping her alive?" the man finally growled. "There's a reason we get rid of every Imperial woman with a drop of highborn blood. Not even this puling, gutless—" he waved at Quinn. "—would have allowed that custom to fall into deadspace. They should have been fucking killed the moment you realized they had more than an inch of those marks on their backs!"

Oona muttered something under her breath, but quieted when Quinn laid a hand on her shoulder.

"Don't be shy," Syrus told the woman before Kizen could start in on the Captain thing again. "I can take it."

She looked up at her husband, frowned, and sighed. "He has a point, milord. There is a reason we do not keep women on board who can use—" She waved her hands slightly. "Sai."

Syrus shook his head. Not even the Navlad were as obsessed with sai as the Fleet. To the Empire, the talent was a resource. These Fleet fuckers acted like it was a monster in the dark, waiting to rip them to pieces the minute their backs were turned.

Up till now, the Fleet hadn't run across any serious resistance from a sai. What they had found was planetside. Easy enough to drop a missile or two. Or ten in some cases. No more sai, no more problem. The shielding panels built into the ships themselves would keep out the rest of their metaphysical enemies. But the panels weren't in the outer hulls, just certain compartments. Everyone else was wide open. Now that it'd hit them on the flagship itself, they didn't know how to handle it. That might be what fueled Oona's temper. She'd just had a very loud alarm blasted in her ear, and it was saying she didn't have enough armor in her ship.

"Here's the deal," he said once everyone was done glaring at each other. "So far, you people have had it easy. Everything we've run into since I came on board has been planetside storm compared to what we'll face once we get inside Hadra's Net. That shit will be like a star going supernova. Everything inside the Net, the Core and all the rest of the little territories? Those are the systems that the local Families are going to protect."

He leaned forward so he could make sure Kizen was looking at him. "One woman. One out-of-control Projective Feel managed to stall our Campaign. We've lost the element of surprise now. Doesn't matter how many Imperial satellites and communications relays our drones take out. They know we're here and they have time to dig in.

"Now, imagine fifteen or twenty of her. Think of what *they* could do to the whole Fleet. Not just one ship." Syrus sat back and hooked his thumbs in his belt.

Kizen opened his mouth, but Oona cut him off. "Hadra's Net?" She was looking from Syrus to her husband, so she didn't see Kizen start to rise, one hand on a knife hilt. Quinn did, though, and he dropped a hand to his own belt. Syrus shifted in place, more because he wished he could get the feel of itching bugs out from under his skin than to help his second or his captain. Nobody had gotten to full-blown rage yet, but the irritation and disgust were as annoying as all get out.

"We have come across mention of it in Imperial records," Quinn said without looking away from Kizen. "It was never much studied, but we can have the Chief Comm-Tech look into what was copied over before the original servers were destroyed. Unless . . ."

All three of them swiveled to look at Syrus.

He growled.

A nasty smile grew on Kizen's face. "Well, Imperial. Seems you're good for something after all."

Syrus hooked the stool over with a foot and sat, fingers still in his belt and ankles crossed. He fucking hated being their walking 'pedia on the Navlad Empire. If the damned Fleet didn't flatten every data center it got near, they might have a better idea of what they were dealing with. Fuckers.

"Well they couldn't build a fucking wall in space," he said. "So they built a trap. Enemy comes through a certain gate, sets off an alarm. All the vamalkuog get their battlegroups together to come thrash whoever it was didn't knock before they came in the door." Syrus shrugged. "That's the theory anyway."

"And in practice?" Kizen sounded like he wished they could run across the Net right now, just so he could try some thrashing of his own.

"Actually tends to work. See, the planets inside the Net? Those are the ones they want to *keep*."

The three of them sat and mulled that over for a minute or so. Syrus let them. As far as he knew, he really was their best source of information on the Empire and its tactics. Which was probably another reason Quinn had kept him alive that first day. Nothing Syrus told them would have been news if they'd been thinking very far ahead in this little trip across the Galaxy. But they hadn't been, and he was.

Kizen, on the other hand... Well, there was a reason Syrus still had his hands so close to the hilts of his knives.

"What does it take to make one of those sai bend to their master's will?" Quinn asked.

Well fuck. Syrus decided he deserved that little surprise. Tell a Fleet man that psychics would be doing everything they could to stop him, and of course he was going to look at ways to use that for himself. They did it with everything else they found, why not this too?

"It takes getting ahold of a baby that's tested positive for the gene and using another sai to condition them so they'll do what you want," Syrus said.

Quinn settled back on his heels and looked at Oona. She looked back.

Oh, that was fucking perfect. The bastard was actually considering it.

"Conditioning," Oona asked. "What is that?"

Syrus tried to figure out a way to word it so they'd understand just how much work it would take and how impossible it was for them to manage. Finally, he shrugged. "Brainwashing. Make her think and do what you want her to, without realizing it's not her will guiding her."

Quinn frowned. "No men? No way to use them in this?"

"Not the way you want. As a rule, men don't have sai. And the ones that do are usually Cracks. Nothing they can do that your com-techs and malware don't do already.

"You want to start making sai do what you want, you need to start saving baby girls and keep them off the Breeder ships until you find out which ones have the gift. Let them hit puberty and see who starts talking to walls."

"What if we cannot condition them?" Oona asked.

Kizen growled under his breath, his frustration ratcheting up a notch.

Syrus threw up another shield and ignored him. He was too busy trying to remember if Barbicans would work as time travel devices as well as transport. Rewinding to the day he'd decided to grab the two women out of cryo would be a really good idea right about now. Leave 'em there, keep on moving. The Fleet would still have the Net somewhere ahead of them, but at least nobody would be asking questions that made him come this close to revealing himself. Now he had to fly along the edge of the gravity well and try not to tell them so much that they'd realize *why* he knew all this.

What to say? Iira would have told Quinn and Oona what he'd found on the women, but did she know what the markings meant? Or why they'd lit up?

"If you can't condition them, you need to find a sai with something to lose and squeeze her until she breaks."

At the edge of his vision, Kizen shifted. An expression Syrus couldn't read flickered across the man's face. Syrus ignored it. He was too busy slamming the lid back on the hole that housed his memories. He wouldn't open up that particular demon pit. He couldn't. Not if he wanted to stay sane. Besides, it looked like Oona had more questions. Syrus figured he could guess what came next.

"And no, you can't crown them if you want to use them. Especially not if you get a kid. Not if you want to be able to tell who's got the gifts and who doesn't." Syrus shook his head when Oona opened her mouth. "Otherwise how will you know if the plan's working?" Woman's head must still be scrambled if she missed something that obvious.

Kizen snorted and crossed his arms. "Why not just grab anyone with more than an inch of those markings on them?"

Syrus bit back a growl. "It's not the size of the maruste on the back that matters as much as which glyphs are in it. Especially when it's in full bloom."

All three gave him identical flat looks. Right. Translator screwing up again. Why was it always the little words that gave it problems?

He backed up in his head and tried to think. "Turned on. Exactly like a switch. A bare back doesn't mean no history. It could just mean they didn't get the basic programming activated in the first place. The people in the backwaters we've been taking are far enough from the Core, they don't usually give two shits about activating the nanites in the first place. Most never update them either. This far out, only the nobility cares."

Telling them how much it hurt wasn't worth it. The children of normal families never remembered it; they were too young when they were brought to the priests. And for people who were old enough to remember? The skin on his back itched.

He kept going. "Best thing to do is catch the girls and their families, stuff them in shielded cells, and give them some of the washouts from training to play with. See who does what."

Like start trying to pull their ears off their heads, or gouge their own eyes out? asked a part of him he'd thought he'd buried ages ago. *Or killing everyone in reach to keep their emotions from infecting you?*

Shut the fuck up, he told the voice. *These bastards will figure it out sooner or later. What happens to kids who can't run fast enough is none of my business.*

The voice obeyed. Just in time, too. He was starting to growl, deep in his chest. Explaining why wasn't something he felt like doing at the moment.

"Look," he said as he straightened and resettled his belt. "You want to make plans to catch sai, fine. We can do that later. Right now we've got the Campaign of this system to sort out and the reserves to pull up. Anything else can wait until we're not short staffed."

Oona opened her mouth again, but Quinn touched her shoulder and she shut up. Kizen curled his lip, and Syrus braced himself as the energy coming off him buzzed from frustration to anger to something Syrus could only think of as jealousy, then right back around again. He waited, feeling the other two close themselves down further and further as the silence stretched out.

Finally, the other warlord dipped his chin. He didn't lower his eyes. "All honor Syrus, Warlord Turan. You have your people well in hand. My troops will be proud to lead the charge. And to take care of your captive women when you set fit to release them to our care."

With that parting shot, the man left just as quickly as he'd arrived, although much more quietly.

"I will have to schedule a meeting with his second," Quinn murmured when the door at the far end of the infirmary slid shut.

Syrus shot a look at his second. "Why? Because he threw a tantrum when he came in?"

"What he said about the Fleet being out of touch with the home planets is true enough, in a way. The Branches are relatively autonomous, as you know. Certain customs have shifted from branch to branch."

"Such as a woman's place in the Fleet?" Syrus asked. He had wondered about it, but since the division of labor seemed to work, he'd left it alone. Now, though . . .

"Indeed." Quinn scooped his slate up from the bedside table and took his seat again. "But one of the duties of a second is to keep our ties to the Root strong. It's the Root that sets the patterns of our lives. Even yours, milord." His lips pulled in a thin smile. "It's part of why there are so few real Challengers for my post, milord. Nobody really wants the job of cultural custodian.

"At least you, milord," the sarcasm practically dripped from the word, "do not attempt to remake us in the image you wish." Oona sniffed and stuck her nose in the air.

"Yeah. Think of how much we'd get done if I tried *that*." Syrus snorted and picked up his slate. "Let's get this deployment shit figured out before someone from engineering starts a mutiny."

ELEVEN -- JOSSA

"They call the common folk rabbits; did you know that? Copulating like the Galaxy is about to end. It makes you wonder, then, who decided that a rabbit should be the symbol of the concubines."
-Chataf Kuchru lis Chuis isk Fuerrus, in conversation with Jossa

When she woke for the second time, she was still disoriented, but not quite as badly as before. For one thing, she recognized that she was lying on a mattress of some sort, and that the lighting above her was more typical of a ship than a palace. For another, her body was draped with a thin blanket, the fabric of which felt nothing like she remembered. Nothing this coarse would ever have been allowed in the vicinity of the fuerrus.

The fear faded a little with that knowledge. What followed was almost enough to throw her right back into the grief.

"'Bout time you woke up."

The voice was harsh, grating on the ears and on the soul. In it she could hear the stark truth of her current reality. The owner of that voice didn't care if she lived or died. She was a thing. An object that just happened to look like a human being.

She cringed. How long had it been since someone had talked to her like that?

Too long. Not long enough.

The voice said something else. Something in a liquid language full of vowels and too many syllables. Another voice, female, answered him back. What? None of *that* fit with what she'd expected.

"What?" she said, before she could think about it.

A pause. More liquid gabble. And then the man's voice again. "Well, at least we don't have to figure out what language you speak. One less problem in my fucked up day."

She lifted her hands to rub at her eyes and realized her head was pounding. And heavy. Why was her head heavy? It felt like she'd been drinking Sender's distilled lozo wine again. What in the name of the Ancestors?

Her fingers touched cool metal—rounded, smooth, and molded to her skull. Yanking her head up, she overbalanced and clutched at the edges of her mattress. No wonder she was off balance! No wonder it felt as if her head was stuffed with padding! No wonder the world was dim! They'd put a crown on her!

"You took out a quarter of our fighting force," the harsh voice said. If anything, he sounded even *less* happy than before. "Would have been more if most of the troops hadn't been out on the base. Congratulations, you're a weapon of mass destruction."

If he was trying to shock her with the news, he was many, *many* years too late. She'd been raised on that knowledge.

Instead of answering, she set herself to learning the boundaries of the crown. They were complete. Nothing from the outer world could make it in. She would not be able affect anyone without touch. Maybe not even then.

How was she going to cope until Del woke up? What if she *never* woke up? What if the crown blocked the bond? She'd never worn one while bonded. She'd never needed one after Del found her. She was alone now, locked inside herself.

She looked over at Delfi and realized that it might not be such a bad thing to have the crown blocking her sai. Yes, it was difficult, but more difficult than trying to survive in new environs without Delfi to anchor her in sanity? She hid a shudder before it manifested further than an ominous quake in her stomach. Focus. Focus on the here and now, and not the possibilities. Not the past. Here and now are what can kill you, and everything that happened before is immutable.

More liquid gabble from the woman. Both the strangers were being very careful to stand where she couldn't see them. Did they think she needed line of sight to use her sai? Did they not trust in the contraption they'd all but welded to her skull? She could feel the tendrils and hair-thin wires feeding in under her skin. Its roots in her brain.

It blocked her sai at the source.

The man replied in the same language, and now that she was no longer swimming through half-consciousness, she could tell he was softening his voice a bit for the unknown woman. His lover? She might not have her talents working at range, but she'd been raised with a crown grafted to her nervous system. She had learned to read emotions in words even without the abilities of a Feel. She just had to remember how to compensate for the enforced lack of Feeling.

But it was so hard! Her soul cried out for her sousi. Her heart cried out for her husband. Neither wanted anything to do with the discipline of the mind. Why couldn't she just curl up and pretend she'd never been taken out of the casket?

"What year were you put under?"

She snapped her head up, shocked out of her haze of grief by the man's words. When she tried to look at him, she nearly toppled over. Someone steadied her with firm hands. Small hands. Very *strong* hands.

"Year?" The face of the woman who'd caught her was impassive, her emotions unreadable, even through contact. Her Imperial was so heavily accented it was almost impossible to tell what she'd said. It wasn't until those hands, so un-ladylike in their strength, squeezed, that the words registered.

"Thirty-four eighty-five, oh five seventeen," she breathed, still trying to compute the disparity between the grip on her arm and the graceful lines of the face in front of her. It wasn't until those strange reddish-brown eyes looked away from her own that she felt able to think again.

"Just over three hundred years," the man said, his voice soft again in its thoughtfulness. "As the Empire reckons a standard year."

The young woman's heart stopped. Tried to restart. Stopped again. Air passed into her lungs and did not come back out. Horror and grief and agony, tamped down to coals, flared to life again. The woman in front of her caught her as she wavered, then eased her center of balance back onto the mattress.

"No," she whimpered, clutching at the smooth metal encasing her head. "No!" She choked on a sob, gasped for air, and curled in on herself. The position didn't help her breathing, but at the moment she would have rather suffocated than keep on with life. They'd *known* the risks. They'd *known* the plan might not work. But still, she'd hoped. Still she'd dreamed that it would be his face. His laughing, loving face, badly in need of a shave—that would be the one to greet her when she woke up. It hadn't. *He* hadn't. Unless...

"Were—" She swallowed and tried again. "Were there any others?"

"Just you two," the man replied. She couldn't tell what he thought from his tone of voice. She didn't put much effort into trying. If she'd lost Rui, then Delfi had lost Denz and they were both that much more the worse off for the loss of their anchors to the real world.

"Oh Del," she murmured, straightening so she could lean across the gap and touch her sister's hand. Her body failed her. If it hadn't been for the strange woman, she would have gotten a very personal look at the decking. Instead, she stared at her rescuer as the woman gabbled in the other language. The woman ended in a word that sounded like "De-el?" as she gestured with her free hand at the other table.

That penetrated the haze of loss. "You will call her Delfi. If you call her Del, she will wake to scratch your eyes out. And put fire-sauce in your bedclothes." Oh, if only it were possible.

A rasping sound like gravel in gears brought her attention back to the man. She stared, then realized he was *laughing*. She knew she'd heard a worse sound somewhere, but she couldn't remember where.

Unfortunately, the horror of his voice was in no way matched by his appearance. He melted out of a shadowed gap in the wall behind the strange woman. He had warm brown skin, lighter than hers. Fine creases, like those of planetside men who spent a great deal of time outdoors, framed hard brown eyes set under arched eyebrows. One eyebrow had a fine scar through it, old but not entirely faded. A small beard capped his chin. His hair was brown as well, pulled back behind his head and probably tied there somehow. His shirt was nearly the color of his skin. The muscles under it bulged as if they were insulted he'd even bothered to clothe himself.

If her heart had been at all fickle, she might have been tempted to fling it at his feet. As it was, she was reminded of the games she'd once played with Delfi and Azia, taunting their men by comparing the finer points of the various longshoremen working the docks around them.

"I said, what's your name?" There was no humor in his voice now. How many times had he repeated the question?

"Jossalyn," she whispered, suddenly reminded of the fact that she was *not* aboard the *Skatasi op Essi* and she was most decidedly *not* surrounded by friends. How long had she been out of the habits of a good concubine?

Too long. Not long enough.

Maybe, if she was lucky, he would kill her soon for her disobedience.

But then what would happen to Delfi? She looked at her sousi from the corner of her eye and wanted to cry all over again. Being the remaining half of a bonded pair was even worse than losing a spouse, if all the stories were true. What would that do to Del, the sane one, the sister who had held them both to sanity all these years?

The man and woman were talking to each other again, ignoring her as they argued. It was a quiet sort of arguing, without the waving about of hands and shouting that she would have expected. The woman wanted something. The man disagreed.

Jossalyn rubbed tears from her eyes and tried to pay attention, but she could only gather that the man held some sort of precedence over the woman. The idea seemed borne out by the crossed arms and mulish look on the woman's face as she glared up at the man. The man's teeth were very white against the dark of his skin, even in this light. To be sure, he wasn't quite smiling. More baring his teeth. But even a person dead to all Feeling would know that he'd won the point.

She shrank back against the pillow when he turned towards her, pulling the thin blanket up around her shoulders in a futile attempt to hide herself. He had a personality as forceful and raw as an unshielded blast of solar energy. Suddenly she was very glad for the crown on her head.

"Well, Jossalyn lis Churus isk Fuerrus. You fucked us up but good, you know that? There's a pile of people here—" He nodded at the strange woman. "Who'd like to fry your brains and throw you to the wolves. Lucky for you, I am who I am and you're more valuable to me alive than in a coma. Got a lot of questions you need to answer."

She stared at him, the sense of his words barely penetrating her daze. Would it never end? Was it not enough that she'd been awakened, three hundred years older and widowed? She'd thought these people were foreign to the Empire. But if they were, how did they know who she was? How could they still be hunting her?

Something dropped into place in her mind. She squinted up at the man, who still hadn't given his name. From the lowest to the highest rank, of, none of the man-hunters in service to the fuerrus would have kept his name from her. If only to gloat that he'd been the one to bring back the prize asjokoj skatbitteogek. And the way he held himself. The words he used . . .

How had someone born in the gutter come to be *in charge* of what sounded like a substantial fighting force? How had someone like him been the one to find her? More surprising yet, how had he known what the glyphs on her back meant? The Savages of the streets had no history, no lineage to their names. The only maruste they could claim was the glyph of nehkeh, a non-person. Such was all they were ever given—and that only if they got caught at some crime, so they would no longer be able sneak into the society of their betters. Better to have a bare back entirely than to wear the mark of a Savage.

Yet here he was, conversant in the glyphs of the highborn.

"You are nehkeh," she whispered in horrified awe.

The man went rigid, jaw clenched and eyes blazing. For one panicked heartbeat, she thought he would kill her. Instead, he leaned forward and braced his hands on the mattress to either side of her hips. Teeth drawn back in a snarl, the growl that rumbled out of his chest nearly made the table vibrate beneath her. She cringed back against the raised head of the table under her. He was huge. Huge and terrifying and not at all human.

As if he could read her thoughts, the snarl stretched wider, turning into a feral grin. "I got one more station to take before the army drops into the gravity well of this fucking planet." He spat the word "fucking" like he expected it to draw blood. Jossa felt her fist clench in the sheets. She forced it to loosen. Ancestors knew how he'd interpret possible aggression. She wasn't strong enough yet to fight.

If he noticed the involuntary movement, he didn't show it. Instead, he leaned closer, breath ghosting over her skin as he ran his nose along the line of her jaw. Jossa shuddered, grateful for the crown that kept his filth from invading her soul.

Hair brushed her cheek. His hair. "I get back, better hope I didn't find any information on the base. I do, I won't need to keep you or your—" He shifted and Jossa closed her eyes, imagining he was looking at Delfi now. "Sister alive." He leaned back far enough so his gaze met hers. "Myself, I'm starting to hope you don't remember shit. Feel free to call me names too. Makes the killing more fun."

Then, with all the care of an engineer in charge of an unstable power core, he turned on his heel and stalked back into the shadowed hole from which he'd emerged. It must have been a doorway, for a moment later a very feminine shriek of alarm pierced the air, followed by a male snarl of rage.

TWELVE -- JOSSA

*They're not happy with flattening a planet. Don't you
see? Whoever they can't load into their ships gets
gassed. Gassed! The whole planet. It's the only thing
they make for themselves. That damned Seed.*
  -survivor of Uzrus System

Eventually the woman finished her work, having poked needles in
every vein and major muscle group from Jossa's shoulders to her
feet. Then she made sure the bag on the end of the catheter tube
was attached properly, the fluids in the IVs were dripping as they
should, and Jossa herself was not about to make an escape attempt.
Or tear the crown from her skull by main force. Jossa didn't bother to
enlighten the woman as to her familiarity with the device. She had
few enough advantages here. The longer they thought she was dazed
and ignorant, the better.

A few female moans and cries filtered through the door when the
woman left, and then Jossa was all alone. Just the quiet hum of
medical equipment at the head of her table, Delfi's near inaudible
breathing, and her own echoing memories. She waited a few
moments just to be sure nobody was coming back, then dropped her
head to her knees and sobbed until she fell asleep.

>>><<<

The pattern of life in the little infirmary was as predictable as the hum of the ship through the deck. The woman, who eventually gave her name as Iira, would come. At first, she only checked the readouts and her charges, changed out the bags at either end of the tables, and made sure Jossa hadn't pulled out any needles or torn any of the sensors free.

She refused to answer questions, except for once when Jossa asked for clothes. A robe, a shift. Anything would be better than relying on the blanket to keep her warm and cover her bits. Iira merely looked at her, then looked at all the various tubes, sensors, and wires, and shook her head. When Jossa pressed the woman, she was rewarded with a short "Not allowed."

The look in Iira's eyes had promised a different sort of denial if her prisoner kept asking. Considering the fact that she was giving Delfi that look, Jossa decided that it would be safer to drop the issue.

After Jossa felt the side of her jaw and found a fresh scar where the small lump of her translator should have been, and a new lump just below that, she stopped trying to make conversation. Her old translator wouldn't have been able to keep up with this new language, but it looked like they'd given her a new one. Since the medic wouldn't speak, that meant she was being purposefully isolated. She could live with that, for now.

Her main worry was that Delfi didn't wake. Iira's refusal to communicate extended to the state of Jossa's sousi. Translator or no, that was unacceptable. When rational queries failed, Jossa moved on to pleas of mercy. When those fell on deaf ears, begging entered the equation. Having progressed through various stages of hysteria and finding them useless against the wall of Iira's indifference, Jossa finally started tearing needles from her arms, intent on reaching her bonded one and determining life or death. She threw curses at Iira, who swatted the flung medical paraphernalia away from her face in the race to find out whether the prisoner could launch herself off the table before the jailor could pin her down. Iira won. Barely.

Jossa retched as Iira caught her around the stomach and all but threw her back onto the mattress. As soon as the opposing force was gone, she made another break for freedom. "Ancestors damn you," she snapped, caught again. "Just tell me! Why hasn't she woken up yet?" She coughed, choked, and coughed again. Made another break for the uncertain freedom that was anywhere but the table. Was pushed back again. Coughed some more and spat a few more curses for good measure.

A hand struck her in the sternum. Jossa's metal-enclosed skull missed the pillow, bounced, and nearly gave her a fine case of whiplash. If she hadn't been trying to figure out if her ribs were intact, she would have been worried about her neck. How could any woman be that *strong*?

"She sleeps so she's not *you*," the medic snarled. "Weak outFleet lungs. She needs serum so she can breathe, before the needles come out! Lay back! Or I'll tell Warlord you died of idiocy."

It took a second to sink in, and it still didn't make sense. "She's not sick from the cryo?" Jossa asked, hardly believing what she'd heard.

Iira just snorted, picked up the loose end of the IV line, and came at her. Jossa decided not to give the medic an excuse to poke any unnecessary holes and held still. So long as she was in the same room as Delfi and so long as her sousi wasn't dead, she could be patient. For now.

>>><<<

Later, after Iira had come and gone a few more times, the warlord returned. He carried a shallow bowl in one hand, and the armor he wore was bloodied. Ancestors only knew if he'd worn a helmet to whatever battle he'd come from. She assumed he must have, because his face was clean of all but a three-day growth of beard and a haze of sweaty grime. So were his hands, which seemed wrong.

For one panicked moment, she thought he was going to rape her. Or bleed her into the bowl. Or, or—well. She didn't actually know *what* she expected. She'd half forgotten about him. Time had no meaning in this room. The dim glow of the lights never changed. As far as she could tell, the displays on the monitors didn't have time markers attached. And the shrieks of the women outside never came at regular intervals. Come to think of it, she hadn't heard *any* loud noises in a while. A great while. Which made the bleeding bowl a not-so-absurd idea, when she gave it another thought.

"You're in luck," he said. "The kemvate of the base melted the hard drives. Everyone on the thing sucked in Seed rather than fight or get captured. Looks like I've still got a use for you." He shoved the bowl at her. "Here."

Jossa shrank away and stared at the grayish-brown half-liquid slopping up the sides.

"I know you can handle it. Iira says the electro-stims in the casket were low priority, but you've got the strength to keep crawling out of bed. Whatever she's hooked you up to should've fixed most of the atrophy. So take the fucking bowl.

Jossa took the bowl, just managing to set it in her lap before she dropped it. She looked at it, wondering how in the universe she was supposed to eat. With her fingers? The stuff wasn't exactly solid, but it looked too thick to drink.

Frowning, she reached for the surface of the mush. Oh, this was going to be unpleasant on *so* many levels.

"Hold on."

Jossa blinked up at the man. He scowled and felt along his belt for something. After a moment or so, he growled and yanked a short metal tube from its clip. A press of some hidden button and a twist of one end, and thin stream of gray flowed from the tube. The substance wobbled for a second as he fiddled with the controls, then solidified into a spoon.

It was a good thing the bowl of food was in her lap, or Jossa would have dropped it. Her jaw certainly fell open. The warlord had taken a living metal weapon and reprogrammed it into a spoon. A spoon! Nevermind figuring out how a Navlad spacer's blade came to be aboard an enemy ship. He'd made it turn into a spoon!

Denz would want to tear the thing apart. Delfi would steal it the moment she found out it existed. And Rui? Rui would tell her that her food was getting cold and she shouldn't waste time staring at fancy new tech when she could be eating.

Once she'd taken a couple spoonfuls of the bland mush, the man leaned against the edge of her mattress and laced his fingers together over his belt, watching her. She fought down a blush and tried to keep eating. It was hard. The food was quite nearly the most tasteless stuff she'd ever eaten, and the texture put her whole digestive tract into revolt. Having a strange man standing over her with greed in his eyes was, sadly, much easier to handle.

He made her scrape the bowl clean, down to the last grain, and then he scooped it from her lap. She blinked back tears as she watched him set it aside. Three hundred years. Spacers' habits hadn't changed in three hundred years. How many times had Rui reminded her, when she and Delfi first came aboard *Skatasi*? Nothing goes to waste.

If she died, would they send her through the recycling processors? Or would they dump her out an airlock? There was no way she could count on a death tablet being made from her maruste. Would Del know what had happened to her?

She had to stay on this man's good side. For the moment, nothing else mattered.

The man saw her tears. Something in his face changed. His free hand lifted, then dropped back to his side. A muscle worked in his jaw. Then, so quickly she almost thought she'd imagined what came before, all the tension seeped out of his body. What replaced it was the predatory ease of a big cat.

Jossa felt her fingers tighten around the handle of the spoon. She wasn't sure what modifications had been made to the original programming, but if she could tap the power switch fast enough, she might be able to get it to retract and reform as a blade faster than he could take it away.

"So," he said, plucking the spoon from her hand and setting it with the bowl on top of the tower that housed the display screens. "Let's try this again. Gonna guess you didn't park yourself on an empty planet full of bajbarog because you needed some alone time. You piss off a Great Family? Pop out a baby nehkeh?"

On the list of things she'd expected to hear, that last one hadn't been anywhere near the top. Jossa stared at him.

"What? That it?" His upper lip quivered, revealing the edge of his teeth. His eyes were hard and entirely unforgiving. "You didn't have any trouble figuring out what I am. Maybe you were fucking one of the garbage men while the fuerrus was having fun with the rest of his whores."

She should have fought to keep the spoon. She could have stabbed him with it. "I belonged to isk Churusimpir lis Kuchruog lis isk Fuerrus himself," she snarled at him. "And that is exactly why you found me on that planet."

One eyebrow went up and he tilted his head to one side. "That so? He put you there, did he? Hide you—sorry, the *two* of you—" The man's teeth flashed as he nodded at Delfi's prone form on the other table. "Away long enough for people to forget about the scandal before he woke you up and the three of you lived happily ever after? Give him time to escape his responsibilities and circle back around to pick you up? Must not have been true love after all, since he forgot you there."

No. No, it hadn't been like that at all. And it had, in so many ways. Someone was supposed to come back for her. For Del. They were *supposed* to have forever with the ones they loved. If there were any justice in the universe, they would have.

Something warm and wet landed on her hand. She looked down. A drop of water slid down her fist where she clenched it in the sheets. Another drop landed as she watched.

Well, this was just perfect. Now the man would know he'd hit a sore spot. Not sore. A point of perfect agony. Any other weaknesses you'd like to show him while you're at it? she asked herself. Anything else you'd like him to use against you?

"Look." The man leaned over and planted his fists on the mattress next to her. This close, she could feel the heat coming off him. See the vein standing out on his forehead. He snapped his fingers in her face and she blinked.

The man growled low in his throat before continuing. "The fuerrus back then jumped the nav beacons and damn near tore the Empire to bits. Did he or did he not put you there?"

Jossa opened her mouth. Closed it. What to tell him? How much to tell him? How dangerous was it for him to know these things? What would he do to her if he knew the whole truth?

"I already told you," she said finally. "We were there because of the fuerrus."

He leaned in closer, his face inches from hers. She could smell sweat, and see the stubble growing across his jaw. But his eyes were what held her attention. He was reading her. Analyzing her face for clues.

"Explain," he whispered. The deep rasp of his voice reached into her nerves and set every one of them on edge.

Jossa clutched at the sheets around her knees and bit her lips to keep her mouth shut.

For a moment, she thought he would hit her. His posture stiffened. The muscles of his neck and arms tightened. Then, with no warning at all, he straightened, stalked around the end of her table, and headed for Delfi.

Oh no.

The warlord stood, one hand hovering over a cluster of tubes near Delfi's shoulder.

"I yank," he said, "and there goes the serum that's helping her breathe. I don't know which one of these is the right one, so I might as well pull them all. Don't know how long she'll have, either. Course," he moved his hand so it rested on Del's cloth-covered chest. "Could just cave in her rib cage."

Jossa gulped.

"Or." He moved his hand back to the tubes. "I call Iira in here and she unplugs your sister. I have her transferred to one of the Breeder ships." The smile on his face looked like a death rictus. "I'm gonna bet you're the unstable element in the arrangement you two have. Bond. Whatever the fuck you people call it."

"Sister," Jossa whispered.

His grin got bigger. She thought she saw insanity around the edges of his eyes. "Sister then. You fucking sai and your fucking soul-bonded shit. More trouble than it's worth, comes down to it. How far will I get before you lose your mind? Thousand miles? Two? Fleet's spread out over a fuck ton of space right now."

"Ok!" The words left Jossa's mouth in an explosion of panic. "Ok! We were running. From the Empire. We stayed on that planet while the rest of our crew went to hide our trail through the Barbicans. Just please. Please don't hurt her."

The man crossed his arms. Jossa breathed again, then realized that she was leaning so far over the edge of the table that she was in serious danger of falling off.

"That Barb only had three keys in the gate," the warlord said as Jossa worked herself back onto the mattress. "This one, the one I came through, and the one the other half of our Fleet used. That's not enough to hide a trail."

"We had a Crack. Denz," Jossa told him. She wished she dared to pull the blanket up around her neck, but she had a feeling doing so would just draw attention to the bits of her anatomy he had so far ignored. Not that they were much worth looking at in the first place.

Focus, you stupid woman. Just because he's not hurting you now doesn't mean he won't if you slip up.

"Rui, my—the captain—had contacts in the Karukap. They told him the planet had been emptied and was about to be sealed out of the Barbican network." She shrugged. "So Denz went into the logs and erased our transport code. Then he was supposed to remove the system from the Barbican databases so the hunters wouldn't know to look for it." She sighed and looked over at Delfi's sleeping form. "It must not have worked."

The man frowned as he tapped a finger on his arm. She watched him, wondering if she'd managed to avert disaster or if he was just sadistic enough to take Del anyway. Finally, his hand stilled. "Go back to the Karukap. They emptied the system on purpose?"

"I don't know that it was ever highly populated," she said. "Just what was on the Ajiri planet?"

One edge of his lip lifted as he looked down at Delfi.

"Yes! Fine, yes!" Jossa lurched in place and was brought up short by the sharp prick of needles being pulled from her skin. "As far as I know, they removed the stations and facilities entirely. We had to bring in all our equipment."

"And the bajbarog? You find a litter and—"

"What? Walk up to a den of blank bajbarog on an empty planet and—" Jossa stopped as she realized what he meant. "No. No. We didn't raid a known breeding program. We had to find the bajbarog without help." And what a miserable experience that had been. Not quite as bad as some of the creatures she'd tended for the fuerrus, but bad enough. She wondered if Rui managed to get the stink out of the ship before—

No. Don't go there.

"Must have been some favor you owed, to get the first pair of cubs. I wonder, how'd you pay it back?" The look on the man's face said he had some specific ideas as to that. Jossa looked back at her hands before her face could give anything away.

"Well, the Fleet's fairly good at forcing Barbs open." Jossa looked up to see that the man had moved around to examine the readouts on Delfi's monitors. Jossa opened her mouth to protest, then stopped. He could move faster than her right now. What did she have to gain by antagonizing him?

As if he'd heard the thought, the man looked up. "Any way to know if someone tracked you down? Power strippers, shield flaws? Alarms?" He wandered towards her. She felt her skin come alive as he passed behind her.

"Anything to let him know your little bait and switch didn't work?"

Jossa twisted as far as the tubes and needles would allow, but the man stood out of view. Hidden as he was by the raised head of her table, his voice was much more terrifying. She bit her lip and fought to keep her voice steady. "Not that I know of. Any program that would alert him could also be used to trace him."

Jossa looked up just in time to see the man reach for the IV bag hanging off the control tower at the head of her bed. "Ah." He grinned, leaned over the medunit, and all but breathed down her neck. "Serum. Should have looked here first. Your man was good with his code. Or did he belong to her?" He nodded at Delfi. Jossa froze. She didn't have anything left to tell him. What else could she give him to keep him away from Del?

His eyes shifted, dropping from her face and lifting back up so quickly she almost didn't catch it.

Oh. Yes. Well of course she could use that.

Slowly, she straightened, pulling her shoulders back and tucking her arms in. She didn't have much in the breast department, but Rui had liked them fine. Odd, how she'd gotten so used to the room that she couldn't feel the air on her bare skin. Once upon a time, she'd spent just as much time in a state of undress as clothed.

"We never wanted to hurt your people. Truly," she said carefully, keeping her eyes focused on the man's chin and the small beard that capped it. "If the bajbarog caused injury or death, I am sorry. They were put there as a temporary guard, nothing more." Her throat closed on the last words and she stopped talking.

He shrugged, but his hand had drifted away from the IV bag as his eyes fixed on her chest. "Not my people, you know that. But they are ejiodiv do trubokoj." He grinned at her shock. "What? Don't think a Savage would know how to say 'responsibility'?

"But we did lose people," he continued. "Most of a squad. One of the techs left a daughter behind. I had to kill her father. I don't need payment for the people we lost. That's not the blood debt that's owed here." He looked down at Delfi, still lying oblivious to all the havoc she could be creating if she were awake. To the terror she caused even while unconscious. The man let one hand drift towards Del's IV bag.

"No! No, please!" The needles pulled again as Jossa lurched towards him. "I'll do anything. Just please—leave her alone!"

"Anything?" He stepped away from Del and over towards Jossa. His eyes were critical, but a smile tugged at his mouth. "That so? Well, you look better than you did when I pulled you out of the casket. I'll give you that."

Jossa told herself to keep still as he reached out and took a strand of her hair. She watched him wind it around a finger, feeling the sheets slide over her legs as she bunched the fabric in her fists.

"Got a bit of a problem though," he said, letting her hair fall free. For a second she thought he'd go back to Del, but he left his hand where it was, hovering over her bare shoulder. "Ain't all that interested in going blind in the process."

Jossa didn't even feel his hand drop. She was too busy being blown to bits by the emotional storm as it consumed her, body and soul.

Thirteen -- Jossa

Feels are too useful to put down with impunity when they lose themselves in the minutia of other people's emotions. But they are also too dangerous leave unbonded. It is advisable to put them in cold storage at the onset of puberty, until someone capable of forming a soul bond can be found.
  -observations, Professor Rusithe, New Hopks College of Medicine

Jossa cried out as rage and fear and deep, deep distrust ripped through her chest and set hooks into her heart. She was going to die. She was going to be torn apart by a man so much in conflict with himself that it was a wonder he could put one coherent thought after another.

Focus, she told herself, panting with the effort. You know how to do this. This is who you are. Now, what is he? It's in there somewhere. It's got to be. Everyone has a base set of emotions. This can't be all of him. It can't—

Reason faded under another onslaught of frustration and desire. He wanted her with something far beyond the lusts of average men. He needed to prove to himself—and to her—that she wasn't better than him. That he had worth in and of himself. It was primal, this feeling. This lust-filled killing rage. Rooted in the core of his being, past the conscious level.

It was familiar somehow. But she couldn't figure out why. Not with the roaring in her ears.

How could *anyone* live like this?

She tried to pull away. Tried to throw up shields between herself and the awful knowledge that he carried within. The certainty that the universe was a place of kill or be killed. And her place in it wasn't what she'd thought. She was to be killed. Everyone was, until he stood alone among the ashes of those who dared touch him.

But she was too weak to fight him, physically or mentally. His grip on her shoulder was unyielding, and her paltry shields disintegrated as fast as she threw them up, until she had nothing left to fight him with. His emotions, his very essence, drove down and stabbed her in the heart, then moved on to boil the blood in her veins and cook her mind.

"Please," she whimpered, tears streaming down her face. "Please stop. It hurts." She gasped for breath, choked on a sob, and gasped again. "It *hurts*!"

She didn't know if she was talking about her heart or her shoulder.

"Open your eyes." The very gentleness of his voice promised that she'd regret any disobedience. She opened her eyes.

And nearly gagged at the flickering light that surrounded her. She knew what it was. Nothing could counterfeit that orange glow. With growing horror, she realized that the patterns on the wall were those of a full maruste. Not just the initial phase, but the Oloteoj Azatlvl in all its glory. He'd activated the Open Blossom.

Her heart quailed.

Jossa tried to curl in on herself. The warlord's grip on her shoulder stopped her. A whimper crawled up her throat. She twisted to look up into the man's face. That hardened, scarred face, with burning eyes and lips drawn back over teeth that suddenly looked far too sharp. Nehkeh. Savage.

A reminder, in the most visceral of ways, exactly what his kind were capable of.

"Which glyph turns it off for good?"

Jossa stared. Worked her mouth.

The warlord snarled and let go of her shoulder. The light went out. Before she could do more than blink in the sudden gloom, he grabbed her again. By the arm this time. The light returned.

"Where the fuck do I cut you open to make it stop?" He all but roared in her face.

She stared at him, her own terror overriding the fury pouring through her nervous system like so many trails of liquid fire. Her eyes snagged on the glyphs shuddering and quaking on the wall, and something in her mind made the connection. Those were *her* glyphs. The warlord wouldn't have the stylized rabbit of isk Churusimpir lis Kuchruog on his shoulder.

"No," she whispered.

The warlord's growl was animal. He let go of her arm, spun, and took the single step needed to bring him to Delfi's side. Once he'd made sure Jossa was watching, he laid his palm on Del's forehead. The sheets and pillow around her turned bright orange as light erupted from her back and leaked out around her body.

Jossa sucked in air. Tried to put her thoughts back together. Failed horribly. Flung a prayer to the Ancestors for guidance and cringed as the man turned back to her. He didn't touch her again, but his expression and body language told her enough. His emotions hadn't changed. If anything, they'd intensified, culminating in a mix of something she could only label as pure frustration.

"Tell me," he growled, so low she almost couldn't hear him.

"Do you know which glyph is which?" she asked. He probably did. She should stop being surprised by him knowing anything.

The lights turned on again as he laid his palm on her shoulder and eased her forward. She managed not to scream this time, mainly by focusing on the difference between the emotions and his actions. He had some control over himself, at least. Or else he'd be pounding her to bloody mush instead of talking to her.

"That's lis Disen isk Fuerrus." He tapped at a spot just over her vertebrae and the lights flickered. "The Imperial family. Not some low level cousin."

He had known exactly where it would lead. Every question. Every threat to Delfi.

He moved his finger to the side, and Jossa stepped on her instinctual urge to swat at the invader. "That's a new one. But it's a big Empire. Or it was."

She reached one trembling hand up and wrapped it around her shoulder, feeling her fingers brush his where they rested on her skin. Fragments of amusement danced over old echoes of the anger and confusion, carrying faint images with them, too blurred for her to visualize clearly. He must be doing something to keep his emotions in check. Probably to keep her from crying instead of talking.

"This," she said. "This is the mark of Churusimpir lis Kuchruog lis isk Fuerrus. I was sold into service before my first birthday, raised to my duty. Bonded to his family line unto eternity. Destined to have my death tablet set below his in the temple. Do you know what that means?"

By the time she was done speaking, she didn't know if the anger in her voice belonged to the warlord or to herself. She didn't care. This man. This Savage. Somehow he had the blood of the fuerrus in his veins, and *now* she was indentured to *him*! It was the only explanation that made sense, given all the time she and Delfi had spent in the caskets.

If he understood the implications, she was doomed. And Delfi with her. If he didn't understand, she and her sousi would still be enslaved and used. Three hundred years! Three hundred years for the turning of time to bring them right back where they started!

Denial and frustration and a sort of resigned anger spread outward from his touch, leaving the fizzing burn of carbonation in her veins even after he took his hand from her back. Jossa huddled in on herself, watching as he paced out from between the two tables and then came back.

Finally, he stopped and looked at her. His face was expressionless, but now that she knew what lay beneath the mask, she wished she'd fought harder to be free of the lines and wires and everything holding her to this table. She shouldn't have accepted Iira's answer in regards to clothing. She should have—

"Well." The man's voice yanked her back to reality. "Now that we've established the problem, mind telling me the answer?"

"Um?" Jossa blinked and eased back as he leaned in close. What had he asked her? The events of the past minute or so had blown the question right out of her mind.

His fist hit the mattress next to her leg with a muffled *thud*. The table shook under her, and Jossa yipped as she clutched at the edges of the mattress.

"How the fuck do I turn it off? My blood. Your blood. It's really easy. Just tell me where I start cutting." A blade appeared in his other hand, the tip solidifying just as it touched Delfi's exposed throat. "Or I'll try hers instead."

"Between!" Jossa reached for his arm and hauled. The lights of her maruste painted the walls around her, splashing across the man's face like a horrible mask. She ignored them. "Between the family and the indenture! Please! Just leave her be!"

"Is it the same for her?" He didn't move. Didn't waver as she tried to pull him away from her sousi. Either she was too light, or he was made of solid silsteel.

"Yes! Yes!" Jossa let go of him and scrabbled for her hair, pulling the loose mass over her shoulder as she twisted to present as much of her back to him as she could manage. "It's right over the vertebra. I promise."

For a second she thought she'd failed. That he'd been faking the anger. That he'd just wanted to see what she knew. What she'd be willing to give up when pushed.

Then a lance of pain shot through her back, and she felt a line of warm wetness creep its way over her skin. The anger hit again, not as turbulent but just as sudden. Jossa gasped and shuddered. Something crawled through her nerves. Her skin itched.

She gritted her teeth and ducked her head. This was just the nanites in her blood adjusting to new information. Assimilating.

Acknowledging the man who owned her not just by virtue of having her on board a ship full of monsters, but down to the very marrow in his bones.

Captive.

Again.

FOURTEEN -- SYRUS

When another covers the gap in your armor instead of taking advantage of your weakness, repayment must be made. Not only in full, but more than—to acknowledge the fact that your life was in his hands.
-Thank-Gifts, Fleet Training Manual

Syrus listened to the door close behind him and tried not to think about what he'd just done. Not that there was any way to deny the reality of the link between himself and the two women. But he'd just made it solid. Unavoidable. Although, now that the women wouldn't be lighting up like bonfires every time he touched them, maybe he could downplay their importance to Quinn. Make him think the activation of their maruste was a fluke. So far the man had kept his peace about the display, but that probably wouldn't last long.

Frowning, he stuck his helmet under one arm and looked down at the cut across his palm. Would it scar? he wondered. The palm was the traditional place to open so the blood of the owner could be mixed with the blood of the owned. He imagined he had scars on his back, but no one had told him one way or another if they were obvious. He'd never noticed scars on the hands of those who owned indentures. It seemed like something that should happen. A reminder that the owner held someone's life in their hands.

Syrus tucked his hand back into the glove he'd stuffed in his belt and headed for the door out of his quarters. The women might not be an issue for him at the moment—not now that they wouldn't light up every time he touched one of them. But the information he'd just gotten was about to completely change this Campaign.

His command room was empty, although someone had left a stack of slates on the corner of the table. He checked to see if any of them were active, but they were all in standby mode. Whoever had left him a load of documentation to look over would just have to wait. He stuffed the slates into one of the storage compartments in the wall and dropped into the quasi-throne at the head of the table. His hand stung when he tapped in the code to light up the wall display, but the bleeding had already stopped. Soon it would scab over.

An aide answered the vid when he keyed in the bridge. No, she said. Oona wasn't there. Her shift was over. Quinn had come and taken her off with Iira. Syrus waved off the woman's apologies and closed the connection.

He thought for a moment before entering the next set of commands. He'd interrupted Quinn and his wives before. But Syrus had only had to track Oona down in her quarters maybe... twice in the time he'd been on the Fleet.

Fuck it. Sitting here and worrying about what he'd find on the other end of the vid was for people with manners. He keyed in the code for his second's vid comm and waited for someone to answer. He didn't have to wait long. In a few seconds, the signal cleared, and he was treated to an up close and personal view of someone's shirt. The person backed up slightly and he realized he'd gotten Quinn himself.

The second blinked once, and then his face settled into its usual impassive mask. Too fast for Syrus to read the expression Quinn had been wearing when he answered the call. "You need Oona, milord?" the man asked.

Syrus nodded. "You too." He pinched the bridge of his nose, remembering too late that he couldn't talk only to his command staff. "Take your time. I need Kizen for this."

Quinn tipped his head in a sort of bow and paused the link. Syrus ground his teeth, called the bridge again and spoke before the aide could get a word in edgewise. "Get the *Ataorl Banso* on the line. I need Kizen patched in on my call to Quinn."

The woman went stiff and opened her mouth.

"Don't let him run you over. Tell him if he doesn't answer his comms, I'm going to start the next Fleet maneuvers without him and he can go park on the sun if he wants."

>>><<<

It didn't take long for Kizen's image to appear on the surface of the table. He was dripping wet, naked, and holding a towel in one hand. The scowl on his face would have done justice to an angry bear. Syrus cut off the complaint the other warlord was about to make by shifting in his seat and asking, "I take it you've got the solar plant locked down?"

Kizen growled something that might have been a yes. Syrus nodded and looked at the image of Quinn and Oona, standing one in front of the other before their own vid capture. If either of them minded dealing with Kizen straight out of a bath, they didn't show it. Syrus swallowed a snort. Why would they? The Fleet's ideas of modesty didn't match the Imperials'.

"Glad to hear it," he said to Kizen. "Head this way. Don't want to give the people down planet too much time to get ready for us. In the meantime, I need you to send out any cloaked stat-sats we have." He looked from the vid of Quinn's quarters to Kizen's. "All over the system."

Kizen opened his mouth, but Quinn beat him to it. "If I may, my lord, it is too early in the campaign for full sweeps. We have the data from the initial sats, plus the records we've pulled from the Customs base and the one we just took. Surely that will be enough to carry us through without risking resources."

From the look on her face, Oona agreed. Syrus shook his head and leaned back. "Kizen, your people find any other keys in this gate?" It was dangerous, giving the man so much power, implying he would know things Syrus's own people didn't. Oona's face went from irritated scowl to full glower, but Quinn stayed quiet. He probably understood what Syrus was up to. Hopefully.

Kizen puffed his chest. "No." He started drying his arms with the towel, as casually arrogant as if he were the one who'd called and he didn't care if he'd gotten them out of bed. "They have gone over the logs again and taken another look at the code. There is the system we passed through to arrive, where you summoned me." He sank enough scorn into the word to drop a ship out of orbit. "And there is the code for the other empty system, which we were about to enter when your summons came. There are no other keys."

Syrus leaned forward and propped his arms on the edge of the table, lacing his fingers together in a loose fist. "So. Once we take this system, where do we go?"

Oona and Kizen stopped for a moment. Quinn lifted his chin slightly and gave Syrus a look through the vid. Syrus let the corner of his mouth curl. Quinn saw it. The other two were so focused on the next battle, they weren't looking any further than the Seeding of the whole system.

"There will be another Barbican." Kizen stopped toweling himself off and stood, wrapping the fabric around his fists. "We just haven't made it far enough into the system yet. Sometimes these outFleet fools stick the fucking things behind a moon and think they're clever."

"True." Syrus looked at Oona's image on the comm screen.

She sighed. "None of the preliminary scans show any indication of another Barbican in the system." She knew what it meant. Now that he had her on board, Syrus could concentrate on talking Kizen around.

"Haven't found it yet doesn't mean it's not there," Syrus said. "Fleet got its masking tech from Imperial colonies. No reason they wouldn't still be using it." He knew for a fact that the military still used the masking tech. Before he'd left Imperial space nearly six years ago, there'd been a very memorable clash between a Kizarard house and a trade guild that ended with both parties nearly flattened by the Imperial Karukap when it restored order. "There are ways to hide the power draw on the solar collectors, too. Easiest is to set up dedicated collector panels instead of shipping in power cells."

Oona nodded and bent over the console that probably bracketed her comm screen. Quinn squeezed her shoulder once, then turned away to work on something else. Syrus would lay money on his sending orders to the men who were working on removing hard drives from the base they'd just finished taking. No captives this time. Just blood. Syrus had left them to the clean up so he could have the conversation with Jossa without an audience. He should have talked to her earlier. Before they launched this latest offensive on the station closest to the occupied planet.

You shouldn't have given yourself away so easily, a voice whispered in his head. *You let her goad you without realizing what she was doing, and you gave her too many weapons. Did you think she wouldn't realize what you are by birth? And then you made it worse by staying away instead of owning it and showing her what you are now.*

Syrus ignored the voice. Regret was too little too late. All he could do was fix the lack of information for the Fleet as fast as he could, before his suspicions turned into reality and they all went down in a blaze of glory.

He looked away from Quinn and Oona's screen to meet Kizen's eyes through the vid. "Once you send out your sats, head this way. Soon as you get here, drop into orbit. I'll wait till you're on this side of the sun and head down planet.

"Not very many people living on the surface of this thing. No hab shields either. I'll take my people deep and fast into the cave systems, then drive them up to meet you. Catch them on the surface." Syrus took a breath and decided to be grateful that emotion couldn't transfer itself over a data connection. "Oona's going to mark the smaller landing fields and space ports. Leave them alone. Take the big ones instead."

Kizen glowered as Syrus gave his instructions. Once or twice he opened his mouth, probably to point out the obvious problems of having one force land before the other was ready to lock down the surface.

When Syrus finished talking, he exploded. "You're ruining everything," the man growled. "There are more holes in this rock than a Breeder ship at full capacity. You know how many of these Imperial fucks are going to escape if we don't flatten those landing fields? We need to make it impossible to fly anything larger than a gnat down there."

He shifted to look at a different part of his vid screen. Probably the section with Quinn and Oona's feed. "Is this the sort of Campaign you let your warlord run?" he snapped at Quinn. "Are you that weak, that you let a man who obviously has no idea how to run a Campaign rule our people?"

Syrus leaned back and crossed his arms. "You're right," he said. "There's a fuck ton of caves on this rock. No way could we block all of them."

"You want to see where the escapees are going," Oona said, realization painted all over her face.

"What do you mean, escapees?"

Syrus nodded, ignoring Kizen. "Tag them, carefully. Especially the smaller ships. Older military models get sold off to traders sometimes. But the military uses them for secret work too. There's going to be a military presence down planet. The base we just took wasn't for trade." He exchanged looks with Quinn over Oona's shoulder while she worked and Kizen growled.

Quinn nodded. He understood. Syrus let himself smile. "Let me know when the sats are out," he told Oona.

He looked back to Kizen's image. The other warlord growled low under his breath and crossed his arms. "Once this Campaign is over, we will have a reckoning, you and I."

And wouldn't that be a thing. Syrus shrugged and leaned in closer. "There is something wrong with this system. Something more than too much resistance too fast. We should've been able to Seed this base and move on. Did you have difficulties with the solar plant?"

Kizen frowned. "Whole sections separated by airlocks. More than usual for a solar plant. The outFleet staff fled to the central area and held there." He lifted one shoulder. "But we have taken systems full of paranoid people before. This is not the first time."

Syrus nodded. "Most of the people in this base were military. Not just separate airlocks here. They divided the base into wedges. Separate life support systems in each. Very few children. Almost no women. None taken." He sat back. "The military emptied two systems linked to the Barb we came through." Better to avoid telling Kizen how Syrus knew that. "Tell me you'd look at this system on your own and not think something is wrong."

Kizen's whole body tightened. His shoulders came up and the veins on his forehead and neck bulged. Syrus waited. He could do that, millions of miles away and not in any danger of getting fried by the man's emotions. Did he realize how much his body gave him away? Syrus wondered if Kizen's second was as unflappable as Quinn or if the warlord drove his underlings to distraction. How fast did he run through them anyway? They couldn't have a high survival rate, given the man's temper.

Of course, Syrus went through his underlings fairly quickly himself.

Finally, when his shoulders were nearly up around his ears, Kizen growled and flung his hands in the air. "Very well, Lord *Turan*," he said. "We will take the larger space ports and send out our cloaked sats. But the thank-gift you bring me had better make it worth my while."

Syrus waited a full ten count after Kizen's image vanished from the table to look back at Quinn and Oona's comm link. Quinn was nowhere in sight. Oona had evidently gone about her business of sending orders and muted the comms. She looked up when he pinged the alert light on her panel. "Milord?"

Syrus crossed his arms. "Thank-gift?"

Something twitched near the woman's eye. Her mouth twisted.

"Oona," Syrus said carefully. He never knew when this woman was going to be helpful and when she was going to roadblock him. "What. The fuck. Did he mean by a *thank-gift*?"

Oona drew herself up straight and focused on some point over the cam. "Milord, a thank-gift is customary when a member of the Fleet has given aid to another member of equal rank. It is commensurate with the degree of assistance given to the one who could not properly perform his duties, and a way to acknowledge that while he may have been temporarily weak, he is not without other resources and is capable of holding his position."

Syrus's translator had to fill in the blanks on some of that, giving him the words milliseconds after they came over the comm. Syrus wondered if Kizen planned *that* little comment, or if he'd really thrown it out as an offhand remark.

Was the man that subtle? Was he even *able* to do anything but crash around like a rampaging bull?

Bastard. Now Syrus was going to have to watch his back for something besides a physical knife. He fucking hated politics.

"Milord?"

Syrus spoke without looking at her. "And if I don't give him... something?"

No answer. He turned his head to look at her. "Oona."

That twitch next to her eye again. She must really hate having to explain Fleet custom. Or maybe she hated having to do her husband's job of wrangling her warlord. "Milord, he could have basis to take your Helm. If you are unworthy of it."

Well, that answered the question of whether the fucker was able to do "subtle." Syrus snarled. He knew what Kizen wanted. The women. And he wouldn't wait long to demand his "gift" either. Probably in public, so all their soldiers could see the warlord of the *Edde Belo* fall flat on his face.

"That will be all, Oona," he told her. "Link the reports to me when you have them."

She murmured something and the light of the comm screen cut out. Syrus sat back and stared at the blank screens in front of him. Just how badly did he want to keep the Helm on his head?

Fifteen -- Jossa

It is possible to design a single medunit to cure all ills. However, the thing would have to be the size of a small house just to hold all the supplies needed. This is why even the poorest town has at least one unit for trauma and another for long-term care.
    -"Basic Operations of Freestanding Medical Units" Professor Ipkus, New Hopks College of Medicine

Jossa's first clue as to her impending eviction came when Iira entered the room and started pulling needles out of her patient's skin. By the time Jossa's brain caught up with what was happening, the medic had moved on from the veins in the arms and was working on the legs instead.

"What?" Jossa tried to take her feet away, but the medic wrapped one hand around her ankle and *held* her in place. Done with that foot, she moved on to the other, catching it before Jossa had a chance to yank it out of the way.

"What are you doing?"

"Bath," the woman said. "You smell. Clothes. Exercise." She yanked another lead and Jossa couldn't help the reflexive jerk of her foot. Iira hauled it back and reached for the next lead.

Jossa wanted to protest, but she couldn't find a single logical argument to use against things like fresh clothes and a bath. What she could use, though, was her imagination. The minute she left this room, she'd be a laser-marked target for the warlord. No matter how hard she tried, she couldn't make herself reconcile with that reality.

So she shook her head and pulled the blanket up around her bare shoulders as she tried to regain possession of her foot. "I'm ok here. Really. Besides, I can't leave Delfi alone."

"No choice," Iira snapped, yanking the last of the leads a little harder than she needed to. Jossa yelped and jumped. Then yelped again as the woman started shoving her legs apart. "Stop fighting," the woman snapped, taking each ankle and forcing it over the edge of the bed. "You want to piss on your own?"

It was so like what Goris might have said that Jossa quit struggling long enough for the woman to flip back the blanket, reach up between Jossa's legs, and start pulling out the catheter they'd fitted her with. Hissing in pain, Jossa clamped her legs around the table to keep from closing them and getting slapped again. Iira had a point. Two, she realized. She might not be an atrophied stick anymore, but she was still weak as a babe. Staying here wouldn't fix that.

She looked over at Delfi, still sleeping the sleep of the coma induced. Her skin looked better than it had. And her face wasn't as hollow as before.

Leaving her sousi in this room was a very bad idea. What if she woke up and found herself alone? What if the warlord came back and Jossa wasn't there to distract him? What would he do to Del? Just because he hadn't taken his rights that Jossa knew of, didn't mean he hadn't while they were *both* asleep.

She could have slapped herself. The maruste, of course. Idiot girl. He hadn't touched her for touching's sake until he'd taken care of the light that could give him away.

Besides—she winced again as Iira did something with the catheter—she'd met any number of men with odd fetishes. So far, a man who would climb on top of an unconscious woman poked full of wires and tubes hadn't made the list.

That decided her. Mostly. "I want to sleep in here."

Iira looked up from what she was doing with the cath tube and the urine bag. Jossa tried to look serious. Like she knew she couldn't be argued with. "At night. When the warlord isn't . . ." She waved a hand, not sure what they called it among the Svis Konanuog. "I want to sleep in here with her."

After a long moment, the woman nodded. "For now. When milord returns, he'll decide. Come." She set the catheter and urine bag and other paraphernalia somewhere out of sight and held out her hand. "Time to go."

Lacking a choice, Jossa allowed herself to be helped off the table. She lost her sheet and blanket in the process, but the promise of a bath was growing too strong to ignore. Iira let her hobble to the door by herself, not even standing ready to catch her. Well, that was in keeping with what she knew of the Kuchen.

"Will she be—" Jossa turned to take a last look at Delfi. And saw it. "Ancestor's Balls," she breathed as she staggered and caught herself against the wall. "Why didn't you just use that? Why *don't* you just use that? It would wake her up! She could be well by now! We both could!"

Tucked under the beds, which she could see weren't beds at all now that she wasn't lying on one, were things that looked remarkably like the hoods of medunits. The kind for healing a person all at once. The kind that left long recoveries a thing of Border worlds and the hospitals of the poor.

Iira's sigh was that of a woman who'd been burdened with a very stupid person to watch over. "Come," she said, and tried to take Jossa by the elbow. Frustration, muted and faint, threaded its way up Jossa's arm.

Jossa planted her feet as best she could. "No. Not until you tell me if I'm right and you could have gotten rid of the cryo sickness the first day."

Iira's hand clamped down. Jossa glared at her. The woman could move her by main force. They both knew it. But there would be injuries involved. Only lira knew what the warlord would say about his new toy being damaged. If they wouldn't use the medunit for cryo sickness, who said they would use it for a twisted or broken arm?

Finally, the other woman stopped squeezing. Instead she glowered even harder. "Can't. It's not the right type. The old warlord liked bones. Blood." She huffed and glared at the door to the outer rooms. "Milord—" The woman cut herself off abruptly. "He had questions. You gave him answers." Her grip on Jossa's arm didn't give any clue as to lira's emotional state. It was as if she was made of stone.

"I gave him the answers I could," Jossa said, fighting the urge to pull away. Who could shut down their feelings like that? Or was the crown adapting to her abilities and extending its reach to her skin?

lira nodded. "His orders are to follow, not kill escapees. Because of the answers you gave. If he has made a bad choice, he will die. Then we will have a new warlord." She pointed at the table. "And you'll see the medunit work.

"Now." She stabbed a finger at a button in the wall. "Come."

Still trying to process the reasons for someone to have a medunit that could only handle trauma but not systemic damage on a cellular level, Jossa allowed herself to be pulled out of the room.

>>><<<

Jossa didn't know what she'd expected, but this wasn't it. The chamber was huge. Egg shaped, with the lines of a door frame capping the narrow end, it was largely unfurnished. A floating slab of metal near the door must be a table, the smaller slabs the seats. They hovered by some invisible means that Jossa couldn't see. Grav boosters, maybe?

At the other end of the room was a gigantic bed. Heavy curtains hung at intervals on either side of the bed. Halfway down the wall between the infirmary and the bed was another door, mirrored on the far side of the room by a slightly larger one. The far wall and most of the ceiling displayed a starscape with a huge blue-and-green planet sitting in one corner and an array of ships strung out into the distance. Every other bit of paneling was taken up with more of the brambles and snakes that had become so familiar in the infirmary.

Considering the noises she'd been hearing, she shouldn't have been surprised that the bed took pride of place, but after days of being stuck in a box of a room with nothing but medical equipment and Delfi to look at, she would have thought there'd be at least a *few* things to mark this as the room of a warlord. Blood, maybe. More armor somewhere.

She didn't have a chance to get a better look. Coming towards her was a cluster of women. That, at least, she had anticipated. What she hadn't expected was the looks on their faces. The women watched her warily, as if she were a snake that might bite them at any moment.

Maybe it was Iira. Glancing to the side, she saw that the medic had gone back to her usual impassive mien. Her body language was no help either. Touching her unasked was out of the question, so Jossa clasped her hands together and turned back to the women instead.

With a start, she realized they all wore crowns over long, loose hair. The same fused-together skullcap and flares that encased her own head. No gaps, no growth plates, no shifters. She'd checked her own crown as soon as Iira had left her to her own devices, after that disastrous first encounter with the warlord. It was nothing like the one the Imperial scientists had tried on her after she'd hit puberty. These were meant to do one thing. Block a woman's sai, totally and completely.

Did that mean each of these women was a sai? Or were the Svis Konanuog just guarding the Barbicans, as it were? The long hair that each wore loose around their shoulders would have weighed things in favor of the Fleet not taking chances. If it weren't for the fact that this most definitely *wasn't* the Empire, if it weren't for the fact that familiar distinctions between commoners and highborns didn't matter much when you were a captive of the enemy.

The floor was cold to her bare feet. She shifted, wondering if she should introduce herself. Was there a protocol for this? Hello, I'm the fresh meat? Is there a rotation or does the warlord take us as he pleases? How many girls does he put in a medunit in a given week? Has anyone died because we were in there taking up space?

That last would go over well. Maybe that was why none of them had stepped away from the little group. And the air of general doom. A person wouldn't need to be a Feel to tell that much.

Iira made a little *tcht*ing noise and turned on her heel. Staring, Jossa watched her vanish back into the other room. Well! So much for guidance.

She was just working up the final nerve to step forward and give her name when the stalemate was broken from the other side. One of the women came out of the pack, dark hair a tumble around her shoulders and the stiffness in her posture all at odds with the welcoming smile on her full lips. She held out her hands as if to take Jossa's.

Jossa shrank away. She didn't need anyone else's thoughts and feelings right now. The woman dropped her hands and sympathy filled her green eyes. "Hello there. It's such a shock, isn't it? So horrible, being taken from everything you know and getting put in here?"

Jossa blinked and tried to come up with an alternative to blurting out her life story. She didn't get a chance to lie.

"Why don't you come with us?" The woman nodded at one of the other doors in the wall. There was fear in that voice, oh so carefully hidden under the confidence. "Milady says you need a bath and clothes." The woman raked her from top to toe with a critical eye. "And probably some real food too, from the sight of you. I'm Julin.

Come now," she said, holding out a hand. "Let's get you taken care of."

"Jossalyn," she replied as she followed, but didn't take the offered hand. Really, what else could she do?

The ship must be as big as an Ajiri city. That was the only thing Jossa could think when presented with the tub large enough to fit the whole crew of the *Skatasi* with room to spare. No crew showers here, timed and cramped. No, this was a small lake. A pond at the very least. And it was full of steaming water. From the patterns and ripples on the surface, it was probably kept full and circulating, warmed at need with heat coils built into the bottom and sides.

It was ridiculous. She wanted to sit in it up to her neck and never come out. Forget clothes. She'd spent a good portion of her life mostly naked. Forget *food*. For the last ten years or so, food had oscillated between the feasts of minor kings and whatever she could scrounge out of the back end of an almost empty cupboard. Predictability had never been in the course projection when it came to food.

But a real bath. A bath! Now that was enough to turn her into a greedy child offered her pick of sweets. She'd expected to be stuffed in a tiny little water closet and told to scrub down as fast as she could. She didn't know why. The warlord had his own private infirmary, so why she'd thought he wouldn't have better bathing facilities than they had on the *Skatasi*, she had no idea.

"Now, if you press this," Julin touched a button along the rim, out of range of all but the most enthusiastic splashing, "there are supplies." True to her words, a section of the wall opened up and shelves of bottles and tubes slid out from behind a panel. Julin took a small bucket stuffed with brushes and sponges and held it out. "Do you need help?"

Jossa couldn't tell if that was polite scorn or genuine worry coloring Julin's voice. She didn't care. She might not be strong enough to do much more than walk, but she could manage a bath without too much trouble. And then she remembered. "Probably with my hair." She sighed as she tried to gather it in her hands. She'd never had hair longer than her earlobes while fully crowned. The crown made it awkward. Her cryo-weakened arms took exception to being raised a moment longer than they thought they should be.

"All right then." The woman started undoing the fastenings of the loose gown she was wearing. "Let's get this over with. Might as well learn to be friends, right?"

Jossa wasn't sure what to make of that, but until this woman was in touching range, she wouldn't know if Julin had an ulterior motive. Without a place to escape to, she'd just have to wait and see. Besides, if they were her jailors, they'd report any bad behavior. And then what would happen to Delfi?

No. For now it was better to sit quiet and go along with things. So she slipped into the tub and prepared to send herself back in time.

Sixteen -- Jossa

We work together as a group. Your sisters may undermine you in petty things. Your mothers may hand down menial chores and play favorites. But when it comes to the safety of the whole, we stand united.
Do you understand, child?
  -Chataf Kuchru lis Chuis isk Fuerrus, to Jossalyn

As it turned out, accepting help with washing her hair was one of her better ideas. She didn't even think about her maruste, and Julin didn't comment on it as she worked on her charge's hair.

Scrub, rinse, and scrub again. Tip the head back and close the eyes so suds and water could make their way under the edges of the crown and through the microscopic channels in the underside of the thing. Another rinse with a pressure jet. Jossa sent a prayer to her Ancestors, hoping that whoever came up with the Kuchen variety of the crown had been as good at covering the circuitry as the Imperials were. Electrocution to the brain pan did not appeal as a way to go. She'd rather have greasy hair and dandruff, and Ancestors knew what else.

But she survived and the crown didn't short, and she never picked up more than genuine worry and concern from Julin. Hope that the new girl would learn her place quickly and a sort of quiet wishfulness that Jossa couldn't put a reason to. Not much curiosity at all. Not a flicker of sai reaching out to meet her where their skin touched. With all the skin-to-skin contact, something should have come through, right?

Then she was clean and it was time to face the others again. Julin wrapped Jossa in a towel after squeezing most of the water out of her hair, then led the way through a different door into what was obviously the women's quarters. "Milord prefers we sleep in the main room when he does not wish us in his bed," the woman said as Jossa padded along behind her, trailing a series of damp footprints. "But when he's away on Campaign, we stay back here." The woman gestured at the room.

Cushions and benches lined the walls near the floor, shelves near the ceiling, with spaces between them for the odd door here and there. Plants covered every horizontal surface in the center of the room, from sprouts to seedlings to small saplings. Ferns, low broadleaves, and various woody stalks. Jossa stopped and stared. "This is . . ."

"We have to do something when he's not around," said a new woman as she came through a door a little further down the wall. "Milord spends a good deal of time planetside at the start of a Campaign. What do you know of growing things?"

Jossa shrugged. "Very little. Our ship—" She stopped to swallow down the grief. "It wasn't big enough for much in the way of hydroponics."

"Oh, they don't let the outFleet near those." The woman laid the armful of cloth she'd been carrying on a nearby chair, then tucked a drifting curl of blond hair behind one ear. "These are for the personal quarters. Ornament. Take some of the load off the air filters. Or so they tell us."

"Mainly it's to give us something to do that's not trying to tear apart the walls." Another woman came with a tray of what looked like cosmetics and jewelry cases. "There're a recreation room through there." She nodded at another door. Her face twisted wryly.

"We're expected to divide our time between the plants and keeping up bone and muscle mass. Now let's see here." She started sorting through the vials, holding them up to the light, and then to Jossa's face. Jossa held still.

"I'm Adafa," the woman said after she'd set aside two or three different containers. "Miss Cynical here is Mivi. She'd love to find a way out, because she can't manage to antagonize milord Syrus nearly as often as she'd like, now that his tempers come fewer and further between than they used to.

"The rest of us are quite happy to stay here and tend plants and know that no one can get into the warlord's quarters." She twisted the top off a small bottle and dabbed a bit on her finger, then onto Jossa's wrist. The light brown stood out against Jossa's dark skin like a beacon. Adafa shook her head and reached for a different bottle. "Now that he's changed the settings on the locks, she's been especially bitchy. We have free run of his quarters, but we need his DNA, fresh, to leave. I gather we have you to thank for that?" The woman grinned up at Jossa as she shook another bottle and popped the cap open.

Jossa blinked and latched on to the least troublesome bit of information she could find in the torrent. "Syrus?"

"He's the warlord, or milord to you," Adafa said sharply, as if she hadn't realized she'd slipped. "Or any of us really. He might be gentler than Warlord Brander—"

Julin, still standing next to Jossa, leaned over and spat. Adafa slapped her. Casually. Without even looking at her. The makeup on her fingers left dark smears on the girl's lighter skin.

"He might be gentler," Adafa continued, as if Julin didn't have a red handprint on her face. "He might have unlocked the infirmary when he brought you in. But he managed to kill Brander. Beat him to a pulp with his bare hands. And if you knew what Brander was . . ." Adafa trailed off as her eyes focused on some point a thousand miles past the wall she was looking at.

Jossa braced herself for the feelings that would come through the grip the woman had on her wrist, but it was as if she'd shut down. An empty shell, with faint rattles of ancient horror echoing down her nerves.

After another heartbeat, Adafa shook her head and straightened. "He'll kill you and never bat an eye," she said. "Don't think he won't.

"We're here for one reason. The sooner you get that through your head, the easier things will be for you and the longer you'll survive. Pray the Ancestors keep him alive through Campaign and that he stays strong enough to hold off any Challengers. We'll all live a lot longer with him than we *ever* would have under a different warlord. And he makes sure our bodies don't go for the rank and file after we're used up."

That last comment almost went right through the Barbican without a safety check. Jossa was still thinking of Delfi and the difficulty of remembering how to be a good concubine instead of Rui's wife. When her too-slow brain finally caught the meaning, she felt the blood drain from her face. "What?"

Adafa sniffed. "Exactly what it sounds like. Milord Syrus may have been born Savage, but there are worse than Savages, and they are Fleet. Whatever hole he found you in, whatever you may have been before you came here, you are the warlord's now. You understand me?"

"I don't think we're going to have to worry about that last part." Mivi had come around behind Jossa without anyone else noticing. Jossa twisted her head to see what the woman was doing, but saw nothing more than blond curls and a bare white shoulder. Unfamiliar fingers gathered up Jossa's dripping hair from where it had plastered itself to her skin. The spike of sick jealousy and rage tripping through her skin and along her nerves nearly staggered Jossa. She bit her lip against the nausea that churned her stomach like a tidal wave and closed her mind as best she could to the images that rode the emotions.

The warlord had deactivated the Open Blossom of her maruste before leaving her to Iira's tender care, so at least she wasn't glowing anymore. But the basic patterns and condensed glyphs of her occupation and lineage were still there for anyone to see.

Mivi knew what Jossa's maruste meant. Somehow. Although Julin hadn't so much as twitched while helping Jossa bathe. How? How dangerous was it for the other women to know?

Suddenly she realized that except for Julin and Adafa, none of them had turned their backs on her. Not that it mattered, since their hair hung loose, instead of up like a proper concubine's. Impossible to tell what anyone's maruste looked like. Not without asking them to pull their hair out of the way.

The warlord, Syrus, had made sure Iira wasn't in earshot when he'd asked his questions. When he'd taken the knife to her back, completed the contract by cutting her shoulder to mix his blood with hers, and sealed the bond so it wouldn't bloom unless he deliberately turned it on. Why hadn't he warned her about the women in his quarters? Had he thought they wouldn't recognize her markings? Did he even care? Probably not, now that she thought about it.

Jossa had no doubt that if she displeased him, the warlord would kill her as easily as Adafa promised. Despite all the effort he'd put in to rescuing her from cryo and getting her healed, he'd gone to great lengths to hide his blood connection to her. She didn't think he'd appreciate her shouting it to the stars.

So many of the men in her childhood would have died for the chance to claim royal blood in their veins. And here he was, doing everything he could to hide it.

No time to wonder why. Right now she had to concentrate on keeping Delfi safe and herself alive. Which meant lying. Which meant using as much truth as she could possibly manage without telling them anything really important.

Other fingers joined Mivi's on Jossa's back. Adafa. The others came around so they could see. More touches. With them came a mix of emotions she couldn't begin to sort out. Reasons and questions and speculation swam in her gut until she had to clench her hands so hard the untrimmed fingernails broke skin. She pressed her fists to her stomach, willing it to settle, grateful they hadn't given her any food yet.

"Mivi is the only highborn any warlord's brought into the quarters," Adafa said, quite as if Jossa wasn't swallowing great gulps of fear. "And Brander only let her in because the ruler of her planet promised she had special skills." Disgust, relief, and an odd sort of pride prickled along Jossa's nerves from where Julin's fingers traced the marks of sire and dam on her skin.

"His promises weren't empty," Mivi snapped. "No one's lasted as long as I have in the warlord's bed." Lust. Joy. And deep, deep self-loathing. If they had been Jossa's—if she'd had to live through the tortures this woman carried within—she would have thrown herself off a cliff eons ago rather than live in such a state.

She clenched her fists harder and bit her lip on a whimper. She could not let these women know she still had some of her sai. If they told the warlord... No, don't think about that.

"So, the rest of you?" she asked, once she had her breath back.

Adafa sniffed and stepped out of the small crowd of women. Coming around in front of Jossa, she picked up one of the dresses Mivi had draped over the chair and held it up. "Most captives go to the Breeder ships. The Fleet men *love* the Breeder ships. All the women they could ever want, and not a one of them able to say no."

She dropped the dress and held up another one, looking from it to Jossa. Her mouth twisted in a hard line, and her blue eyes glittered with what Jossa could only assume was hate. "But the warlords are above regulated leave time. Why shuttle over to a ship when you can keep a herd in your rooms and dip your usik whenever you please? And if everything lines up just right, he might get a squalling little brat out of the bargain. More fodder for their war." Adafa's eyes went sad for a second or so, before she blinked hard and scowled. "Not that milord Syrus has gotten any offspring on us."

Jossa blinked, unsure if the woman was mad at the warlord for *not* siring children, or if she was relieved that none of them had born half-blood babies.

Some of the women behind her tittered nervously. The emotional onslaught eased as they took their hands off her back.

Adafa caught her small gasp of relief and misread it. She raised one elegant eyebrow, dropped the dress, and picked up another. It was deep gold, held together at the shoulders with knots of bronze, and almost completely see through. She nodded and waved at the cluster of concubines. "Shoo you."

They shooed.

Adafa grabbed the towel wrapped around Jossa before she could escape and yanked. "Yes," the woman said. "Milord has survived almost three years here on the Fleet. I am not a—" She stopped gathering the hem of the dress in her hands and gave Jossa a look. "What's the word you highborn use?"

"Nehkeh."

"Ah. The odd language you use. Adafa shrugged and jerked her chin at Julin, then at the tray of cosmetics. The girl jumped to obey. Jossa decided not to correct her. Not many people knew that He'la was the prophetic language, completely unrelated to highborn Imperial. Explaining the difference to commoners and those without the sai for Foreseeing was a waste of time.

"Anyway, spend enough time keeping milord happy and you'll pick up a few things. From replanting seedlings to colorful new words for your genitalia. Arms up."

Jossa obeyed just in time, barely managing to find the shoulders of the dress as Adafa threw it over her head. Then they pushed her into a chair. Someone gathered up her hair, Julin came at her with the tray of cosmetics, and Mivi snatched up a hand and attacked it with a nail file. It occurred to her in that moment that if they'd been told to get information out of her, they were doing a singularly bad job of it.

But if the life of a concubine among the Svis Konanuog was as dangerous as they implied, maybe their lack of curiosity was simple self-preservation. Why get to know a woman who could be dead soon?

If that was the case, then maybe she could survive this. Keep her eyes open. Hide her reactions when touched. Do everything she could to learn everything possible about the warlord. Then, when he came for her at last, do her level best to make her body remember every lesson she had ever learned in her childhood. Life in a harem was one great game of Survival. She'd won it before. She would win it again.

Seventeen -- Jossa

A concubine's primary function is breeding. Our
people may number in the trillions, but our natural
birthrate is too low to worry about pleasure. If our
master brings you to the peak, so be it. But woe to
the woman who does so on her own.
    -Chataf Kuchru lis Chuis isk Fuerrus, to Jossalyn

Water ran down her arm and dripped from her elbow as Jossa
squeezed the cloth out over the bowel. She waited for it to stop
before leaning over to wipe the last traces of cleanser off Delfi's
stomach. As with every time she touched her sousi, she pushed down
the bond between them, praying she'd get a response.

Nothing.

By now she was so far past tears that she was operating in a dull
haze of despair instead. Iira had allowed her to detach the mag
tethers on one of the chairs out in the main room and rehook it here
in the infirmary, so she could sit with Del when she wasn't in the back
rooms with the other women. But it wasn't the consolation she'd
thought it would be.

Two and a half weeks now. Two and a half she'd been up and
walking around, and still Delfi lay there. Iira had vanished after the
first couple days, and none of the writing on the medunit made any
sense. Not that Jossa was any sort of medic. If Goris had been here,
she might have been able to tell what was going on and when Del

would wake. But Jossa was left waiting. Wondering. On her own in a ship full of tainted air and people who didn't care if she lived or died, except in how it affected their own lives.

"Oh Del," she whispered, dropping into the chair next to the medunit. "They put a crown on me, did I tell you? I think I told you." She laid her chin on the edge of the bed and ran a finger up her sousi's arm. The veins showed blue under Delfi's pale skin.

"No growth plates or seepage points like the Imperial doctors tried. You know, before . . ." She might as well be touching a corpse, for all the emotional feedback Del put out. It was almost as if her own emotions were being sucked *in* to her sister.

She sighed. "It's probably a good thing. Not that I'll tell *them* that. Except they crowned you too, and when you wake up, I have no idea what that's going to do to the bond." When. Not if. Delfi had to wake up. She had to. They were just weaning her off the cryo drugs and on to whatever it was that made it possible for the outFleet to breathe on this ship.

She still hadn't figured that part out. None of the concubines had been particularly forthcoming with answers. The few questions she *had* managed to ease into conversations had painted a very bleak picture. Especially when she put it all together with some of the things Iira had said. Weak lungs and breathing. Some sort of inoculation anyone who wasn't Fleet born had to get before they could spend more than an hour or so aboard. Or down on the planets after they'd been conquered, if the stories the girls told amongst themselves were true.

"Guess that answers the question of why people call them Svis Konanuog." Jossa stretched, feeling the vertebrae in her back pop and snap, then winced as a muscle pulled. "Such a long way from the Palace," she said, taking the bowl of water and setting it on the floor at her feet. She should have finished cleaning Del up, but she just didn't have the heart for it right now. There was that skin ink on Del's hip, entirely mundane and inert. Another down by her ankle. Poor man's decoration, when there wasn't much in the way of maruste on the back. She'd gotten them on some backwater space station, twins to a set Denz had done the same day. They'd thought it was a great joke.

Jossa didn't want to look at those right now. They meant more than a maruste ever would. Yet another reminder of a life she'd never have again. She couldn't even run away to find it. They were gone. All of them. Rui and Denz and the *Skatasi*, and even those who'd been chasing them. Ancestors, if she were to walk into the Palace tomorrow, not a person there would know why she had a right to stand in that building. Not if the warlord had told her the truth of things.

She wiped her eyes on the sheet and laid her head on her arms. "Well, that was one thing about being a kuchru in the palace of the fuerrus. Attendants. I haven't had a decent massage in . . ." She stopped to tally up the time, then laughed. "Three hundred and eight years. Give or take."

Once the laugh started, she couldn't stop. It just kept going. She clung to the edge of the bed and bumped her head against the mattress, laughing under her breath. "Oh Del. Del. Do you remember? Azia said she wanted to learn some of the tricks. And you said you'd teach her that one thing with your hips?" Jossa choked on the laugh. "Adan walked in just as you were demonstrating and looked like he'd died and gone to heaven."

No answer from the girl on the bed.

"And then when we talked Rui into extra water tanks? Told him he had five women on the ship now and a three-minute shower only meant we'd reset the timer so often it'd break within a month." She wiped more tears from her cheeks and gasped for breath. It had been a thing of beauty, what came next. The giant copper tub that Del bought from some poor junk dealer. Gotten it all the way to the ship and into the hold without anyone realizing it. What in the name of Ancestors she'd been thinking, Jossa had never found out. But she'd done it. She'd even managed to get it full of hot water. And keep it that way.

"Poor Denz. You were both so *sure* he was too tall to slip down like that. Nearly drowning in the middle of an orgasm. There have to be more ridiculous ways to go, but—"

"She sounds like a very unique person."

Jossa whipped around. Only the fact that she had a death grip on Del's hand kept her from completely shaming herself and landing on the floor. For a moment she gaped, trying to figure out how Mivi had snuck up on her. Then she caught herself and regained control of her flapping jaw. "Yes," she managed. "Very much so."

What in the universe brought the woman in here *now*? Very carefully, Jossa laid Delfi's hand back on the mattress and rearranged her fingers. The IV needle was taped to the back of the opposite hand, so at least there hadn't been a risk of pulling that loose. When she looked up again, Mivi was still there, straightening the sheets on the other mattress.

"I always dreamed of being soul bonded," the woman said softly as she pulled out the corner and retucked it. Her wealth of honey blond hair fell in curls and waves, shielding her face from view. "I thought it must be the most wonderful thing."

It is, Jossa wanted to tell her. And the most horrible. Delfi had quite literally saved her. Many times over, in fact. But if she ever lost her sousi. That didn't bear thinking about. There was a reason all the most overwrought stories featured a broken bond pairing. Those who survived, well. The stories had a nugget of truth at their center. The remaining half of a bond generally wasn't considered useful to society. Especially if the one who survived was the unstable half, instead of the anchor holding them to sanity.

She realized she'd laced her fingers with Del's and was gripping them hard enough to hurt. Hurt herself, if not her sister. She let go and concentrated on keeping her hands in her lap.

Mivi didn't seem to need an answer. She moved up to the head of the medunit and pulled the thin pillow out of its casing, squeezing it as if trying to force comfort into it. Or out of it. Jossa decided to swap it for Delfi's when it was time for bed. Del wouldn't know any different. She hoped.

"I still got to be special, though. Even though they said I didn't have enough sai to fill an ovary. Isn't that nice?" Mivi's smile was too bright, and her green eyes all but shone in the dim light of the room.

Jossa managed a weak smile in return. "It is." So long as the woman stayed out of touching range, Jossa could go on pretending to be happy for her.

Mivi narrowed her eyes, lips tightening slightly. Jossa kept the smile on her face and willed herself to believe that yes, it was good that the woman believed herself special. And it was, in a way. It was a trick she'd learned long ago. Whatever her real thoughts, so long as she could see some part of a person's opinion as truth or reality, she could make them think she agreed with them. Invaluable when it came to life among the kuchruog. Something she was probably going to need more and more often when dealing with the warlord and his. This one in particular.

"Four months," Mivi said, looking down at the pillow she held. "He wouldn't touch us. Wouldn't hardly look at us. Now? Now, I'm the one he comes to. When something goes wrong on Campaign. When he wakes up raging in the night. I make him forget why he killed Brander. So for a little while, he can forget that the bitch he came for was dead before he even made it to the infirmary."

Oblivious to Jossa's reaction, Mivi stuffed the pillow back in its case. If the covering had been fabric instead of prefabbed synthsilk, she would have ripped the seams. Instead, she crushed the pillow down until it took up half the space it should have. And kept on pushing, face twisted in concentration.

Jossa fought to close her mouth before the other woman abandoned her abuse of the poor pillow. What? Who?

"Of course, it took him a while to realize I was there for him." Mivi stopped punching the pillow long enough to let it fluff up a bit before jamming a fist back down into the case, "He's usually so nice. So gentle with us all."

Apparently satisfied with her work, she tucked the loose ends of the case in on themselves and slipped the whole thing under the sheets at the head of the table. She smiled as she smoothed the covers and tucked them in. Perfectly. Not a wrinkle to be seen.

Jossa eyed the medunit mattress she'd spent however many days occupying, then looked at the one Delfi still had possession of. It was wide enough for the both of them, wasn't it? She slept quietly, and Del wasn't in any shape to thrash around. She never had to touch the other mattress again.

Then she had the horrified realization of what would happen when Delfi actually woke up and learned the truth of their current situation. Assuming she didn't come up kicking, and that Jossa could explain things before the warlord lost his temper. Because as sure as Barbicans needed keys, she'd get the job done. Del could anger a monk sworn to pacifism, and do it in record time.

And if she took it upon herself to try and protect Jossa? To offer herself in Jossa's place? As Mivi apparently had?

Many a room and the furniture within had fallen victim to the enthusiasm of Delfi and her husband. Teeth marks and sprains and bandages had not been uncommon. Traveling for miles just to get out of range of their broadcasted feelings had been a necessity for Jossa, just so she could tell her own emotions apart from those of Delfi and Denz. Rui had nearly booted them off the ship a time or two. Only that fact that Del's departure would mean Jossa's as well had kept them safe.

All that had happened when Delfi was in a *good* mood. Now? Just the two of them on this ship? Jossa couldn't keep the shudder from crawling down her spine at the thought. How she would take the fact that they'd lost their gamble, Jossa couldn't be sure. But it would probably have something to do with sinking her hooks into the nearest man and torturing him in every way possible.

"I said, are you listening to me?" Jealousy and anger oozed up Jossa's arm, sending spikes of chill pain through her nerves.

"I'm sorry." Jossa covered the Mivi's hand with her own and loaded as much calm acceptance into her voice as she could manage. "I guess I got a little distracted." She tried a smile.

It worked. Somewhat. Mivi smiled back, her emotions stepping back down into the realm of mild frustration. Jossa left her hand where it was, just in case, and shored up her defenses. It had been a long time since she'd done this particular dance, and last time she'd had Delfi to help. "What was it you were saying?" she asked when she thought it was safe enough.

"Oh!" Mivi took her hand back and went to perch on the bed she'd just made up. "Just hoping she recovers soon." She nodded at Del's still form on the mattress of her medunit. "It is so odd, having someone in here. Milord hasn't come within ten feet of the door since, well—" She shrugged.

Jossa pulled her feet up to the edge of the seat and wrapped her arms around her knees, eying the door to the main room. It would be just her luck for the warlord to come back now and discover them having this discussion.

Mivi must have seen her nervousness. She laughed and waved a hand. "Oh, don't worry about him. There's an alert, you see. He made one of the techs set it up so we'd know when he came in the main room." She sneered elegantly. "Milord Brander liked to keep us on edge. Liked to ambush us and make us run scared through the quarters. Milord Syrus, though, he doesn't think like a Fleet man."

Jossa blinked, then tucked her head down to hide her face. Worried for his women, her mother's uncle. The warlord just wanted to know if someone else was trying to get at what was his.

"It's remarkable, isn't it?" Mivi sat back and crossed her ankles under her. "Even I haven't managed to get him to open this place up;

he's that careful with us. Well, with me I guess. Like I said, he's absolutely *gentle* with everyone else. I guess you could say I walk that line." She held her hands up as if balancing an ancient set of scales. "It's there, you know. There's only so far you can go before the bruises turn to broken bones. The old warlord, he was harder to gauge." She rubbed a hand along the edge of the mattress she was sitting on, as if it was an old friend.

Jossa decided right there that she was squeezing in with Delfi, no matter what. If there was ever a time to be grateful for a crown, this was it. Right now. Her taste of this woman a few minutes earlier had been quite enough. If she had to endure the poisonous mix of emotions that comprised Mivi's being for more than a few seconds, Jossa thought she might go just as mad as the woman herself.

Then she realized that Mivi was waiting for an answer of some sort. "You are very special," Jossa said, with every ounce of truth she could muster. "To be able to do what so few can master."

It was like giving water to a parched plant. Mivi beamed, eyes practically glowing. She hopped off the mattress and stroked a hand along Delfi's hair. "She'll be fine, you know. These Fleet medics really do know what they're doing. They can put almost anyone back together. If it hadn't been for that bitch Rissa going catatonic, they might even have gotten *her* patched up in time."

She turned to smile at Jossa. "You won't tell anyone I talked about her, will you? We're not supposed to mention her. Everyone gets so very upset when she's talked about."

"I promise," Jossa told her, meaning it with every ounce of her being. Mivi was as subtle as a battle cruiser dropping out of orbit. Whatever reason she had for wanting Jossa to ask about old concubines, it couldn't be good.

"Oh, thank you!" Mivi fluttered a hand and flounced to the door. "I'll have someone bring you something to eat, ok?"

Jossa waited until the woman was gone before leaning her head against Del's cool hand and praying to every Ancestor she had that her sousi would wake soon. The sooner she was awake, the sooner they could start figuring a way out of here.

EIGHTEEN -- SYRUS

It has been found that each subject has a certain range. Inside which they may feel or hear or otherwise sense another being. Depending on the strength of the psychic ability, the subject may have a variety of reactions. In the strongest, it has been known to cause madness before training can be initiated.
     -recovered data, date unknown

Almost three weeks after the first assault on the planet below, Syrus didn't have an answer for the issue of the thank-gift. He knew what Kizen expected. By now, half the Fleet knew that Kizen wasn't just after the Helm of the Turan. And three quarters of the Fleet would be thrilled if the bastard got his way.

Luckily for Syrus, the Campaign was going well. Well enough that he could leave the surface forces and catch a ride up to the *Edde Belo* to coordinate contingencies for the whole system instead of worrying about the one planet. Kizen's ralenen needed to meet the outFleet warlord for themselves before they would tell their men to follow orders. Fucking politics. Maybe he should leave the bath until after he'd done the meet and greet and maybe even pummeled a few of them into submission.

But no. He needed to recenter his mind, so he *wouldn't* jump the nav beacons and start ripping people apart. Fucking war, so much more complicated than it needed to be. Fucking planets full of people driving him fucking insane. Fucking people, getting in his way just because they could.

Parents clinging to his legs as they begged him for mercy. Piles of dead men stacked like levees against the bloody rivers. Children watching with hollow eyes as their mothers were marched into the bowels of the Fleet ships. The same children crying as they were hauled off and stuffed in other ships, the better to keep the Fleet going on down the line.

It wasn't the worst thing he'd ever agreed to, this warlord fuckery. He wanted to grab every single one of the survivors by the hair and tell them that at least they'd had each other for a little while.

But warlords didn't get sentimental. Neither did he, usually. He just got pissed at all the motherfucking idiots who didn't realize they were being saved. Innocked and shipped off planet. Out of the way of what was about to happen to the people who were a little too good at hiding. The same type of person he'd been, a long time ago.

Not so many this time. In the way of rats and desperate people through time immemorial, people took any way off the planet they could find. Even if they knew Oona's people were tagging every ship that left atmo, there weren't many places to hide. Soon enough she'd have the data to tell them where to find the leak in this fucking system. Then they could work on plugging it.

If his guess about Hadra's Net played out, the Fleet was both in trouble and in a position to cause a hell of a lot of havoc in the Empire in the next couple years. So long as they could make it through the next Barb.

He checked the slate in his hand as he palmed open the door to his quarters, but there hadn't been an update. No messages one way or another. It could mean the techs were still getting acquainted with the computer system. It could mean they were still trying. It could mean anything.

All it really meant was that his own commanders would keep doubting their warlord's decision to let so many escapees succeed, and Kizen would needle him at the banquet later. So maybe he'd be dead in a few days, if the techs didn't come up with something.

In the meantime, he had several weeks of blood and grime to clean off and enough sexual frustration pent up to go through at least three or four of the women. Maybe lira'd gotten the new one out of the infirmary. Maybe the other one was awake. He might have two fresh bits of meat to try instead of just the one.

He started shedding armor and clothes and putting them in the cleaner next to the door. None of the women came out to the main room. They'd know he was here and start the heat in the bath, but he didn't expect them to come running out to fawn all over him the minute he set foot in his rooms. It had taken a while to break them of that. But they'd finally learned that he'd come and find whichever ones he wanted for the moment and leave the rest alone. Otherwise they were just tripping hazards.

At least that's what he told them. They also pissed him off, shoving weeks' worth of worry and petty arguments under his skin. Right now he was so sick of the emotions of a planet's worth of terrified and angry people that a few minutes of peace were like an eon of relief.

He pulled off his pants, wincing as caked in dirt flaked off and week-old bruises made themselves known all over his torso. The best armor in the universe couldn't save a person from cracked ribs.

His slate dinged. An automated message told him that lira'd set an alert to go off once he made it back. She'd locked the infirmary and put the women in their rooms, where no one else could get to them. She said she'd gone down to Med Bay and was taking care of the incoming casualties. If he was going to be breaking anyone's bones or wanted to have his way with the remaining cryo patient, he'd have to take care of the aftermath himself.

He stopped. Reread the message. Snorted to himself and deleted it. Tired of babysitting his strays, was she? Not surprising. Quinn had been snippy on the flight up from the surface about how much time Iira had spent in Syrus's quarters since the two foundlings had been brought on board. Not that Syrus would ever lay a finger on the woman. He preferred someone who wasn't a walking glacier, thank you very much. Whatever Quinn and Iira and Oona had between themselves seemed to work itself out better than any *normal* marriage he'd ever seen, but it wasn't something he wanted to get in the middle of.

Besides, med-techs might be viewed as a short step up from cockroaches by any Fleet warrior, but *someone* had to run Med Bay. Iira's place was down with the injured while they were on Campaign, not babysitting concubines.

Locking the women in though? That was new. Even the dumbest Fleet bastards had quit trying to break into his quarters months ago. So why would she lock the women in the back?

Dropping his clothes into the cleaner, he decided he might as well check the infirmary first. It wasn't hard to find a half-healed wound, this one along his neck where the gorget joined the helmet. He picked up almost as much dirt out of it as blood when he broke it open. Definitely time to get washed up, before something closed over and started to fester.

When he saw that only one of the beds was occupied, he almost turned around and reached for his slate. He caught himself mid stomp. Iira must have decided Jossalyn was well enough to be turned loose of the infirmary. That was probably why she'd locked the women into the back rooms. Added protection and to cut the risk of anyone trying to escape.

It didn't look like she'd been trying very hard, though, if the rumpled sheets on the empty bed were any indication. He chuckled when he got close enough to lean in and take a deep breath. Iira wasn't as much of a stone-hearted bitch as she liked to pretend. The table didn't have the antiseptic med-bay smell that clung through a night or two. The new woman had set up camp in here and probably refused to leave her sousi without a promise that she wouldn't be kept away.

Well that was on course with how the breed acted. Even the weakest, most fragile bit of a thing would turn into a snarling terror if someone tried to separate her from her partner for long. He'd seen that often enough. With one of them laid out like this, well, the reaction would be even worse.

Good thing everyone had managed to compromise before he'd gotten back. Otherwise Iira's message probably would have said that she'd broken his new toy in half instead of healing her up. Maybe she was being less soft hearted and more practical. He would've had to punish her for injuring any of his women. He took a moment to look the redhead over, but didn't bother checking her very close. He wanted to be clean and he wanted to fuck the living daylights out of someone, not necessarily in that order. Now that he knew Jossa was up, this was as good a time as any to see what sort of woman the fuerrus had access to back when the throne was worth something.

The women had turned the heat on in the bath, but they hadn't stuck around. For a minute he debated grabbing one of them and dragging her out to join him. But the lure of a tub full of water was stronger. At some point in his life, he'd learned an ancient phrase about cleanliness and godliness. The godliness part was a crock of shit. The cleanliness? It took someone who knew what true filth was to really appreciate that part.

He scrubbed down the Imperial way, kneeling at the edge of the tub and dipping a bucket of water out to get rid of the worst of the grime before he contaminated the whole thing. He had to literally scrape the stuff off his skin. He and his men had gone from the surface almost to the core on the first push, down in the dregs and sewage, before they'd started herding people upwards. Short of an eeva suit, there wasn't a set of armor made that could keep all that dirt out.

If it hadn't been for his own brand of street rat's genes, he'd have probably ended up with sepsis or who the fuck knew what else, poking around down in the lowest levels of the caves. He hated Kovavek planets. Cesspools, every one. Science hadn't even discovered the cause of half the diseases you could catch in the lower levels of a Kovavek planet.

Once he'd rinsed off the crusted blood, dirt, and bits of what might have been other people, he slid into the tub. Forget a double armful of women. Forget a real bed. Forget people kneeling at his feet. At any point in his life, this right here was something he would have killed for.

Not just being physically clean, but alone. Completely alone inside his head. In a few minutes he'd start to get twitchy, like a mental patient expecting to hear the voices he'd been cured of. But for now, he was going to enjoy the solitude.

Syrus lasted about half an hour before his dick made up his mind for him. He didn't have to worry about what parasites the women might have. Or whether they'd rigged themselves to kill him. No bombs going off. None of the soldiers waiting for him to let his guard down. There were a hundred reasons not to grab someone out of the slave pens before they'd been cleared and shipped up to the Breeder ships.

He didn't have to worry about any of that. The women weren't exactly standing at attention when he opened the door between the bathing room and their quarters. Neither were they draped around the room like some of the more ridiculous holos he'd seen. They kept their eyes on him, the acid whisper of fear all but hidden in the low thrum of anticipation. They knew the drill. All except the new one.

She sat at one of the tables, holding a plant over a small glass container. Her long fingers cradled the dirt, thin roots escaping to drip water on the table. A thin sheen of cosmetics dusted her face in golds and rubies. The leaf-green dress she was wearing made her skin glow. She looked far, far better than she had when he'd pulled her out of that casket. Almost healthy, even though her collarbone still jutted and he could see every tendon in the back of her hands. That could have been from tension. Even from halfway across the room, he could see she was trembling.

His erection bobbed against his stomach as he breathed. The tension in the room ratcheted up another notch. His nerves sang with it, his lust settled a bit deeper in his balls, and he felt a smile work its way across his face. "You." He crooked a finger at the new one. "Come here."

She took the time to put the plant back in its container, clean the dirt from her fingers, and shake out the folds of her dress before stepping away from the table and the other women. Nobody moved, either to encourage her or block her.

Standing in front of him, she was just as blank to him as Quinn or his wives. Right. The crown. It locked her in as much as it kept her from Feeling. That was ok. She couldn't hide her physical reactions. Her breath came in pants as she clenched and unclenched her hands in the fine gauze of her dress. He tilted his head and eyed her. Looked like he was going to have to do all the work here.

"You're out of practice," he told her, stepping in to catch one wrist and pull her a few steps closer. His hand lit on fire with nerves, sending tingling jolts of pain all the way up his arm. But she didn't try to pull away, so she was about three steps ahead of what the others had done when he first took the Helm. A tick in the plus column.

Her throat worked as he counted her ribs with his hand. The slight smell of dirt and plants overlaid perfumes and cosmetics, filling his nose as he leaned in close. She stayed put, watching him out of the corner of her eye as he reached with his free hand and palmed the lock on the door between the bathing room and the women's quarters.

"You know, I hate doin' all the work." He backed up a step, bringing the woman with him. "This doesn't have to hurt you. Might even enjoy it, you loosen up."

What he needed her to do was relax, just a bit. Enough that he could find whatever it was that would turn her from a bundle of fear and nervous energy to something else. Right now, the lust and need singing in his veins were strong enough to outweigh what sang through her skin. If he could bring the same things up in her; get her other emotions to step down, then this would be a lot more fun. For both of them.

She wavered. Her hands came up to his hips, dropped away, and then settled into place. Not really helpful, since she brought more of that electric nervousness with her. Better than nothing though. There was determination under all that sting and fizz. Was she using it for courage? Trying to keep from running?

He circled a nipple with his thumb and it pebbled up hard and tight. She gasped, and her breast filled his hand. Small, yes, but he got tired of the huge, swinging udders Brander had filled the place with.

His dick twitched and he grinned. "See," he murmured into her ear, running his nose around its outside curve. Her hair smelled like a meadow full of flowers. "Not so bad."

She trembled as he moved from ear to jaw, then down the line of her neck. Her fingers on his hips fluttered, like she'd forgotten she'd put them there. She didn't back away when he took another step to close the space between them. He cupped her ass, pulling her even closer, fitting her up against him, right where she belonged.

But she was still scared of something. Still holding onto herself with both hands and what must be an iron will.

That lasted until he lipped at the base of her neck, then bit gently. She melted. It was the only word for it. Arousal ran down her neck and crawled up her body from where they touched. She sucked in a breath. Her head fell back a little further, giving him better access to the rest of her neck. He grinned against her skin and bit again, a little harder.

This time she mewled under her breath.

He had her skirt up around her hips, one hand cupping the back of her head and his teeth working over a nipple before she flipped the switch. One minute he was riding high on arousal, just getting to the point where he could start the feedback loop. Then, between one heartbeat and the next, grief hit. Lust drained out of him like air from a ruptured hull, leaving only loss. Deep, heart-wrenching loss. Once he caught his balance and managed to squeeze back the tears, he found the source. Not himself. The woman. Jossalyn.

She was curled up on the floor, her back to the door. Her arms were over her head as she sobbed like the world had ended. Some small part of him, buried deep, reminded him that her world *had* ended not that long ago. The rest of him was flat pissed off, roaring in the sort of animal fury that usually sent him off into a killing Frenzy.

He grabbed her by the hair. He had her halfway across the room before she came to life again. Her feet slipped and skidded on the wet floor. Her hands came up in a futile effort to get her hair free of his grip. But she was too crippled by her own internal agony. She kept crying too. He didn't think it was with pain so much as self-loathing. At least, that was what he thought he was picking up from her. He wasn't so familiar with that emotion from the outside, but he knew what it felt like when it came from himself.

He cursed her as he went, in every language he knew. High Imperial, street Savage and Kuchen. He cursed her for a kuchek who should have known her place and how to do her job and a bitch who couldn't keep herself under control and an outFleet oiyao who should have taken what was offered and been grateful that some other oversexed jackass hadn't gotten hold of her first. He also cursed himself for forgetting that she was a projective empath.

Locked under a crown maybe, but crowns didn't always work when the wearer was strong. And the best way to strengthen a connection was skin to skin contact. He'd been a moron to forget that.

Yes, said the part of him that sympathized with the grief-stricken woman, *you were*.

Shut up, he growled at the voice.

He damn near punched a hole in the control panel for the infirmary. With more strength than precision, he all but threw her through the opening in the wall. She landed in a heap of green gauze and tangled hair against the base of the other foundling's table. If she noticed where she was, she didn't show it. She kept crying, gasping sobs that racked her whole body and made him want to either stuff her in an airlock and hit the release, or hold her until she stopped.

Snarling to himself for the weakness, wondering what else she'd pulled to the surface when she hit him with all that grief, he grabbed her and hauled her upright. "Look," he roared in her ear. "You see her?"

She looked. She saw. If anything, the wish for death got worse. The feeling that joined it was something he'd only ever described as "It's all my fault." He knew that one like he knew the pattern of his soul. It went light years past guilt. Right out into the emptiness of dead space itself.

Beating her to a bloody pulp would only make a mess he'd have to scrape off the floor and shove down the reclamation tubes. He had to remember that. Had to brand that into his brain before he forgot that he'd been looking for a good fuck, not cleanup detail.

"You don't pull your shit together," he snarled, "I'm going to drop you on a Breeder ship. You know the average lifespan of a woman on one of those things?"

When she didn't answer, he shook her by the hair, hard. She whimpered, hanging there, hands fisted against her stomach, but didn't speak. Didn't even try to fight.

"A year. If they're lucky. Pump you full of fertility drugs and mount as many men on you as they can in a day. There's a whole Fleet out there looking to blow their load into an actual living cunt. One of them's bound to get lucky. You live long enough to pop out a kid, they'll cut the umbilical and start the whole show over again. Fight too much and they'll just stick you in a coma instead. Ready-made incubator. How long you think you'll last?"

She kept staring at the young woman on the medunit table. Growling, he spun her around and took her by the shoulders. "I don't need both of you. Don't know why I'm keeping either of you. Whole Fleet wants you dead. So you get your head on straight. Do whatever you fucking Feels have to do to keep emotion from mixing things up. Or I'll take her instead."

That got her attention. A jolt of alarm and the burning heat of anger hit his hands. He clenched his fingers tighter on her bony shoulders and glared at her, daring her to read him. She was the one person on this boat who could blow his cover; but right now, he was betting she was too wrapped up in what she was feeling to notice much outside herself.

"She'll kill you first," the woman whispered, voice broken but clear.

He laughed and dropped her. She staggered and landed up against her sousi's table. "Funny to see her try. People been trying to kill me since before I can remember. Stay there. Got something for you."

He came back twenty minutes later, having snagged one of the women to help him go through their stash of dresses. He'd brought her to screaming orgasm and destroyed half the closet in the process, but she'd managed to salvage a dress from the wreckage. He might finally be calm enough now to walk the corridors of the ship and not pick a fight with everyone who looked at him sideways.

Jossa was huddled on the floor next to the other woman's table. Somehow, she'd gotten her sister's hand down without disconnecting any of the leads and was clinging to it like it was her last hope in the universe. He couldn't tell what she was whispering against that translucent skin, but from the reverent tone, he wouldn't have been surprised if it was a prayer.

"Put this on," he said, dropping the dress into her lap. "I've got warlord things to do. You're going to see what the rest of the Fleet looks like. And be glad you ended up with me.

Nineteen -- Jossa

You try to stand between two halves of a sousi, you're signing your own death certificate. Don't matter what you aim their way. They'll kill themselves to get past you.
-advice to a young recruit

The warlord led Jossa halfway down the corridor outside his quarters before he spat a curse and halted midstride. Jossa stumbled to a stop, barely aware of the pain in her arm where his fingers dug into her muscle. Her dress had sleeves, so the full force of his emotions were blunted by the fabric. But it wouldn't have been any different if she was naked and plastered to him. Nothing could make much of a dent in the dull throb of grief running through her veins.

"Come on."

Jossa felt him haul her around and pull her back the way they'd come. Her toes barked against the decking as she scrambled first for balance, then speed, trying to catch up with the fuming warlord. Her legs were long enough, but he moved with a purpose that threw her off balance and made it hard to find the rhythm of her steps.

No sooner had she caught her balance and managed to shrink the distance between them than he stopped again. Jossa almost smashed her nose into his shoulder.

It was disturbing, she thought absently, how the doors here opened. She half expected them to make some sort of suction noise, or to burble and pop with little liquid sounds. Something, at least, to go with the stomach-turning ooze of metal flowing back into the frame around the door. But the process was silent. As silent as the bond between herself and Delfi. As silent as the years that had taken her from—

Jossa grunted as the warlord shoved something into her stomach with enough force to back her up a step or two. She swallowed, *hard*, to convince her breakfast to stay where it belonged, and looked down.

He gave her half a second to see that he was still holding on to the object before letting go. Jossa yipped in surprise and grabbed for the thing. No thought involved, just a grab and a grunt when she misjudged its weight. Her fingers scrabbled for purchase on its rounded surface, catching and slipping from raised bumps and grooves. Just as she lost her grip entirely, she found an edge. A rim? And caught hold for real.

Then she discovered the slimy grit that covered the thing, and the fact that something was all but stabbing her hand, and nearly let go anyway.

The warlord caught it before she lost her grip entirely and shoved it at her again, harder. Jossa fetched up against the wall of the corridor this time and tried to wrap her arms around the disgusting thing before he let go again.

"What in the—" she started to ask.

The warlord growled, grabbed her arm, and they were off again.

"Ow!" Jossa couldn't help the little yelp of pain. She hitched the mysterious object over to one hip, hooked her fingers around one of its curved edges, and tried to ignore the wires poking her from wrist to elbow as she stretched her legs to catch up with the nehkeh man in front of her.

His grip on her arm eased as she drew alongside him. Jossa did her best to match her steps to his, just a little behind and to one side as he all but stalked down the hall. For a moment she had difficulties with her skirts, but she managed to get a pinch of fabric in the hand not clinging to the mysterious slimy thing. After that she just had to keep from stepping on his heels—less tempting than it might have been given her bare feet—and make sure she didn't lag too far behind him as he made turns, went up small ramps, and occasionally stopped short in front of her.

Twice she lost her grip of the thing he'd handed her. Once she lost it entirely and nearly had her arm wrenched out of its sockets as a reward for stooping to get it. The second time, she caught it in the tips of her fingers. After that, whether out of pity or because some of his anger had worn off, the warlord slowed and she had less trouble.

That only made for more opportunity to look around. What she saw was not designed to inspire hope in a person. Quite the opposite.

The theme of twisting brambles, thorns, and winding snakes must be something universal to the Fleet as a whole. Every hall, every door, every ceiling crawled with sinuous lines and barbed angles. Enameled eyes, red and gold and silver, watched her from dark, burnished metal leaves as bas-relief bodies slid and caught on long thorns. Occasionally the creatures and plants protruded from the walls, forming hooks, clasps for safety lights, and the borders of what she assumed must be security hatches and other safety measures. Once she flinched away from a hooded snake, convinced she'd seen it move.

The warlord ignored her, stalking down yet another curved hallway. Men and women scattered in front of him, staring as Jossa trotted past, and re-formed in clusters to whisper in their liquid language once the pair had moved on. Jossa could only guess at what they might be saying; they were too quiet and too far away for her to gauge tone of voice. Their faces, though, were not promising. If she hadn't known it before, she knew it now. She'd have no help in any escape, assuming she could come up with a viable plan.

Assuming Del woke up in any shape to help her.

Jossa lost track of time. Surely this ship had faster means of transportation than walking. She wouldn't ask though. This was part of his punishment for her, and she didn't want to make it worse.

Eventually, the warlord halted again. Jossa overshot him by two or three steps and he yanked her back to his side without so much as looking at her. She braced her feet and panted for breath, feeling the sour Fleet air sting the back of her throat as she looked around and tried to figure out what she'd done wrong this time.

"Back up," the warlord growled. Jossa stared at him. He glared and yanked her in closer to his body, then used his free hand to slap a blank space in the wall next to him. Jossa hissed in pain and tried to resettle her burden on her hip before the man could take it into his head to run off again.

The vines covering the wall next to the warlord slid and retracted. The snakes slithered up and out, forming an oval half a foot taller than the warlord himself. Then a seam formed in the blank metal, and the halves of the oval hissed, dropped slightly, and moved apart to reveal . . .

A lift? Jossa shrank back against the warlord as a crowd of women emerged from the little room and out into the corridor. Some of them saw the warlord and dipped their heads. Then they saw Jossa and sneered. From the back of the lift stepped a pair of men. One with an ornate helmet shading ice-blue eyes, and another with florid skin and a fine webbing of purple veins creeping up his neck and down his cheeks. The two men bowed at the waist, and the man with the icy eyes said something in the Fleet language.

Jossa flinched as the translator in her jaw parsed the words for her.

"We'll see you shortly in the banquet hall?" The man's voice as reproduced by the translator was slightly stiffer than the real thing, but the lack of emotion in it was just the same as the original.

"I'll get there when I get there," the warlord replied in the same language, then pulled Jossa into the lift while the words were still filtering into her brain. She looked up from making sure her skirt was all the way inside and saw the strange man watching her. She couldn't read his eyes under the rim of his helmet, but his mouth was a thin line in his face, and she thought she saw a muscle tic in his jaw.

The door of the lift closed, the floor jerked, and he was gone.

>>><<<

The warlord hauled her out and down a short corridor. He wasn't even looking at her now. Hadn't spoken, hadn't shifted his hold on her arm. He just brought her along, like baggage. Baggage that made him really, really angry. Jossa wrapped her arm more tightly around the thing he'd made her carry, ducked her head, and tried not to let her skirt catch on any of the thorns sticking out from the walls of the hallway as he stalked towards the murmur of voices at the other end.

She knew what she could do to make him less angry. Maybe. But he hadn't given her a chance to offer. Even if she could get him to listen, she didn't know that she had it in her to service him out in the open like this. In a past life, yes. But that had been the Palace where she was raised. Here? Where even the ship itself was trying to hurt her?

As if in answer to the thought, she tripped over a seam in the floor and ran face first into the warlord's shoulder.

He didn't move.

Jossa got her feet under her and tried to figure out if her nose was bleeding. She'd just decided she was safe when a sound make her look up.

A roomful of women stared at her.

These weren't women like those who occupied the warlord's quarters. These, like the one getting off the lift, wore dark uniforms, slashed at the shoulder and breast to show various brighter colors under the fabric. Ranks? Differences in their duties? More snakes and thorns wrapped themselves around the women's necks in ornate torcs. Hair was either short or wrapped up and pinned in place.

Jossa tried to square her shoulders and stand straight under the weight of so many hostile eyes. She didn't manage as well as she would have liked.

"Milord. We did not expect you."

A woman came up the low steps that ran down the center of the room. The others shifted out of her way as needed, going back to their duties at terminals and handheld screens. One had her fingers in a holo, turning it this way and that as another poked at little yellow lights inside. The lights brightened, then followed the second woman's hand as she pulled them out of the display and down to the screen she had propped against the edge of the holo projector.

"Show or tell," the warlord growled at the woman as she stopped in front of him. Jossa resisted the urge to rub her ear against her shoulder. His voice vibrating in her jawbone via the translator was not a fun feeling. He kept going, either not noticing or ignoring the involuntary twitch of her head, "Easier to show your girls what to look for. Telling them hasn't worked."

The woman's full lips tightened, and her dark eyes narrowed.

"Now, Oona. Got places to be."

Oona bowed, a short jerk of her upper body that almost didn't count, and walked away. The warlord followed. Jossa followed in his wake. She made it two steps before something caught her bare ankle. Only the fact that the warlord still had hold of her arm kept her from falling flat on her face. The thing he'd given her to carry went flying as she let go and flailed for balance. Her downward motion halted with a jerk. Jossa hung in midair for half a heartbeat before the warlord yanked her again and she stumbled down a step. Another yank and she was able to get her feet under her to straighten herself.

The room around them was silent. Worse than laughter. Worse than whispers.

Never had she been so glad to be crowned. Not even the burn of frustration and anger, coming through her dress where the warlord had hold of her, was enough to stave off her relief. What these women must think of her. What they must be feeling right now.

Something hit her in the gut. Jossa grunted and curled in on herself. Cold, sticky fabric clung to her skin as the slime from the thing she'd been carrying glued her dress to her body. Ridges and wires poked at her belly.

Jossa looked up into the hard, brown eyes of Oona. Except for those eyes and the downturned corners of her mouth, the woman could have been a doll, an inanimate prop piece, for all the expression she showed.

Jossa looked down at the dirty, sticky thing the woman held. Half of it had rubbed itself shiny. The other half was just as disgusting as before. Even more so, because the stuff covering it had started to dry. And the smell was horrible—of rubbing alcohol and the dregs of a water tank.

With a sigh, Jossa hooked her fingers around the edge of the thing, hitched it back over to her hip, and followed the warlord as he started moving again. Nobody tripped her this time.

"She is a disruption," Oona said as they walked. "A distraction from purpose."

"She's learning a lesson," the warlord growled, moving past a cluster of women gathered around a screen mounted in the wall. They shifted and bunched to make room for him but stepped out and away from their object of focus as Jossa tried to get by. The warlord pulled her through with a tug and a snarl over his shoulder.

"Then give her the back of your hand," Oona replied, without looking back to see what was going on. "And teach her."

"Already learned that one, thank you." The words came out before Jossa could stop them.

Next thing she knew, there was an arm in front of her face. Dark and corded with muscle. The warlord. He had hold of Oona's wrist.

Jossa jerked away. The warlord's fingers tightened on her arm, halting her attempt at escape as easily as he'd stopped Oona from slapping her.

"Not that lesson," he snarled. "But I'll teach you, if that's what you need."

Jossa stared at Oona as the woman curled a lip at the warlord. He watched her back, teeth bared. Finally, the woman dropped her eyes and dipped her head. "As you say, milord."

The warlord let go of the woman's hand and they started moving again. Only then did Jossa realize that what was coming through her contact with the warlord wasn't anger. Or even frustration. Those emotions seemed to have melted away somewhere since they'd come off the lift. She couldn't quite tell what the man was feeling, beyond the fact that he was feeling something. Resignation? Pain of some sort?

Jossa tightened her hold on the contraption she carried and caught her skirt in the tips of her fingers. She wouldn't complain. As long as the fires of fury were banked, she could survive.

>>><<<

The thing the warlord had come to show Oona dealt mainly with the holo display in the upper corner of the room. Jossa stood as the other poked and prodded at the lights and watched the activity of the room around her. Women gathered, talked, and dispersed. Some had communications devices clipped to their jaws and ears. They spoke to thin air in tones that her translator couldn't pick up or parse. Snatches of conversation in closer proximity resolved themselves into coordinates, flight groups, and water levels. Nothing complete. Nothing more than two or three words. But as she listened, Jossa realized what this place must be.

The bridge. The command deck not only for this ship, but for the Fleet as a whole. And, if what she was hearing was correct, a Fleet in the middle of an offensive action. And... scouts? She couldn't quite bridge the gap between the terminology these people used and what she had been used to hearing as a concubine to the fuerrus, but that seemed to be the best guess.

What was it lira had said? The warlord was using Jossa's answers to the questions he'd asked when she first woke up, and he was doing... something with the information she'd given him. Something that might endanger his position at the head of the Fleet?

"Smaller." The growl of the man himself pulled Jossa's attention back to the cluster of people next to her. "Coasting too."

"But milord," said one of the women. "How—"

"You saying I don't know what I'm talking about?" The warlord poked at the holo in front of him and pulled out a light. As he drew the yellow glimmer away from the lines and dots that must have been a map of this solar system, the light resolved itself into a ship. Cargo class, small crew. Not a model Jossa recognized. Well, why should she?

"They're trying to hide," the warlord said. "You've been looking for military signals. Military profiles. And diplomatic markings. No one in their right mind is going to paint a target on their back like that." He gave the ship a spin along its axis and left it there, wobbling in midair. "Rework your figures, go back over the tracking since the first push, and see what you get."

"Not earlier, milord?"

He shrugged. "If this doesn't work, sure. But they'll have wanted to see exactly what they were dealing with. To be sure the comms weren't intercepted or translated."

The women nodded and bent their heads to their task. The warlord stepped away from the holo display and looked at Jossa. "You're learning."

She stared at him. He held up his hands. His empty hands. She realized he hadn't touched her the entire time he'd been working at the holo. And she'd stayed put. Hadn't tried to run. Hadn't tried to find a sympathizer in this room of women. Had just... stayed.

Jossa glared at him and the warlord laughed. A few heads turned and someone in the holo group muttered in surprise, but otherwise, the women in the room ignored him to continue with their work. Why shouldn't they? Jossa thought sourly. They *had* work. Actual work that meant something.

"Come on." The warlord moved back towards the door and looked over his shoulder at Jossa. "We're not done."

Oona appeared next to Jossa, face flat but eyes full of of meaning. Without context, though, or a better knowledge of the woman's personality, the warning or message was going to have to stay hidden. Jossa dipped her head to the woman, just in case that was what she was waiting for, and followed the warlord down the shallow steps and out the door. The thing he'd given her to carry dug into her fingers, and her dress stuck and pulled where the slime had saturated it. She knew she was trailing the reek of the stuff like a beacon for a wolfhound. Jossa stuck her nose in the air and kept going. Her place in life right now might not have much meaning, but she could make them think it did.

The piece of metal, wire, and sharp edges turned out to be part of the warlord's armor. Jossa didn't make the connection until she found herself at the opposite end of the ship from the bridge, surely, in an armory surrounded by snarling men. The warlord wove through the crowd, one hand on her back as a guide, ignoring the shouts, calls, and looks of hostile intent that followed the pair as they passed.

She could feel his temper rising as they moved deeper into the room. The touch of his hand on her back was light enough that she only felt bits and pieces, but the more looks of greed came her way, the more insistent the warlord's guiding hand. He was all but shoving her along by the time they reached a floating table at the back of the room.

A woman with pale skin and green eyes glowered at them from behind the table when the warlord finally stopped. He yanked the piece of armor away from Jossa, growled something to the effect of "Fix it" at the woman, and dropped the thing on the table next to a set of half-melted greaves. Jossa had just enough time to see that the thing she was carrying had probably been a pauldron before it was damaged. Then she found herself spun around and facing a wall of muscled, armored manflesh that went on the entire length of the room.

They were all looking at her.

She couldn't help it. Her heart quailed.

Someone reached a hand out in her direction. Bare, reddish tan under the purple of day-old bruises. Jossa looked up at the owner of the hand, who leered at her with a mouth of broken teeth. His lip was split and bleeding sluggishly. Dark brown hair straggled over his face, clotted with... something she didn't want to identify.

Jossa shrank back against the warlord, trying to get her hands behind her body so she could grope for the knife hilt on his belt. Hopefully it wouldn't be keyed to his DNA. Hopefully she could activate it in time.

It wasn't there.

The man in front of her yelled and flailed away. Something hit the deck with a thud. Something else, warm and wet, hit Jossa in the chest and face. She looked down.

Not only was her dress covered in a crust of slime and dirt, but now there was blood in the mix. She looked back at the man. He clutched the stump sticking out of his shirt sleeve and snarled in pain as he glared at her.

No. Not at her. At the warlord. Who was holding the knife she'd been looking for. "You know better than to touch what's mine," he snarled at the man whose hand he'd just cut off. He glanced over at Jossa. "Pick it up."

She looked at the warlord and then at the hand on the floor, oozing blood. He wanted her to give the man his hand back? Really?

Slowly, not taking her eyes off the one who'd tried to touch her in the first place, Jossa crouched and took the thing by one finger. It was still warm. Still *warm*.

Suddenly she was very, very, very glad for the crown on her head. As glad as she had ever been for a crown, to block out the emotions of others and contain what she herself was feeling. If she had been free, unguarded by anything at all, she would have tainted this whole room with her revulsion. Maybe permanently.

She was holding a severed hand. A hand that had tried to touch her.

Ew.

"Stick it in his belt," the warlord said in a low voice. He hadn't lowered his blade.

Jossa side stepped around the man until she found a mostly empty pouch hanging from his belt. The crowd in the room moved away from her like water from oil, but she was more focused on the fact that she'd have to touch this man. That she'd have to stick his *hand* in his *belt*. Never in all her time as a kuchru to the fuerrus had she been told to deal with severed limbs.

She finally managed to tuck the thing, wrist first, into the pouch on the man's left side. She would have winced for the unsanitary condition it was going to be in, but given the circumstances, she hoped it turned septic.

"Come on." Jossa had barely stepped away from the injured man when the warlord grabbed her elbow and started moving. "And get down to Med Bay," he yelled over his shoulder as he moved through the room. Jossa heard a general shuffle and clatter of armored men behind her as she trotted along in the warlord's wake. The men between them and the door moved out of the way, watching her with eyes that burned.

But none of them tried to touch her.

The warlord pulled her out into the corridor and kept on going. Apparently, she wasn't done learning for the day. Jossa wanted to ask him why he'd cut that man's hand off. Why he was dragging her all over a ship full of people who hated him so much. But she kept her mouth shut. The emotions coming to her through the filter of her sleeve roiled and churned so much that she couldn't pick out anything but the ever-present thrum of dull anger.

Eventually he slowed down, then stopped. Jossa kept her mouth shut on her questions, sucking in air to her complaining lungs instead. After a second or two she realized he was watching her. She straightened, trying not to look as flattened as she felt.

He kept watching her. Not saying anything. Just.... watching. Finally, Jossa ducked her head and asked, "Milord?"

"You're learning." It wasn't quite a statement. Wasn't quite a question either. Jossa opened her mouth to reply. Or to ask him what he meant. But he went on. "Keep learning."

The wall behind him oozed open, revealing a door twice as wide as any she'd seen on the ship so far. And more people too.

Jossa gulped and looked at the warlord, but his attention wasn't on her. It was on the milling throng in front of them, turning as a unit to watch the newcomers. The warlord moved into the room, and since he had hold of her arm, Jossa moved with him.

The room bowed as a collective whole, fist to shoulders, and then its occupants went back to whatever they'd been doing.

Jossa wished she'd known what was coming. Wished her dress wasn't covered in muck and slime. Wished... so many things. But the warlord had hold of her elbow and seemed to be looking for someone in particular, so she stayed quiet and concentrated on keeping the hem of her dress from getting caught under everyone else's feet.

Occasionally that meant brushing up against this or that person. Luckily they were all clothed, in looser versions of the uniforms she'd seen so far. The slashes of color became flowing falls of synthsilk and gauze, depending on the gender of the wearer. The women's torcs were on full display instead of tucked partially behind the collars of their shirts. Snakes and thorny brambles decorated sleeves and the occasional belt.

And every step she took brought more hard eyes to watch her passage. More bared teeth and flared nostrils.

Why the obsession with snakes, when the people reminded her so much of wolves?

The warlord stopped, yanking on her elbow to make her stop too. Jossa bit back a yelp as his fingers dug into the half-formed bruises he'd already given her. She nearly crumbled as his emotional state finally clarified, bright and sharp. Hate. He'd happily kill this monster, as soon as he could.

Jossa looked up to see who the warlord meant. He was right. This man *was* a monster. She didn't even have to touch him to see that. The twist of his mouth, the shadows of insanity in his eyes. She knew that look. She'd been intimately acquainted with that look in a life long ago.

"You are going to keep Warlord Kizen company," said Warlord Syrus.

For a second, Jossa couldn't understand what he meant. Who? Do what? The sharp pain in her elbow wasn't going away, and it was a little hard to think with all the half-formed images coming through the contact with her warlord. Bloody images. Full of anticipated satisfaction and... relief?

She didn't get a chance to figure that one out. He shoved her forward, and she stumbled into the waiting arms of the Warlord

Kizen. No space in between. No way to gain a moment of sanity between one dangerous man and the next. The only saving grace was that Warlord Syrus let go of her as soon as Kizen laid hands on her. Which was a good thing, because those hands had a grip so strong as to break bones. And a heart so twisted, it might have been an experiment gone wrong.

Jossa screamed. She couldn't help it. The things he felt. The images and thoughts that came to her through those feelings. The pain remembered. Relished. The pain he looked forward to inflicting. No reason. No logic. Just pain. Such a love of pain.

Some corner of her mind, protected by the crown or the leftovers of her bond with Delfi, managed to parse the images. The women she'd just met in the bridge, dead. The women in the warlord's quarters, dead. The man from earlier, the one with ice-blue eyes, handing Kizen an ornate helmet covered in gilded snakes. Syrus's head falling out of the helmet as Kizen opened the faceplate. The warlord putting the helmet on, gore and all, before pulling a gun and shooting his benefactor.

Triumph.

Satisfaction.

Someone had hold of her. Someone familiar. Someone with huge hands and shadows in his heart.

But not the monster. Or rather, not the worst monster.

"Still learning?" asked a rough voice in her ear.

Jossa nearly melted. Syrus. *Her* warlord. Never had she thought she'd be glad for his existence.

But she wasn't allowed to relax. Wasn't safe yet. The other warlord, Kizen, came for her. Spittle flew as he roared incoherently. Her translator was reduced to mechanical gibberish as it tried to translate the madman's words at the same time that it worked on the ruckus that erupted around them. People shouted, pushed, and shrieked. Syrus wrapped an arm around her ribcage and braced himself. Jossa would have been ashamed to find herself clinging to his arm for protection, if it hadn't been for the fact that there was a knife blade forming itself in Kizen's hand. Then she panicked. She couldn't *move*. Couldn't get away. A soldier was one thing, but she wasn't so stupid as to think Syrus would protect her here the same way he had in the armory.

A new man appeared. He grabbed Kizen's waving arm and twisted, then pushed. The warlord staggered back, ran into the crowd behind him, and bounced to his feet with a snarl. He made it a full step in Jossa's direction before Syrus's voice stopped him in his tracks.

"Not so fun, is it?" Jossa's warlord asked, the low rasp of his voice all the more dangerous for how softly he spoke. He shifted Jossa to his side with one arm and then set her down so that the new man was between her and the other warlord.

The rim of the man's helmet cast stark shadows over his face, but the blue eyes that turned to look at her were unmistakable. Jossa gulped. Apparently the man who'd met them coming off the lift earlier was more important than she'd guessed.

"Move, Quinn," Warlord Syrus said. The man with the blue eyes looked at him, then bowed and moved back. Exposing Jossa to Warlord Kizen in full. She nearly shivered.

"What did she do to me," the warlord snarled. "Fucking bitch. The fuck did she do?"

Syrus opened his mouth to answer. The door at the far end of the hall slid open and an armored man staggered in. He hit the nearest table and stumbled along its length. Women scrambled out of the way and men grabbed for their weapons.

Jossa stared. Standing in the door, holding a blade that was far too big for her, was a very familiar figure. Coils of flaming red hair flared out from under the crown that capped her head. Blood covered her naked body from head to toe. A few sensor pads clung to her chest and forehead. An IV line hung from one arm.

Delfi.

The men in the room moved almost as one, surging forward like a planetside tide of death. Jossa snatched the hilt of a knife from her warlord's hip and launched herself into the fray before he could do more than bark a surprised curse.

She had another weapon in moments, stolen from the belt of a Fleet warrior. Half a heartbeat to remember what one of the concubines told her—that the Fleet men didn't fight amongst themselves while on Campaign, and so went more lightly armored while on ship. Then her training took over. The first knife went into the man's unarmored cervical vertebrae just as the blade solidified. She left it there, snatched another from his belt, and plunged the second into the eye of the next man.

She made it about twenty feet before anyone realized they were being hit from behind. By that time, she'd lost half her dress and both shoes. All around her people shouted in the Kuchen tongue. She didn't need a translator to know what they were saying. Somewhere ahead of her, Delfi was silent, in keeping with their upbringing. Shrieks and showy outcries were for exhibition matches. When it came down to business, you saved your breath for surviving the fight in front of you.

Which made what she was about to do all the more idiotic. Ducking low, she swept a man's legs out from under him at the ankle, lunged forward to bury her blade in his throat, and filled her lungs with as much tainted ship air as she could. "Delfi!"

All the time spent in the infirmary paid off. Her throat was healed of its three hundred years of disuse. Her lungs worked far better than they had when she'd first woken up. She'd successfully drawn the attention of at least half the room.

Her enemies split. Those who couldn't get to Del came for her instead. For a moment, her rational mind quailed in terror at the solid wall of warriors, each intent on breaking her in half and probably raping her after. Then her body kicked back to life.

Blessing all her Ancestors for the fact that no one had a firearm, she came in under a wild swing and drove a fist into the man's throat. As he choked, she stabbed him in the eye with the blade in her other hand. She was on to the next by the time he toppled forward.

Three more went down, but she could feel herself tiring. Not enough stamina. Not enough strength. Delfi hadn't answered her cry, but she couldn't worry about that now. She had no idea if the clothing these men wore was armored. She couldn't afford a wasted attack to find out, which made her targets that much smaller. Blunt force only did so much. She had no idea what she'd been thinking, throwing herself in the middle of them. Except that Delfi was here. If they were both going to die, better to do it fighting. Like they should have in the first place.

She kicked someone in the groin and found light armor plating instead. Reversing course, she slammed her heel into the nose of the man coming up behind her. And made the fatal mistake. The one in front of her caught her hair and pulled. She staggered and fell, twisting away from the reaching hand of the other man. She hit the floor on her side and gasped as her breath left her. No time to recover. Her knife went into the knee of her captor easily enough. He roared in pain and let go of her hair.

Jossa felt more than saw the boot coming for her spine. This was it. She wouldn't get to see the person who would kill her. He'd break her. Beat her to a pulp and leave her a smear on the floor. The fuerrus would have had a fit if she'd still been in his service. Every instructor she'd studied with was screaming at her from beyond the grave. What did they expect, two against the might of enemies such as these?

She clawed for the bond. Screamed for Delfi with voice and spirit. Felt nothing. Thrice-cursed crown! Damn the man who'd put it on her!

The blow never came. None of them did. Except one. Someone grabbed her by the hair and pulled her upright. She tried to jam her blade into his elbow. He caught her hand in his. "Get your head together," the warlord snarled. "Stay here."

Before she could figure out what had happened, he shoved her into the arms of someone else. The man caught her in a grip of solid silsteel. She righted herself just in time to see the warlord dive into the pile of men surrounding Delfi, fists flying, roaring in the Fleet language.

"What?" she gasped, trying to come to terms with the fact that she was alive. Still scrambling inside herself for the bond and coming up empty. She prayed that it was only the crown blocking her and not Delfi's death in the melee. "What?"

"In the Fleet, if you kill, you are strong." The man hauled her around so she could look at the room behind her. The groaning, bleeding bodies of a good twenty or so men lay scattered between them at the dais. "OutFleet woman, you are very strong."

She hiccupped, choked, and doubled over laughing.

Twenty -- Syrus

- - - test group has improved on the last one by nearly twenty-three percent. However, the problem of the mood swings remains. They're too unstable. We're still cleaning bits of Garcia out of - - -
  -audio recordings, New Hopks College of Medicine

Syrus clamped his arm around the blood-slicked thighs of the girl he was carrying and snarled under his breath. Her anger raged around him like a wild animal, sinking hooks in his arm and shoulder and tearing at his veins. Her physical claws raked at his back, caught in his hair, and pulled his clothes in all the wrong directions. He'd already taken an elbow to the back of the head and had one ear nearly pulled free of his skull. He'd thumped and scraped her against every wall and corner he could manage in retaliation, and still she fought.

Bitch. As if he didn't have enough problems on this Campaign. Now she'd had to wake up and ruin the one political event he'd tried to suffer through since—he blew out a breath. He couldn't remember the last time he'd done the meet-and-greet bullshit. Probably when they'd given him the fucking armor in the first place.

At least none of the new techs had gotten killed. They'd all been smart enough to clear out. There were a lot of fresh widows on board tonight, but that was nothing new. They'd either be claimed by new husbands or end up down in crew bunks soon enough. Oona's problem, not his. So long as one of them got him some concrete data on this system and did it soon, he didn't care who was married and who wasn't.

No, his problems came in the form of lunatic women who shouldn't have even been able to walk straight after spending hundreds of years in cryo and then weeks in an infirmary bed. Never mind fighting like demons. Where the hell had that come from anyway? They were supposed to be fucking concubines. Operative word there being fucking.

He looked over at the other one, stumbling along behind him. Iira had taken hold of her as soon as they'd gotten clear of the banquet hall and was all but dragging her down the hall by her elbow. She kept on giggling. Tears leaked down her cheeks as she gasped for breath and lost her balance and hiccupped and was hauled to her feet, then repeated the process a dozen times over.

Syrus shook his head, got caught in the back of the skull by some bony bit of the she-demon he had slung over his shoulder, and decided enough was enough. His rooms weren't far, but he didn't want them destroyed either.

"Here." He palmed open a small conference room and went inside. The shriek and near loss of his captive told him that he'd forgotten to duck down far enough and nearly scraped her off on the frame. He caught her before she could land on her head, flipped her upright, and tossed her on the table that floated in the center of the room.

She came up snarling and spitting, feet and fists flying. Syrus let the feet connect so he could get close, her emotions hitting him harder than her body could. She was running out of power. He ducked inside her guard and caught a wrist in each hand. "Calm the fuck down," he snarled into her red face. "Gonna get yourself killed, you know that?"

"Why isn't she dead already? You soft outFleet piece of hydro scum. Is this how all the Empire treats its women? Indulging them? Allowing displays of temper? First one and now the other! I think you are *trying* to get everyone on the ship killed. Is that it? Is that why you came to this Fleet and assassinated your way to the Helm? So you could halt the Invasion?"

Syrus stared at Kizen. He should have known the man would follow them. How had he not noticed him?

The sense in the man's words hit him. Syrus let go of the girl's arms and clamped a hand over her face instead. Turning so he could face the man fully, he said, "You want to bitch about me wearing the Helm, you talk to him." He pointed at Quinn, who'd slipped into the room behind the other warlord and was talking quietly with Oona. "I came to the Fleet looking to kill Brander."

He leaned forward and glared at the other man. "Now. If you have something to contribute besides 'kill everyone in sight,' I'm all ears. But if you can't remember that the base tenet of the Fleet is Strength Over All, then maybe you should go work on your strength of will. On your own ship. I'm sure your second would like to go over the next push with you, now that we've rearranged our troops."

Kizen's face turned the darkest shade of purple Syrus had seen this side of a beet, and his eyes nearly bulged out of his head. One of these days the man was going to fall over of an aneurysm and they'd have a hell of a time figuring out who got to replace him. His hands wrapped around the knife hilts on his belt. For a moment, Syrus thought he'd actually try something.

The girl on the table behind him finally decided she'd had enough of trying to get his hand off her face and started aiming her kicks instead. Two solid hits to the ribcage were enough to get Syrus's attention, though not enough to injure or wind him. Snarling, he dragged her forward, fingers still clamped over her jaw. "You kick me again," he told her, "and I'm going to find new ways to hurt your sousi. Got me?"

She froze.

"Now sit still, you little bitch. I'll get to you in a minute."

She glared at him, nostrils flaring as she sucked in air. Her rage made his entire arm feel like someone was mainlining hot coals through his veins. He gritted his teeth and glared back at her.

Finally, she crossed her arms and slumped in place. The fire didn't dim, but it was as good as he was going to get. "Oona," he called over his shoulder. "Warlord Kizen is going to be heading back to the *Ataorl Banso*. Get that started, would you? Then get the new techs working on parsing the data. Might as well get some work done while someone's sorting out the living quarters."

"Milord." Her disapproval was like ice. If he could have gotten away with it, Syrus would have grabbed hold of *her* with his rage-burned hand, to see if her skin would give him any relief. "Milord Kizen, if you would follow me?"

Miracle of miracles, Kizen went. Grumbling and cursing, but at least he went. Two people out of his hair now. Holding up one finger to warn the girl on the table, Syrus took his hand off her face. Slowly, in case he needed to flatten her again. One step. Two. She stayed put, eyes flickering between him and her sousi behind him.

"You can let her go, lira," he said quietly.

Jossa blew past him, aiming for the redhead. As she brushed against him, frantic worry and relief sizzled in his mouth like carbonated water and mint. Sharp and cool all at the same time. She wasn't quite as beat up as the other sai, but she'd taken her share of hits and lost most of her clothing in the fight. It was hard to tell on her darker skin, but he figured she'd be covered in bruises before a couple days passed.

"Go get your kit," he told lira. "Might as well patch them up in here."

She murmured, bowed, and went. Leaving him with two women hugging the life out of each other and Quinn, who still hadn't said a word one way or another.

"Well," Syrus said when the other man didn't speak up. "Say it. I should have left them where I found them."

"Perhaps." His second stepped up next to him, but even this close, he was unreadable. "But as you said to Warlord Kizen, Strength Over All. It is what allows us to absorb outFleet men as our warriors. It's what enables those grafted in to the fighting force to survive at all. It is what drives us. These two . . ." He gestured at the women in front of them. "They are not average women, are they?"

"You mean, for the Empire? Or for sai?"

Quinn looked at him from under the rim of his helmet.

Syrus snorted. "Average women don't wind up in long-term cryo on empty planets. There *are* women who fight. You don't notice them so much on Campaign because they aren't where *you* usually find women. They don't hide in locked rooms and they don't cower. They either take their families and run, or they join the guerilla strikes the local resistance starts after our first push. Very few make it into the prisoner population. "Ones who're left—" He shrugged. "They figure out what's coming and shove dick-eating mechanicals up their own cunts. Or bombs." He frowned at Iira. "What *was* that thing that woman had inside her?"

"Not all are suitable," Quinn said before his wife could answer. His voice was quiet, emotionless. "Even for the Breeder ships."

Well, that was one way of putting it.

There was a pause as Syrus watched Jossa go over her sousi's injuries like a mother with a child. The girl, or young woman, took it like a child too. Swatting at hands, pulling her feet away. Hissing when cuts were poked at. "What was the damage?" he asked.

"Oona is still making a tally. It appears she tore the locks in your rooms apart and overrode the programming. All the guards between your quarters and the banquet hall are dead. At least thirty within the hall itself." Quinn took a breath and uncertainty threaded its way to the surface. "If I may, milord?"

Syrus looked at him.

"You touched them. They did not light up."

He frowned at his second. Why did the man have to notice so much? Syrus was just about to ask him that when he was interrupted by a coughing, guttural noise he'd only heard a few times in his life.

He swung around. The second woman, Delfi, was speaking. But it wasn't Imperial. Or Kuchen. Or even one of the hundreds of pidgin languages the Edge worlds used. No. This was full-blown He'la. The language of the Foreseers.

Fucking hell, just what he needed.

Then he saw what Jossa was doing. "What the fuck," he snarled, lunging forward to pull her hands off the flares of her crown before she could yank on them any harder. "The hell you think you're doing, woman? You'll kill yourself and you know it." Touching her was like touching a live wire. Pure panic burned through his nerves. Syrus gritted his teeth against the urge to scream in frustration. Claustrophobia closed in around him, and his skull suddenly felt six sizes too small. If he didn't get the top of it off somehow, he was going to fail and die and then they'd all be lost because—

The monster rose inside him. The monster that he knew, beyond all doubt, was his. Emotions he'd never had words for, but he knew them as well as he knew his soul. Black and twisted, burning like acid and drowning like water. Aimed at everything and everyone who tried to make him what he wasn't. He grabbed it, gave it the fear for its fuel and snarled as it flowed up through his veins and out through his skin. Someone cried out in the distance, but he was too pissed to care why. He just wanted the fucking noise to stop. They all needed to shut up and leave him alone, fuck it all. Why couldn't they leave him alone?

The caustic mix running through his veins overflowed, sizzling out along his nervous system. He felt his mouth stretching in a roar—the monster's roar, teeth bared. If they wouldn't give him some peace and quiet, he'd have to *make* them. Once they were all dead, it would all go away. He'd wake up in another puddle of blood and finally, finally, be alone in his head.

"Milord?"

His punch would have hit Quinn in the face, if the man hadn't dodged. Fast bastard. Syrus snarled and balled up the other fist, then frowned. Why couldn't he use that hand? What was in the way? And why did he hear screaming when he tried?

He looked. He was holding someone's arm. Slim. Darker brown than his. Female. Oh.

He dropped Jossa, who curled over her wrist and whimpered quietly. Shaking out his hand, he looked back at Quinn. "What do you nee—"

Something hammered him from the side. Ribs and face. And it kept hitting him. The guttural shrieking identified his attacker as the other foundling. She'd used up most of her energy breaking into the banquet, so the blows didn't carry much force. The corona of her rage just added to the toxic mix still boiling through his veins. He only had to take five or six hits to the head before he could duck through her guard and plant a fist in her jaw. Quinn caught her before she landed, but she was already out, limp in the man's arms.

"Milord? Do I need to go prep the medunits?" Iira was standing in the doorway, questions on her face and the low-need med kit in her hands.

Syrus looked from the unconscious and bloody young woman his second was lying on the table to the other one crouched on the floor, cradling her wrist. He sighed and rubbed at the bridge of his nose. The comedown off this high would hit soon, and he could already feel the cold creep of its sewer sludge along his skin. "Just do what you can for that one," he said, waving at Delfi.

Iira bowed her head and moved over to set up shop next to her husband. Syrus dropped down on his haunches next to Jossa. "Hey."

She didn't look up, still muttering to herself, too quiet for him to make out. Grumbling, he hooked a finger under her chin and dragged her face around to his. "Look at me you fucking bitch."

If she realized what she was fighting against, she didn't show it. Jossa's eyes went past him, to where Iira was working on the other woman. "I need it off. Please take it off. I need it off. I don't know what's coming. I know what was said, but I don't know what's coming." She clutched at his hand. Panic shot through his nerves, making his heart stutter. "Please!" Her voice was hoarse. "I need it off! I need to know! I don't know! Please!"

Tears streamed down her face. She was chewing her lip bloody. Grief mixed with regret and self-hatred turned his hand numb, but climbed no further. He was still too close to Frenzy for her emotions to make much of a dent in his.

He shook himself free and she all but fell over. Growling, he caught her and set her back upright. She fell again. Syrus snarled and dragged her to her knees. Stupid bitch. Blind, dumb, crazy bitch. So lost in her panic she didn't see the obvious hitting her over the head.

"Listen to me," he rasped when he finally got her face pointed in his direction. Her eyes were wild. He knew she wasn't seeing him at all. Her hands kept trying to reach for the crown, but his grip kept her from managing it. "Jossa, listen!" Her head jerked back and forth as he shook her.

She hiccupped and clung to his shirt. "Please," she whispered. "Need it off. Take it off. Can't under—" She hiccupped again. "Please!"

Behind him, Delfi moaned and muttered in He'la. Jossa nearly climbed over the top of him before Syrus could hook an arm around her waist and pin her to the table. Fuck it all, how was he supposed to get her to calm down if they kept setting each other off?

"*Oloteoj duparodivek tukavaf kamogek*," he snarled in High Imperial. "Fucking bitch, open your eyes and look! It doesn't matter if you get that thing off. See?"

She went still. Syrus didn't care if it was because he'd used Imperial on her, or if she'd actually gotten a good look at her sousi. The numbness in his arm eased. Settled into something different.

Syrus didn't try to figure out what it was. This might be his only chance to get through to her. "She's crowned too," he growled in her ear. "Remember? Can't make predictions if her sai is cut off."

Something beeped behind him. Oona's voice cut in over a speaker. "Milord? Iira said you'd be here."

Leaving the stunned woman in a heap on the floor, he stood and went over to the comm unit. "Let me have it then."

"Milord, the techs have found a second Barbican in the system. It's not showing up on our scans."

TWENTY-ONE -- SYRUS

Gravity. No matter how we fight it. No matter what we build to negate it. It will not leave us alone.
   -spacer proverb

Syrus frowned and leaned forward. The map of the system was a mess of projected orbits, markers for known satellites of the sun, and recorded flight paths. The latter, traced in purple, burst out from the planet below the *Edde Belo* in a crazy corona. The trails led all over the system, almost completely at random. Almost.

Something yellow and faint flickered to life near the bottom of the y-axis. Purple crossed it here and there. But the amorphous blob of light was large enough to be visible under the projected trails.

The door to the hall slid open. Kizen came back in, followed by the tech who'd been taking him back to his shuttle. Her lip was split and bleeding. She bowed and escaped as soon as Kizen's attention snagged on the wall. The warlord breathed a curse in Fleet that Syrus's translator couldn't parse. He got the gist of it though.

"Zoom in on the point," Syrus told the invisible tech as he leaned in for a closer look. "And replay traffic from the time we took the trading post. Twenty-four, thirty."

She obeyed. The yellow light grew larger and the edges of the system faded and shifted onto the ceiling and floor, then wrapped around the other walls of the room. The days since the Fleet's first attack on the system sped by, compressed into thirty-second increments. The purple lines grew and twined and snarled. Syrus settled his weight on his heels. "I fucking hate being right."

"Milord?" Quinn nearly made his warlord jump in place. Syrus bit down on a snarl and looked at his second, who traced a finger over one particular line leading from the planet the Fleet was parked over. It looped twice, ducked behind a moon of the third planet, and vanished into the asteroid belt between planets six and seven.

"There's nothing there," Kizen growled on Syrus's other side. He had his nose nearly stuck to the point where the yellow light flickered, as if he could make the outline of a satellite appear just by glaring it into existence. Even the emotions he gave off were all aimed at the wall. For once, Syrus didn't feel like the man was trying to personally roast him alive.

"Give me the gravity readings," Syrus told the tech. He knew what they'd show, but conjecture and insider knowledge weren't going to work on Kizen. He needed cold facts.

The woman obeyed, and light blue strands of light blinked into existence. Thin and pale compared to the purple, the net effect still looked like someone had tipped a basket of knitting over and let a bunch of cats play with it. Quinn shot his lord a look as Syrus coughed on a laugh, but Kizen straightened and scowled. "This amuses you? It tells you nothing! Except where to hunt *later*, when we are done with the planet-bound Imperials and their sniveling excuses for armies."

Syrus swallowed another dry laugh and shook his head. "Look." He stabbed the yellow light with a finger. "Remember where the Fleet got their masking tech in the first place? All those fun toys you have that let you sneak up on a planet." He tapped the wall. "Gravity doesn't lie. There's something there. And it's going to get us all killed. The whole fucking Fleet."

Now he had everyone's attention. Kizen glared. Quinn's eyebrows climbed up his head. Iira scowled and went back to patching up the women. Ok, not everyone's attention. Jossa was still staring into space. One hand clutched a flare of her crown. The other was laced with her that of her sousi, chalky brown to pale white. Whiter, because the redhead had a grip on her counterpart strong enough to cut circulation.

Syrus yanked his attention back to Kizen as the heat levels in the room climbed.

"You're telling us what?" the man ground out. "That there's an installation there? Some secret army is going to try and wipe us out? Try, I say, because if there's anything the puling Imperials *can't* do, it's fight a proper battle."

Syrus stepped on the impulse to clap like the audience at a stage play and tried to think of where to start.

"When you found us, how many keys did your originating Barbican have?" he asked. Maybe he was wrong. Maybe this was just a fluke. The local lord getting clever.

"We've been over this already." Kizen said. "Two. The one we found you in, and another empty system. We hadn't sent more than a dummy-sat through before you called us through your Barb."

"No other keys in *that* Barb? No signs of previous use?" Syrus had to hammer this home, because they would do their best to ignore the rest of what else had to say.

"It was in regular use by the outFleet curs before we conquered the system. No other keys though. We blockaded it early. No one escaped from the system as we took it." Scorn practically dripped off his voice, sizzling like acid in the air and burning imaginary holes in the floor.

"Our techs checked the Barb as we came through to this system. The only key out leads to the same coordinates as your other, empty, system. The one you *didn't* come through." Syrus looked at Quinn. "We have confirmation now. We've hit Hadra's Net."

"Hadra's Net?"

"What fucking net?"

The two Fleet men spoke over each other. Syrus ignored them, doing calculations in his head as he ran a finger along one of the purple travel lines, following it from the trading post near the Barb, past the fourth planet, behind its moon, and down past an orbital station siphoning gas off one of the giant planets. He would have bet money on the ship that left this trail being one of the first off the base when the Fleet attacked. Other lines went for planets, or the solar collector, or the asteroid belt. But this one . . .

He eyed the flickering yellow light of the phantom base down at the lower end of the y-axis and then laid his palm over the large wobble in the gravitational field almost a hand span below it. Then he put his other hand over the Barbican they'd come through.

Same size. The lower one was bigger, maybe. Which made an even worse kind of sense, when he thought on it.

"The fucking hell are you doing?" Kizen snapped. "You gonna hump the wall now, is that it? Not getting enough—"

"Shut your mouth or I'll shut it for you," Syrus told the warlord. "This is more important than our egos."

Kizen drew himself up and opened his mouth.

Syrus didn't wait to hear what the bastard had to say. He turned, hooked a foot around Kizen's ankle, and clapped his hand over the man's face. A slide of the hip, a push of the hand, and the other warlord fell flat on his back. Syrus followed him down and pinned him with the hand still over his face and a knee to the chest.

Kizen grunted and gasped for air, scrabbling for a pressure point on Syrus's wrist as Syrus pinched the man's nostrils shut. Before Kizen could lash out, Syrus wrestled one of Kizen's arms down and pinned it. His weight balanced now, he leaned in.

Kizen croaked and gasped for breath as Syrus forced the air out of his lungs. Syrus's hand on the man's skin was scalding. Syrus snarled and leaned a little harder on Kizen's chest. The monster, that caustic mix of things he couldn't name, wanted *fear*. Not rage. Kizen flailed with his free hand, scrabbling for a knife.

Syrus settled all his weight on the man's chest. Kizen's trapped arm came free, a wild strike catching his attacker along the inner thigh. Syrus barely felt it. The fucker's face was finally turning purple. His teeth gnashed, but he couldn't do any real damage.

"Milord!"

Syrus rammed his elbow up towards the source of the voice and the owner of the hand on his shoulder. He followed through as he stood, bringing his other fist around to pulverize the fucking moron who dared—

Something caught his wrist and twisted just enough to shift the momentum of the swing in a lateral direction. Syrus staggered, nearly tripped over Kizen's legs, and caught himself. Nothingness flooded up his arm, driving the monster back. His vision cleared of the red haze and he could see clearly again.

"Milord," Quinn said in a flat voice. "This gets us nowhere."

Twice. Twice in less than an hour, he'd nearly lost his shit. Not just the little bit he let himself have during battle. He'd nearly gone completely bug-fuck *twice* after how many years?

Months, his imaginary conscience reminded him. *You're not that much in control.*

You shut up, he told the voice.

"You." Kizen surged to his feet. "I'm going to kill you!"

Somehow Syrus found himself standing on the other side of Quinn as his second put his hands on the other warlord's shoulders and *moved*. Kizen ended up three feet away, on his feet, perfectly steady. "Milord," Quinn said in that same voice. "I believe Warlord Syrus said we are all about to die. If we may put off the Challenge until we ascertain the validity of that statement?"

Over in the corner, Syrus heard Iira snort softly. Quinn was watching him though, so he found the edge of the table again, hitched a hip up, and laced his fingers across his leg. See. Nice and safe. He could be semi-civilized when he wanted to be. "The Net is a last line of defense and a first line, depending on how you look at it. And depending on what sector you come in on. Long and short, it's a tripwire. Way I learned it, about the time the Navlad Empire realized you lot were serious about this whole 'conquer the Galaxy' business—"

Kizen growled. Syrus ignored him. "'Bout that time, they decided they needed some sort of defense. Something that would tell them it was time to scramble troops, aim them one direction, and pull the triggers on their heavy artillery. And just in case the islosteog fail and the battlegroups get pounded into so many pieces of scrap, they built a failsafe."

He ran his fingers through his hair, caught the tie that kept it all back and yanked the thing out. Scraping the loose strands back into their queue, he started to wrap the tie back around his hair. It snapped in his fingers. Growling, Syrus chucked it at the door. "Don't matter if we sit here and wait for the battlegroup to land on our head. Don't matter if we fight them and win. There's an outpost sunward of the Barb." He pointed at the map on the wall, where a slight wobble showed in the gravity lines above the blob of the Barbican. "They want to control traffic to the rest of the Empire. Best way to do that is to make it impossible to open the Barb to start with. Which means keys. We don't get those keys, the *correct* keys, to the Barb they got sitting at the bottom of this system, we die. If not here, then in the next set of planets. They'll drag a solar collector through the gate and we'll be so much matter in an accretion disc."

He stopped trying to get his hair out of his eyes and looked at the two Fleet men. Kizen stood still, face a black cloud. Quinn still blocked the way between the two warlords, but he had his hands hooked into his belt and an almost thoughtful look on his face. Well. At least they weren't laughing.

"How do you know this?" Kizen finally asked. For a wonder, he didn't shout. "Nothing my people retrieved from any database has mentioned a trap." He stopped and snorted. "Beyond the usual shit the Impie pukes try to pull."

"Well they wouldn't, would they? Not if they didn't know." Syrus shrugged. "Who's going to settle in a system set to blow when the wrong person trips over a line of code? Who wants to live *outside* the bounds of that line and risk being cut off from the Core of the Empire?"

"That leaves the question of who told *you*," Quinn said quietly.

Syrus looked at his second and wondered how much to say. What had the man guessed, in the three years or so he'd had Syrus on board? How much had he guessed just in the past couple weeks?

"You hear things," Syrus said finally. "Scraping along the edges of society. Especially high society. They think the help doesn't have ears and a brain to listen with."

Something shifted in Quinn's eyes. Before he could say anything, Kizen spoke up. "Say we accept that the system is rigged. Say there *is* a Net and this other Barbican needs to be accessed. We can deal with it once we've finished Conquering this system. I don't see a need to worry about it until we're much closer to the outer satellites."

"By then we'll be even further away from the Barb and its guard post," Syrus said. "They'll have even more time to get ready for us, if we're lucky. If we're not lucky." He shrugged. "Remember what I said about vamalkuog and battlegroups and heavy artillery? They're not going to wait for us to come through the Barb if they can help it. They *might* wait for us to waste time and resources here. Wait till we're weaker." He held up a hand before Kizen could do more than bark a negative to that. "Think, you bastard," Syrus growled. "Think. What would you do? What do *we* do? Attack a strong position? A strong force? Or hammer the shit out of them from orbit and *then* drop a battalion of soldiers on their heads?"

Kizen opened his mouth again, shut it, and looked at the display on the wall. Syrus waited. The man was a fucking hot-head. A half-operable impact weapon just waiting for someone to jiggle it wrong and explode it in someone's face. But he had to have *some* brain in there, to keep his section of the Fleet moving forward through the Barbicans. Hell, he'd been trying to force Syrus himself into a Challenge fight for how long now?

Quinn sidled closer to his warlord as Kizen ran his fingers over the system map, muttering calculations to himself. Syrus raised an eyebrow at his second. "You see it yet?" he asked quietly.

A bubble of faint amusement surfaced in Quinn and threaded through the air between them. It was gone as quickly as it had come. "Milord, the only question is who? And how?"

Syrus snorted and looked back at Kizen. The other man had told the still invisible tech to expand the map again. He had one hand on the hidden Barbican and the other running flight patterns from the various satellites around the system's star. "Think you know the answer to that too."

"And if you're wrong, milord? If it's just a smuggler's base? Or a shipyard or other military installation? We have two Fleets here now. More than might be expected otherwise."

Syrus looked over at the corner with the two captive women. Iira was done patching up Jossa and had started in on the redhead. The young woman growled and hissed as the med-tech poked and prodded and wiped at blood tracks, but her sousi had a death grip on her hands, so she couldn't lash out. He looked away before Kizen could notice his counterpart's attention was wandering. Jossa wouldn't have anything new to offer. Her sousi would likely try to gut anyone who came near with her bare hands.

"Is it safe to assume I'm wrong?" he asked Quinn. "Or should we act like it *is* a threat and deal with it?"

"The Fleet is strong," Kizen said. He stepped away from the wall and crossed his arms. "We take the place. With two Fleets here instead of the one *you'd* have if I hadn't come along, we can send a strike force and enough Seed to deal with the Barbican and its outpost easily." He looked over at the captives. "Even after what your pets have done to your forces."

The redhead chose that moment to slap Iira's hand away from her legs and shrink back against her sousi. Jossa roused a bit, leaning forward to lay a hand on Iira's shoulder. Her lips moved, but the translators issued by the Fleet weren't set up for High Imperial, so only Syrus knew that she was warning the med-tech what would happen if she went poking in places she wasn't equipped to handle.

"You send a strike force," Syrus said, pulling the men's attention away from the scuffle among the women as Iira reminded the strays who was in charge. "And you could take the outpost. Maybe. But were you listening when I said you'd need the *right* codes? Hammering your way past the security protocols leaves tracks in the system. In this case, you'll probably set off alarms from here to the Core if you try. You'll blow us all up anyway, you do that." He leaned forward to get in Kizen's face. The heat in the air around the man ratcheted up a notch or two. "We need to make it think it *gave* us those keys. Like it's supposed to. Even if you take out the guards and Seed that outpost, how are you going to manage that?"

Kizen crossed his arms and glared over at the map on the wall. "Then we—"

"No we." Syrus moved around to block his view. "Me. I go. Take one of the ships we captured, run like a scared rabbit, and follow all those people looking for safety. Right into the outpost. One more refugee." He tapped the blob of yellow. "I get in, get the keys, lock the Barb against any incoming traffic, and get the fuck back to the Fleet."

Assuming his security clearances still worked. Assuming whoever ran his blood test on the other end didn't just execute him the minute they got the results. Assuming a lot of stuff, actually.

But if he didn't at least try, they were all fucked.

"You?" Kizen snorted and bared his teeth. "We are to trust you? An Imperial outsider *offering* to save us from annihilation? That's convenient."

"Offering to save himself," Quinn said quietly.

Syrus raised an eyebrow, but when his second didn't add anything to the statement, he shrugged and let it go. "He's got a point," he said to Kizen. "Something doesn't get done about this, we have to etaevatoj bekig."

All the Fleet natives, even Iira, turned to look at him. Half a second later, Syrus's ears caught up with him and he realized what had happened. Growling, he looked for a new way to say what he meant. Fucking Fleet language and fucking Fleet mentality that went with it. They didn't have a word for "go back" and either his translator or theirs must have fucked things up. What language was he speaking anyway?

Something like razors skittered over his face and neck, slicing imaginary lines into the veins of his arms. He was pretty sure the derision came from Kizen, but for all he knew Iira was adding a dose of it as well. It was hard to tell where that feeling came from when it made his whole body burn with pain.

Syrus sorted through what he'd said, focusing on the words instead of the mockery. Fleet, fleet, fleet... and he'd dropped into Imperial for the last bit without even thinking about it, filling in the gaps between words and meanings out of habit, trusting to the translators to parse things into something usable when he missed a word here and there.

"Bekig," he said again in Imperial, then went on in Fleet. "A place that isn't *here*, the time that isn't *now*, and neither in the future. Past place."

These fucking people, so obsessed with going forward that they didn't have a way to say "reverse course" or "turn around" without fucking up the syntax. Syrus crossed his arms and glared at the wall, not really seeing the map on it, while he waited for the others to wrap their minds around what he meant.

"Absolutely not," Kizen said in a flat voice. "There is nowhere in the past timeplaces to go. Not for—" He snarled wordlessly and waved his fists. "No. You would have us go all the way to the Root, out of cowardice and unconfirmed guesses."

"Very, very well-educated guesses," Syrus reminded him. "Based on experience, observation, and the fact that there is a *hidden* Barbican in this system with an even *better* hidden satellite guarding it." He stabbed a finger at the wall. "You ignore me, ignore that—" He waved his hand again. "Then it's not just embarrassment. It's *death*." He leaned into Kizen's personal space until he could smell the alcohol the man had been drinking at the banquet. "Is that a risk you want to run? I'll be dead, sure. But you won't get my Helm and you won't get to gloat about how paranoid I am, because you'll be *dead* too."

The other warlord drew back until they weren't sharing the same breathing space, but the heat he gave off tightened the skin of Syrus's face, stretching over muscle and bone. "Fuck you," the man growled. "Fuck you, and the bitches who keep your balls, and the cunts who suck your cock. You go. Make a fool of yourself flying all over the system after imaginary threats. I will do as we have always done, those of us who are true Fleet. I will Conquer this system. Then, when I have done that, I will deal with those har izrumeor Imperials. And we will see who *truly* wears a Helm." Still growling and muttering under his breath, Kizen turned on his heel and stalked out of the room, nearly ramming himself into the wall before the door finished melting open.

Syrus watched him go, then looked over at Quinn. If he didn't know better, he'd call the look on the man's face amused. But Quinn was never amused, entertained, or even a little bit smug, not that Syrus had seen. "Well," the second said. "Milord, I think you will have to make do on your own in this case."

Syrus snorted. Maybe Quinn really was enjoying this. "I didn't need his help anyway. So long as I get this done fast, he won't have a chance to send anyone down there and blow the thing to bits."

"No." Quinn walked up and laid a hand on the wobble in the gravitational waves that marked the next Barbican. "Not if this is our only way out of the system."

"Well, you're going to keep an eye on him," Syrus said. "Sweeps, rabbit hunts, you name it. Keep him occupied until I get back. And if I don't make it back—"

"Will you stop that?" lira snapped. The soft *whack* of skin on skin cracked through the suddenly quiet room. Syrus turned to look. The redheaded sai had her sister wrapped up in her arms, guarding the other woman's head as she hissed at lira like a pissed-off cat. lira raised her hand again, probably to dole out a little more discipline.

Syrus reached over and caught her wrist before she had a chance to strike. "Hold on," he told her, eyeing the ball of arms and legs and bloody clothing that might or might not have been two people at one point. The redhead started hissing at him instead.

"Quinn," Syrus said over his shoulder. "I still owe Kizen a thank-gift, right?"

"Yes milord,"

The germ of an idea sprouted and took root. Syrus turned to look at his second. "There's a blond in my quarters. Back full of scars. Blue eyes. Don't let her talk you into beating her. Take her over to the *Ataorl Banso*. Make sure he keeps pounding the shit out of this system like he said he would.

Quinn's lips twitched, but he bowed. "And you, milord?"

"I'm going to sneak into that outpost and bring back the keys for the Barbican. And these two—" He jerked a thumb at the girls on the floor. "Are my ticket in."

Twenty-Two -- Syrus

They're untrustworthy as Hell, but who else are you going to send on the suicide missions? So long as teams keep comin' back, alive or in pieces, we'll keep sending 'em out. No good for anything else.
    -recording, private quarters, Admiral Utten, 1567.602 F.K.

Syrus could drop a space station though the holes in this plan. His old clearances were probably enough to get him aboard the base guarding the Barbican, but they could also get him killed right in the hangar. He'd have to survive long enough to get new ones, fast. So much depended on being able to move around the base instead of getting stuck in a holding cell or floating dead in vacuum.

Add in the fact that he was bringing the two women along for the ride and this was a shitstorm just waiting to happen.

He stomped on his conscience when it tried to speak up and turned his brain back to the puzzle of getting them to cooperate. Hopefully he could keep them off balance. Keep them from realizing how badly they could fuck this thing up for him. If not, well, it wouldn't be the first time he'd opened an outer hatch on someone. But it could be his last.

Somewhere behind Syrus, something hit the deck of the hangar with a ringing clang. He looked up, pulled out of his thoughts. A tech bent, cursing under her breath, and picked up the piece of equipment that had fallen off her cart. Once it was back in place, she trotted off across the hangar towards the mechanic shops, pushing the cart ahead of her. Syrus clipped the knife hilt back on his belt and took a deep breath to center himself. He was on edge. That was all. Oona and her team were doing a last check of the ship he'd be using, one of many captured from a landing field down planet and brought up to be retrofitted with Fleet systems. He'd commandeered it mainly because Engineering hadn't started tearing it apart yet.

The scuff of a boot on metal announced Quinn's presence. Syrus waited.

"Milord, if I may?"

Syrus swallowed the smile that would have wrecked the serious mood and glanced over at Quinn. "You don't understand why I'm bringing the women."

"No milord." Quinn tipped his head slightly, the rim of his helmet shadowing his eyes.

Syrus turned on one heel so he could look the man in the face. "Think about it. They're sai. There are two of them. Which, granted," he lifted a shoulder, "isn't really a guarantee of them being bonded. Whoever answers my hail on that base might know that, he might not. But no Imperial is going to turn away two sai. From their point of view, they might as well cut off their arms and legs and feed them to a bajbar."

Quinn frowned slightly. "You wish to fly in there and hand them the women?"

Syrus eyed Quinn. The little pinched line between his eyebrows said he wasn't happy. The line had been there since Syrus had declared he was bringing the strays along. It was the longest any expression had lived on Quinn's face in the entire time Syrus had known him.

Well, he could go fuck himself. The women might break this plan all to bits, but they could also be what made it work. Trying to explain the particulars of Foreseers and sousi to a Fleet man was like trying to tell a cat how a space elevator operated. Not worth it.

Admit it, his brain told him. *You're not bringing them because you think you can get them to work for you. You're bringing them because the minute you take off and leave them here, Oona is going to chuck them out an airlock.*

He growled at the voice.

It's called guilt, his conscience said. *And you have it in spades.*

He snarled. Out loud this time. Quinn's face tightened. Syrus opened his mouth, then shut it. And there was always an airlock. Better he do it himself than someone else.

Someone who would probably torture them first.

Syrus shook his head. Quinn was still waiting for an answer.

"Maybe. Maybe not." There was more, of course, but not even Quinn needed to know the fine details of how he planned to pull this off. "Depends on how long it takes me to get the keys. I'm not occupying the fucking base all by my lonesome. In and out is all. If getting the job done means I have to make them think I've given them the women, that's what I'll do." He curled a lip. "Not like they'll live long enough to use them."

"When can we expect you back, milord?"

"Day or two out. If Oona's vacfighters don't blow my ass all over the solar system. A couple days on the base. Another two or three back. Might have to circle the system if they try to follow." He hitched his carry bag higher on his shoulder

Quinn raised an eyebrow. "As you wish, milord." He picked up another carry bag, this one tattered and burned, blazoned with the sign of this planet's government. "Oona had one of the outFleet pick this out of stores. Will it suffice?"

Syrus took it, rifled through the contents, and shrugged. "Should. She cleared the ship yet?"

Quinn gestured. Oona and one of the mech-techs were coming down the ramp of the ship. The captain dusted off her hands as she came forward. She didn't look impressed.

Syrus raised an eyebrow at her.

"It will fly, milord," she said, coming to rest in front of him. "Badly, but it will fly."

"All relative to what you expect," he told her. "That right there was some officer's baby, before we got here."

Oona frowned harder, but a commotion on the other side of the hangar interrupted what she was about to say. Iira, leading the two strays by a set of tethers shackled around their wrists. Someone had found clothes for the redheaded one. A shirt and pants, not one of the dresses his women wore. The girl swam in them. She was also guiding her sister across the deck, moving her around crates and clusters of people like she had charge of a child, not a woman six inches taller than her and weaving like a drunk.

"If I may, milord?" Oona's voice was the closest thing to disrespectful he'd ever heard from her.

He looked at her. "You may, Captain."

Her mouth twisted. "They've served their purpose. We're forewarned of the Imperial Net."

She shut up when he scowled at her. The closed-down ball of emotions under her skin shifted slightly before righting.

"We need to have the 'Who's Warlord here?' discussion again? You know you never win. If you're so worried about it though, talk to your husband. He's not complaining." He turned to look at the mech-tech standing off to the side. "Get them on board." He nodded at the women still making their way across the deck. "In one piece. Tether them in the galley—" He stopped and thought better of it. "Alive."

The woman sputtered. He ignored her, turning on his heel and stalking up the ramp of the ship. "And make sure they get the walls in my rooms fixed before I get back," he called over his shoulder. "Want the locks working again. Tired of crazies tearing things apart."

>>><<<

One hour and a very convincing firefight later, Syrus latched the control yoke into place against the console. He shouldn't leave the bridge. It wasn't smart.

But he could hear the women moving around down in the galley. Whatever Iira had dosed Jossa with to calm her down must be wearing off. Syrus shook his head and checked the nav system one last time, just to be sure. He had a little while before the women managed to break free of their shackles and sabotaged the engine.

Well, those would actually be minor problems, considering the alternatives. The techs hadsaid that the ship was spaceworthy. And it might be. They'd told him the deck plates weren't rigged, the core wasn't set to blow, and as far as they could tell, the nav system was clear of worms that might fly him into the local star.

That didn't mean they'd found everything. He hadn't given them much time once he'd picked the ship he planned to use. Even if he trusted that they'd gone over every line of code in the nav banks, it didn't mean this heap of metal wouldn't drop him down a gravity well. He'd commandeered a Karukap vessel. There were fail-safes built into these things to keep them from wandering off, even if the person who took one had clearance to fly it.

No. No. Clear. Stupid nav beacons and their overrides. Ah. No wonder this ship had been sitting on that planet instead of on the base in orbit. Whatever poor fuck took his last breath back there had been smuggling some sort of plant matter out to a satellite around the fourth planet in the system. Or maybe it was fungus. Hell, there might even be eggs rotting in some cubbyhole under the deck plates. There'd been chickens down there. Who knew?

Syrus hoped there wasn't any of that shit on board right now. Probably not, what with the going over the techs had given it. He'd check later. For now, he erased the smuggler's port of call from the system, then got to work telling the autopilot to skate them around the third moon on the second planet. Hide from the smuggler's sensors, but still make it look like they were taking the usual route back to the Barbican. Hopefully the people guarding the back door would be too buried in panicky civilians to take much of a look at where he came from and how he'd gotten this ship.

Of course, if he'd missed something and the ship decided to slide out from under him, he'd just wasted his time. Syrus double checked his course and shook his head. Fiddling wouldn't make it perfect. He'd just have to take what he could get. That there was a second Barb system was a mixed blessing in and of itself. Just the sort of fucked up thing most Imperials thought their Ancestors handed out like carnival treats. Sweet and full of promise on the outside, acid sour on the inside. Then, when you got too many of those "blessings," they had to replace your teeth.

Somebody wanted to funnel people through the Barbs and make them *work* to get anywhere else. Preferably, with scans of their maruste before they were let through.

He tapped a few keys on the autopilot and looked at the course. Still there.

In the meantime, he had two shackled women to check on. He needed to get some answers. See what he was dealing with before they had to put up a front for any Navlad officers. It'd be a pity to go to so much trouble to keep them alive just to find out that the risk of them flipping the switch from sex toys to killer women was bigger than getting shot by the Navlad Karukap.

Scooping his bags from under the pilot's chair, he toggled the intercom and headed aft.

>>><<<

Syrus stopped when he made it to the galley. It was empty. What the fuck?

The space was narrow, more a widening in the hall that ran through the ship than a room at all. Not meant for a large crew. Sink and counter on the starboard side, with a metal basin set over the hotbox for cooking. Storage and table to port. The table was bolted down, not floating like the Fleet version. More storage under the bench that wrapped around three sides of the table. Everything a solid Karukap gray. Not an inch of extra space to hide in.

He'd stuck them at the table. Tethered them there with mag cuffs. How the hell had they managed to get free so fast? It took him ages to get out of those things, and even he had a hard time resisting the pull of the tethers long enough to get the job done.

A muffled whimper told him where at least one of them was. The flare of anger and confusion told him how to find the other one. Squatting on his heels, he ducked his head so he could see under the table. "The hell you doing under there?" he asked. And how the fuck had they managed it? Sheer force of will?

Jossa was on the bench, curled on her side. The other one, Delfi, had pulled her tethers to their limit and was wrapped around the head of her sousi, cradling the weeping woman's face against her breast. It looked uncomfortable as hell, what with the flares of Jossa's crown jabbing her in the ribs, but she was managing.

Delfi turned her head in his direction and hissed. He couldn't see her expression behind the snaking mass of hair billowing out from under her crown. But he could guess what it looked like. Little bitch. He bared his teeth at her and stood up, grabbing the bag Iira had given him before takeoff. The girl under the table hissed again when he dropped it on the surface over her head.

He ignored her halfhearted swat at his leg and started unloading the gear. "Now," he told them. "Got a whole bunch of electronic shit up here. Gonna use it on you whether you like it or not. Personally—" He dodged another strike and kicked back, gently. He didn't connect. "Stop that, or I won't tell you what I've got for you."

A barking stream of the Foreseers' language answered him. Rage and frustration and confusion burned his legs. Jossa's whimpers had escalated to muffled sobs. He let a small fist make contact with his kneecap before he crouched down again. "Listen. Those crowns are coming off. Difference in what happens after depends on how you answer my questions and whether you keep trying to knock my kneecaps off. Got that?"

Delfi all but spat another string of garble at him. The girl was so wound up he couldn't tell which emotion he'd made worse. There was grief under it all. He could feel it now that he was nearly touching her. The fury and frustration overlaying it were so blinding that he had a hard time telling one from the other.

Then there was Jossa. She just lay there, hiccupping into Delfi's shirt. Nothing at all like the woman who'd stolen his weapons and gone barreling into a pile of Fleet warriors.

He stood, growling to himself, and snapped the tethers that held Jossa to the bench. Then he reached down and grabbed her by the collar. Delfi flailed at him from under the table, but she couldn't do much damage from where she was and the tethers wouldn't let her scramble out the other side.

He could feel Jossa now that he was touching her. If he hadn't been hit by it before, he would have dropped her. He nearly went down anyway, as the weight of guilt and self-hatred sliced its way up his arm and punched in under his ribcage. All his fault. Should have never. All his fault. Better to have died than go through life like this.

He set her on the bench seat a little harder than he'd meant to. She gave a strangled cry that dissolved into a sob. He tried letting go of her and she toppled forward, face buried in her hands, nearly hitting her forehead on the edge of the table. Gritting his teeth, he took her by the shoulders and pushed her back upright long enough to relink the tethers to her shackles. She stayed put for the process, weaving in her seat like a drunk.

"Jossa," he growled at her once he had her attached to the wall again. Delfi tried to use his leg to help claw her way free of the table. He ignored her. "Dammit woman, look at me!"

Nothing. Delfi managed to make it upright and started pulling at his arm, snarling like a demented kitten. Now he had fury, regret, self-hatred and frustration hitting him from both sides. The emotions churned under his skin, mixing with his own and bubbling through his body as the monster reached for control.

Fucking women. So wrapped up in their own problems. Didn't even realize that without him, they'd be worse than dead right now. Either stuck back on that planet as their life support killed them in inches, or on the *Edde Belo* as Kizen and the rest of the Fleet tore them apart. He'd brought them along, hoping they'd be useful—and now he'd been turned into a fucking babysitter!

"Alright, enough!" His hands moved. One grabbed a body and threw it. The other struck out blindly.

Delfi hit the end of her tethers and snapped back. The crown protected her skull from the impact when she struck the bulkhead. Jossa's head whipped back, and she stared at him, his handprint turning half her face bright reddish brown.

"Now. What the *hell* was that back on the ship?"

For a moment he thought it hadn't been enough. He had no idea, short of beating them senseless, what he'd have to do to get their attention elsewise. Then Jossa wavered, caught herself, and looked over at Delfi. "I broke her." Her voice was hoarse and scratchy, like she'd been screaming for weeks instead of crying quietly in a corner.

He blinked. Not really what he meant, but at least it was something. He'd take it for now.

"Aren't there rumors?" She looked back at him. Her eyes had glazed over again. Her voice cracked on every other word and she kept having to stop to gasp for breath. "There used to be rumors." Her hands came up to clutch at his, fingernails digging into his skin. It was like someone had stabbed him with spikes of dry ice. He couldn't feel his arms.

Delfi croaked something derogatory, then cackled. Jossa looked down. Syrus followed her eyes. Delfi was leaning over, one pale hand wrapped around her sousi's ankle. From the look of concentration on her face, she was trying to do something. If the rising level of anger was any clue, she was failing.

He decided that calling attention to whatever was going on would backfire in a massive way. Might as well get what he could out of Jossa while she was using real words. "Been over two hundred years since we had a fuerrus worth the name. None of them last more than five or ten years. None of them keep stables of women anymore."

Delfi spat something at him. He glared at her. "Get up here."

She didn't move.

"You want that crown off or not?"

She narrowed her eyes at him. He snarled and tore a hand free of Jossa so he could point at the bag he'd left on the table. "That's the shit that'll get it off. Keep her upright. You." He glared at Jossa. "What about the concubines? Why would any man want a pile of women around who could kill him in his sleep?"

Delfi got up on her knees and waddled along the bench. She watched him like she expected him to reach out and hit her again; but she took her bonded's shoulders when he let go and held her upright as he eased out from the bench and went back to the bag. He was fucked if they could communicate subvocally. If the crown didn't block Jossa's sai skin to skin, it wouldn't work on any communication through the bond, but he'd just have to take the chance. Delfi was the only one in any shape to kill him anyway.

"Conditioned," Jossa said after a moment. "We weren't just there for sex. We were his guards, too. Allow no harm to come to him." She laughed. There was enough bitterness in the noise to turn the whole galley sour. "Have to start it early, you know. Doesn't take. Have to find them young and teach them well. Lucky, you know." Her head lolled on her shoulders as she tried to look at him. Delfi nearly lost her as the taller woman started to flop over sideways. Cursing, the young woman wrestled her back upright.

When it looked like she'd lose the fight with gravity and dump her sousi off the edge of the bench seat instead, Syrus reached over to help. Touching the crown didn't hurt, so he shoved Jossa's head in the direction of Delfi's shoulder. She hit with a yelp and they both landed in the bench with a mingled squawk and a sprawl of arms and legs.

"Know conditioning," he said. "Seen it started too late. Think that's what fucked up . . ." He frowned. "What's her name. Likes bruises."

Jossa muttered something he couldn't understand, probably because she had a lock of her bonded's hair stuck in her mouth. Delfi's hands flailed and she barked out a couple words that could only be curses. For a moment he considered leaving them to sort themselves out, but with his luck they'd get themselves all the way sorted and he'd wind up having to kill them. Not really something he wanted to do right now.

Instead he held up the neural interfacer he'd just put together. "See this? Who wants to go first?"

They just looked at him.

Bitches. You'd think they'd want a chance at freedom. He was waving it under their noses. Literally. Now they got all scared and meek? It was true what they said. People from the Core were crazy.

"Fine." He grabbed a fistful of Jossa's shirt and pulled her off Delfi. "You then. I take this off, you going to be able to translate for me?"

Of course, if the red-headed Foreseer really *did* have a prophecy locked in her head, he might already be fucked. But somehow, what little he'd heard about that particular breed of sai didn't make him think she could to get around the crown the way Jossa had. They either knew something or they didn't. Touch didn't factor into the equation.

No. Chances were, the words she spouted were a result of something in her brain having gotten scrambled, either by the long-term cryo or whatever woke her up without any of Iira's alerts going off. Fuck, it could have been the fact that she'd been crowned before regaining consciousness.

Jossa was either too far gone to think of any of that, or she was more lucid than he knew. "Can't," she whispered. Her lips were cracked. Her skin was starting to take on a texture that reminded him of plant husks covered in dust. "Know the words. Words aren't the problem. Translation comes from . . ." She fluttered her hands near her chest, then reached for her head. "It's the bond. The pairing. Takes the meaning *behind* words and sets it in order.

"Del," she choked and tried to turn in his grip, reaching for her sousi with trembling fingers. "Del has been calling you names. And—"

"Yeah, got that part. Can't get anything done with you crying and her speaking in tongues. So. I take off the crowns. She," he pointed at Delfi, who glared. "Will stop acting like a spoiled child. Then you'll find out if it's just the crown making her talk like that or if it's something else. Deal?"

She frowned. "And what then?"

"If you hadn't noticed, we're on our own. Headed away from the Fleet." She blinked at that. Hope and suspicion bubbled and crawled over his skin. He raised an eyebrow at her. He was about to crush the hope flat. "Right now we're aimed straight at the most secure Karukap facility this side of the Core. You're going to help me get inside.

"Now hold still. This is probably going to hurt."

Twenty-Three -- Jossa

Crowns were one of the first things developed, child. How else are we to keep gifts of such strength as yours from bursting you at the seams? How else can we hold you inside your skin until you're sane enough to do it yourself?
    -Chataf Kuchru lis Churus isk Fuerrus, to Jossalyn

Having a crown removed almost hurt worse than having one attached to her skull and its insides. Jossa couldn't remember her first crown. She'd been too young when it was placed. She did remember when Iira had forced this most recent one on her. Now, as then, there was nothing to dull the pain. From one breath to the next, her brain ignited as a million threads of fire retreated along neural pathways. She knew she screamed, but it wasn't until someone slapped her lightly on the face that she realized she'd actually passed out.

The warlord held a cup in one hand. In the other, he had a jumble of curved metal plates loosely joined by the wires running along their undersides. It took her a moment to recognize the crown, now that it wasn't on her head.

She groaned and tried to touch her face. Her hands came up short. Frowning, she tried again. She didn't make it half as far that time. What?

"Didn't kill you." The warlord set the crown somewhere out of sight and reached for her. She cringed away. Her back met a soft, but resistant surface. Nowhere to run. If she could even get her feet moving.

His frustration reached her first. She tried to pull away. Stars and black dots swam in front of her eyes and the room spun. His hand cupped her head, fingers threading through the hair near her ear, his emotions grinding at her mind, and half-formed visions of people she couldn't recognize floated before her eyes. Jossa nearly cried with relief. Not even the pain was enough to dampen that reaction. She wasn't a prisoner in her own mind anymore. She'd been able to feel him coming. Before he'd touched her!

He held the cup to her mouth. Jossa sipped on reflex. The water was tepid, but he didn't make her drink faster than she could handle. When she closed her lips against the flow, he took the cup back. He didn't let go of her head.

He was closing himself down. Even through contact, the grinding frustration and its odd echoes of... Sorrow? Loss? ...faded to nearly nothing. The ghosts dancing at the edges of her mind faded too, though she reached for them. For a man who seemed to exist on the edge of his temper, he was remarkably good at hiding his feelings when he chose. Especially considering that he *was* a man. And a Savage at that.

His mouth twisted and his eyes hardened. Standing, he walked away from her and over to the other end of the table. "Your sousi likes to sleep. She always this lazy?"

Jossa blinked. She'd been so focused on the warlord, she hadn't noticed Delfi sitting across from her. Unconscious. De-crowned. The panic rising to swamp her dropped just as fast as it had risen. She slumped back against the bulkhead, swallowing down the last of her fear. "Maybe it's just you," she whispered. Then gulped and added, "Milord," before he could round on her.

He laughed. "It's Syrus for now. I know you know it. You 'milord' me where we're headed, we'll all die." He scooped the cup of water off the table, amusement rising in the air, and grinned down at her. "Let's see how good you are at translating."

He dumped the water over Delfi's head.

She came up shrieking. "Jekkawyj neh! A'lih de'o niayj lu kidda'yjo ch zo'yj iya'zaks neh! Uksu lu zo'yj shavih zi we'ryj neh! Go'oyj lu zo'yj iuriweh fennao lu nuh zo'yj neh! Joss! A'apallih zotturyj nihba?"

Jossa stared at her sister. She couldn't look at the warlord. Couldn't meet his eyes. Couldn't do anything but gape in horror and claw frantically for the most important part of her sai.

It wasn't there. She'd been so sure it would be there. How could she have lost her ability to translate? Half her talent was *gone*. Was the bond permanently damaged? Was it Delfi? Was her sousi the one who was broken? But Del had always been the strong one! Delfi had always been the one who—

"I'jekkea'oks ysho'yj ekki uyrru jekkawyjks neh! Jephilli lu no ysho'yj—" The smack of flesh on flesh cut Del's tirade off aborning. Jossa heard it, but didn't react. She'd gone deep, diving into parts of her mind she hadn't touched in... far too long. Where was it? Where was the pull? Where was the soul deep tug that told her what the words really meant? Nothing. Just the echoing ring of Del's voice off the wall.

Del had told the warlord that all his children should be born with two heads, and that his usik should fall off and his seed poison all his women. Something in that mess should tell her what lay in the warlord's future. Something! He deserved every word.

Nothing. No deeper meaning, no translation. Where was it? The crowns were off. There was someone present to hear the prophecy, as required. Even if Delfi's prophecy had originated in something old and buried—even if it had been an echo caught in Del's head until the crown was off—it should be freed now! The translation should still come through the bond! She should *know*! It was why they paired! It was how they worked!

"Well, this is a fucking nightmare. Should've spaced you both, you know that?"

::Joss!::

The fear and rage and shame in Delfi's mental voice were enough to rock Jossa where she sat. She shook her head and clamped her mouth shut.

Delfi had pushed herself as far as the tethers would allow, clinging to the edges of the table to keep herself in place. ::Joss, focus! Look at me!::

Just like that, Jossa's mind cleared. The fear and horror were still there. She'd lose it again in a moment. But for now, she had her anchor. Delfi was here. She hadn't completely lost her mind. Really, how bad could things be if her sister was awake and decrowned? They'd muddle through somehow. They always did. The two of them and the crew and . . .

Here came the grief. The suction her sister had set up through the bond failed, letting all the memories come rushing back. Twofold, now that Del's could touch her in return. Of all the times not to be crowned. This part had been easier to deal with when she was still locked inside herself. How could she have let this happen? All her fault. It was all her fault. Everything.

"The two of you don't quit babbling about whose fault it was and whatever the fuck it is you're saying, I'm sticking both of you in the airlock. Then I'm going to depressurize it. Really slow. Got me?"

"Should have never made Chethalin try to kill him," Jossa whispered, half to herself, half to the warlord. She felt her hands hit the end of their tethers as she clutched at the ends of her hair. "It's all my fault. Ran and ran and ran. Shouldn't have run, either, except the truthsayers would have found us sooner. Not later. Reconditioning is worse than conditioning started late. Wanted to be *free*."

"O'zo iike'ao nih," Del said softly from the other side of the table, voice cracking on her grief. She was still holding on to the edges of the table, her eyes burning behind the curtain of hair. "O'zo iike'ao nih," she crooned, softer.

"Until they found us!" Jossa rubbed the tears in her eyes off onto her shoulder, feeling the tethers pull at her arms and not caring. "Until—" she gulped down a sob. "Ancestor's Seed, I should have known he wouldn't let us go so easy!"

"Who?" The warlord's grip on his emotions had slipped somewhat; she could feel curiosity dancing over her skin.

"liphilih," Delfi snarled, and then she yelped.

Jossa looked up. The warlord had Del by the ear. But he wasn't looking at the Foreseer. He was looking straight at Jossa. "Who?" His voice was quiet. Dangerously so. Something unnamable and dark leaked out of him like radiation from a cracked core.

She sighed. "The feuerrus datevataf. He had a very minor sai of Hearing."

The dark stuff transmuted to something else, then pulled in before she could identify what it was. Syrus sat there on the edge of the table, still holding Del by the ear, ignoring her flailing hands and the scratch marks she was leaving on his arm. Just when she thought he'd forgotten about them entirely, he frowned. "What happened to concubines when the fuerrus died?"

::Finally,:: Delfi muttered. ::The right questions.::

::You're going to get us both killed,:: Jossa shot back. Delfi's flare of anger along the bond told her she'd struck a nerve. If the warlord had been any sort of sai, they might have been in trouble for it.

Steeling herself, Jossa looked up, praying he hadn't noticed her lack of attention. If he had, he didn't give any indication beyond a raised eyebrow. Like one of her instructors when she hadn't given an answer in time.

::We'd be free right *now* if I'd been able to find a gun!::

Jossa blinked. How had she not thought of that?

"Got that fucking sousi look on your faces." The warlord leaned over to glare at Del. "What did she say?" Delfi twisted against his grip on her ear and stuck out her tongue.

"Guns," Jossa whispered. Then louder: "Guns. Why weren't there any?"

"Oh. That." He settled his weight back and shrugged. "Keep them locked up. They fight each other to gain rank. Things are bad enough when they Challenge each other with knives. We'd all end up in vacuum or fixing life support and the locks every other day if they could have guns outside of active combat. Can you imagine letting a bunch of lunatics run around with pulse rifles and random projectile weapons on a fucking spaceship?"

She stared at him, trying to decide if he was serious.

"Back to the story," he said. "I don't have a full chrono to wait here."

"Guards in life, guards in death," Jossa told him. It was easier to answer than arguing about gun safety on a ship. "When the fuerrus died, we took up residence around his tomb. When *we* passed on, our death tablets would stand around his, closer even than his children's. Until then, none but his Progeny were allowed to approach. For worship."

He snorted, but rolled his hand in a keep-going gesture.

"The prince wanted to change the order of things. He—" She stopped and shuddered.

"You were already brood mares." The warlord let go of Delfi's ear so he could lean forward and meet Jossa's eyes. "He wanted to stack the odds, see if he couldn't turn his own recessive throw into another. Strengthen the bloodlines."

"Jannudyj neh," Del spat, rubbing her ear against her shoulder. "Tahts aksyi'krys nih. Tsets lo'teks jekkehsaks ska'eks kasheks i'rhithaks nih." She slammed a fist down on the table, narrowly missing the warlord's hand. "Kashyj kessacks o'zo l'kehaoks nih."

Syrus looked at Jossa and growled, his irritation warring with her own despair as it crept up under her skin. She didn't need to be told twice. Not that she thought he needed translation for that last bit, considering Del's tone of voice.

"We'd spent our lives dancing to the whim of the fuerrus," she said. Translating directly from He'la to Imperial was almost harder than translating a prophecy. She looked down, trying to pick the clearest words she could. The surface of the table had little chips of reflective material embedded in it. "He forgot that while we might be the most powerful sousi pairing in isk Churusimpir lis Kuchruog lis isk Fuerrus, we were also a Foreseer and her translator. We didn't have much warning of what he'd planned, but we had enough. We attacked him. We ran. Rui—" She stopped to swallow down tears. "Rui and his crew took us in. Hid us. We thought we were safe."

Syrus snorted and levered himself off the table, taking the cup with him. Liquid ran. She looked up to find him standing by the little sink, holding the cup under a stream of water. "Figures." he said. "People with power don't give it up if they can help it. No matter how far you run; take something they think is theirs, they'll fucking come for you. Just a matter of time." He set the cup in front of Del, who stared at him through her hair.

The warlord might as well have been wrapped in shielding panels, for all Jossa could read his emotions. She knew he was angry. The thread of grief was back as well. But for the life of her, she couldn't tell why.

::Del? Can you get anything off him?:: Delfi's secondary talent was to Hear the thoughts of others. If she could glean some hint of what the warlord was thinking, maybe they could figure out which way to jump when he exploded.

Delfi didn't answer. Instead, she reached out and caught the cup of water with her fingertips, then inched it closer to herself and sipped, staring at the warlord the entire time.

One eyebrow climbed up his forehead, but he looked back at Jossa instead of commenting. "So," he said. "You ran. Someone decided they still wanted you. Obviously they found you."

Jossa snorted. "Every concubine and noblewoman worth the name is a sai. Of course they found us." She looked down at her hands, laced together in her lap. At least the tethers let her do that much. "Twenty generations of breeding in our veins. When my parents sent me to isk Fuerrus, they received three solar systems and the accompanying Barbicans as payment. They were rich systems. Each had an Ajiri planet and several Kovavek facilities. Delfi's family didn't need any more planets. They took promises of future breeding stock—children—when the lines were diluted enough that inbreeding was less of a risk. A direct link to the fuerrus into perpetuity." She looked up at him. "Do you know what that would have been worth? If a son of their line had ever shown sai?"

He took the cup from the table where Delfi'd left it, refilled it at the sink, and set it down in front of Jossa. "Sure. He'd be the Fuerrus. Right now there are so many people fighting over the throne, no one can sort out who's really got sai and who's making their women fake it for them."

Well, there was that. But that had been going on since time immemorial. Even the occasional commoner had turned up, claiming some member of the Progeny either sired or birthed them in an alley somewhere. Some had even managed to parlay that supposed blood tie into positions at court. There were just too few children in the Imperial line to pass up the chance that a spare scion might be useful at some point or another.

They were certainly good for keeping the legitimate Progeny in line.

"Dikoch kezs i'wehricks nih," Delfi sang, laying her head on the table with a giggle.

The warlord looked at Jossa. She translated, then reached for that inner pull. Still nothing.

He laughed. "Truth in death? That's the oldest fucking wise man's saying there is. Problem is, by that time there's no use in knowing the truth. Can't rule the Galaxy if you're dead." He frowned. "Drink your water."

Jossa looked at the cup, then back up at him. He bared his teeth in an unpleasant grin. "Drink it. This isn't a choice." From the way he hooked his thumbs in his belt loops, she didn't think he'd stop with making her drink just the water.

She picked up the cup and drank. He watched her, leaning against the table, emotions still held tight under his skin. He was considering something. But what? Without Feeling, without reaching out, she wouldn't know.

She didn't want to reach. She'd already spent too much time with this man. Jossa shook her head. She should be grateful to have her sai back. That he was hiding his emotions and the insights they brought was an extra blessing, unlooked for and doubly precious because of it.

::Joss.:: Delfi's voice in her head was quiet. Almost gentle. ::Joss, just tell him the rest.::

"Why?" she muttered. "He's the one who found us. He knows more about that Ancestors-be-damned system than we ever did."

There went the curiosity again, paired with a shipload of speculation. They crawled over her skin, settling in through her pores and burrowing into her brain. He wanted to know what just happened, and what other talents her sister had that he hadn't read in her maruste.

Jossa wished she dared to give him a taste of her talent again. Whatever he was, he wasn't stupid. He could tell when she was manipulating his emotions. The bathing room had been an accident, and look what he'd done then.

But it was so tempting.

Delfi leaned around the warlord and glared. Jossa glared back. And lost, just as she had every time she'd ever tried to out-stubborn her sister. "Fine," she snapped. "Fine. Have it your way!" She tried to fling her hands in Delfi's direction, but the tethers yanked her back. "I broke her, ok?" She scowled at the table and clenched her fists on the bench. "I broke my sousi."

Syrus raised an eyebrow, but didn't say anything. His emotional barometer didn't change either. She wanted to hit him. Get a reaction of some sort. But even if she could, he'd probably break her arm in retaliation.

"If I hadn't been the one to find the system, we would have kept on running. We might have been caught, but at least—" Jossa sniffed. "At least Rui and Denz and the crew wouldn't have thrown themselves away trying to draw the hunters off. At least we would have died together! Not three hundred years apart and stuck on a ship with—" she waved her hands out at her sides. "Slaves, Del. Again! That's what we are! You just haven't been awake long enough to realize it!

"And now your words are all scrambled up and the translation isn't coming, and I've broken you! It's all my fault, and if we'd just stayed with the crew! Just stayed put and never gotten in those *tukovafek* caskets!" Jossa scrubbed her cheek on her shoulder, feeling the synthcot of her borrowed shirt scrape and rasp at her skin.

Same as her guilt was doing to her soul.

"You'd be dead now anyway. If you were lucky, you would've gone out in a blaze of glory and taken the rest of your crew with you." Syrus planted his hands on the table and leaned down to look her in the eye. His emotions were locked down, his face serious. "Said it yourself. They wanted to pump you full of come and pop as many brats out of you as they could. Don't need your mind for that." He straightened and picked up the cup again. "Instead, you're alive. At least you've got that."

"We're still slaves," she spat at him.

He shrugged and turned back to the sink. "So'm I, in a way."

She gaped at him. What made him think he was in any way a slave? Even if it were true, what was wrong with him that he could say so and accept it?

She was still staring as he came back to the table and set the cup in front of Delfi again. He stood there for a second, his hand on the rim of the little silplat cup, and met Jossa's eyes. And, very deliberately, he slipped his shields. The rage hit her in the face, bringing with it ghost images of beatings, the sting of an activated maruste, and shouts she couldn't understand.

She clutched at the table with fingers that blistered and bled as she groped along her bond to Delfi, looking for sanctuary. Delfi caught her, reeled her in, and pulled the emotions along with her. Jossa cried out as the hurt and anger of a lifetime poured through her and down, deep into the abyss that was Delfi.

Somehow, as the cold numbness of Delfi's blessing moved through the bond, Jossa managed to form words. "You—" Her breath caught in her throat and she groped for different words. Better words. Something to say that might, *might*, be enough to turn his attention away from the topic at hand. "You said your plan included us?"

The warlord—for that was what he was, no matter what he might call himself—let go of the cup and curled a lip. "Sure do. But I'm not done with the questions. Not just yet." He pulled his shields back into place and Jossa felt some of the ominous pressure in the room ease. She licked her lips, found them whole, and risked a look at her fingers. Smooth skin, whitened by her grip on the table.

A hand, huge and work worn, seamed with small scars, landed gently on the surface in front of her. The other hand, its fingers careful, gentle even, cupped her chin and pulled her face up. The warlord bared white teeth. "Still got plenty of time before I need you to play rescued slave. And plenty of questions." His snarl turned to a malicious grin. His shields wavered. Something flickered out and licked at Jossa's mind, sharp and hard. It vanished under a wave of oily smugness. "Such as the rumor that the sai of isk Churusimpir lis Kuchruog lis isk Fuerrus—" he grinned wider at their reaction to the name, "—would put on shows for him, when he needed a bit of entertainment."

Twenty-Four --Jossa

Leaving aside the issue of the soul's existence, it is an apt metaphor. How else would you describe a mental link this strong? Not even marriages have the endurance shown by those with the soul-sibling bond.
      -observations, Professor Rusithe, New Hopks College of Medicine

Jossa stared up at the underside of the bunk above her. What was that ancient saying? One engine forward, two in reverse? It certainly fit. Staying alive counted as forward movement, but Ancestors knew how long that would last.

She thumped her head against the wall behind her a couple times, wishing she'd managed to keep her mouth shut and not completely infuriate the man. But no. She'd added scalding water to the burn of Delfi's words, and now she and her sousi were stuck in here, shackled to the wall.

Jossa thought about it, then thumped her head again, this time to enjoy the feel of impact against her skull. If she was going to die, at least she wouldn't be wearing a crown to the event.

Still, she was probably going to die.

"I blame you," she said.

At the other end of the bunk, Delfi kicked her sister's ankle. Lightly.

Jossa brought her head down and glared. "You little! You're the one who started calling him names!"

Delfi spared a glance from behind the curtain of red hair over her face and went back to fighting the shackles holding her to the wall. Her arms shook as she pulled against the tether between the metal cuffs and the anchors stuck to the wall.

"What are you doing?" Jossa asked, leaning forward to see. The shackle and tether assembly on her wrists brought her up short, and she slumped back rather than fight them.

"Gahtsylii a'liksii yahzi'ii neh. Gahtsylii wekkach dikoksii kaeshy nih," Delfi snarled. "Jennia'yj nehkeh kaeshyj neh!"

Jossa groaned and thumped her head on the wall again. "That right there is what got us locked in here instead of keeping us where we could learn anything. You and your mouth."

Delfi threw up her hands and gave a wordless cry. Frustration blew down the mind bond like air before an explosion. ::My mouth?:: Delfi wailed down the mind bond. ::What about yours? He couldn't understand anything I said! Nobody ever will again!::

Jossa moaned and pulled her knees up to her chest, trying to hold herself together. She was going to fly apart soon. She was going to lose all control, and she couldn't do anything with it, because she was chained to this fikekoj wall while that piece of filth hid where she couldn't get to him. She was going to kill him when she got loose. She was going to—

::Oh no. No, please. Jossa, no.:: Delfi's tone of voice changed abruptly. Jossa felt the anger drain out of her, sucked towards Delfi and swallowed up. Gone. Taking the murderous thoughts with it.

::I'm sorry, Jossa. I'm so sorry. I didn't mean-:: Delfi lurched forward against her tethers and held for a moment before they snapped her back. ::I shouldn't have.::

Jossa coughed and uncurled, letting her arms drop to the mattress. "It's ok," she managed. Her throat didn't want to work. Her tongue felt thick.

Delfi writhed in the mind bond like an unsettled cat and Jossa put out a mental hand to soothe her. ::Shhh. No harm done.::

::Everything is all wrong,:: Delfi whimpered. ::How can it have been so long? Will we ever know why they didn't come back? Denz—:: She cut herself off with a choked sob.

Jossa put one foot out and rubbed at Delfi's leg with her toes. "I know, I know. Just a few weeks ago, I had hope. We were going to see our family again. And now?" She tipped her head back, this time to keep the tears from falling out her eyes. It didn't work. They trickled along her cheekbones and down her neck. "Now we're . . ." She fluttered her hands helplessly and shrugged.

::We're stuck,:: Delfi said, her mental voice a little firmer. She fed warmth to Jossa, the warmth of love and family. ::But we still have each other.::

Jossa swallowed hard and took the comfort offered, letting it wrap around her mind like a warm blanket. Oh, Del. What would the world be like without Del? What did it cost her sousi to shove all her feelings down and away? To offer peace when she herself hurt so?

At the other end of the bunk, Del snorted and went back to fiddling with her shackles. ::If we're going to lay blame for why we're tied to the walls, he didn't get truly angry until you opened your mouth and asked him if the first thing he does with a pair of sai in front of him is ask if they fingerbang each other for people's entertainment.::

"Maybe." Jossa sighed and rolled her shoulders, trying to find a position that didn't strain the tethers too much. They were already starting to pull. Too much longer down here, with the anchors reeling her in tighter every time she moved, and she'd be trussed up like a bird for roasting. "But he may not have lost it if you hadn't already been cursing him and his lineage."

Delfi looked up and frowned. ::I'm speaking gibberish. He wouldn't know what I'd called him.::

Jossa raised an eyebrow. "You used the word."

Puzzlement fizzed along the mind bond. Delfi's fingers stilled. ::I said his mother was a whore, his father must have been a blind drunk who didn't know where he was sticking his prick, and it was amazing a barbarian—:: She stopped. Jossa decided Del must have done the mental translation and figured out what He'la word she'd used to set the warlord off.

"He's more sensitive than most to being called nehkeh." Jossa settled her back more firmly against the wall and hitched her hips so she could stretch out her legs. One of her feet landed on Del's thigh. She draped the other over the edge of the bunk. "The He'la meaning is less . . ." She *hmmed* and tried to think of the right way to put it. "Less caustic than what it's come to mean with High Navlad."

::But they boil down to the same thing in the end.:: Delfi looked down at her hands. She had a thin piece of metal that blinked at one end buried in a seam of the shackles. Jossa didn't know where she'd gotten the makeshift lock pick, but knowing Del, she'd taken the keys off the warlord himself when he grabbed them and hauled them down here.

Jossa nodded. "Yes. And to make it worse, he really is nehkeh. He doesn't like having his nose rubbed in it."

::Of course he's nehkeh. Aside from the truly spectacular muscles, there's the way he talks." Delfi wiggled the piece of metal in her shackle and something creaked. Something else made a little spitting noise, and the shackle fell apart in her lap. ::This Fleet is the perfect place for him. They're all violent lunatics who get off on killing people.::

"Figure that out just from a little rampage down the halls?" Jossa grinned as her sister's face twisted. The warm blanket of comfort didn't go away, though, so she couldn't have been too put out.

::They might have noticed how naked I was, but they were much, much more interested in the blood. Honestly, there might have been a little drool.::

Jossa laughed. She couldn't help it. The image Delfi sent along the mind bond was so ridiculous. All those hard-faced men, panting and drooling like dogs.

::There you go.:: Delfi smiled and started in on the second shackle. ::You just need a little humor to hold you over. Then we'll go up to the bridge and take care of the warlord. Between your sex appeal and my fists, we'll get this boat headed someplace safe.::

And just like that, the real world came crashing in. Jossa took her foot off Delfi's leg, pulled the other one up from where it dangled over the edge of the bunk, and curled in on herself. "No. We won't. He won't allow it."

Delfi's hands stilled. She stared at the shackle around her wrist, face hidden behind her hair. ::What do you mean, won't?::

Now Jossa had used the word *Del* hated most. She would have smacked herself in the forehead for her own stupidity, if she'd been able to move her arms that far. She almost opened her mouth to answer, when something else occurred to her. So she shut her teeth with a click and used the mind bond instead. ::I mean that he may be nehkeh, but he holds our bonds. And he knows exactly what that means.::

The warm blanket Delfi had been holding around Jossa's mind fell away as fear surged in the younger woman's body. Jossa felt the acid burn of it in her throat and eyes for all of a second, before the scalding heat of fury seared her face and chest. Then, just as quickly, it was all gone. No comfort in its place. Just a gaping, empty maw, devoid of thought or feeling.

Delfi sat frozen, skin covered in gooseflesh, barely breathing. Jossa quested along the link towards her, inching carefully into Del's mind, clinging to the edges lest the vacuum of emotions pull her in. ::Del?::

Delfi's body gave a single convulsive quake, but she didn't answer.

Jossa reached one foot out and ran it gently up Delfi's leg. She felt the fine hairs, evidence of too long in cryo. She felt the chill of a body with compromised circulation, still realigning with life instead of sleep. But she didn't feel Delfi. "Del," Jossa barked, scared now. Had she broken her sister? *Again*?

Delfi quaked again and raised her head, using her free hand to brush her hair out of her face. ::I'm here.::

The words were there. The emotion wasn't. Jossa took a deep breath and nudged Delfi's shackled hand with her toes. ::You going to finish that or not? Where did you even get a lock pick?::

The glowing bit on the end of the piece of metal shimmered as Delfi waved her hand a little. Her laugh was shaky, but it was still a laugh. ::He left the crown taker-offer sitting on the counter. I managed to grab this off it while he was carrying us out.::

::You little sneak. So it was all a show? The insults and the—::

::Oh no, I meant every word.:: Delfi wiggled the lock pick one more time. The shackle popped open. Grinning, she stuck the bit of metal between her teeth and crawled over to plant herself in Jossa's lap.

Jossa grunted at the impact. "You were too big for this when you were six, you know that? He decides to come back in here right now, you'll have to do a lot worse than call him names to convince him that sousi don't engage in sex as part of their bond. We're practically giving him the show he asked for."

Delfi snorted and tucked her head under Jossa's chin for a moment. Jossa closed her eyes and breathed, letting the presence of her sister ease the worry and fear and heartache. It wasn't permanent. But for now, she could sit and revel in the fact that Delfi wasn't dead. That their bond was still in place. And that whatever happened, they'd face it together. For the first time in nearly a month, Jossa felt true peace. Quiet. Calm.

Then Del sat up, wiggled back so she could get to Jossa's shackles without undue strain on the tethers, and got to work on the first lock. ::Tell me about the warlord.::

Jossa shifted her arm so Delfi had better access to the seam and tried to think of where to start. With her first waking? The second? The things the other concubines had told her? ::That will take too long,:: she said finally. Carefully, making sure she got as many details as she could remember, she bundled the whole into a metaphorical package and pushed it down the mind bond.

Delfi wavered, sinking back on her heels as she absorbed the information. A blink, then another, and she shook her head. ::He is…
.::

Jossa nodded. ::He is many things. But stupid isn't one of them.::

Delfi bent over her work again, makeshift lock pick wiggling furiously. ::True. But he's also made a grave miscalculation.::

"What?" In her surprise, Jossa forgot to keep the words in her head.

The shackle around her wrist popped open. Del dug into the other one as Jossa shook her hand out. ::Do you have any idea what his plan is? Where we're going?::

"I was a little preoccupied. What with you being awake and the language mix-up and all that." Jossa winced. She didn't want to remind her sister of that right now. Although they would have to deal with it at some point. Had they lost the gift of Foreseeing too? She locked that question away in a deep corner of her brain before Del could pick up on it. As horrible as the Foreseeings could be, she prayed to the Ancestors that they were still somewhere in Delfi. They were too useful to lose.

::Hey.:: A hard finger poked Jossa in the breastbone. ::Wake up, sister mine. We don't have time for daydreaming over muscles.::

::Excuse me?:: Jossa shot up straight and grabbed for Delfi's shoulders. ::I dropped out of orbit when he came for me. Not a day ago! You think I'm—:: She looked at her hands. Both hands. Free.

Delfi doubled over laughing.

Jossa shook her head. "You are an evil child, you know that?"

Delfi gulped down a couple more chuckles and nodded. Then she wrapped her arms around Jossa and squeezed tight. For the second time in ten minutes, all was right with the world. Then Delfi sat back and moved so she could dangle her legs off the edge of the bunk.

Jossa did the same, eyes on the door. ::What's your plan?::

Delfi leaned against her sister's side, toying with the lock pick. ::You won't like it.::

::I usually don't. Although if you plan to have us run out there, one carrying the other and yelling "Help, she's hurt," I will brain you myself.::

::But that one works so well! Especially if one of us is really bleeding.:: Delfi grinned up at Jossa.

Jossa arched an eyebrow.

Del pouted, but it was just for show. Anticipation and glee thrilled down the mind bond. ::He thinks we are only good for sex, though he has seen us fight.:: She reached a mental hand along the bond. ::We need to know what he's planning.::

It took Jossa a moment to understand. A heartbeat to see what her sister meant. Her heart stopped altogether. "I can't," she whispered. "I can't. I—"

Delfi covered Jossa's mouth with one slim hand and wrapped her other arm around Jossa's torso. ::Then don't. You've already done so much. I will do this thing. I have enough Hearing to get past his shields. Especially if I'm touching him. You be ready to fry his mind if he resists.:: Her lips quirked and she looked back at Jossa. ::One way or another, we'll make it happen.::

Fear punched Jossa in the gut. Fear entirely of her own making. She lurched to her feet. "No."

Delfi turned and reached up to take Jossa's face in her hands. ::We are sisters, aren't we?::

Jossa opened her mouth and then shut it, trying to think of how to explain this to Del. ::He doesn't know you. He knows what I'm willing to do for you. But not the other way around.

::His shields are strong. He isn't stupid. You try to glean from his mind, or I try to read him. He catches either of us sneaking into his head and we won't get a second chance. I nearly killed him with my emotions twice already.:: The look on his face when he'd told her how many Fleet soldiers she'd destroyed. The rage that poured off him after she'd lost herself to grief and forgot her duty in the bathing chamber. Jossa slipped her hand into Del's and squeezed. ::He expects sex. He wants entertainment. But he might talk if we ask.:: She looked at the door to the rest of the ship and took a deep breath. ::And if we come armed.::

TWENTY-FIVE -- SYRUS

May your Ancestors see you.
May your Ancestors know you.
May you carry them with you always.
    -Benediction of the Activator-Priests

Syrus locked the last couple code changes into the masker and switched to the third set of parameters as he listened for movement in the hall leading to the bridge. The women would show up once they'd made a thorough sweep of the ship. They couldn't *not* confront him. He'd rather they'd had the decency to stay locked up in the crew bunk, but from what he'd heard over the shipwide comms, that idea never made it to orbit.

He didn't have to wait long. He was just making the first changes when the faint ring of feet on hollow stairs announced their arrival. He snorted to himself. People made the mistake of thinking they walked quieter in bare feet than in boots, but they forgot that hollow metal made noise when stepped on. He saved the program and switched over to the completed one. Hopefully the right woman would attack first. Hitting someone with this thing twice in a row was risky.

And except for when you're having a temper tantrum, you don't really want to kill them, do you?

He snorted and leaned back in his chair, propping his feet up on the copilot's seat as he imagined stuffing the voice in a cage and locking it. It should be so easy.

The women stopped outside the door to the bridge. Syrus waited, listening, but if they were coming up with a plan, they were doing it along the mind bond that made them sousi. Smart.

He could feel them, though—their emotions a quiet turmoil of anticipation, fear, anger, and glee. The redhead must be shielding somehow, to keep them so muted. He couldn't tell what came from which woman, but he had a fairly good guess.

After another minute or two, the wait got boring. Whatever they had planned, it apparently included letting him die of old age. "Thought you two weren't interested in giving me a show," he said finally. "You breathe any louder, I'm going to think you're about to come." He looked at the door. "If that's what you're up to, might as well get in here so I can watch."

Surprise and embarrassment flared. Fabric rustled as one of them moved. Slowly, first a foot, then a shoulder, then the rest of her eased through the door. Jossa watched him with hooded eyes, mouth set in an unhappy line as Delfi slid around the opposite side of the doorframe. Both women held spanners, their fingers wrapped around metal bars almost as thick as their wrists.

"Thought Oona's people checked the boat for possible weapons."

"They missed a storage locker," Jossa said. Now that she was close enough, he felt the steady thrum of determination emanating from her. Its rhythm was uneven, pulling to the side. Towards Delfi.

Syrus dropped his feet off the copilot's chair and leaned forward to rest his elbows on his knees, dangling the masker in loose fingers. The women tensed. He raised an eyebrow. "You gonna use that on me? Or the controls?"

Delfi said something sour in He'la. Syrus guessed it meant "What do you think?" He laughed. Jossa flinched, fear spiking through the air like an electrostatic charge. The end of her spanner wavered, but she didn't drop it. Delfi raised her weapon a little higher.

"Look," Syrus said. "You wanted to know the plan, right? Where we're headed? That sort of shit?" He straightened and waggled the masker at them. "Otherwise you wouldn't have sat out there in the hall debating who gets to hit first."

The women exchanged a look. And probably a good number of subvocal words. Syrus wondered if the feeling of a hundred tentacle suckers pulling free of his arms signaled chagrin.

Neither woman spoke, so he kept going. "Here's the deal. You make things easier, in a way. We get where we're going, I say I've got a couple sai I rescued before the Fleet got to them—"

Delfi snorted. Jossa made a disbelieving noise. Syrus jerked his chin at Delfi. "I say I figure this one's a Foreseer. Unless she plans to keep her mouth shut"—he eyed Delfi, who glowered at him—"there's no way around telling them."

The two women traded another look. Syrus decided to ignore it. He thumbed the toggle on the device and started working on the third set of parameters again, taking out the original glyph and replacing it with the one for Foreseer, then hiding it under the death-only condition.

The women stood there, watching him. He kept one eye on them as he worked, wondering when they'd get the nerve to attack. Place of birth, switched. Family, fixed. Erase the indenture link for sure. He pulled information from one of the other samples stored in the masker's memory and dropped it into place instead.

"Why?" Jossa broke the silence at last, her voice huskier than usual. "Why leave the Fleet at all? Won't that—" She took one hand off her weapon to make a rude gesture. "Other warlord take over? Why give it up? I thought you *liked* ruining planets."

Syrus looked up. Was that what she thought he was doing? Escaping? Just how out of it had she been in that conference room?

Jossa flinched. Syrus realized he'd slipped his internal shields. For a second he thought about leaving them down, to keep her off balance. Then he yanked them back up. She was too strong, and he had no idea if the redhead had secondary sai that could bite him in the ass. Jossa eased back onto her heels as he settled the shields again and Syrus hid a smirk. The redhead still watched him like a snake about to strike, but Jossa thought she knew him. Thought she knew why he did things.

Syrus bared his teeth at them and leaned forward, masker clenched in one hand. The plastic casing creaked. He loosened his grip before it cracked. "I like flattening solar systems just fine. Once I'm done with this trip, I'm going to go right back to it."

His conscience wiggled free of the cage he'd built for it and gave him the evil eye. He ignored it. Easier to do that than try and stuff it back in its hole. At least right now.

Delfi hitched her makeshift weapon a little higher and growled at him. Syrus nearly laughed. If it hadn't been for the pop-fizz of frustration bursting in his skull, he would have. She almost sounded... cute. But she was serious, and so was the situation.

Fuck it, he thought. They'd come up here to attack him and make their escape from the Fleet a reality. Telling them where the ship was going wouldn't hurt much. It might keep them from screaming their true identities to the stars on arrival.

"There's a hidden Barbican in this system," he told them. "Part of Hadra's Net. We're headed for the base guarding it."

The women stared at him, faces blank. He didn't even get the satisfaction of surprise. Nothing. So much for his big reveal.

Jossa must have caught his disappointment, because she smiled. Just a little. Delfi snorted. He raised an eyebrow, but kept going. "The Karukap started building the Net before you went under. They must not have gotten to this section by the time you went in the caskets. Would have thought you'd at least heard rumors."

"Oh," Jossa said, glancing at Delfi, who shrugged. "The Barrier Wall. We weren't sure it was actually going through. We thought it might be. But we'd been away from the Palace for nearly ten years when the hunters caught up with us." She stopped and curled her shoulders in. Next to her, Delfi shifted her weight to lean towards her sousi. Jossa leaned a bit in return. Her hold on the spanner loosened again. "We should have asked *why* the place was being emptied," she said in a small voice. "But there were so many being closed off and quarantined, we didn't think anything of it."

Delfi said something, frustration coloring every word. Syrus waited, but Jossa didn't translate. He eyed her until she looked away from her sister and saw him. Her mouth twisted. "We should have known when Denz wouldn't tell us exactly how he'd found the place. Hiding us under guard of the Karukap . . ."

Yes. They should have. But desperate times and all that shit. Shit he knew far too well. Rubbing it in now wouldn't do him any favors. "You know what the contingency plans were in case of a breach?"

"Khe," Delfi said, with venom. Was that fear coming off her? Jossa blinked and stared at the redhead. Syrus waited. They had that look on their faces again. The sousi look that meant they were talking to each other. Whatever Delfi told Jossa, it wasn't good. Jossa's surprise rippled out, along with indignation. He hid a wince as the emotions struck his face.

"Is it even possible?" Jossa whispered, looking back at him. "I thought you said the Empire was crumbling. How does it have the resources to mass a battlegroup? Or give up a Barbican and its systems?"

"The Empire is crumbling. The Karukap . . ." He shrugged, made the last couple changes on the masker, and locked the code in place. "Opinions differ. So do priorities."

She looked at him. "They'll stall first. They have to. It has to have been tried before."

He nodded. "More than a few times. It's more likely to work now that it's the Karukap and not just whatever the Border Rardog can scrape together."

That made him think of what was coming. He tightened up his shields a bit. No telling if the sai on the base ahead of them could feel anything at this range. If they could, his only defense was to make his mental footprint as innocent as possible.

"Larachah nih," Delfi said in a hard voice. "Lujko'ksii yzo ykspuch esho, o'zo keha'oksii ekka uethga ykspuch esho nih." And then she swung the spanner at his head.

Syrus lunged to his feet, catching the metal bar in his free hand. Jossa came alive and stepped in, aiming her weapon at his face. He dropped the masker, ducked under the strike, and drove his fist up under Jossa's ribcage. The air left her lungs in a muted squeak. She folded around his fist. He shoved, and she dropped back into the copilot's chair. The spanner hit the floor with a clang.

Delfi's heel took him in the knee. Syrus grunted and caught his balance, then yanked on her spanner. She'd already let go. Instead she came at him, hands reaching for his shoulders, her leg swinging up for another kick. Dumb move. Panicked move.

Syrus let her get hold of his shirt, crouched slightly from his already hunched-over position, and scooped the masker off the pilot's seat where it'd landed. Then he stood. Delfi staggered, her balance thrown, her feet slipping as she tried to gather herself. Syrus grabbed her by the shirt front, hit the power button on the device, and rammed the business end into her stomach.

Electricity popped. The girl went rigid, eyes bulging. Surprise tore up his arm and ripped at his neck before flaying the skin from his face and chest.

Syrus snarled and shoved the masker harder into her abdomen. Bitch! Think she could hurt him, did she? Think she and her precious sousi would take him out and fly off, free and clear? She had no *idea* who she was fucking with!

Something hit him from the side. No finesse. No technique. Desperation and fear overwhelmed the surprise. His right side went numb, then flared in agony. Syrus fell back a step, then another as Jossa caught her balance and swung her fist at his face. Syrus backhanded her with the hand that held the masker. She twisted with the force of the blow, fetching up against the pilot's chair. Syrus let go of Delfi, turned so he could catch Jossa by the shoulder with his free hand, and dropped down next to Delfi. Jossa dropped with him. He heard her cry of pain as her knees hit the deck, but all he felt was rage. Rage and desperation. He wasn't sure if it came from Jossa or himself.

"Shut the fuck up," he roared in her ear. He yanked. She lost her balance. The thin fabric of her dress tore. She landed in an ungainly heap on her sousi. Syrus grabbed by the hair and pulled her back. She fought him, trying to cling to her sister. Trying to shield her.

Bitch. Fucking sousi and their fucking stupidity! Throw themselves out an airlock if they thought it would save their bonded.

Somehow he got Jossa off the redhead without giving in to the urge to snap her neck. He didn't know how, what with the feeling gone in his arms and the monster in his head about to tear free of its prison.

"Shut up," he roared at her again. "Look. At. Me." Jossa jammed the business end of a knife hilt into his armpit. A hilt that had come from *his* belt. Syrus stopped short. The monster paused its tirade. So she hadn't been flailing around to no purpose after all.

Jossa stared up at him, eyes wide, chest heaving. Syrus raised an eyebrow and dredged up some mockery to dance along his skin and tickle her extra sense. She growled and jabbed him harder with the hilt, but she didn't activate it. He chuckled. "You go ahead with that," he told her. "I'll live long enough to hit your girl with this again." He waggled the masker in his other hand. "I zap her again so soon, her heart goes into v-fib. You know what happens after that?"

Jossa bit her lip and looked at her sousi, stretched out and unconscious on the floor. Syrus loosened his hold on her hair just enough to allow her the movement. "She dies," Jossa whispered.

He smiled. "She does."

Jossa looked back at him. "But you'll still be dead."

He shrugged. "Maybe. Lived through worse. Question is, will you?"

She swayed and he let her go. She wasn't going to attack him. She was too afraid of life without her sousi.

The perennial weakness of a bonded sai, his conscience reminded him in a caustic voice.

He ignored it. Instead he reached out and took Jossa's chin in his hand, pulling her face around so she'd pay attention to him instead of staring at Delfi. Fear etched a pattern of sorrow and hopelessness over his skin. "So," he said, "you going to work with me on this? Or do I have to keep threatening you two all the way to the base?"

She licked her lips and opened her mouth, then shut it.

He leaned down to look her more fully in the face. "I'm exactly what you think I am. Savage. You got lucky just now. Wanna take the risk I lose my temper and don't get it back? I can get into the base on my own. Just easier to have you."

"You never hurt the women in your quarters like that," she whispered. The acid faded slightly. He couldn't read what replaced it, but it was cool and firm. If something intangible could feel firm.

"They're not sai, sousi, or so infuriating that I want to wring their necks every time I see them," he replied. Then frowned. "Except the one, and she likes it. Which is fucked up."

Jossa snapped her mouth shut on whatever answer she had for that and looked back at Delfi. He waited and tried to breathe, to tamp down on the thing inside. He hadn't lied. It lived too close to the surface these days. And he *could* do this job without her or Delfi, although getting access to the base on his credentials alone would be much riskier.

No, the real danger was losing himself, killing both of them, and not coming back. Or not coming back in time. If he lost his shit out here, and the Karukap found him like that?

Well. At least he'd be dead before Quinn or Kizen realized he hadn't delivered on his promise.

Jossa flinched and looked at him. He realized she'd Felt some of that. His shields must have degraded enough for her to catch his frustration. He glared at her, daring her to comment. To prove him right.

Her mouth twisted, but she kept it shut. Instead, she settled her balance on her knees and then stood, pulling him up in the same fluid motion. Syrus blinked at her, not quite sure how she'd done it. When he opened his mouth to say something, she put her fingers over it, cutting him off. With the other hand, she took his wrist and pulled his hand to her waist.

Syrus felt his eyebrows climb up his forehead. He didn't think she'd hit her head. Maybe it was some sort of delayed effect of the drugs Iira had dosed her with back on the *Edde Belo*. He looked at his hand on her waist, then at the redhead on the floor. If that was the case, why wasn't Delfi affected?

Jossa stepped in closer, her hips bumping his. Her hand slid from his mouth to his chest, fingertips resting on his sternum.

Oh, now he got it.

Syrus wove the fingers of his free hand through the hair at the back of her head and pulled. Just enough to expose her neck. The scent of the shampoo his women used drifted up from her hair, a mix of spices and honey. "So," he said, leaning down so his lips brushed the soft skin just over the carotid. Her heartbeat hammered against his mouth. He felt arousal bloom from the spot under his lips, wiping out the fear, but leaving that other emotion floating like fog on a lake. "This the deal then? You going to pull all that experience out and dust it off for me? For real this time?"

"Need to promise me something," Jossa whispered.

"Promise?" He bit down. She shuddered and sagged as her knees went out from under her. He caught her. His shields cracked slightly. He braced them back up. He wouldn't be able to set up the loop this time. Couldn't afford to let her get inside his head. He'd put too much work into keeping her alive to have to kill her so soon, given what she'd find rattling around his skull. Had to get her worked up enough the hard way. Syrus stepped back towards the pilot's chair, pulling at her waist to bring her along.

"Just me," Jossa gasped in his ear, following him in a one-two step pattern. Kind of like a dance. "Don't touch her. Please."

He pulled away to look at her. The arousal was there. That was real enough. But so was everything under it. She was afraid of what would happen if he went for her sousi instead.

This reaction was beyond what he'd gotten when he made the suggestion that they get each other off for him to watch. This was something to do with Delfi herself. But it wasn't about jealousy. Some bonded pairs let that shit mangle their lives. Not these two. Not with the grief Jossa felt when her husband came up.

He looked down at Jossa, rubbing a thumb along the back of her neck as he thought. She watched him, breathing uneven as her body responded to his touch. But she kept her mind closed off.

Syrus leaned down to graze his teeth along the line of her throat, up to her ear. She quivered against him. Her hands plucked at his waist in feathery little movements. "You keep her in line," he breathed. Her arousal spiked, setting his body on fire where he touched her. "Keep her in line, I don't mess with her. Violent . . ." He paused to bite her earlobe gently. "Or otherwise."

She leaned against him. He was more than half holding her up by now. His dick was trying to fight through his pants. From the raggedness of her breathing, she was picking up on the reaction. He waited while she found the air to speak. At last, she turned her face to his. "Agreed," she whispered.

Syrus grinned and moved back to sit in the pilot's chair, pulling the startled woman down to straddle him. "Then you better get to work." He ran his hands up her arms and undid the catches that held the shoulders of her dress together. The fabric puddled around her hips, giving him an eyeful of bare stomach and breasts, all quivering glory as she panted for air. Pale scars marked her dusky brown skin. Some small. Some larger.

"Only got so much time," he said, tracing a finger over a pale ridge just under her sternum. It looked like a knife wound someone had stitched up in the dark, without bothering to match the edges.

Long fingers wove their way through his hair. Her lips were softer than he'd expected. Perfect, actually. He managed to get rid of the weapons on his belt and tighten his shields one last time before she hitched herself up to fit her hips against his.

His control didn't last, of course. He had the choice of enjoying himself or keeping her out of his head. By the time he lost his grip on the outer guards, she was a whimpering, shivering mess of white-hot need. He clung to the inner barriers by the barest thread of determination when she convulsed over him, hair straggling into his face as her orgasm ground her into dust.

Not more than a heartbeat later, he lost it too; his hands on her hips pulling her down, down, down. She went from whimpering to screaming, hands tearing at his hair, and he followed her through the black hole. His ears rang. He might have gone permanently blind. All he could think was that *this* was what the fuerrus had had in his palace. In his bed. Now he could see why a man would chase her for ten years just to get this back. He might literally fuck himself to death.

Twenty-Six -- Syrus

If we link the nanites to the DNA, it should give us a complete record of how the breeding program went, even if the original data banks are lost. So long as the subject doesn't get electrocuted, retrieving their genealogical history should be as easy as taking a blood sample.
    -recovered data, date unknown

He dreamt of blood and dust. So thick at the back of his throat, he needed to claw it out so he could breathe. There were bodies at his feet. Their blood mixed with the dirt of the street, turning it to a tacky red-brown mud that stuck to his toes and plastered the rags he wore to his skin.

Plastered. There was a word. He couldn't remember where he'd learned it. None of the builders had taught it to him. They always chased him off.

Something made a noise nearby. His head shot up. He stared, feelings he didn't recognize burning and twisting in his gut. Pounding at his head. The only other person in the alley cowered against the wall, sucking air as she bit her hand and stared at the bodies.

She was also silent.

Good. If she'd tried to talk to him, he would have had to kill her. Instead, he was going to figure out where these new feelings came from. They hurt. He didn't like it. Bad enough the whole city hurt him, just by existing. Bad enough the fuckers burned his skin and made him want to hide in the coldrooms to escape. But now something was messing with his stomach. Son of a bitch.

He kicked the bodies. Nothing. Dead. No feelings there. Was it him?

Another noise. Low and whining. Like a dog growl. Coming from his throat. It made sense once he thought about it. You're less than an animal, part of him said. Why wouldn't you make noises like one? Except now, the dogs will come after you too, because you're not one of them either.

Something scraped against stone. He looked up. The girl was inching away from him. He glared at her. Something was wrong with her face. It kept changing.

He pointed at the ground in front of his feet and snarled again. She shook her head and backed away again. Words sprouted in his head like weeds after spring rain, but didn't reach his mouth. All that came out was another growl as he stomped over the bodies, right through the blood puddle, and after the girl.

This is wrong. This isn't how it happened.

He snorted to himself. Wasn't like she was alive to complain, was it? His child-self reached the girl, grabbed a fistful of hair in one sticky hand, and yanked her head back.

A stomach-churning meld of faces cracked wide in an insane smile. He saw Delfi's hair, Jossa's bone structure, and Rissa's—

His child-self smashed the girl's head against the wall as hard as he could. Her skull cracked like an egg.

No! Syrus tried to stop the kid. No! That wasn't what was supposed to happen. You touched her. Or she touched you. Who did what doesn't matter. But you didn't kill her!

Didn't you?

He opened his eyes in time to see Delfi hefting a spanner over one shoulder. He reached up to deflect it. Not soon enough. He kept her from caving in his skull, but not from giving him a solid tap on the head. Glaring at the snarling young woman, he growled. "You're all temper and no brains, you know that, girl?"

Delfi hissed something derogatory at him and hauled on the spanner. He let her have it. She staggered backwards, flailing for balance. And she *was* in a temper. Not that he needed to guess why. Jossa lay against his chest, not quite asleep, but dozing. He remembered that he'd lost all his interior shields. For a heartbeat, panic froze his brain. Fuck. Would she realize?

Then he came to his senses and slammed them all back up. No point in leaving anything out there for her to catch.

Jossa groaned a little and shifted against him. He couldn't worry about her right now. Delfi had her balance. If she wasn't planning to murder him outright, she was definitely going to cause as much pain as she could. Too bad for her, he was ready.

Syrus grabbed the masker from where he'd left it on the console. Thumbing the toggle on the side of the case, he jabbed the thing into her ribcage as soon as she came in reach. Hopefully it had been long enough that this wouldn't kill her.

Delfi went up on tiptoe, a high-pitched keening noise clawing its way out of her throat. Fear hit him this time, not surprise. He was aware enough to notice it, now that the monster slept. Her body twisted and turned, hands scrabbling to get at her back. He knew the feeling. It was an absolute bitch. Like being lit on fire from the inside out.

The masker beeped a warning and he pulled it away. She dropped. Jossa writhed in his lap, moaning and clutching at his chest. His dick twitched. He told it to settle down. In a few minutes they'd all be electrocuted and nobody would want anything to do with sex.

Speaking of which. He tilted the masker up so he could read the screen at the top of the device. Well look at that, he'd gotten the right settings for the right person. He flipped the toggle for the next setting and looked down at Jossa.

Hitting her was even easier than Delfi. He shut his ears to her half-aware cry of pain as she thrashed against him. He shut his eyes too. He could see right down her bare back. Watching someone's maruste rearrange itself into a new pattern was disturbing on so many levels. Who would have thought the one thing the Empire managed to grind into him was the collective obsession with people's lives being written on their backs? Fucking bastards.

Of course, he probably should have done this when he didn't have the woman in his lap and his pants down past his ass. Grumbling, he set the still-twitching woman on the floor next to her sousi. Once he'd yanked his pants back over his hips, he picked the women up, and took them back to their bunk. He'd have to come back with the kit for the blood draws, but that could wait. On the way out, he grabbed the broken bits of the cuffs. No point in trying to shackle them again. Now, to get this shit over with. Syrus flipped to his own setting once he got back to the bridge and stood there for a moment, trying not to think of how long it had been since he'd worn his real maruste.

He jabbed himself in the neck before his brain could calculate the exact times and dates, cryo included. Or how many times he'd done this. Or any of the rest of it. Time travel was a fucking bitch. That was his last thought before the needles went through his skin and the program hit his bloodstream along with far too many volts of electricity.

It was so stupid that he laughed. And laughed. And laughed some more as the fire burned through his veins and his blood shifted back into the old familiar patterns.

He laughed until unconsciousness claimed him and he slipped into deep dreams of a different time.

TWENTY-SEVEN -- JOSSA

No one knows where the prophetic language originated. What we do know is that all subjects with the ability to foresee started using it around the same time. It can be parsed word by word, but without the translator half of the pairing, its warnings are useless.
  -"Etymology of He'la" Professor Sandini, New Hopks College of Language

Jossa had known for a long time now that something was very wrong. And like a fool, she'd walked head first into danger anyway.

Anything to keep Del from sinking into the same pit.

Now she lay in a place somewhere between agony and bliss, sore and stretched and a half step off tempo. She wished her skin would peel off and prove she wasn't this person she pretended to be. Somewhere under all this was Rui's wife. She knew it. She just couldn't find her through the haze.

A shriek slammed into her skull and vibrated through her eardrums. Her cheek burned, first with physical pain, then with residual terror. Another shriek, this time with words. ::Joss, wake up!::

What she meant to do was to sit up and look for whatever it was that had Del in a panic. What she managed to do was raise her head and blink at her sousi through eyes so heavy they nearly refused to open. "Del? Wha?"

::I can't stop it! It's coming—it's still working!:: Del's face swam into focus. She looked queasy and panicked. The feelings rolling off her had enough force to sear themselves straight into Jossa's brain. It hurt. Oh Ancestors, it *hurt*.

"Joss!" Another slap across the face.

"Ow. Del, stop it." Everything felt heavy. Her tongue, the weight in her stomach, the—

She stopped. Backed her thoughts up. Went over her body again. Felt Delfi follow her with her mind, pushing pushing pushing as the urgency built. Three parts joy. Half a part horror. Another part pure and unadulterated terror.

It was there. It was working. Her true sai. The talent that made her continued existence worthwhile.

::You are a moron.:: Del doubled over and fell off the bed. "Hunters seek and hunters find," she croaked in Imperial. "Keys to turn and keys to hide. Ghosts will know, ghosts can save. Run, rabbit, run. Hawk invisible stoops from a cloudless sky!"

Jossa wanted to cry. Wanted to bundle her sister up in her arms and scream in despair. The whole time. They'd had the answer the whole time, if only she'd put some thought to it. Stupid, stupid, stupid.

No time for that. She needed to get moving.

Words rose like bile in her throat, threatening to spill out into uselessness. She swallowed them down, then forced her feet, followed by the rest of her body, off the bed. The air was cool on her skin. She was naked again. No time. No time for the little things. Had to go. Had to—

She tripped over Del and nearly fell against the door. Catching her balance, she tried the keypad. Unlocked, thank all the Ancestors and bless all her Progeny.

She found the warlord aft, coming out of a hatch in the floor. She got a brief glimpse of machinery before he saw her and kicked it shut. Wary anger colored the air around him. She didn't care. She had her audience. Now she could let the translation out.

"They've found us," she gasped, clinging to the corner of a box sitting in the corridor. "Patrols. Something about a ghost knowing what to do about keys. And something else. Something hidden that's going to come later."

He stared at her. Every one of his shields were locked in place. As far as her sai was concerned, he wasn't there. Behind her, she heard Del stagger down the hall.

Jossa ignored her. The man in front of her needed convincing. "We're still broken," she said, pushing herself to stand straighter. "But the prophecies still work. They're backwards. Imperial, not He'la." Delfi rounded the corner and nearly ran into the wall. Jossa reached out to steady her. "I have the translation. But I don't know what it *means* until someone else hears it!" Later she'd try to figure out why they were so scrambled. For now, it was enough to know the prophecies still worked. *They* still worked. After a fashion.

Syrus just watched her with flat eyes. She could have screamed. Would have thrown something at him if there'd been anything to throw. He chose now to shut down? To go from a man of high emotion and action to an asjokojek *statue*? Ancestors' balls!

But she was trying to keep Del upright and hold on to the contents of her stomach at the same time. She didn't have any attention to spare for an infuriating man who couldn't take a prophecy when she dropped it on his head.

And then they ran out of time. Alarms blared over the shipwide. The comm alert attached to Syrus's belt started blinking and beeping. All at once, he came alive. Next thing she knew, he had them turned around and was hustling them down the corridor. Headed towards the bridge, if she had her guess.

"Hey," she yelped, then clapped a hand over her mouth.

Delfi retched.

The warlord made a disgusted noise, but didn't stop. "You're right. Got maybe an hour before the patrol's knocking on the door. Kemvate at the base must have them out further than I thought. I'm the ghost, by the way. Don't know about the rest. 'Cept the key. That's obvious, isn't it?"

Jossa urped and leaned to the side, leaving a trail of stomach contents on the deck. He growled and scooped her up in one arm, Delfi in the other. It didn't help very much, except that they weren't trying to move and vomit at the same time. Jossa bit her lip to keep her mouth shut on the rest of her stomach's rebellion. There wasn't anything left down there but bile. Maybe not even that.

"You two always get like this when you foretell?" He was almost conversational about it, damn the man.

Delfi croaked a negative. Jossa shook her head. "Not in a long time. Cryo probably had something to do with it. We're out of—Wait. You didn't have that before." Forgetting her stomach, the alarms, and the fact that she was so much baggage to the man carrying her, Jossa squirmed around and pulled at his shirt. He growled and tried to drag her away, but the hall was too narrow for him to do much more than make her reach a little further.

"Get the fuck off or I'll drop both of you."

A bare foot caught Jossa in the ribs. Delfi. Her sister was climbing the man like a tree. Jossa wished she'd thought of that. On the other hand, she didn't exactly want to go wrapping her legs around him again. While he was busy trying to detach the bipedal shellfish he'd acquired on the one side, Jossa reached up and yanked on his collar.

She was right. The seven-ringed gas planet of a mechute, with a unit number under it, stared back at her from the skin over his carotid artery. He snarled at her and let go. She hit the deck with a thud and a yelp, scrambled to her feet, and went limping after him. "Why do you have that now when you didn't before?" she half yelled at his back.

"Maybe you just weren't paying attention," he snarled over his shoulder. How he was making any forward progress while trying to get Delfi loose was a mystery, but he was managing. Oddly enough, his emotions were still locked under heavy shields. Jossa tried to touch Del's mind to see what her sister might be picking up, but Del was focused on the warlord. Nothing Jossa could do would get through to her.

"I'm not some Edgeworld commoner. I was practically chewing on that spot. I would have noticed if you had tha—Del! Look out!" The warlord turned and rammed himself backwards at the wall. Del, who'd worked her way around to his back and was trying to pull his shirt out of his pants, dropped just in time.

Before she could pop back up, he spun, picked her up by the shoulder, and turned her around to face him. "Take a look at your sousi then." Before Del could wiggle away or fight back, he pulled her hair to the front, exposing her back, and shoved her towards Jossa.

Jossa felt her jaw go slack. She would have never believed it was possible if the proof hadn't been staring her in the face. But there it was.

Jossa reached out a trembling hand and traced it down Delfi's spine. She felt a distant echo of triumph ring in her head as the warlord's shields slipped. But she couldn't take her eyes off what had happened to Del.

::What did he do?:: her sister asked, her voice more subdued than ever before.

"Your maruste," Jossa whispered. She'd seen this pattern. How long ago? On one of the concubines in his quarters, maybe? Yes, that seemed right.

"Did yours too. Memorize them. Don't take all day about it. Then get dressed. Your clothes are in your bunk. Next set of alarms means they're about to board." With that comforting remark, the warlord left them there in the hallway.

Delfi managed to stand still for all of two seconds before spinning around and pawing at her sister. Jossa let her, still trying to process the implications. Now she understood why she felt like someone had plugged her into a power pack and cranked the levels up to eleven. She'd been erased. In one of the most basic ways possible. He'd taken away her identity. Her history. And given her an entirely new one. It was sacrilege of the worst sort. It was a blessing of the highest order.

In all the years they'd run, she and Del had never managed that. They'd used every other method of disguise they could think of. But how hard had they tried to actually *change* their maruste instead of camouflaging it? Could they have found someone with the technology to do so? Obviously, it existed. He had it. How did he have it? How did he just have it *lying around*? He'd been with Fleet for... years, at least! How was this possible? How long had it been possible? Had it existed before they'd got into cryo? She could have stayed with Rui. They could have just vanished. Could have kept running. If only they'd had something like—She should have looked for more ways to hide. Then she would never have had to—

"Joss!" Panic again, burning its way through her skin like acid. And then calm. Cool hands on her face, a slight pulling sensation, and the swirling thoughts settled. Laid themselves out in an orderly fashion. Became themselves again.

::Joss.:: Delfi crouched in front of her on the deck, holding Jossa's face in her hands, forehead pressed to hers.

"I did it again?" Jossa said, lacing her fingers with Delfi's. It wasn't a question that needed answering. "I'm so glad you're awake, Del."

::Maudlin.:: Del kissed her on the forehead, then stood. ::Come on. He's planning something. But he's still shielded. And if we're about to be boarded by Imperial forces, you need clothes.::

Jossa flushed as she remembered that she'd run right out of their bunk and up to the warlord without a stitch on. Without even checking to see where her clothes were. She'd forgotten how disorienting the translations could be.

Then she noticed that the insides of her thighs were sticky all the way to the knee. Right on the heels of that came the awareness that she stank like a whorehouse.

She opened her mouth to ask Delfi if she remembered where the head was from their previous exploration of the ship, then stopped.

::What?:: Del asked, tugging on Jossa's hands.

Jossa let herself be pulled to her feet, still thinking.

"Joss . . ." Even accented in He'la, Delfi's voice was equal parts amused and exasperated.

"I need a rag," Jossa said. "Fast, before he notices we're taking too long."

TWENTY-EIGHT -- JOSSA

A masker doesn't work on empty air and dreams. To rewrite someone's life history, you need to splice in the parts you want to replace. In short, you need new DNA. Blood works best. Easiest to get and to test.
    -advice to a young recruit

Jossa and Delfi found clothes in a battered travel bag in their bunk. Jossa hadn't realized how much she'd missed pants. Even though she didn't have any underthings. No rags either. Delfi sacrificed the hem of her shirt and Jossa did her best to clean the mess of drying seminal fluid from her legs. Ancestors be praised, Delfi's clothes had pockets, although Jossa's didn't. Del frowned as Jossa tucked the sticky rag into one of the hip pockets, but didn't try to get away. ::That's just gross,:: she muttered through the mind bond.

Jossa grabbed her sister by the wrist and dragged her out the door, heart pounding with fear. Any second now he'd be back, wanting to know what was taking them so long. He'd realize they were hiding something. She couldn't let him figure it out. Nobody could know.

::Not even me?:: Del yanked her hand away from Jossa, but trotted to keep up with her sister's longer stride. ::Or are you going to let me flail around in the dark?::

They stepped into the bridge and Jossa felt the reply fly right out of her brain. She halted mid-stride, barely noticing when Delfi barked in surprise and stumbled into her. Grumbling and rubbing her nose, Delfi elbowed her way around her sister and onto the bridge.

The warlord had a blood-sample tube stuck in his arm.

"Took you long enough," the warlord said. No—Syrus. She had to remember his name was Syrus; he wasn't Warlord here. He pulled the needle free, not bothering to put pressure on the vein he'd been drawing from. Popping the tube loose from the syringe, he laid it on the console, where two others already lay.

Jossa snagged Delfi by the back of the shirt before she could go poke at the tube. Knowing her, she'd destroy them, just because she could. Syrus looked up from bending the tip of the needle against the control panel in time to catch the motion and laughed. "Wouldn't mess with those. You get her to cooperate with the plan yet?"

It took Jossa a second to realize the last bit was directed at her. "I haven't had the time, what with the vomit and the panic," Jossa said faintly, pushing ::Wait, wait, wait:: down the bond at Delfi. She couldn't deflect Syrus and explain to her sister at the same time.

"Do it fast. They'll be locking on in a few minutes." He dropped the damaged needle in a refuse slot in the wall and rolled his shirt sleeve back down. "You'll want to put up whatever shields you can. Looks like fucking someone's brains out anywhere within half a solar system of the Barbican's guard base is enough to have their Feels send out the scouts."

It wasn't until the wave of smugness hit her that Jossa realized she hadn't been able to find him with her sai since she'd entered the bridge. Not ten feet away, and it was as if he wasn't even there.

The ship-to-ship beeped, cutting off any reply Jossa might have made. It was just as well. She was so busy gasping in fury that the next thing she said might have brought her death instead. Delfi knew what to call him though. The things she muttered in He'la were enough to turn the air colors.

Jossa put her hands on her hips, knowing she looked the farthest thing from threatening. He might have his emotions contained so she couldn't read them, but she could still push *hers* at him. He'd feel *something.*

He did. His body stiffened and his hand clenched on the back of the pilot's chair, but he kept his face relaxed. "Running out of time here. Jossa made a deal." He gave her a look that could only be described as hungry. Then he turned to Del. "You were knocked out. Might want to reconsider your temperamental inclinations, if you don't want them to find out who you really are and stuff you in lockup till they find a high bidder for your ovaries."

"Zhuzhu he'lao wessia'e kashyj," Del snarled. "Okshua'e nih."

Syrus raised an eyebrow. Jossa glared and translated for him. He laughed. "I *do* know big words. Oughta get paid extra for the syllables too." All humor left his face. "You gonna cooperate or what?"

Delfi told him she'd rather muck out dragonets' stables.

Feet on toes made for a horrible weapon when you were trying to distract someone as oblivious and angry as Del was, but Jossa gave it a try anyway. "Shut up," she hissed. Just because the warlord didn't understand, it didn't mean Delfi was helping the situation any.

"Look, told you before, I can improvise here," the warlord said, apparently ignoring Delfi. She'd moved on to less far-fetched and more practical insults. Jossa was glad the tirade was in He'la. If Syrus got some of that in his head, he might actually follow through.

Oblivious to Jossa's worries, the warlord kept going. "It'll be shittier and it's not part of the plan, but step one of improvising is to kill the two of you and tell them you panicked. Couldn't be helped." He held one hand over the call button and the other over one of the hilts clipped to his belt. His teeth were white in his face, but he wasn't smiling. His face was a rictus of death.

Jossa shifted her weight to the balls of her feet. Next to her, Del shut up and followed suit. If Syrus thought they'd go down without a fight, he was highly mistaken.

His mockery of a smile stretched wider. "Or the two of you can keep quiet and think of *why* you ran from the Empire in the first place."

Jossa dropped back on her heels, staring. Ancestors behind, he was right. She kept getting caught up in dominance games with this man when she should be thinking of how best to escape as soon as they made it to this base.

Apparently, he took her lack of reply as agreement, because his hand hit the call button.

Del reached out and slipped her hand into Jossa's, squeezing so hard her bones creaked. ::Now's a good time to explain,:: she said, her mental voice flat.

Jossa squeezed back and leaned in to lay her head on Delfi's shoulder. The encrypted garble on the viewport cleared, revealing a man's face, smooth and young. Dimly, Jossa heard something about time and not enough of it, but she wasn't paying attention. ::*Look* at me,:: she said, opening up the bond so Delfi could see into her mind. ::Look at why I kept the rag. He's Imperial. Remember. Blood opens all doors.::

Twenty-Nine -- Syrus

Stay out of the Uvlaku quarters. They're animals. The only reason they're here instead of dead is because the high-ups think turning berserker killers loose on the enemy is ok, so long as we hide the unit inside the command structure and deny it ever existed.
    -advice to a young recruit

Syrus stood in front of the hatch, waiting. He'd stripped himself of weapons, piling them on the deck by his feet, and held the tubes of blood out away from his body. Jossa's and Delfi's in one hand, his in the other.

None of the prep work would matter if the soldiers on the other side of the airlock couldn't get the fucking thing open. He must have cut things a little closer than he'd thought in that mock battle against Oona's vacuum jockeys as they'd left the Fleet. Or else the fighters had been putting more effort into the ruse than they were supposed to. Either way, he hoped the damage to the airlock hadn't made it completely inoperable. The Jikujoj class fighters covering the patrol cruiser would blow the whole ship to bits rather than let him near the base without verifying his identity.

Not his. He had a handle on himself. The women, though. He turned to look. They stood behind him, holding hands and doing a passable impression of terrified children.

He didn't trust them for a moment. If they waited more than half a second after the hatch opened to scream for help, he'd be surprised. Shoulda just killed them once they came to their senses and started digging in their heels. Hell, shoulda never brought them along. He'd known it was a risk. Quinn and Iira and Oona had been right. They could blow this whole thing out into vacuum.

Why the fuck had he even pulled them out of cryo in the first place? Stupid soft-hearted pity. He might as well have overripe fruit for a brain, as much good as it did him.

Too late now. There were people right outside. Having the hatch open on a couple of dead bodies would move his execution date up from "sometime soon" to "right the hell now". Definitely not what he needed. He'd just have to—

On cue, the last of the manual overrides kicked in and the damaged machinery of the ship's airlock ground and squealed its way into motion. He winced at the noise. The women behind him went from worry to alarm. And then, of all things, humor. He twitched. The cool, bubbling feeling was beyond bizarre. He locked himself down again before his surprise could escape the shield he held over himself.

Luckily, he expected the guns the soldiers aimed his way.

He raised his hands, making sure the man saw the three vials of blood. And waited. If he hadn't known Jossa and Delfi were capable of their own brand of mayhem and mental destruction, he would have believed the terror radiating off them as they squeaked and edged closer to him. Quick on the uptake, those two. And well trained, to be able to fake emotions so well that another Feel would think they were for real.

"Mechute, sar," said one of the soldiers. Respect to a ranking officer in High Imperial, as was proper. That would change here in a minute. "Turn around and remove your shirt please, sar."

"Someone better take these first." He held the blood samples out to the soldiers. "Me." He waggled his right hand. "Them." He jerked his chin at the girls and tipped his left hand. "Don't drop them. Had a hell of a time getting them to sit still long enough to make the draw. They got issues with needles."

One of the men reached out carefully and took the samples, then edged back and passed them off behind him. Someone else took them, then vanished around the corner. Leaving Syrus with nothing to do but turn around and take off his shirt.

Well, it was going to happen sooner or later.

Reminding himself that he was the one who'd come up with this plan in the first place, knowing full well that it would come to this, he eased his arms up over his head as he turned slowly on his heel.

The women watched him, still holding on to their masks of terror. But now he knew them a little better. Much better than the soldiers behind him. Speculation hid in Jossa's eyes. Delfi had both arms wrapped around her sousi and her face hidden in Jossa's shoulder. But they knew something. What had they picked up? When?

He clamped his shields tighter and pulled his shirt off. Then stood there and waited. One of the soldiers behind him inched forward and pressed the muzzle of his weapon to the back of Syrus's head. A heartbeat later, the other one touched the cold tip of an activator to his neck.

The air lit up a deep orange.

The soldiers behind him went from closed and guarded, seeping just a bit of suspicion, to full-blown contempt. Then their training kicked in and they clammed right up again. Jossa flinched. Delfi's eyes narrowed. He glared at them, daring them to say anything, even in He'la. He'd know it. There was one He'la word that everyone knew.

It hovered in the air over his shoulders. Brighter and larger than the two bond-contracts, the only other marks he'd been given. The word overrode anything else his nanites, his blood, would have shown.

Nehkeh. Savage. No family lineage. No House, adoptions, or background. Nehkeh didn't get their histories activated in childhood.

No. They got the loopy, fucked-up scribble the Foreseers used. It told everyone exactly what he was. Animal. Non-human. A gutter rat thrown to the Karukap when it was decided he was too dangerous running around loose. The rank and unit number on his neck weren't points in his favor, either. Everyone in the Uvlaku came from the same place as him. All the rejects, sent to die together.

Jossa and Delfi's eyes grew bigger, if it were possible. Their false fronts were getting shaky.

"You check out, Mechute," said the man who'd gone to test his blood for matching nanites.

Syrus made his lip uncurl, then reached up behind himself and found the knob of his third cervical vertebra. A slip and a push, and the lights went out. He pulled his shirt back on as he turned around. The men still had their guns trained on the three of them, but not with the same air of high alert.

"You know, sir, you could have just sent the confirmation over the ship-to-ship," the man said. He'd come up out of the shadows holding a screen in one hand.

The glyphs and shields on the man's rank belt made him a vundate. If Syrus had been anyone or anywhere else, the man would have just set himself up for disciplinary action. Using that tone of voice on a superior officer would have landed him in whatever degree of trouble the officer wanted to hand out. But he'd get away with it *because* of what Syrus was, and they all knew it.

"Took damage on the way out," Syrus replied. "Half my communications array got wiped out. C'mon you two, turn around."

The women looked at him.

"How long were you stuck with those bastards, anyway?" He went over and put a hand on Jossa's shoulder. She was slightly less likely than Del to blow this whole thing by taking a bite out of him. "They need to check your maruste."

If he dropped any bigger hints, he might as well start broadcasting clues from satellites.

He ended up turning the girls as a unit, but at least they straightened and quit clinging to each other. The sheer-backed shirts Iira had brought him in the go bag were meant for just this sort of thing. Display of the maruste. There were advantages to raiding Imperial storage lockers to clothe his women.

The soldier with the activator eased forward. Syrus backed off. Jossa's eyes went wide and she clamped down on Delfi's hand, but the read off both of them was still fear and unease. He was starting to wonder if it wasn't real after all.

The maruste of two of his concubines back on the Fleet lit the air over their backs. He'd stripped the code of all the garble their nanites had tried to parse from the Seed virus and Brander's influence. Then added just enough of Jossa and Delfi's true glyphs that if either one of them started spouting crazy shit, they should have an excuse. Considering how often they babbled stuff that could break a man's brain, he deserved a pat on the back for managing to do that without corrupting the programming. So long as his work held up to scrutiny. He was more than a bit out of practice.

"Gabala," said the man with the screen. "Isn't that one of the Edge systems that went dark a few years back?"

It was. Three Barbicans before Syrus had caught up with the Fleet.

"Yes sir," Jossa murmured, ducking her head.

And just like that, the air shifted. His cover story was being taken as truth; at least for now. The soldiers would still treat him like shit because of where he'd been born, but the girls had gotten him in. He was useful now, and not just for having made it off a planet under siege.

"And you, ma'am?" The guy was thorough. Not that it'd help him with Delfi. "When did you get taken from Ejkeka?"

She looked at him, all wide blue eyes in a pale terrified face. And babbled at him in He'la. Jossa choked. Her mask slipped slightly. Not much, but enough for Syrus to tell that it really was a mask. He would've worried about the calculation he felt under the humor that oozed out around the fear, but if she didn't get hold of herself, she'd infect them all with mirth.

What the hell had Delfi said?

It didn't matter, really. Now the soldiers had gone from suspicion to awe. As well they should. They kept their positions, but the muzzles of their weapons dropped another inch or two. Idiots.

Delfi gabbled again and cringed away from the man with the activator. Jossa caught her before she could do anything catastrophic. Syrus went to hover over both of them. "You done scaring them now? I barely got them settled down to begin with."

"Y-yes." The man with the screen stepped back and waved them towards the hatch of the intercept vessel. "Right this way, sir." *Now* there was respect in his voice. Fucker. "Ma'am, if I may." He laid a hand on Jossa's arm. She flinched away and nearly ran right into Syrus. He steadied her, frowning. That hadn't been acting. The jolts of alarm firing up his nerves felt too real to be a front. What the?

"Are you her translator?" the soldier asked her.

Jossa shook her head furiously. "She keeps talking like that. Has ever since—" She stopped, gulped, and looked up at Syrus. He watched her back. If she blew this whole thing now, he'd kill her. Fuck the plan.

"She got hit, when we ran. Then he found us." Jossa ducked her head. "I don't know what any of it means."

The man shrugged. "Pity. Maybe one of the other refugees will be able to match with her. Would be nice to know what those fikeknuog are going to do next. Hate to have to stick such a pretty lady in cold storage just 'cause we couldn't find you a Translator."

That last bit was aimed at Delfi. She frowned and barked something else. Something bad, if Syrus had any guess. He was starting to recognize insults. Jossa's shoulder shook under his hand as humor bubbled through his skin.

"Think it's a fair bet they plan to kill everyone in the system. Won't need to worry about cold storage then. Speaking of, can we get going? Now that everyone's who they say they are?"

It was like throwing a switch. Just like that, the scorn was back. "Yes sir," the man said. "If you'll follow me. Koalski! Go get Rali." One of the soldiers peeled off and headed back into the ship ahead of them. "Alivte Rali will take your ship back to base. You three will ride with us."

Syrus swallowed a sigh and nudged Jossa forward into the airlock of the other ship.

THIRTY -- JOSSA

Hadra's Net isn't a transit hub. It's a series of defensive watch posts meant to hold the enemy and give the Karukap time to retaliate. If we let the civilians dictate its design, we'll be overrun within years, if not months.
          -Isloste Kuskik, in conversation with the fuerrus

Two full squads of Navlad soldiers were waiting when they emerged from the patrol ship into the hangar of what must be the base guarding the shadow Barbican. High, high ceilings gave incoming and outgoing ships clearance to move freely, though they still followed the little guide carts along the white lines painted on the deck plates, each to their assigned slot.

Other ships sat waiting, some battered Karukap craft, some sleek civilian skimmers. Scooter bots shuttled around underneath the vessels as mechanics tore open engine compartments, shouted at each other over repairs, and scratched their heads as they puzzled over botched upgrades of past services.

The air shimmered with waves of determination and fear. It looked like your average orbital hangar, albeit in Karukap form. It felt like a pressure-plate bomb, waiting for the next piece of bad news to set it off. Jossa closed her eyes and looked for something else to focus her sai, something that didn't inundate her brain with images of dead bodies. The men in front of her weren't afraid. Despite, or maybe in defiance of, the atmosphere in the hangar, the soldiers were quiet, wrapped in watchful anticipation. Not eager. Just ready.

Looking from the guns pointed in her direction to the blank face of Syrus next to her, Jossa decided that, given the chance, she would happily kill the warlord.

She'd been taught better than to end up a hostage. She was supposed to use her brain, not give in to her feelings. If she'd come up with an escape plan sooner—if she'd realized the implication of having a member of the Imperial bloodline in arm's reach. She should have been able to keep herself in operating condition after Del woke up. Instead of jumping headfirst into a roomful of soldiers, she could have gone for his heart.

Ancestors, she'd stood there on the bridge of the ship and let him talk her into complacency! If Delfi hadn't made her move, he might have talked her right back into those shackles. She should have bashed his skull in instead of listening to a word he said. *Fikekoj veltukov!* From the minute she'd woken up, she'd had a multitude of chances. Every time he'd touched her, she'd had an opportunity to flatten him. Why hadn't she done so? The day in the bathing room, she could have used her grief to overload his mental circuits. Instead, she'd turned into a wailing child. And again, after he'd knocked Delfi out.

She could have taken out the crew of the scout ship. She could have even overwhelmed the warlord, if she'd worked fast enough. He was unnaturally fast in the physical sense. His shields were strong enough to keep all but the faintest of surface emotions from leaking through. But being able to keep something in and keep something out were two different things.

On top of all that, Syrus was a man. He didn't have the natural defenses a sai did. He'd be far more susceptible than Chethalin had been, all those years ago. She and Del could have taken the ship and his cooling blood and used them to get through the Barbican on their own. Without ever worrying about the base. Two women or trillions of people? She could guess which the invaders would worry about most.

But she hadn't. She'd been too slow to come up with the plan for escape. Too slow in putting the pieces together. Stupid, stupid, stupid.

The hangar around her was built on familiar lines. All square corners and oblique angles. It should have been comforting. But it wasn't the *Skatasi*. It wasn't her ship, with her crew and her husband. The architecture may not have changed. People were still people. But this wasn't her home. There was no comfort here.

It was time to put her mind back to work. Too late to think of should haves. They could still escape. They had a plan, such as it was. She and Del would very likely be taken for questioning. Away from Syrus. All she had to do was pick her moment. The emotions they'd been faking were already sinking into her, becoming real. If she could keep them from consuming her, she could turn them on the guards.

Delfi stumbled on the edge of the boarding ramp. The soldier nearest her put out a hand to steady her. Jossa braced her sister from the other side. Not difficult, considering the fact that Del was clinging like a limpet. Necessary even, because if her sousi went down, Joss would go down too.

Then she started to overbalance, and she realized that the soldier wasn't just supporting Delfi against a fall. He was trying to separate her from Jossa.

Unfortunately, the ship dropped down to an idle just as Delfi started to shriek. Jossa clapped a hand over her sister's mouth. ::Be afraid,:: she snapped over the mind bond. ::Little fool!::

The soldier kept pulling. Delfi's cry of anger turned to one of fear. Huge tears spilled out her eyes. She cringed away from the man, waving her arms and shaking. Same as she had the last two times the soldiers had tried to separate them.

Tension poured off the men waiting on the deck. Jossa could almost *hear* them getting ready to shoot her. She tried not to cringe, but the fear wasn't a façade anymore. It was very real.

A heavy hand landed on her shoulder, bringing with it amusement and irritation. Jossa jumped and looked up at Syrus, who watched her with something like a smile pulling on his mouth. She managed to keep her snarl internal, but he wasn't paying attention to her. He'd moved on to talking at the soldier instead. Just as well. Whatever was about to come out of her mouth right now couldn't be good.

In fact, considering the mess he'd just landed them in, she should probably stop planning ways to infect the soldiers' emotions and start figuring out how she'd keep them from killing her out of hand.

How had she not seen this coming?

She knew. She just couldn't admit it. The gun barrels she was looking at were proof enough. They'd walked into this open eyed and blind. She and Del both. Arrogant in their self-assurance and clinging to their illogical assumption that past knowledge of the Karukap meant they could expect the same behavior of it now.

::Dummy,:: Del whispered in her mind, her voice ragged and strained by the tightest shielding she could manage. Jossa would have kicked her if it wouldn't have given them away. ::We'll do it the first way if we need to.::

Because emotional assassination had worked so perfectly when they'd attacked the fuerrus datevataf. Trying it on an entire squad of soldiers and their commander would make things go even better. Yes. Of course.

Jossa dug her fingers into Delfi's shoulder and hugged her a little tighter. That was in character. Any civilian surrounded by this much firepower would be cowering and praying that their Ancestors would welcome them in the afterlife. The fear settled its hooks deeper into her skin, raising goosebumps and sending her heart racing. Jossa cursed herself. She was out of practice. Too long in cryo. Too long with the crown on.

Del tucked her head up under Jossa's chin and squeezed her fingers a little harder, siphoning some of that paralyzing uncertainty out of Jossa's side of the bond in the process. Whatever Syrus said must have convinced the men to halt their attempts to split the sisters. Now the soldiers guarded them as a unit, letting the two of them shuffle along behind the warlord at their own pace.

Jossa shoved a bit more fear over for Del to take care of and tried to get a read on the men around them. None of them were wearing much in the way of sai shielding. All of them were confident in their actions. In the soldiers' eyes, neither of the women was a threat to life, limb, or mind.

In front of them, the warlord had his hands out at his sides. Facing him was a man with the blown-out nebula of a kemvate on his neck, lights under his skin shifting in time with his pulse. His rank belt had more flourishes and medals than Jossa owned jewelry as a concubine. He was shirtless. Muscles bulged and flexed under spacer-pale skin, obviously the result of conducting all his business from a weight room.

She tamped down the disgust and kept herself from making a face only by the barest of margins. This sort. Setting the example of a perfect officer. Always ready for inspection. His shields were too strong to get much of a read on his emotions, but she could tell what he was just by the way he stood and the expression he wore.

If Warlord Syrus was an arrogant, manipulative achek who believed he could twist the universe to his liking, this man was a belligerent ox who just plain *forced* it in the direction he wanted it to go. There was no compromise or bargain here.

If the weight of impending doom had been bad before, it was nearly suffocating now.

Derision seeped through the bond and settled into her bones like slow-acting acid. With it came an image. They were still in the hangar, weren't they? Not twenty feet from the ship that had brought them in. Play panic, get inside, run.

Del's plans always did cut down to the bare bones of things.

But it didn't make her feel any better. There was still something. Sitting there on the edge of her consciousness. Telling her it was a hopeless cause. How could they ever make it beyond the Karukap's sphere of influence? The minute they ran, there'd be pursuit.

::Not if we play it right. Not if we do it when the warlord makes his move.::

Jossa blinked at the square grid of the deck plates, wondering how Del could be so confident that Syrus would take risks so soon. His maruste was real. The way the scouts treated him, the fact that there was a high-ranking officer waiting to meet them. It all spoke to a level of authenticity that two Border women didn't rate. They'd bring him in and he'd be safe to go with them. Whatever tests they ran on him, whatever questioning they had for him, he'd be in the clear. Because he had truth on his side. They didn't.

"Well now, Mechute lis Tova af Mitachte."

Jossa shot a glance in Syrus's direction, and the sigil on the side of his neck seemed to glow. The Karukap had rearranged ranks and imagery at some point, if a kemvate was coming to greet a mechute-ranked soldier.

The kemvate kept talking, oblivious to the workings of Jossa's mind. "Most men don't look as fresh and juicy as you after being dead almost twenty years." His voice was dry.

The warlord didn't move. Jossa would have been more impressed if she hadn't just sagged against Delfi. Twenty years? How long had he been on the Fleet? He didn't look old enough to have been *anywhere* for twenty years, unless the Karukap was taking trainees at ten.

Who knew? Maybe they were.

An alarm blatted overhead. The soldiers went from alert to high alert. The kemvate's hand came up to his ear in the unconscious gesture of everyone who'd ever worn an implant.

::*Odavek!*::

For one panicked second, Jossa thought she'd slipped. Scrambling with metaphysical hands, she checked her shields and the layer of false fear that had grafted itself into her bones. Had the sai sentries heard her? Had she leaked anything?

::Don't you dare,:: Del snarled as she straightened and stepped in front of her sister. Just as the kemvate looked over at them.

No. Not at them. Past them. At the grav-shielded entrance to the hangar bay itself.

Jossa gulped and turned to look, but from her angle all she could see was the aft tailfin of the patrol ship and the flash of alarm lights set in the walls around the hangar.

::Joss, get ahold of yourself!::

But she'd held on to the fear for too long. It had taken root in her mind, and she hadn't shifted enough of it over to Del. Now something had happened. Was happening. And here she was, crippled. She couldn't pull her own weight anymore. She was useless. Always useless! They were trapped. Trapped on this Ancestors-be-damned base on the edge of a system about to get eaten alive by the Kuchen Fleet. Svis Konanuog. Those who devoured the stars. The bloated faces of the dead walking into the twisted ships. Fodder for their sick appetites. Why should they fight? Why run?

They were going to die. All going to die. They were all . . .

Oh no.

Here it came again. Someone fired a weapon nearby. People shouted. The alarm blared its staccato pattern of one two, one two. Perimeter breach.

Pain exploded in her head. She shrieked and clawed at whatever had hold of her hair. Rage and frustration seared their way through her scalp and threatened to boil the blood right out of her veins, leaving after images of weapons and dead bodies covering the ground. Her foot connected with something solid, but pushing only made her head hurt more.

"You're a fucking piece of work, you know that?"

Syrus.

She quit trying to tear herself free and dangled, clutching at his hand where it tangled in her hair. Doing her best to take as much of her own weight as she could.

"Couldn't hold it together just a little longer, could you? Come on, woman, get your feet under you and *run!*"

Del was still on the deck, babbling about flies and carrion. If Jossa didn't speak soon, she was going to vomit. If she waited too long, there'd be blood with the bile.

Something struck the ship behind her. Sparks flew. Something else whined through the air right after it. The warlord cursed and dropped her. She landed badly, an ankle twisting under her on impact. Before she could figure out who was firing or from where, he'd grabbed her by the arm and pulled her along behind him.

"Del!" Jossa managed to reach out and get a fistful of Delfi's shirt before Syrus dragged her too far. Then she wrapped her legs around her sister's torso for good measure. Not the best. Probably the most awkward way to attempt a rescue. But leaving Del out there was unacceptable.

She caught a glimpse of the kemvate's body past the wild tangle of Delfi's hair. He was down, a gaping hole in his chest. None of his men were visible, but the streaks of weapons fire coloring the air put them behind the next ship over.

She didn't get a chance to see who they were aiming at. Syrus pulled hard on her arm. Jossa screamed in pain as he levered her around the open ship's hatch, but kept her hold on Delfi.

"The flies and the carrion. Is it dead? It will be soon. Maggots, maggots, maggots!"

"The fuck is she talking about?" Syrus started flipping up the seats built into the hull of the ship they'd just exited, hunting for Ancestors knew what in the storage compartments underneath.

Finally. "The thing I told you was coming," Jossa gasped. "They're here. We're all going to die."

He froze and looked at her, a string of low-impact grenades in one hand and a medium-spread haze gun in the other. Some corner of her brain noticed that basic weapon design hadn't changed in three hundred years. Another corner wondered if the old designs had been repurposed. A bolt hit the bulkhead near Syrus's shoulder and fizzled, showering him with sparks. He ignored it. "What did you just say?"

Jossa lost the battle with her stomach and retched. The ration bars the soldiers had given her on the flight in tasted so much worse coming back up. At least they matched the color of the warlord's pants.

That was when the long, shrill wail of a biohazard alarm went off outside the ship. A greenish haze curled around the edge of the hatch. Out in the hangar, people started to scream.

Syrus cursed and lunged for the controls. "Hold your breath!"

She didn't get a chance to obey. Neither did Delfi. They were too busy being sick as the ramp retracted and the hatch closed, and the warlord sat there, cursing the Fleet in more languages than she'd ever heard of.

THIRTY-ONE -- SYRUS

The practice of using a wife and children to
demoralize a man is older than our recorded history.
On occasion, it has been known to work on soldiers of
the Fleet as well. But not often enough to justify the
time it takes.
    -Tactics of Demoralization, Fleet Officer Training
    Manual

By the time Syrus managed to convince the two women not to stab him in the back when he went to open the outer hatch, the Fleet had its soldiers sweeping the hangar outside. He'd been watching them on the monitors up in the bridge as the troop transports dropped their loads just inside the grav shield that separated the vacuum of space from breathable atmosphere.

The air outside the little patrol ship was still faintly green. Bodies lay scattered around the deck of the hangar, Karukap and civilian alike. Anyone who hadn't been shot had gone down in a puddle of vomit and liquefied lung tissue. The Fleet soldiers wore breathers for the first sweeps of the base around them. Syrus wished he could shoot them all. But that meant firing up the engine. Which just meant the men outside would call in a vacuum jockey to blow the ship to bits.

Go outside, get caught, find whoever was in charge and feed them their own teeth? Or go up in a ball of shrapnel and flame because the

Fleet figured out someone was in here and decided not to take any chances?

That was the logic he used on the women. Or tried to. What actually happened was every time he went for the button that would open up the hatch, Delfi snarled something in He'la and pointed a gun at him that would spread his cooking innards over the entire forward bulkhead. Why the fuck had he taken his eyes off her anyway? Should have known she'd dig another weapon out from under the seats.

"Look," he told her, as calmly and quietly as he could manage. "We stay here, air's gonna run out. We go out there, we got a better chance of living."

She coughed and spat her words at him. Frustration popped and sizzled off her like water drops in hot oil. Syrus bit down on a growl and looked at Jossa. She had a spacer's blade in one hand and a grenade in the other, and she didn't look at all sure of whose side she should be on. If he'd been any sort of Projective, he could have tried to ease her over to his way of thinking. "Well?" he asked. "What'd she call me this time?"

"I like living, thank you," she replied as she eased forward and leaned through the hatch to the bridge. Syrus growled and started to get up. If she touched the ignition—

But she came back just as he was reaching out to grab her arm. The look she gave him was half nerves, half anger. She was lucky they were in this fucked-up situation, or he might not have let it slide.

Fuck. He was losing it again. Get away from those Fleet bastards for a couple days and he forgot what it was like to put up with their constant emotional hammering. Forgot how to keep himself from giving in to it.

Focus, you dumb bastard.

He caught a flicker of movement on a screen over Jossa's shoulder. Another ship was landing, right in the center of the hangar. Syrus frowned as he tried to make out the markings on the hull. It was too small to have made the same trip he'd just botched. Ship-to-ship transport then, probably from a carrier in orbit around this base. But which flagship did it answer to?

The outer hull of the ship melted open and erased the need to read the ship's designation. No one else on the Fleet wore armor that ornate. Or with a thorned serpent gilded in silver wrapped around the helm.

And behind him came a woman. Limping and in rags, golden hair a snarled mess around her face. She was barefoot, and from the rust-colored spatters covering the lower half of her legs, she had been for a while now.

"Fucking hell," he snarled, and grabbed Jossa. She yelped and zapped him with a shot of adrenaline-laced fear. Delfi yelled when he punched the button for the doors of their own ship, but Syrus pulled Jossa around so she was between himself and mad Foreseer. Delfi spat again, Jossa tried twist around to stab him, and Syrus shook her hard enough he heard her teeth rattle. "Shut the fuck up," he told them.

Reaching out with his free hand, he yanked the away from Delfi and tossed it on one of the passenger seats behind him. She lunged for it and he caught her around the waist. Frustrated rage seared his skin, but he hung on.

Some fifty odd pulse rifles turned in his direction as he stalked down the ramp, dragging the women along with him.

"Kizen," he roared across the hangar. "The fuck you think you're doing?" He didn't want to think about *why* one of his own women was standing here. Standing *there*, like a whipped dog. Where the fuck was Quinn? The fuck had happened to the plan?

Kizen looked up from whatever the woman had given him. He was too far away for Syrus to get a read on his body language. One hand came up, and he keyed the comms built into his helmet. In front of Syrus, the soldiers went rigid. Then a letten stepped forward. "This way," he barked in Fleet. "Sir."

There was a sea of contempt in that word. An ocean of it, like mucus coming off the men surrounding them. Syrus looked at them. So that was it, then?

For a second, he actually considered attacking. Going down fighting instead of letting himself be led off like livestock to slaughter. He'd take a few with him. Kizen wouldn't have anyone to gloat over in the end.

Delfi muttered under her breath as she tried to wiggle free of his grip. Jossa shushed her, but didn't move. She hung at the end of his other arm, her fear etching his nerve endings.

His imaginary conscience wasn't impressed with that plan. Sure, he could take on his own men turned traitors. He could die in a rain of pulse bolts. The women on either side of him would have an extra thirty seconds to curse his name before the soldiers turned on them, too. And what, exactly, would that gain anyone?

Not a fucking thing. Not even answers. And right now, if he had the chance to cut someone's throat to get a few, he'd do it and laugh.

So you buy some time, his conscience whispered. *Just buy some time, keep your shields up, and work out how you'll get free.*

Syrus didn't bother trying to shove the thought back down its hole. Instead, he eased the two women around so they were standing next to him, and then raised his head to meet the blank face of Kizen's helm across the hangar. "All right," he said once he'd added a few more layers to his mental shields. "Get this over with."

»»««

It looked like Kizen had it all planned out. Probably from the minute Syrus had told him what he was going to do about the base. Instead of getting shot, or beaten, or marched down to a brig, Syrus and the women were escorted out of the hangar, through a maze of corridors, and into a conference room. Jossa didn't put up much of a fight, stumbling along like a drunk again. Delfi held her up on one side and spat He'la at anyone and everyone who came in reach as she blasted Syrus with her fury. The slimy mucus feel of the soldiers around him didn't do anything to help.

Every breath was a struggle. He made the walk to their makeshift prison mainly by clinging to that quiet voice in his head. Buy some time. Don't lose your shit and turn this place into a bloodbath. Don't give yourself away and suffocate on thin air and emotions.

The monster that lived in him crept out to do battle with his conscience. He shoved them both back down, hammered the lid on tight again, and focused on putting one foot in front of the other.

Focus, fuck you.

That's the spirit, something in him replied.

He didn't answer. They'd made it.

Someone had come in advance of their group and unbolted the table and all the seats, clearing it for use. The fact that the lock on the door was the easiest thing to crack this side of an old-fashioned metal-and-wood affair didn't matter. The search the guards made of their bodies stopped just short of cavities and radiated exams.

The women were stripped and shackled with grav cuffs. None of the anchors holding them to the wall were anywhere near the panel access points. No picking any locks. No getting to the wiring inside the walls.

Where the women were forced into sitting positions, Syrus was left standing. They'd also given him an extra set of cuffs around his ankles.

Even if he'd gotten a chance to speak, he wouldn't have told the sousi pair what that meant. The two would probably stop sitting there and emanating and actually start trying to get free, and he'd lose any chance he might have at keeping some sort of lid on the situation. The last thing he needed was those two dropping out of orbit and infecting whatever Fleet soldiers might be around with their emotions. Armor or not, the men would feel something. And after the first time, they'd know where it was coming from.

His men. He'd stopped keeping track of how long he'd been with these people, bleeding and nearly dying next to them. At least a couple of standard years. Maybe more. The minute his back was turned, they'd flipped on him. Hadn't even given him a chance to get the job done.

Morons. Whoever had programmed those drone-sats had fucked up the shields on the little bastards. Probably Kizen's people. His knew better than to let the enemy know they were being attacked. Instead, they'd let themselves be detected and the fucking security on the base had clamped down tighter than a virgin during her first lay. They'd turned what should have been a fairly simple crack-and-grab job into something exponentially worse. The key codes would be impossible to get to now.

Well, Syrus thought, at least he could die knowing the Fleet had run themselves into the metaphorical wall. Now they'd have to reverse course through the Barbicans. Or else sit in this system and get pounded to pieces by the Imperial Armada. Hopefully Kizen liked radiation and extreme gravity, because that was on the menu too.

Syrus decided he really *should* have been making someone pay him for all those big words over the years. Then he could have taken the money and hidden in some backwater Border system instead of running around known space with a pack of psychotic necrophiliacs. Gotten a farm in walking distance of a forest, hunted when he felt like killing something. Had some peace for Ris—

He hauled his mind back to the present. The girls were coming out of their daze, testing the limits of their tethers and making the obvious conclusion. When things finally started happening, they'd be shit out of luck. Trapped.

He craned his neck around to get a look at the anchors on his own cuffs. The air around the cuffs shimmered and sizzled, a side effect of not having any slack in the tether. He squinted. Had they? They had.

He checked the other side. Same. Looked around the room and did the math. It wouldn't have worked for Jossa, or Delfi, even if she'd been standing. They didn't have the freakish strength that came from being Savage. Even if he did get loose, he couldn't pull the same trick on their tethers. Not with where they were anchored.

Assuming they weren't already dead by the time he broke the tether.

Here he was thinking of a rescue again. He checked his mind for quiet little voices telling him what to do and came up dry. Perfect. There had to be something wrong with him on the cellular level. Those two were pissy, annoying, and over-emotional in every sense of the word. He'd done his good deed for the day, keeping them from being beaten to a pulp on the hangar deck. Not even fucking Jossa was worth risking his life for a second go round. Even if he *did* get hard remembering it.

"Zhuzhuch nehkch kashe'yj i'innaks e'vah o'li neh!"

He blinked and looked over at Delfi. Whatever she'd just said, the jagged spikes of disgust and scorn coming off her were clear. He followed the line of her eyes and realized she was glaring at his erection.

"What, you think I need some help with something? Feel free."

"There really is something wrong with you." He couldn't tell if Jossa was putting a good face on her fear or not. If she was trying to act like it wasn't messing with her head, she wasn't doing a very good job. Hopefully she'd get a handle on herself before the next stage of this little drama went into action. It was a safe bet that she hadn't put all the pieces of her situation together yet. When she did, well. He wasn't putting money on the fact that she was the stable half of her sousi pairing. Not anymore.

"What? I'm here. Tied up. Two naked women in the same room. Give me a variable noose around my neck and I won't even need you. I can get myself off." His dick twitched and he shoved those thoughts down. He wanted to mess with their heads and distract them, not actually work himself up. Besides, taking care of himself without the feedback from someone else was like flying a ship with a half-crippled navigational computer. Possible, but not all that fun.

Delfi spat something insulting, probably about his lineage, and went back to trying to look at her cuffs. Jossa thumped her head against the wall. "Why didn't you just take the ship? We were in it! We could have—"

"I told you, we would have died. If they didn't get us in the hangar, they would have gotten us leaving the base. He's probably got half the Fleet in orbit around this place." If not the whole Fleet. Where was Quinn in all this anyway? Bastard had said he was loyal. Hell, he'd *acted* loyal for nearly three years now. Had he just been waiting?

"And we're not going to die now?" She looked downright indignant. Well, he was pretty pissed himself. Except he wasn't about to be gang raped. They were.

"Not dead yet, are we?" They would be soon. Unless he managed to get loose without bringing the whole base down on his head.

That hail of pulse bolts was looking better by the second.

Delfi coughed out something under her breath. He didn't catch all of it, but Jossa went rigid, her attention fixed on the door. He frowned, trying to figure out what had made her start sucking in all that fear. It was almost like she was trying to turn it into something else and build a shield out of it.

He felt the smug confidence a heartbeat before the door slid open, mixed with anger so strong it could only mean one person. Kizen stepped into the room. There was some shifting around in the corridor outside the room, and Syrus wondered if the woman from his quarters was out there. It wouldn't surprise him. Bastard didn't have an original idea in his head. Probably thought that pulling the same stunt as Syrus had with Jossa would prove some sort of point.

But when he saw the man shuffling through the doorway, Syrus nearly lost his mind to fury. Quinn? Quinn was the one who betrayed him? Quinn, who'd put the fucking Helm on him in the *first* place?

A low growl started in his throat. The monster inside lunged at the end of its chain, and he felt the familiar burn start in his veins.

Then he saw the way his second was holding himself. One arm hanging loose at his side. A bruise purpled his face from jaw to temple. Blood trickled down the other side of his forehead from an already healing gash. His *bare* forehead, with the line across it from where his helm always sat.

Syrus couldn't remember the last time he'd seen the man without a helmet of some sort. In battle or shipside, he never took it off. That he wasn't wearing clothes didn't matter. It was the lack of helmet that made him look naked.

Quinn's close-cropped white-blond hair was clotted with blood. His eyes were focused on something in the middle distance, and there was a rapid tic in his jaw. Those were the only outward signs of the one-man supernova he'd carried into the room. How the man hadn't self-combusted was a mystery.

The cage wrapped around his torso didn't have anything to do with it. Glimmers of electricity sparked along the copper-colored bands of metal that followed the line of the man's ribs around his torso. Their ends hooked into his sternum on the front of his body, down into the bone itself. On the backside, they attached to a framework hooked into his vertebrae.

The whole mess looked like a psychotic jeweler had decided to start working on people instead of gems. A soldier standing behind him had a silplat lead in one hand. It had an activation button and a voltage meter, and that was it. You didn't need much else to electrocute a man whenever he got out of line.

Of course, whatever moron thought sticking the second-in-command of Kuchen Fleet Turan in a torture cage was a good idea obviously didn't know the first thing about him. The things were designed to keep Imperials in check, not to tame Fleet soldiers. Any minute now, Quinn would decide he didn't really *mind* the tickling in his nerve endings.

New plan. Get out of this room before Quinn lost his shit. When normal Fleet men went into Frenzy, people ended up pulped messes on the deck. When this man finally broke, there'd probably be body parts flying. Syrus had dealt with plenty enraged Fleet soldiers and come out battered, but alive. Right now, he was just some highborn's piece of art waiting to happen. And so were the girls.

Which was probably Kizen's plan all along, now that he thought about it. The only question was how the bastard had managed this in the first place.

Two more people appeared in the doorway, nudged in by the muzzles of the soldiers behind them. Iira and Oona, naked bodies a mosaic of bruises in all stages of healing. Quinn lurched in their direction, face twisting into a mask of pain and animal savagery. A Numb would have been able to feel the surge of animal lust that came off the man, followed by an even bigger pulse of rage. Quinn watched the women as they limped past him, all the brains of a berserker bull showing in his eyes.

"Get the fuck over here." Kizen grabbed Iira by the arm before she'd made it more than a foot past her husband. He hauled her over to the wall and shoved her down. Quinn snarled and jerked against the collar around his throat.

Most Imperials died before they ever got past the lowest level of current in the cage. Fleet people might be strong and heal fast, but even for them, resetting the heart wasn't the same as taking a bullet. However many volts the soldiers had the thing set for, they barely fazed the man trapped in it. Once the current was gone, he came down off his tiptoes and braced his feet, glaring as Kizen set the anchors further down the wall and shackled Oona in place.

"Did you know," Kizen said in a conversational tone, "that the Imperial medunits aren't portable?" He grinned down at Oona as he took a handful of her breast and squeezed. Syrus watched her face. He couldn't tell what Oona was feeling through the morass of blind fury Quinn emanated, but damned if the woman didn't keep her face completely still.

About the time Syrus started imagining the damage Kizen must be doing, Oona gave in. "You can't decouple them from the base." Her voice was rasping, but that could have been a side effect of having had her windpipe nearly crushed. At least he guessed that was what had happened, if the marks on her neck were anything to go by. "All the saline and sanguine solutions are plumbed in. Along with most of the common drugs."

"Exactly! Their portable units are for shit. Not near capable of keeping up with what's about to happen here. You know what that means, don't you *milord*?"

Syrus raised an eyebrow at Kizen. Whatever he was planning, he'd get around to telling them all soon. Man couldn't keep his mouth shut to save his life.

First chance Syrus got, he'd rip the swaggering bastard's jaw off and beat him to death with it.

"Of course he does," Kizen said, when the silence had stretched on just a little too long. "He knows how this works. He's supervised a Breaking or two, hasn't he? Watched outFleet men scream for their families when they go into the medunits. And scream louder when the cunts come out, all shiny new and ready for the next round of fun with the rank and file." The warlord left Oona and came over to stand in front of Syrus. "You are a *very* good spy. Milord. Stealing the Helm for yourself. Taking advantage of our beliefs; the very things that sent us out to the stars to begin with. Following all the old rules and customs as if you weren't here to fly us all into a trap. But you know, you didn't have to hide what you were . . ." He grinned again.

Syrus imagined those white teeth scattered all over the deck, and lost a bit of time. His shields were starting to fail again. He'd known they would eventually. Quinn's arrival had weakened them more. He just had to hold on a little longer. Had to keep the anger in the room from mixing with the molten pit at the center of his being. Just a little longer.

A fist hammering its way into his gut fixed his attention problems.

"I said, your second's been playing you for a fool." Kizen grabbed a fistful of hair and yanked Syrus's head around so he could look at the battered man being tethered to the wall. "Your *second* has had your whole record in his private files now for months. Karukap, personal. Everything. He's been stripping it out of the Imperial networks since you first set foot on the *Belo.* He knew exactly who you were. And what you are."

Panic. For all of a heartbeat, Syrus thought it might actually be true. It would mean Quinn had been working behind his back, saving stuff he'd thought the Fleet had flattened. He'd thought it was idiotic at the time, the way they threw away so much intel.

Then he snorted at his own stupidity. What did it matter now— what they thought they knew? He was either going to die here, or he was going to break the seal holding the shackles to the wall and kill every motherfucking bastard in this place. This wasn't blackmail. Or leverage for something else. It was just an empty threat.

Either Kizen didn't care or didn't realize he might have used that little revelation for something better. He had his stage; and like every two-credit actor from here to the first migration, he was playing to the only audience he thought mattered. Himself.

"There are some interesting gaps, though." A smile split Kizen's face in half. There was nothing like sanity in his eyes. All Syrus could feel now was the oily slickness of the man's pride. "None of the techs could break the encryptions. Same with the ones he caught and brought in from the Campaigns. No matter what punishments he delivered for failure. Wonder why that is. How high up in the Empire does this little operation of yours go?

"You realize that now that we have this base, we'll be able to decrypt everything we've ever had on the Empire." Kizen ran a thumb down Syrus's jaw, then cupped the other side. His other fingers rested on the marks of rank on either side of his prisoner's neck.

Syrus clenched his teeth on a snarl, telling himself that giving this man any more ammunition would just drag things out longer. At some point, he had to let go. And take the feeling of drowning in raw sewage with him.

Kizen didn't notice Syrus's reaction. Or maybe he assumed it was for some other reason. The crazed smile stretched wider. "Thank you, by the way, for breaking this place open. But you must have known we'd find out, yes?" He leaned in to whisper in Syrus's ear, bringing with him all the smug certainty and righteous anger of a man who'd had finally won his game against the universe. "Enjoy the show, milord. You tried to save the bitches, but they're going first.

"And if—which is a very big if, as you know. If the men leave enough of them for the medunits to put back together, well. Guess we'll just have to see how effective the Imperial models are, won't we?"

He stepped back. Syrus forced himself not to twitch away as Kizen ran his armored hands down his neck once more before finally leaving him alone in his own skin. Though not with his own emotions. Not with everything going on in the room. At least the bastard wasn't touching him anymore. One more second with the feeling of crawling worms under his skin and he probably would have vomited for the first time since... Well, he couldn't remember the last time that hadn't involved nearly a kegger of brew. A long time.

"Now, I plan to make a preliminary test of the units' capabilities. The poor excuse for a thank-gift you had sent to me. What was her name?"

Syrus managed a shrug. "Never kept track."

"Really now?" Kizen looked over at Jossa and Delfi sitting huddled up against the wall. "Pity. I think I will appreciate her much more than you ever did. She doesn't mind the bruises at all. Begs for them, as a matter of fact.

"In the meantime, I'll leave you to entertain yourselves." He clapped Syrus on the shoulder, brushed past the soldiers setting the tethers on Quinn's legs, and was gone.

Thirty-Two -- Jossa

What I propose is that the two subjects also balance each other emotionally. One focused on reality and one, as they say, with her head in the clouds. Stable and Unstable, if you will.
> -"Behavioral Patterns of the Psychically Mind-Linked" Professor Rusithe, New Hopks College of Medicine

Jossa inched herself into a tighter ball and tried to decide if the results would be worth the effort of moving her wrist in its shackle. Probably not. No slack in the tether, no reason to rub her skin raw trying.

Del was quiet in Jossa's mind, her attention off somewhere else. A quick skim of her sister's surface was all Jossa could manage before having to withdraw, stomach roiling. Her sousi was tracking the warlord back through the halls.

Jossa wrenched her mind away before the slime of the man could wrap her in its grip, but escape was a near thing. Stupid, stupid, stupid. Don't go chasing poison. Should be keeping the shields up!

Shields. Hah! If there'd been six of her, she wouldn't have enough strength to block everything going on in the base around them. Ancestors, it was a miracle the people in this room hadn't incinerated her on the cellular level.

Jossa dropped her forehead to her knees and tried to breathe. It was hard. So hard. Superheated air scorched her lungs and dried her sinuses so quickly that each breath was a new form of torture. Vague images coalesced from the heat shimmers in her mind's eye. Glimpses of Warlord Kizen. Of his soldiers overrunning Oona's bridge. Of an alley, the dirt that surfaced it churned to bloody mud. Delfi was angry. Iira and the other woman were twin coals of fury. Syrus teetered on the edge of some sort of berserker state.

And his second? Well, that man had passed beyond berserker and into full insanity long before the Fleet had brought him in the room. If the rest of the Fleet soldiers had anger at their core, central to their very being; *this* man was akin to some of the things she'd learned about in philosophy class. The perfect embodiment of rage, in the light of which all other manifestations of the emotion were reduced to shadow. What was the word her teachers had used? Platonic?

She hoped the tethers keeping him in place held. She didn't think he'd kill anyone quickly if he got free.

Syrus waited a full minute to speak after Kizen had left. His voice rasped and growled. "So, what the hell happened to taking over the system and letting me get the keys?"

Jossa kept her head down and pretended she hadn't heard. Del was still off in the base somewhere, watching the other warlord's mind as he gloated to himself. There must not have been much shielding built into this place, for her to be able to manage it so easily.

"Any minute now, they're going to come in here and get the show started. Talk, dammit."

That brought Jossa's head up. She yanked at her connection to Delfi. Del twitched and shoved an image through the bond—Mivi strapped to the table of a medunit—and went back to what she was doing.

Syrus wasn't looking at his second. He was looking at Iira and the woman tethered a few feet further down the wall.

Start the show? Oh.

Oh.

Delfi yanked her out of the pit before the sticky tentacles of horror could drag her any further than the edge of despair. ::Stop that,:: Del snarled as she drove a stake through Jossa's psyche and into her own. Jossa winced, but didn't fight her. The more solidly she was anchored to Del, the less chance she'd lose control and infect them all. ::And pay attention,:: Del snarled.

"He went back to his ship. Sent word that he was rearranging the troops for another push into the caves." Iira shifted and hissed in pain. "Quinn also requested a meeting with Kizen's second, to examine the details of the plan."

"And to see how he managed to let his warlord get so out of control?"

Iira started in surprise. Jossa hissed at the sudden change in the emotional temperature, then cringed as the anger returned, stronger for the slight relief she'd felt.

"What, think I didn't realize? Think I didn't know the minute I stepped too far out of line, he'd find a Challenger for the Helm who could take me?" Syrus snarled. Actually snarled. "Give me some credit, woman."

Jossa cried out as a flurry of information hit her brain. Chagrin, for all the times Iira had spoken to her warlord as a child. Anger, for having been caught. Jossa hung from the shackles, gasping. The others didn't seem to have noticed. Jossa threw up as many shields as she could manage, praying they'd hold. They started to erode as soon as she put them up.

At the far end of the room, the second growled and pulled against his tethers. They gave, just a little. Jossa's imagination fed her the heart-stopping image of what could be done by a man who might be stronger than the artificial grav generators holding him to the wall. But technology won. He snapped back, head bouncing off the metal paneling with a low *thud.*

Another layer of shields crumbled under the fresh surge of anger. Her resolve pulled against the mental stake keeping her anchored in Del's mind.

::Del!::

::Just hold still already. You with the panic. Them with the arguing. Only so much I can—:: Delfi's voice was strained.

::Del, if you don't help me right *now*, I swear.::

Grumbling, her sister reached. A trickle of fear siphoned over to Del's side of the bond. Jossa took the scraps of peace that streamed towards her and fused them into place over her shields, patching the weak spots. Please hold, she prayed. Please don't let anyone get any angrier.

The conversation had moved on while Jossa was distracted. "Something was wrong a great deal longer than that," the captain of the Fleet ship snapped at Iira. "No Trueborn Son of Kuch would have made another wait before meeting face to face. Should have—"

"Oona!" Iira leaned forward, hissing something in Fleet under her breath. Jossa couldn't make it out. Either because she couldn't hear; or because her translator hadn't had time to assimilate the words it needed to make sense of something so muffled.

"A'lih pa'richo odeh lu kashezs ya'eks ajzs nihba?"

Jossa looked over at Delfi, who was staring at the ceiling. She couldn't feel anything but frustration in the bond. But then this *was* Del. Whatever other feelings she had, she kept them down where Jossa couldn't see them.

That was good. This may not be the first hopeless situation they'd ever been in, but it had been a long time since they'd had to manage one entirely without backup. Or hope of rescue. Or anyone really, working from the outside. The fewer distractions they had, the better. That included the distractions they themselves created.

Jossa snorted. Rui would have charged in here, Denz covering for him like some giant out of legend, and gotten her free, even if it meant he had to do it with two broken arms and stumps for legs. And he would have called her six kinds of idiot for ever getting caught like this in the first place. Then he would have grumped about how she always ended up naked in these situations and how much it cost to replace her clothes.

None of that was the point right now, but still. It hurt to imagine, knowing it wouldn't happen.

"Joss," Syrus growled, just as tears filled her eyes. "Tell me what she's saying. You two." He glared at Iira and Oona. "Quit gossiping and finish explaining why your husband's walked himself out into space without a suit."

Jossa blinked, opened her mouth to snap at the warlord, and felt her outer shields crumble to ash as the second beat her to the mark. She clawed at the bond, scrambling for the peace of mind to slap up more defenses. They toppled almost as fast as she built them. Del groaned and leaned her weight on the stake holding their minds together as the metaphysical anchor threatened to rip free.

"Fucking piece of lying—" The translator chirped and squeaked as it tried to keep up with the second. His words were slurred and garbled by his gritted teeth. But it was the veins standing out on his forehead, and the way every muscle in his body had gone rigid, that had Jossa truly worried. The soldiers had left the electric cage wrapped around him. It popped and hummed as he thrashed. His pale skin was striped with contact burns. She could smell the cooking flesh from across the room. He didn't notice.

Syrus did, though. From the look on his face, the proportionate increase in the second's injuries to the lack of attention the man paid them wasn't a good sign.

"Why are you the only one still wearing clothes?" Jossa said, praying the translation of Delfi's words would be enough of a distraction.

Every head turned in her direction. For a moment, even the second's rage eased slightly, shifting over to the slip slide of curiosity.

Jossa pulled her knees up to her chest. "It's what Delfi said." More or less.

In her mind, Del laughed. The sound was as cynical as a noise could be while still being called a laugh.

From the way Syrus's face twisted, he wasn't much impressed. Color rose under his skin. The muscles of his neck bulged. Jossa waited, holding her shaky mental barriers and praying he wouldn't explode. He'd better not. She didn't know how much of this she could take.

"Because," he said finally. Quietly. "I'm not about to rape anyone. Or be raped. I'm here to watch you all get beaten to death. Then they'll probably turn him loose." He jerked his chin at his snarling second. "So he can blow off some steam. Once Quinn's done skullfucking us, Kizen will cut the life support to this room and kill him too. Claim he went berserk and couldn't be brought off the edge. Killed his own wives. Can't aim him at the enemy anymore. Can't trust him to do what he's told once you've taken away the only people he cares about. Needed to be put down and a replacement found who *can* be manipulated." He looked at Iira and raised an eyebrow as she scowled. "Isn't that right?"

"A Trueborn Son of Kuch without his wives is a loose cannon." Oona sighed and shifted where she sat. Quinn jerked in her direction, and the tethers yanked him back to the wall again. His head bounced. He snarled. Jossa wondered if any of the captive Fleet realized they were leaning in each other's direction. Probably.

Jossa sat there, feeling the lava-like crawl of the man's rage as it seeped through the last of her defenses. On an intellectual level, she'd known what was planned. Even on an instinctual one, when their clothes were cut off and they'd been forced into position. But the reality of it was only now sinking in. This was actually going to happen. There would be no escape. No talking or bribing their way out of this. She and Del were—

Del's mind screamed *fight*. Same as it always did. She didn't have the frame of reference, of experience, to know what would happen. What it would be like. She'd been too young for service to the fuerrus when they'd escaped the Palace.

Jossa knew. She'd been the one to keep them in food until they'd learned how to pick pockets and steal. She'd been the one to do the protecting. The distracting. She knew what was coming.

Her mind gibbered. Froze. The only thing left was to cling to the bond. So she did. Her mental fingers dug into the place where Delfi had pinned their minds together. She held on with everything she had left. Peace, Jossa told herself, trying to slow her breathing enough to think. The bond brings peace. So long as we have that, we'll get through this.

::Will you pay attention? No point in planning to survive if you don't know what happened in the middle.:: Del took a metaphysical elbow and rammed it into her sister's ribcage, slamming her out of her fugue and back into reality.

Jossa gasped for breath.

"We found out after you left. When Quinn went to the *Ataorl Banso*." Iira looked up at Syrus and sighed. "One of Kizen's predecessors started the degradation of Fleet tradition within their Branch." She ducked her head so she could tuck a piece of hair behind one ear. "He got the second to kill his wives. When he became unmanageable, the warlord put him down. Instead of sending to Kuch for a true second as he should have, he filled the position with an icotusorl child instead. A Falseborn."

Jossa decided she'd need a nav computer and a week to figure out what all that was supposed to mean. Time and brainpower weren't on her side. The door slid open and a Fleet soldier swaggered in, armored from head to toe. He brought with him an oily wave of smug anticipation.

It couldn't overtake the miasma that already filled the room; but if each of the double handful of men standing behind him brought the same sort of feeling, soon she'd be more concerned with not vomiting than anything else.

A long-ago lesson, mutilated almost beyond recognition, flittered through her brain. Something about ancient plays and a chorus to back up the main players. Except this chorus wasn't singing; they were about to perform unspeakable acts to underscore what had gone before and what was to come.

Delfi snarled, her brain full of images detailing what she would do to these men given the chance. Jossa tucked her knees up closer to her chest, wishing she had enough slack in the tether to wrap her arms around them.

Why hadn't they just stayed with Rui and Denz and the crew? Why oh why oh why? Syrus's warning hadn't been worth the breath he'd used to give it. It didn't take a Feel *or* a Hear to figure out what was about to happen.

Over on the far side of the room, the second started yanking at his restraints. He didn't seem to notice the electricity from the cage or the fact that his burns were getting worse by the second. The smell of cooked meat got stronger.

She tried wedge her nose between her knees without success. If the man had been angry before, there weren't words for what emanated from him now. Every shield she put up crumbled in the making. The stake holding her mind to Del's started to char. There was no peace in the bond. No comfort.

Couldn't her sousi see what was happening? Didn't she realize the danger wasn't just these men? Or was she too focused on the soldiers and what she planned to do to them when they got in kicking range? Self-absorbed, shallow little asjokoj bittehek. How was the unstable half of the equation supposed to function without her anchor?

The men started sorting out the pile of shackles and anchors they'd carried in. "Hello milord." One of the men stopped in front of the warlord pinned to the wall. "Does the entertainment satisfy?"

The comment snagged on the edge of her consciousness, startling Jossa out of her building irritation. The lack of answer on Syrus's part, coupled with the glazed look in his eyes, was puzzling enough to hold her attention for a few more moments. Was it just her, or had the heat in the room risen a few more degrees?

The soldier didn't seem to care if he got an answer or not. He hammered a fist into Syrus's stomach, and while his victim gasped for breath, drove the other one into the side of his head. Jossa stared. She'd seen any number of fights in her life. She'd trained for all manner of possible assassin. Men, women, small and quick to big and strong. The blow should have shattered the warlord's jaw. Or at least popped it out of joint. No normal man should have been able to withstand that. Her brain rebelled against the alternative, that Syrus was simply impervious. Physics said one of them should have taken major damage.

Del didn't pay any attention to the little display. She was still glaring at the cluster of soldiers and thinking of ways to hurt them.

The stake holding their minds together wiggled a bit and slid. Anger crept in around the tattered remains of Jossa's shields. She growled and tried to hammer the stake back into the ground. Stupid Del! When was she going to focus on the real problem?

A strangled yelp pulled her out of the bond and back into reality. The soldier in front of Syrus had taken another swing. The warlord— was he Warlord now that he was caught like a fly in a spider's web? The warlord dodged, and the other man's fist hit the wall instead.

Given how he cradled his hand, he'd broken at least two or three bones. From the way the undercurrent of arrogant satisfaction transformed to the whine of an engine overheating, the Fleet man was about to quit playing and lose his temper for true.

Syrus laughed. It was wheezing and strangled, but it was still a laugh. "Come on. Try again."

The soldier's individual tone vanished into the heat-shimmering haze that dominated the room.

"Hey!" One of the others grabbed the man by the back of the shirt and hauled him away. "He'll get his when the time comes. Fucker. Got four bitches here, don't gotta mess with the Impie spy."

At the other end of the bond, Del's mind twisted. She was searching for something. Something these unshielded, unarmored men were keeping hidden. Jossa tried to pull on her end of the bond. Tried to tell Delfi that she was slipping, and would she please come keep her sister from losing her mind? Nothing. No siphon. No awareness.

Ancestor's Seed. For once, couldn't the girl just explain what she was doing? Leaving her sister out here to follow along like some sort of, of... Jossa had no idea what. Something tame and following. Some creature that stood and waited for the slaughter to come and did *nothing* to save herself.

How could Jossa do anything if she didn't know what her *tukovafek sousi* was doing?

::Del,:: she shrieked in her head. She was done waiting for an answer. The men were still joking with each other, the bastards. Why should they hurry? Nobody was going anywhere. They had their prey all wrapped up in a bow, just waiting for them. Motherless, fatherless *bastards!*

The stake tugged at her mind as it slipped a little further. Its blackened edges cracked and split as heat worked its way further into the wood, weakening its structure. For half a moment her head was clear, and then the anger came swarming back through her pores. ::Damn you,:: she screamed at Del. ::Tell me—::

The man who'd pulled his fellow soldier away from Syrus came out of the cluster, a set of shackles in one hand and anchors in the other. Why was he the only soldier moving? Why was he the only one getting ready to restrain the prisoners? Did they think they only needed one set of shackles? How stupid could they be? Bastards. Did they think she wouldn't fight them when they tried to take her? Did they think they'd be safe if they left her legs free?

Dread trickled through the bond, flavored with something she almost never felt from Del. Fear. This didn't add up. Something else— math and men and the number of available women. Why couldn't she do the *tukovafek* math?! Stupid fucking anger in the air, clouding her head!

He took a step towards Del.

Jossa understood. "No. No, no, no, no, no . . ."

Delfi snarled and spat, cursing him and his ancestors and the sheep they must have bred with. When he grabbed for her ankle, she kicked him in the teeth.

"No, no, no, no, no . . ." They wouldn't. They couldn't.

Jossa pulled at the stake holding their minds together. Of course, now that she was trying, it wouldn't come free. Of course! Because what else could go wrong today?

Did these men realize what was going to *happen* to them when she got loose? Forget getting loose, forget killing them the old-fashioned way—she'd fry them from here! Fatherless trash! Motherless dregs of the universe! They'd *pay* for this.

Some last shred of sanity clawed its way out of her mind just as the man spat out a tooth and grabbed at Del.

Use me. Me. Please! She's never had to. She was too young. I've always been the one. She's never had to give herself up. She's never done anything but love Denz. Please!

Her mouth refused the words. All she heard was "No, no, no, no, no . . ." All she could see was red.

The stake left blackened splinters in her psyche as she dug and pulled, trying desperately to free herself. Delfi's fear and horror and rage burrowed into Jossa's brain. She fought them; and the more she fought, the more *Del* fought, the deeper they went. Her exterior shields were long gone. Now she was losing the interior ones. The ones that kept her rooted. The ones that drew their strength from the bond. From the outside came volcanic fury, hot and implacable as gravity itself. A veritable bonfire burned her from the inside out as Delfi lost her fight with the Fleet man.

Jossa couldn't tell who was screaming now. Delfi? Herself?

The soldier locked the last restraint around Del's leg and tethered it to the anchor. She lay, struggling, spread eagled and shrieking in fear and helpless anger as the man dropped to his knees between her legs and reached for the front of his pants. In the center of the room, the other soldiers laughed, but their voices were dim. Someone roared into the distance. Someone else wailed.

The sounds faded. Too late, the stake holding Jossa to Del incinerated, charred by the wave of emotion Delfi brought with her as she reached along the bond.

Just before the lava closed over her head, Jossa managed to get what she really wanted to say around the denials filling her head. "Me! Please. Me instead!"

Then there was only heat and pain.

THIRTY-THREE -- SYRUS

*If it's done right, you can turn any enemy sai into
your weapon. Especially if they're untrained. Get in
close and overwhelm their mind. Even the lowest-
level Projective will start infecting the people around
her if you hit her hard enough.*
        -advice to a young recruit

From somewhere out of the roaring, screaming insanity, a memory
worked its way into his brain. It floated down through the caustic
ooze, breaking to pieces and sliding around the monster, evading the
wild swipes of its talons.

Somewhere under all that chaos, in a place he rarely visited, Syrus
held his breath and helped the ghost of his conscience put the pieces
back together. His lungs burned, begging for air, but the last shreds of
his sanity told him that as soon as he gave in—as soon as he opened
up to the murk around him—he'd be gone for good. Nothing left but
killing, killing, and more killing.

He wondered what was so wrong with killing. It was the only thing
he'd ever been good at.

Not true, a voice told him. A ragged mental image flashed in front
of him, shedding the dust of the street and the heat of the sun as he
dug tubers out of a garden. He growled at the voice and snatched the
image, hearing the old man's voice echo through his ears. The

muffled words became clear as Syrus laid the image in the center of the rebuilt memory.

Once, many years ago, he'd been asked how he kept from going insane. How he'd survived for so long on the streets without getting himself chopped into little bits and shoved in with some butcher's daily grindings. The question had been asked in anger, after he'd pissed someone off for the umpteenth time. He'd answered by saying that he was Savage and hard to kill, and nobody in his little territory thought he was worth coming after once he'd done some of his own chopping.

The answer had been the truth.

But it hadn't been the whole truth.

There was a system down there in the subcity of pariahs and outcasts that real citizens pretended didn't exist. Everyone was Savage. But some were true nehkeh. And the one rule held above all else was that when a nehkeh found a child who'd bred true, someone was supposed to catch the kid and teach them how to stay alive.

Pick a target, a goal, the old man had told him as he'd supervised the harvest that blistering hot day. Hold it in your head before you go under. Focus on it, even when you're about to tear someone limb from limb and cave their skull in on the cobbles. The man told him that over and over. On quiet days. On busy days. On days he beat the child-Syrus to the edge of sanity. Over and over. When you feel yourself slipping, find yourself a goal.

Syrus had learned how to aim himself before he'd learned to read. The same man who'd taught him to decipher letters on signs had picked him up out of the dirt, brought him to the basement he shared with four others, and made Syrus learn the hard way. Six months later, the man had kicked him back out on the street.

Now Syrus held on to the memory as he tried to learn the lesson over again. The screaming howl still battered at his defenses. His lungs still burned. But he could hear the rasp of the man's voice in his ears, reminding him of his goal. Get free. Kill the soldiers. Get free. Kill the soldiers.

It was all he could do to keep the mantra up. The thing inside him was free again. It wanted to kill everyone in sight. Paint the walls with their blood.

But slowly, bit by bit, the churning Frenzy started to fade. Something smelled like cooking meat. It got worse every time he heard the *smack-thud* of flesh hitting metal. A man roared at the top of his lungs, wordless and enraged. Quinn. Maybe.

Two female voices shrieked in Kuchen. His brain wasn't working well enough to make sense of it. His translator couldn't keep up either. He didn't need to know the words. They were pissed. Terrified, and all the angrier for it because they didn't know how to live with being scared.

They'd be dead soon. Bitches shouldn't waste their breath.

He managed to focus through the red haze long enough to get a picture of the room. Four of the soldiers were beating each other to a pulp, their armor scattered in pieces on the floor.

Another had hold of Iira. Her feet flailed and scrabbled for leverage as she twisted and screamed under him. Syrus couldn't tell if the puddle of blood she was lying in came from her or the soldier.

The blood under Oona was her own. A soldier, half naked and snarling like an animal, kept hitting her with a helmet, bashing at any part of her she couldn't protect. Which was pretty much everywhere but her stomach. Quinn looked like a pig left to burn over a fire. The second had run out of slack in the tethers, but he kept thrashing, trying to get at anyone and anything. Spittle flew from his mouth. He'd burst a blood vessel in one eye.

Nobody'd gone near Jossa. Why?

He didn't so much hear the snap as he felt it in his bones. Delfi was already making enough noise to wake the dead, trying to fight the soldier on top of her. Her scream when the bone went was three octaves higher than anything she'd managed so far. One of the soldiers was doing to her what could be expected of an enraged Fleet man with more testosterone in his veins than blood.

For a moment, all Syrus could feel was the agony of a shattered femur and a dislocated hip being forced further out of place as indescribable weight bore down on top of him.

He nearly lost his grip on the memory and its lesson. No. Focus. Hold to the target. Don't forget the target. Remember who you're going to kill and how. The monster has you by the balls and by the brain. It's using every hormone and nerve in your body to drive you mad. But so long as *you* know what your goal is, you can aim the rage. Once you've killed the thing you plan to kill, you can come out of it.

A new pain stabbed him in the groin as Delfi screamed again. Penetration. Fucking hell.

Fear blistered through his nerves, small points of agony that combined in his brain and stopped all function. Something came thundering on its heels, a feeling without label. Words like "star" and "corona" flashed through his mind and vanished just as fast. They didn't come close to describing it.

Syrus lost control of his lungs. He sucked in a breath, both real and metaphorical, as the monster reared up and bit the head off the man who'd taught him. Then it turned, all hissing corrosion and dripping acid, and swallowed him whole.

And for a long time, all he knew was the searing, baking heat of fury, underscored by the electric current of absolute terror. His mouth opened. And all the curses and profanities of a life stuck at the bottom of existence spilled out in one wordless roar.

>>><<<

It was the despair, creeping in around the edges, that finally damped the flames. But not before they burned his soul to a crisp. Every thought, every breath brought agony . Not physical. Emotional.

The pain of knowing it would not end. That nothing could stop it. No hope of escape. No way to survive this. There was no enduring. There was only the final release. It would come, but not soon enough. The agony would go on much longer than the body could handle it.

He knew that feeling. He'd felt it before. Inside and out. He'd taken it, stuffed it down, and walled it up with as much determination as he'd ever felt in his life. He'd thought he'd hidden it forever. It must have escaped when his willpower failed.

A mewling gasp of pain scraped inside his ears. The voice was quiet. Broken. A rasping mutter in He'la answered it. And he realized where the despair was coming from.

Him, yes. But it was answering someone else. Delfi or Jossa. He couldn't tell. The air against his skin was still superheated, the mental manifestation of all the pissed-as-fuck people turning him into some sort of half-baked roast. Burnt on one side, raw on the other. They should have stuck him on a spit and rotated it so he'd cook straight through.

Now he was hungry. Fuck it all. The fuck was wrong with him?

You're looking for any way to distract yourself from what you know you're going to do.

Growling, he stomped on the voice in his head. She was dead. She couldn't feel it.

The wet *slap slap* of skin on skin alternated with the gasps and hisses of a woman in pain. He forced his eyes to focus. Delfi. The first man to take her had ended up knifed in the neck. Probably by the man currently working her over. Two more soldiers were dead on the floor in the middle of the room. Blunt-force trauma by the look of it. By the door, a couple more still struggled. They'd shed almost all their armor.

Iira was still flat on her back under one soldier, growling like a pissed-off cat. She'd stopped kicking. Instead, it looked like she was trying to peel strips off the man's arms with her nails. She'd already managed a few long gouges, but the man ignored them as he pounded away. The emotions coming off her were faint compared to the rage filling the room.

Oona watched the pair with murder in her eyes. One eye was swollen shut. Her mouth was a bloody mess. Her knees looked like someone had inflated them. The bruises hadn't risen yet, but she'd go from her usual tan to black and purple soon enough.

Quinn... He'd managed to pull one of the tethers on his legs free of the deck. None of the men had payed attention to where they were while they fought. The man who'd been beating Oona with his helmet lay with one kneecap poking through his skin. Or maybe that was a leg bone. Not the worst thing that could have happened. He could have kept fighting. Except for the fact that Quinn was in the process of shoving his heel through the man's temple. An erection the size of the *Edde Belo* lay against the second's stomach, bobbing in time with the kicks.

All right then. Get loose before Quinn.

Another broken cry pulled his attention around and threatened to drown him all over again. The despair rose a little higher. Not much better than the anger, all things considered.

If Jossa knew what she was doing, Syrus would throw himself out an airlock right now. Her eyes were glazed, tears streaming down her face. Blood leaked around the edges of the cuffs and ran down her arms. Somehow she'd twisted around and gotten her feet braced against the wall, straining in the direction of her sousi. She hadn't dislocated her shoulder, but she was about to.

Jossa was the oven of fury and fear still burning him down to char. She was the despair too.

No wonder it felt so familiar.

Remember the target. Remember. Focus on the target. He'd be worse than useless if he gave in to the soul-crushing grief she was feeling. She was about to be the leftover half of a sousi pairing. She had no idea how to survive that. If she hadn't infected the whole base by now, anti-sai armor or not, what she would do when Delfi died under this sort of torture . . .

It would make her reaction when she'd woken up alone on the *Edde Belo* look like the work of a Numb. She was the unstable half of her bond. Anyone could see that. Fuck Delfi and her flash-bang fits of temper, camouflaging the truth.

How had Kizen figured all this out? Did he *know* what he'd set free when he turned the men on the Foreseer?

A scrap of conversation. What does it take to make one of those sai bend to their master's will?

If you can't condition them, you need to find a sai with something to lose and squeeze her until she breaks.

He'd handed this plan to Kizen with a fucking bow on it. Sure, the man might get Syrus's Helm out of it. If he didn't die. Which was likely, since the sai Kizen was trying to break was about to go insane and kill them all with her mind.

You could help her with that.

He told his conscience to shut up—not that she ever listened to him—and concentrated. He could do this. The soldiers had set the anchors wrong. They were over a seam in the wall, and that weakened the seal. If Kizen knew what it meant to be Savage, to be nehkeh, he would have made sure the men didn't do something that stupid. And if Syrus had been Fleet born, the bastard would have checked the anchors himself. The man had no idea how much like the Svis Konanuog Syrus really was.

Fucker.

He must have done some struggling of his own while he was lost in the inferno. His arms hurt like hell. They were about to hurt even worse.

Syrus braced his feet, sucked in as much of the free-floating anger as he could manage, and made sure the target sat in the front of his brain. Get free. Get. Free.

For heartbeat after heartbeat, nothing happened. Syrus snarled, blocking his ears to the pained whimpering at the other end of the room and the rhythmic slapping that went with it. The smell of burnt flesh filled his nose. He ignored it. His day had gone from a possible shitstorm to full-blown Hell. He was too pissed to let himself get distracted by something as simple as cooking meat. He wanted free, fuck it all. He'd spent too long chained up and helpless. Never again. He'd promised. Now look where he was. Stuck on a wall like a fucking museum exhibit.

Sons of bitches thought they could hold him, did they? Thought they'd leave him here to rot? Here's the freak from planetside. Thought he could escape his birth. Look how far he made it.

He'd show them. First he'd break free. Then he'd show them just how *much* he'd been holding back.

Snarling and growling, feeling blood trickle down his arm as the edges of the cuffs cut into his skin, he pulled. Get free. That was all he had to do. Get free. Then he could pound every single beating heart in this place down into silence, and he'd finally have some peace. He just had to get free so he could use his hands.

The left arm popped loose a fraction of a second before the right. Anchors, tether, cuffs and all. He lurched forward and almost landed face first on the dead soldier in front of him. Flailing, Syrus tried to catch himself, then lost his fight with gravity and tripped instead. His roll brought him up near Quinn's feet. Syrus jerked his head back. The second's bloody heel skidded along his cheekbone.

He punched at the foot, just on principle. Something cracked and Quinn grunted in pain, then kicked again.

Fix the target. Remember the target. What the fuck was the other part of that again? He was free now. That was what he'd wanted. He could kill anyone he wanted. Make them all shut up. Leave him alone.

Turn the emotions off and let him have a little quiet. Then go out and finish off the rest of the base.

You know that's not what peace is, the voice told him.

That sort of peace wasn't going to help now.

Moron. This is exactly what that sort of peace is for.

Fucking dead people talking in his head. Why couldn't she just shut the fuck up and let him think to himself?

Something hit him in the gut. He turned over to see that the two soldiers trying to beat each other to death had finally noticed him.

Oh yeah. That was the second thing. The soldiers. People he could kill. Legitimately. Gladly.

Maybe they'd have some credit bits on them and he could get paid for all these extra big words he'd been using today. In the meantime, his too-vocal conscience wasn't going to kick a fuss about him pounding their heads in.

He rolled out of the way of Quinn's second kick, grabbed a knife hilt off the body of the soldier he'd tripped over, and came up in a crouch near Oona. She screeched and kicked at him, still lost in Jossa's emotions. He ignored her. He knew his target now. This was going to be the most fun he'd had in a long time.

The first man was missing his breastplate and greaves. Bastard had also forgotten every bit of discipline he'd ever learned when it came to hand-to-hand fighting. Syrus ducked in under one flailing fist and drove his activated blade into the gap between the fifth and sixth ribs. Lung strike. Not a fast kill.

Jamming his knife into the side of the man's neck won him an artery. Much better.

The soldier hadn't even hit the floor before Syrus stepped and pivoted around him. The second man still had his gorget and breastplate. His helmet was gone, along with his belt.

Syrus didn't get a chance to wonder about the belt. It whipped at him, empty holsters and all. He let it hit him on the shoulder instead of in the face. He caught the soldier's other wrist before he could connect fist to flesh, then twisted. Cartilage crunched. Too far gone in the rage to notice his elbow had just popped free of the joint, the man struggled forward, snapping his teeth.

Syrus slid his knife home in the underside of the man's jaw, pinning the soldier's mouth closed.

Don't forget your target. Remember. Use the anger inside. Let it control you, yes. But unless you can stay focused on the goal, you just end up dead. Apparently, while he'd been swimming in lunacy, his conscience had decided that moral guidance was for the dogs.

This was why he hated having mental breakdowns. Someone was always telling him how to pull himself out of it.

Despair seeped through the anger as he remembered that he didn't actually *have* anyone to force him out of the berserker state. No one to silence the agony running rampant in his soul. Not anymore.

A whimper and a breath of pain brushed against his mind, almost too faint for him to notice.

Iira.

The last two soldiers.

Right. Targets.

They were easy enough to take care of. Too caught up in what they were doing to notice the danger. He hauled the first one off Iira, feeling ripples of lust shoot up his arm. It felt like poison. Fuck. The shit Jossa was putting out had blown his defenses wide open. Any other day, a jolt like that would have damn near made him cream his pants. But not now. The monster still rode him too hard.

He wrapped his arms around the man's head and shoulders, then twisted. A cracking crunch announced the breaking of the man's spine. Syrus threw the man back towards the pile of bodies in the middle of the room. Idiot. Should have listened to whoever told him to come in here with a helmet on. No chance it would have kept him from losing control, but he might have lasted a bit longer.

Iira lay on the floor, gasping quietly. Her face was misshapen. The man who'd gone after her must have decided she needed some softening up before he took her. Every time she tried to pull her legs together, she winced. But she wasn't crying. If she felt anything but impotent fury, he couldn't tell. There was something in her eyes though. Something . . .

He shook his arm free of the leftover lust and went to finish off the last soldier. This man *was* coming, driving deeper and deeper into Delfi as he all but convulsed. She was screaming again, the hoarse cry of overused vocal cords. Syrus could hear her. The sound was distant, echoing in his skull. But there. Real. He curled his lip. Watched his hand reach out to wrap itself around the man's neck. Motherfucking sonofabitch! The hell did he think he was doing?

The overlapping plates that made up the gorget of Fleet armor were designed to brace the spine. Protect it. They weren't designed to stop a pissed off Savage who'd just decided to rip someone's head off their shoulders.

He didn't quite manage it, but he did snap the spinal cord. That was good enough to cut the sick flow of emotion off at the source. The body landed on the pile with a dull thump.

Leaving him still pissed—and aroused in ways he'd never wanted. Before him lay a woman spread eagled and broken. Her hips were deformed, her thighs covered in blood. Her breath rattled as she lay there and stared at the ceiling. She'd stopped struggling.

Delfi, a woman he'd known barely a week. The biggest pain in his ass since—And she'd stopped fighting. If he hadn't seen her ribs move, hadn't felt the agony rising off her like a cloud, he would have thought she was dead. From the way she breathed and the look of her abdomen, she wasn't going to be among the living for much longer.

"No. No, please. Leave her alone."

The words weren't spoken above a whisper. He managed to turn his head from the ruin at his feet. Jossa was still trying to pull free of the wall. Her feet scrabbled on the deck, slipping in the blood dripping from her arms. The tethers didn't have any slack left. Her hands were pinned to the wall.

"No," she said again, voice cracking. "Please don't."

He walked over and crouched in front of her. She didn't even look at him. She was focused on Delfi. On her sousi, battered and dying not five feet away. So close and so far.

What would his target be when the stable one died and he was left locked in a room with this one? Kizen? He could go for Kizen. Given her range, he'd still have a shitstorm of emotion to fuel him when he found the man. Bastard. Fucking piece of shit. He'd find him, all right. He'd show him just how stupid it was to—

The voice in his head laughed her manic laugh. *To what?* she asked. *Leave an ignition source near a compressed container of combustible gas? What do you think the Fleet's made of? Think these men weren't expendable? Why didn't they set up surveillance? This's gone to Hell in a handbasket; you'd think someone would do something about it before it got so bad.*

Delfi coughed and whimpered. Jossa sobbed and lurched against her tethers. Syrus reached out and caught her jaw without thinking, forcing her head around so he could see her face. Blind panic mixed with fury and turned to a sort of liquid explosive. His arm, already burning, nearly charred itself to the bone. She pulled against him, eyes rolling like a panicked animal. "Del," she whispered. "Del, no."

Here was something beyond despair. She knew what was coming. She could feel it. The bond would break and she'd be left alone. Half a soul, half alive. Forever a wanderer. Bereft.

At least that was what all the stories said.

He should just kill her now. Put her out of her misery. Do it before Delfi died, so that when the Foreseer breathed her last, Jossa wouldn't turn him back into a raging maniac. He had his mind for now, although the half-formed shields he'd managed to throw up wouldn't hold very long when he was skin-to-skin like this. Kill Jossa.

Get her out of his head for good and ever. Purge himself of the voices she'd resurrected. Kill Delfi, so she wouldn't keep struggling along with the one lung she had left. Then go find Kizen and smear his brains all over the inside of a medunit.

You know better than that. You know how to fix this.

I'd have to set up a link, he told his conscience. *It's not like sex. That's easy. I don't even know if it will work. I don't have time anyway.*

Then remember.

Fucking voice. He made it out of this alive, he was stuffing her back down so he'd never have to hear from her again. He'd enjoyed the peace and quiet since he'd took up the Helm of Warlord.

No you didn't. You missed me. You've enjoyed having me nag you these past few weeks.

Cool hands reached into his soul and pulled out one of his first good memories. *Now, like this, but a little different. You know. I showed you.*

THIRTY-FOUR -- JOSSA

Contrary to what the commoners think, peace is not the absence of troubles. It's knowing you have shelter in the storms that life brings. That, my dear, is the essence of the bond.
Never forget.
    -Chataf Kuchru lis Chuis isk Fuerrus, to Delfi

When the peace first touched her, Jossa thought Delfi had come back. It felt right. So right. Like the bond at its strongest, when everything just dropped into place. She reached for it, so relieved that she wasn't even worried about the fact that the bond wouldn't let her speak to Del in its current condition. What she found was like a slap in the face.

Delfi still hurt. Was still lost in agony and fear. The stake holding Jossa's mind to her sousi's had vanished. Her sister couldn't even tell what was real and what she imagined. There was no way in the universe she could have done anything for Jossa. What in the name of—

Frustration. Mixed with that eerie calm, like a petrol slick on water. A sense of resignation, as if the owner half expected his efforts to be ignored. And then another push of cool water along her nerves, the raw heat of anger and the burn of fear dissipating beneath the wave.

Someone had their hands on her. She nearly screamed when she realized. She smelled sweat and the musk of man and almost lost her stomach.

"Don't you start that again. Can't keep this up forever."

She froze mid-thrash. She knew that voice.

Another push along her veins. He'd worked himself under her somehow. Seated himself cross legged and arranged her across his lap so she was half facing him. She looked down on reflex. The front of his pants still bulged, but she couldn't feel anything like desire from him.

"Now who's got the sick mind?"

Humor, bitter and sharp. It was gone as fast as it came, lost in the cool waters. His breath was warm on her neck as he hooked his chin over her shoulder. "Hold still dammit."

"What?" What was this feeling? How could it be?

He stopped moving for a second. She almost thought something moved under the incredible calm. Something familiar. Had she felt this from him before? Another wave of peace and certainty swamped her, and the feeling of *other* was gone.

"Gotta get these off you." One huge hand wrapped around her wrist. She gasped in pain. "Your own fault," he told her. "Going batshit like that."

"Batshit," she whispered. She wasn't sure if she was asking a question or not.

He stilled for a moment. "Yeah. Don't ask me where it came from. I've got too many languages up in here." He knocked his forehead against her temple, gently, and went back to whatever he was doing with the cuff. "Be glad I'm managing words at all. I could be beating the shit out of you." Anger bubbled up and dissolved before she fully registered its existence.

She reached for the bond. For Del. Got pain and labored breathing. Agony in every fiber of her being. A sob stuck in her throat and she bit down on the shoulder in front of her to keep from screaming.

"Fucking hell, woman." The warlord went rigid under her. "Stay the fuck out of her head, will you? Barely holding you together as it is."

Something about that was all wrong. She couldn't think of what. All she could feel was the newest wave of sanity coming to wash away the pain. No. Not wash it away. It wasn't gone. It was... manageable. It was—

Syrus let go of her arm and she lost the thought. New pain, physical pain, tore up her shoulder and into her neck. She whimpered and leaned in the direction of the still-tethered wrist, resisting the urge to curl into a ball. There was a muscled wall of torso in the way of the maneuver. A muscled wall of torso that belonged to a man who had bullied and threatened and stomped all over her existence. Who'd saved her from a slow death and delivered her into torture instead.

A man who was picking the locks on her shackles and keeping her from losing her mind all over again. Almost like Delfi could. Almost like the bond.

Her head shot up so fast she nearly fell over. She would have if he hadn't caught her around the shoulders and hauled her back upright. "What the hell," he growled, irritation threatening to burn up all the good he'd done. "Stop moving. We don't have much ti—"

"Sai." She leaned back so she could look him in the eyes. "You're sai."

The dam he'd made for her vanished. Pain, despair, and every other emotion permeating the air around them came flooding in. He stared at her, muscles working in his jaw, pupils blown and skin an ashen brown. He was about to lose his grip on her shoulders. She clutched at him with her free hand as she overbalanced.

Hitching herself upright, she took his jaw in her palm. Oddly, he wasn't giving off any emotions at all. Like a stunned ox. Which was a fairly apt description, all things considered. "Deny it," she told him, putting as much command into the words as she could manage. Her voice cracked. Her throat hurt. She ignored the pain. She had to do this before she lost herself again. Delfi was hurting too badly and everyone else was still too angry for him to be able to drag her back to sanity a second time. "Or help me."

Another moment passed. He breathed under her, a sharp staccato of panic. His fingers on her shoulder clenched and loosened in short little spasms. She still didn't Feel anything from him. Not anger, not fear. Nothing. On the floor nearby, Delfi hitched another breath and whimpered quietly. Agony lanced through Jossa's chest. She convulsed, dropping her hand from Syrus's face to clutch at her heart.

Not long now. Oh, Del. This wasn't how it was supposed to end. How long would she last once her sousi was gone? Would Syrus be able to put her down before she went completely crazy? Could he even try to help her? To hold her sanity to her body? Probably not. It wasn't instinctual for him. That he had managed it to begin with was a miracle. Or torture.

Her mind was wandering. Again. Ancestors, they should have never put her in storage to begin with, all those years ago. Should have dealt with her then. She just kept breaking things. How many had she tainted? How much of this damage was irreparable? How many of the people in this room would keep their psyches intact, assuming the warlord didn't kill them all once she snapped. What about Delfi? Would this be the time Jossa ruined her for good?

"Dunno what you're talking about." Syrus fisted one hand in her hair and pulled her head back. It was such a contrast to the waterfall of sanity hitting her in the face that she gasped and let him twist her around. One rough thumb, tacky with blood, wiped at her cheek. "We get you loose, get her to a medunit quick enough, she might have a chance. Hold on to this feeling." Another rush of calm. "Do what you can to project it."

Jossa stared at him.

He shook his head and went back to working on the hand that was still tethered to the wall. "Never mind. Just sit still."

Leaning her forehead against his collarbone, she sat. Blocked her ears to the sounds that the second was still making and concentrated on her breathing instead. For now, she had her sanity. It would have to be enough.

>>><<<

Jossa rubbed her wrists as she leaned against the wall and watched Syrus check Delfi over. Under the outpouring of calm the warlord kept shoving her way, she could feel her sister's pain. It was a distant thing, not the sharp agony it had been. Jossa tried to ignore it.

"Brace yourself," he said. Jossa frowned. Why was he telling Del to—

He laid his hand on Delfi's neck, and the sudden slack in the false bond he had created was staggering. Jossa clawed for the remnants, pulled them back together, and pushed them out again. Along the other wall, Iira's and Oona's quiet gasps eased.

The second continued with whatever he was doing to the corpse at his feet. Jossa looked hard at Syrus rather than focus on the lunatic and his toy.

The warlord knelt over Del, one ear to her chest. Jossa opened her mouth to ask him what he was doing. He got up, took the hilt of a spacer's blade from the corpse next to her sister and started twisting the dial. A long, thin section of the metal grew from the working end. When Syrus set the knife blade over Del's ribs and got ready to push it in, Jossa nearly fell on her face trying to get the thing out of his hands. He caught her one handed. "Calm the fuck down," he said once she was steady again.

Jossa opened her mouth to yell and got blasted with another wave of sanity. Syrus ignored her and went back to Del.

"Not there," someone said. Jossa paused in the middle of bringing her fist down on the warlord's head and turned to stare. Iira. Half sitting, half slumped against the wall, one eye swelling shut and the other watching them from behind her tangled hair. "'Tween second and third. Close to third. Clav—" The woman coughed. "Clavicle."

Syrus looked at her, shifted his fingers on Delfi's ribs, moved the knife, and pushed it in before Jossa could do more than yelp a protest.

Del tried to shriek, but it came out as a gasp. Jossa yelped and lurched forward, nearly losing her grip on the bubble of sanity. "Calm down," Syrus said. "You want her lung reinflated or not?" He leaned over and did something with the hilt. Delfi gasped, a full breath this time.

The warlord sat back on his heels. "Get Iira and Oona loose. We're going to find the infirmary."

Jossa stared at him, then at the gray tube sticking out of her sister's chest. The peace still covered her, and by extension, the others. That incredible calm he'd managed to dredge out of somewhere. But what if it vanished? What if she got too far away from him and lost the feeling?

"Just do it." His voice was tight. But he didn't let go of the calm. "Sooner before later."

She obeyed. One step. Two. The relief weakened, but remained. Enough to keep her balanced. So long as she didn't touch either of the women directly. She could feel them through the barrier Syrus held between her and the world. Fleet. Angry. Right down to the core of their being. And she'd only managed to make them worse. Beautiful.

"And stop thinking about it."

Apparently he'd decided that since she knew what he was, he had the right to get even more dictatorial. Bastard.

Del shifted in the back of her mind at that, but she was too occupied with breathing to make any comment. Jossa could have wept. Just for the feeling of her sousi along the bond. Syrus growled again, his eyes narrow and the muscles on his jaw working. She sent Del a swift caress to the cheek along the bond and then moved around Iira to get to the anchors. Time enough to break down later. Right now she had to try to stay calm. "Who had the key?" she asked the woman as she examined the locking mechanism. At least it wasn't a combination dial.

The medic nodded in the direction of her husband and the dead soldier at his feet. "He did."

Jossa swallowed as she met the maddened gaze of the captive second as he pulled and thrashed against the tethers. Somehow he'd gotten his other leg loose. He was trying to stand, but his feet kept slipping in the red mess that was the soldier's skull. "Please tell me you don't mean the second."

The other woman, Oona, snorted. The second lurched and snarled, just in case she didn't understand that he was a threat. Iira shook her head. "Bad humor. No. The soldier." She jerked her chin at the body. "Him."

"Syrus," Jossa called over her shoulder, keeping her voice low. "Can you leave Delfi a moment?"

Pain trickled through the bond as the warlord did... something to her sousi. Then he was standing next to her. "Names now. That's new."

"You're in a horribly good mood," she replied. "That soldier had the key for the anchors. And probably the cuffs." She looked at her wrists, surprised. "How did you?"

"You think Delfi's the only one who knows how to break those things open?"

She looked at his wrists as he eased around Iira and her companion and crouched near the body of the soldier. The cuff and anchors were still attached.

"I didn't have time to go hunting for keys. Savage, remember? We're freaks of nature." He didn't look at her, but white teeth flashed in a grin. Something like acid dripped past the calm. It was gone before she could identify it. Jossa frowned.

The second yanked at his arms and kicked out, snarling and snapping. Syrus hooked the dead soldier's belt and pulled the impromptu footstool closer, away from his underling. Jossa eyed the second's remaining anchors and prayed the Fleet didn't have any more men who were the equal of a nehkeh.

>>><<<

The second didn't get any more limbs free before Syrus untethered Delfi and the two Fleet women. Although it wasn't for lack of trying.

Jossa looked at the gun holstered on the belt of the dead soldier at her feet. Could she move fast enough to grab it if things spun out of control again?

While the second snarled and snapped and tugged on his restraints, the rest of them waited in various stages of pain as Syrus worked on getting them out of the room. He tapped at the control panel for the door, pried out the housing around the lock with another stolen knife, ripped out a handful of wires, and growled.

His frustration made the serenity of the false bond waver. Jossa clutched at it with both hands. As if he'd heard her mentally telling him to control himself, he sighed, put his shoulder to the door, and pushed. It slid open a couple inches.

Another minute or so and he had it all the way open. "Either you got everyone to kill each other," he said to Jossa, poking his head through the gap. "Or he emptied the base. We're clear." He ducked around the edge of the door and leaned down. "Guess he wasn't kidding about testing the medunits."

"What?" Jossa was still clinging to the peace of the bond he was generating. It was stronger now. Steadier. The more she projected, the easier it was for him to strengthen it. But her control wavered every time he let one of his other emotions surface for a moment. She was walking a piece of razor wire over a ravine, praying she'd make it to the other side before it sliced her feet to ribbons.

"You say that a lot, you know." He came back in the room and tamped down on the irritation without being asked. He had a folded piece of metal tucked under one arm. "Oona, how banged up are you?"

Oona glared at him, then lurched out of the way when her husband lashed out at her with a heel. "Not so bad," she said through gritted teeth. Jossa bit her lip. The woman was covered in blood and minced as she walked.

A look at Iira told her that whatever the captain's condition, the med-tech was even worse off.

"Good." He said to Oona. "You're helping." Syrus took the piece of metal, unfolded it, and set a stretcher down on the floor next to Delfi. "Take her feet. Jossa, stay put." How he'd seen her getting ready to help, she didn't know, but she could feel his attention. "You touch her and we're all fucked."

She opened her mouth to snap. At least Delfi knew when it was her sousi and not someone *else* about to lay hands on her. He'd stabbed her in the chest with a needle made of living metal. What did he think would happen when *he* touched Del?

The warlord swiveled on the balls of his feet and glared at her. Jossa gulped, and her grip on the peace faltered. He looked like a mad thing, all bloody and feral, his pupils blown and the whites of his eyes so bright against his skin. Right. No mentioning the fact that he was sai.

He turned back to Del. "I'm not interested in losing any teeth," he told her. "You fight me and I'll leave you here to die. Got that?"

Delfi turned over in Jossa's mind, but she didn't try to speak. She was in too much pain. Too full of anger and fear. Syrus was right. Jossa would do more harm than good if she touched her sister. Nothing left for now but to cling to that all-encompassing grace. It was the only thing that would keep them all sane until they could get away from this room.

Something niggled at her. Something about hows and whys. Delfi gasped again and Jossa felt the thought slip away. She could worry about all that later. Right now she had to concentrate on her task. Transmuting what Syrus gave her into the true peace of a sai bond.

She didn't know how well she was doing though. She hadn't been on the giving end of this very often.

It must have been good enough, because even though Del whimpered when the warlord and Oona crouched down to ease the stretcher under her shivering body, she didn't struggle. Jossa stepped aside to let them pass through the door and into the corridor, and she found her eyes catching on the dead soldier's gun again.

The second snarled and lunged against his bonds as Iira limped out after the others. The grav tethers on his shackles hummed as they gave slightly, then pulled him back. Monstrous rage boiled out of him to batter at the bubble of peace Jossa clung to with everything she could manage. The second lurched forward again, and again the tethers yanked him back.

But now he had his feet under him. He'd managed to tuck himself into a sort of ball as he landed. He worked first one foot under his hips, then the other. Now he had leverage.

The fear welling within her was Jossa's alone. She crouched and grabbed blindly as the man made another desperate attempt to free himself. The *hummmm-thunk* of the grav bonds snapping him back to the wall was accompanied by a slight metal crunch. Voices shouted somewhere nearby, but she ignored them. She had the gun now. Oh please, oh please, don't let it have some sort of safety.

She didn't get to find out. One second she was rising from her crouch near the dead soldier, clinging to the last shreds of the false bond as she brought the muzzle to bear on the lunatic in front of her, the next she found herself yanked backwards and around as something hard struck her across the face.

Jossa cried out as the fresh surge of heat drove its way through her jawbone. She lost the gun and heard it clatter across the floor. Someone shouted at her in a different language; her translator couldn't work fast enough to keep up with it.

"The hell you doing?" Syrus snarled as he caught her and pulled her around to face him. "We don't have time for this shit."

Oona was right behind him. She was the source of the shouting. Something about fucking outFleet bitches and what was going to happen to Jossa if she tried that again.

Jossa opened her mouth to yell back. How stupid was this bitch anyway? Didn't she realize what would happen if her husband got loose?

The peace of the bond clamped over her mind and smothered the words before they became actuality. Jossa gasped for breath and felt her head wobble on her neck. What? What had just—

"I can't hold this against them." The warlord leaned down to whisper the warning in her ear. "Not against what they'll do if you kill him." The rumble of his voice was almost comforting. Jossa let it sink into her bones as she basked in the restoration of the false bond. "Think, woman. We're all free. What do you think will happen if either one of us loses our shit?"

She could feel his frustration straining at the leash as he straightened and tipped her face up to his. There was something in his eyes. Something she couldn't identify, but knew anyway. He wasn't scowling. Or snarling. Or wearing any of his usual expressions. His face was calm. Flat. The same way Rui used to get when a deal went bad and he didn't want to show it.

The warlord rubbed a thumb lightly along her sore jaw. "I don't rape when I lose my mind," he said after a moment. "Ain't the way I'm wired." Jossa flinched as he took her chin in his fingers and shook her slightly. "I kill people and play in the blood. You got that?" He stepped aside, pulling her face around so she could see Delfi lying on the stretcher and panting in pain.

Jossa took a deep breath. She got it. She'd been stupid to think they were safe. So stupid.

The warlord seemed to understand. He let go of her chin. Jossa reached with her mental hands for the false bond and did her best to shelter the others with it.

It was hard. Almost harder than it had been while she was chained to the wall. Somehow it was easier to reach for grace when she knew it was the only thing saving her from imminent death. When the knife was off her neck, she slipped into complacency far too easily.

Once she was sure of her grip on the Feeling, she nodded at Syrus. He nodded back and turned to speak quietly to Oona. She had to stop making death threats so she could listen to him. After another moment, she hissed something under her breath, turned on her heel, and limped out to the hall to stand next to Iira.

Syrus waved Jossa after her, then followed them out. They all waited as he forced the door to the room shut again. Then he and Oona gathered up Delfi's stretcher and they all limped off down the hall.

It wasn't far, but it was far enough. Syrus closed every door he found behind them. Probably to create as much of a barrier as possible between the second in his prison and any survivors.

Lucky for them, there were a lot of doors. Imperials didn't build on curved lines like the Fleet. The halls were straight, but they were mazelike on purpose. Each crossing could be closed off to block invaders and give soldiers time to fight in sections if needed. Nobody could storm the place without heavy losses.

Unfortunately for the men and women who'd staffed this place, the air ducts hadn't had as many failsafes. Bodies lay here and there, faces still. Suffocated. Stinking, too, of loosed bowels and the other indignities of death. Some had breathers on. It hadn't saved them. The air had been too tainted.

She breathed through her mouth and closed her eyes to the condition of the few women. Wondering how long the five of them had been raving in that room would only make it worse. She couldn't think about that. Instead, she grabbed the peace of the false bond and tried to mainline it to her heart. It worked, for all of a minute.

The other warlord must have moved most of his people out once they'd taken the base. Syrus had been right about her range though. And the ineffectiveness of their armor. The few Fleet soldiers they saw were dead. Torn apart with the same ferocity as the ones in the room where she and the others had been held. Jossa stared at the crumpled and broken bodies. Ancestors' Seed, she had hoped she'd never see this again. And here she was... again.

"Don't look," Syrus said as his emotions wavered, leeching anger like lava into the waters. "Seriously. Don't fuck this up."

She stared at his feet in front of her and concentrated on listening to Delfi's breathing. It was better. Somewhat. Not as labored. But she still needed a medunit. And her mind was still twisted in on itself. The only thing Jossa could parse from the morass of her sister's head was pain. Every ripple of agony echoed from her sister's body to her own.

The two Fleet women had locked themselves down somehow. They were just echoes in her head. Slightly out of step with Delfi and herself. Completely out of sync with Syrus. But still there. Still injured. Still angry.

Juggling them all plus the false bond turned walking into a new form of torture. She'd thought losing her virginity hurt. Having to give herself to the fuerrus. What she'd done to keep herself and Del alive during that first year of freedom. She'd thought *that* was bad. Giving herself to Syrus had been a betrayal of everything she'd tried to build with Rui. But this. What had been done to Delfi. What she'd done to them all. This was desecration.

"And stop thinking. Fuck, woman."

She stared at his heels and walked. And walked. Until she ran right into his shoulder. Startled, she staggered back and rubbed her nose. Questions bubbled inside her. She squashed them. Asking him "What?" again wouldn't help matters.

"You stay here." He steadied her with one hand on her shoulder. "All of you."

She was still getting her bearings when he moved away. There was a red insignia on the wall nearby, two short bars crossed in the middle. The origins of the symbol had been lost in time. Now it just meant "infirmary." Good. Now, all they needed to do was get inside. Judging by the tangle of Fleet armor and the trail of blood leading down the hall, whatever guards had been stationed here were dead. So why was he being cautious?

The door slid open. A searing mix of anger, pain, and lust slapped her in the face and clogged her lungs. Every nerve leapt to attention. Her body tried to simultaneously melt and get ready for battle. Jossa slumped against the wall behind her, clawing for sanity. Delfi's, Syrus's—even her own would do if she could manage it. She was going to send them all into an orgy if she didn't manage to balance herself out again.

The door slid shut behind the warlord. The emotions vanished, leaving only the residual anger of the Fleet women and Delfi's pained breathing. Right. Shielding plates. Of course an infirmary would be shielded. The Karukap trained its people to ward themselves against sai. But if a person was injured, their defenses were more likely to fall.

Now she just had to hold herself together until—until what? Until Delfi or the warlord could do it for her? Again?

"How are you feeling?" Iira had come to stand next to her. "Any hurts besides," she gestured at Jossa's wrists.

"Not so bad as you or Del," Jossa told her. "It's all inside." She tapped a finger to her breastbone. "I'll live."

Iira opened her mouth to say something else, but the door to the infirmary slid open again. Syrus stood there. His shirt was gone; his pants were torn. He bled from a dozen fresh wounds. In one hand, he held a knife, its blade long and wide. From the other hand dangled the head of Warlord Kizen, snarling in death as he had in life.

The soft *pat pat pat* of blood dripping on the floor was the only sound in the corridor. The pyroclastic flow of rage that had filled the room behind him was gone. Only the Savage remained. "Come on then," Syrus said as he met her eyes. The cool calm filled the air between them, shaky, but undeniably there. "Let's get this shit over with."

Thirty-Five -- Syrus

You cannot collar the soul. Not once it's seen its way to freedom.
    -proverb of the Edge Planets

Eventually, Syrus looked up and realized Jossa was gone. Looking over at the other units in use, he saw that Iira hadn't moved. She'd been perched on the edge of that same stool ever since they'd closed the lid on Oona, doing a very good impression of a statue. A bloody, battered statue.

Oona and even Jossa had tried to talk her into getting into a unit right away, but the woman refused. She was the Chief Med-Tech of the *Edde Belo*, flagship of the Turan of the Kuchen Fleet, and by Strength and Will, she'd make sure her co-wife was up and walking before she'd let them stuff her in a box herself.

Syrus hadn't bothered arguing. Del's breathing was too shallow and her heart rate too fast. He didn't know if Jossa thought of it, but the possibility of internal organ damage hung over the young woman just as certainly as her collapsed lungs. And far more dangerously. Jossa *seemed* to be holding her own fairly well. He didn't want to send her back over the edge by mentioning the danger, so rather than bring it up, he'd let her distract herself by arguing with Iira.

Syrus sighed. If he hadn't noticed an unstable Feel wander out of one of the most heavily shielded rooms in the base, Iira probably hadn't even batted an eye.

He looked over at the third unit. It had at least another two hours on the chrono. The concubine bitch, Mivi, hadn't had much to say for herself after he'd killed Kizen. Partly because the man had broken her jaw in three places. But she'd also been looking for more, even through her half-conscious stupor. Whoever tried to condition her before she came to the Fleet, they'd fucked her over but good.

Now that he thought about it, he could see how this had happened. He hadn't given her nearly enough of what she wanted. She wouldn't have been able resist Kizen. And Syrus'd handed her right over to the fucker.

He kicked the mental door shut on the memory of the walls coated in blood. It was almost a guarantee that he'd be going back to empty rooms. He'd be surprised if Jossa and Delfi came quietly. Or agreed to stay put once he got them there.

Come on, what'll you do? Drag them back in shackles? Is that really what you want to be?

Arguing with the voice in his head was stupid. And a losing battle.

All this assumed he had a Fleet to go back to. So far, they were holding off. Kizen hadn't expected anyone but Quinn to get loose. He might have even had a tech tamper with the anchors of the second's grav tethers, weakening the seal. From what the man said before Syrus severed his spinal column, Quinn was supposed to be turning them all into bloody mush right about now.

Syrus looked at the display screen propped up on Iira's medunit. It showed the room they'd left. It looked very different now. At some point, his second had managed to pull the last grav tethers free of the wall. And, true to Kizen's plan, he was turning the other occupants of the room to bloody mush.

Syrus decided that he never, ever, wanted to know how Quinn and Iira and Oona managed to keep their weird idea of marriage going. Although what was happening in that room certainly explained why Quinn had been so upset over the waste of a dead body. And Iira's promise to Mivi just before she prodded the concubine's broken bits back inside her medunit and closed the lid on her. There were great things in store for the shattered woman. She just wouldn't enjoy them for long.

He should have let Jossa take her shot. Hell, he should have done it himself. Maybe he would have been able to hold out against the emotions the man gave off. Maybe he even would have been able to use them to channel his own blowup.

Maybe, maybe, maybe. Why don't you find a gun and take care of him right now?

Why don't I just seal off the room and suffocate the bastard? he replied. *Then Iira will try to gut me and I'll have to kill her. While I'm at it, I might as well set Oona's medunit to "cremate" and be done with it. It gets me fuck nowhere as far as keeping the Fleet running. Now. Keep your opinions to yourself, would you?*

She went quiet.

If it came to that, he could take care of Quinn later. There were four blast-sealed doors locked to Syrus's genetic code between them and the lunatic, and nobody was going anywhere. Nobody but Jossa. Who the fuck knew what she was up to. She could be starting a self-destruct sequence somewhere. In fact, she probably was.

Syrus snagged a spare slate from one of the counters along the wall and set its chrono to match the timer on Delfi's medunit. Then he headed out. He stopped at the door, thought about letting Iira know he was going for a walk, then shrugged and kept going. She'd notice. Or she wouldn't.

For safety's sake, he logged in to the controls in the hall. A swipe of one bloody thumb gave him basic access. Once the door slid shut behind him, the women were locked in. Quinn wouldn't make it into the infirmary if he decided to go for a walk. They couldn't go set him loose, either. Win win.

Loose ends taken care of, he went hunting.

The Fleet hadn't sucked all the Seed out of the air vents when they'd boarded the base. Just enough to make it breathable for a baseline conscript with the innock in his system. That was plenty enough for Syrus to manage. Not run a marathon, maybe, but who the hell wanted to do that?

When he finally found Jossa, he cursed himself for an idiot. And cursed the voice inside that told him he should have known. Of course he should have known. What he didn't know, but wanted to, was how to stuff the voice back in the hole and *keep* her there. With his luck, he couldn't. Fuck.

He stood in the door and looked at her, wondering how someone so battered could have so much dignity. Jossa had turned her chair to face him. She sat in it like some sort of queen out of legend. If queens were naked, bruised, with tangled hair, bloodshot eyes, and bloody wrists. The lights of the control board screens painted her skin with blues and greens. Her eyes were eerie in the shadows that hid most of her face.

Syrus slammed his shields back up, hoping she hadn't gotten much of a read on him. The room was quiet, except for the whir of processors and fans. Whatever she felt, she had a strong enough hold on herself to keep it contained. Although not to keep herself from trembling once a minute or so. He thought he felt something like bravado shimmer through the air.

"Trusting," he said after a few minutes. "Leaving Del up there with me and Iira."

She snorted, and transformed from the statue of a slave queen into a real person. It was a shaky snort, but it was a sign of life. "She's locked in a medunit. Somehow I doubt you're desperate enough to pry the thing open and violate her in the state she's in."

He decided not to tell her that Quinn had gotten free of his shackles. The man was too big to fit in any of the maintenance shafts.

"Thought all this would have locked down," he said.

"It did." She held up a piece of cloth in one hand. Syrus realized it was a scrap of his shirt. When had she gotten hold of that? "Strange thing about the Empire. It's obsessed with bloodlines."

Something in one of the machines growled quietly. Humor trickled through the air, canceling out his irritation. He realized the noise came from him, not the computers. Muttering curses in his head, he leaned against the doorway and crossed his arms. "You say that like it's news."

"Ah. He reminds me of the things he knows. Things that everybody knows." The dried blood on her wrists flaked off as she gripped the armrests of her seat and leaned forward. She was more fragile than she let on. Her knuckles were white on the armrests. Her voice had a brittle edge. "He doesn't explain how he knows things he *shouldn't*."

He ignored the mocking laugh bouncing around his brain. The last thing he needed was to get all sentimental and do something stupid. Like give Jossa his life story. Or a reason to doubt his sanity.

She watched him, eyes narrowed and breathing almost normal. As if pretending she *wasn't* naked and bruised. As if she had every right to sit there and demand answers. Maybe she was trying to convince herself that she did. Ha.

There was something off about her though. Something different than it had been, under the nerves she was doing shit all to hide.

After a second, he realized the humor leaking out of her was really the bravado from earlier, transmuted slightly. It hit as a bubbly cascade, like the fermented fruit drinks he'd stolen as a kid. Was she *trying* to get him drunk? Or did she even realize what was happening? Either way, he could wait her out. She was the one who had a sousi to get back to, not him.

Of course, when Delfi emerged from the medunit and found Jossa gone, she'd come to get her sister. Then they'd have one of those mental discussions and figure out the best way to fuck up the rest of his day. Delfi would eventually try to attack him, which would mean he'd have to put her back in the medunit. Which would waste even *more* time. And then someone up in the Fleet would get impatient and blow them all to bits.

The odd drunk feeling tickled, damn it all. She wasn't even *trying* to hide it anymore.

Fine. If that was the way she wanted to play things.

Syrus dropped into the chair across from her and stretched his legs out in front of him, crossing his ankles. "This is all you get," he warned her. "No questions."

She smiled slightly, as if she knew something he didn't. Her hands eased a bit on the armrests and she sat back. Syrus decided he liked her better when she was off balance and panicky. Wherever she'd found this new personality, it could only mean trouble.

Syrus took a breath and exhaled slowly. Get the hard stuff out of the way fast, like ripping off synthskin that bonded wrong. "They told you about Rissa, yeah?" The women in his quarters were smart enough not to run their mouths where he could hear, but no way they'd kept that secret.

She nodded. "A little."

He folded his hands and propped his elbows on the armrest of the chair. "Rissa found me on the streets. She had sai." Which was a bit like saying a star put out light and heat. She'd had so much talent they'd had to stick her in cold storage to keep her from following him after he left.

"Her family ran the system. She realized what I had. Talked me into coming home with her." And hadn't that been a poor man's drama, when her sire found out she'd brought the trash home, covered in blood and feral as a stray dog. "She had a sousi. Fresh bonded. Neither of them could take care of themselves. Protect themselves. Things were going sour in the quadrant and her sire liked to play politics. You know what they say about Savages?"

"Bring one into your house and you bring ruin unto your family," Jossa said quietly.

Syrus clamped down on his shields again and sighed. "She wouldn't let me go. Only way he let me stay was if I let them do a contract binding. Lifetime indenture."

He could see the understanding dawn. "Oh."

For a moment he debated what else to say. In his head, Rissa was going nuts, but she'd been dead for years now. You couldn't read emotions off a figment of your imagination. He wished he could claw her out of his brain, since she refused to go back in the hole where he'd been keeping her. But taking a knife to his skull would be crazy. Crazier than sitting here having a civil conversation with a woman who'd just watched her sister get raped and was about to go back to being a sex toy. But not as crazy as what Rissa wanted him to say.

What happened in this room could stay in this room, he decided. He didn't have to let it affect him.

Liar, Rissa snarled at him. *You are a horrible liar.*

He ignored her. The drunken mix of humor and courage that Jossa had been putting out was starting to mutate into the pop-fizz of frustration.

"I figured out that if I kept from killing everyone in sight," Syrus said, "I'd get three meals a day and a clean place to sleep. Better, Rissa and her sousi were teaching me how to tell what feelings were mine and what came from other people." He met Jossa's eyes. "And how to mimic what the bond felt like. More I learned . . ." He shrugged. "Less likely I was to kill someone to make it stop."

Her hands on the armrests clenched and she looked away. Ok. Whatever that meant. She'd locked her shields up tight again. Even the bravado was gone. Reflexively, he reached for it, like a drunk who'd just lost the wall keeping him up. Syrus gritted his teeth and glared at Rissa's mental image as she laughed at him.

But Jossa didn't say anything or ask him to explain, so she probably knew what "make it stop" was all about.

"Some point, Rissa's sire decided I was old enough to be a threat. I wasn't a pet anymore." Syrus let his shields slip to show her what he'd thought of *that.* "Her sousi liked me fine. Probably wouldn't have gotten in my way if I'd decided fucking Rissa was the thing to do. Leastwise, that's what her sire thought. So he sold me to the Karukap."

Jossa opened her mouth, got half a syllable out, and clamped her teeth together. Yeah, that's right. No questions. His sharing mood only went so far.

Syrus waited to be sure she wasn't going to try again, then leaned forward. "They stuck me in the Uvlaku."

Understanding mixed with awe, coloring the air around her, and her eyes went wide. "Ghost."

He nodded.

She didn't say anything for a minute or so. He looked at the chrono on the console and tried not to think of how his so-called career had ended. Tried not to remember how he'd come to be in the Fleet.

A battered body, barely recognizable as human. He'd missed her by hours. If he hadn't wasted time on stealth, she might have had a chance. He could still hear her screams. Remember her eyes. Brander avoided hitting her in the face. Bastard had known someone was coming for her.

You tried, he told himself. You tried, fuck it all.

Jossa watched him. She'd pulled her shields back up. All the way this time. No hints. No teasing. No guidance. He tried to stuff the emotions back down, but they churned and boiled under the surface. The pain was almost physical. He'd never told anyone this much about his life. Not all at once. And he'd never mentioned it once he'd boarded the Fleet.

Rissa was quiet in his head. As quiet as if she'd never been there to start with. He couldn't tell if she agreed with what he'd told Jossa or not. It wasn't the whole truth. It wasn't even most of the truth; but it was enough.

"Well." Jossa leaned forward so she could set her elbows on her knees. "That explains how you learned so much about the nobility."

Syrus decided she must have forgotten she was naked. He stared at her small breasts and nearly lost what she said next.

"I suspect, though, that if the Karukap had done a full DNA analysis when they took you on, they would have gotten rid of you completely."

Uh-huh. Like the Karukap didn't keep tabs on the political situation in the Empire. Just because none of the vamalkuog had managed a successful coup *so far* didn't mean they hadn't tried. His Savage background was probably the only thing that had saved him from being shackled to a throne and made a figurehead. However he'd wound up with Imperial blood, nobody in their right mind wanted an uncontrollable lunatic in charge.

"Especially given the fact that one of the oldest secrets of the Empire is that blood *is* everything." Jossa kept talking, oblivious to the thoughts going through his head.

He glared at her. Apparently she'd forgotten how she'd wound up in this situation to start with.

She glared back, but her shields didn't slip.

"Think you're forgetting the order of things around here," he told her. "Me Warlord. You Concubine."

"Exactly." Her voice held a lifetime of regret and hurt. Suddenly he wished he hadn't been so flip with his answer.

Rissa was still silent. It was starting to make him nervous.

He waited another second or so to see if Jossa planned to say anything else. When she didn't speak again, he waved at the control console and its screens. The bluish light showed green here and there, where the data feeds spat information. "Not sure what you're trying to do here. Especially since Delfi's still in the box."

Her shields wavered, then firmed. He couldn't make anything of the weakness. Hell, it could have been plain exhaustion. She pulled a synthcot cloth from an opening in the console and started wiping down the board. "There's a thing concubines knew," she said in a quiet voice. "And the immediate imperial family. I'm not sure who's aware of it now, what with the state of things.

"All government facilities were mandated to have back doors in the programming. Answerable only to the fuerrus and his bloodline." She waved a hand at the receptor for the blood sample and the pattern of needles in the palmar area. "And in certain locations, the concubines." Her teeth flashed. "Guards aren't effective if they can't work the locks."

He leaned back in his chair and took a breath. "So you're telling me I've got access to . . ." Syrus trailed off, not sure if he wanted to finish that thought.

"The Barbican keys were always yours for the taking. Still are." She tipped her head and squinted at the console. "There will be a record. But since I assume this place is getting destroyed anyway . . ." She shrugged and looked back at him.

He stared at the console. Then at his own hand. All the doors in the Galaxy. Well, the most important doors anyway. Open to him because of an accident of breeding.

That didn't mean he had to be happy about it.

Rissa still hadn't given her opinion. He kept waiting for it, like a satellite about to fall out of orbit. If she'd been alive, he wouldn't have had to wait at all. Fuck it anyway.

He didn't realize he'd bared his teeth until Jossa wrapped slim brown fingers around his wrist, pulling his hand into her lap. Now that she was touching him, he could feel her emotions again. No more bravado. Just a cold sort of determination, giving root to the wobbling rattle of her nerves as they buzzed their way over her skin.

He let her open his hand, her broken nails tracing the lines of his palm. "The ancients claimed they could tell your fortune by these," she murmured. "You know what I see?"

He raised an eyebrow at her. The corner of her mouth twisted. "The past. At some point, someone in the Imperial lineage sired a child on a nehkeh woman."

Some part of him, the part that remembered a childhood in the streets of an Ajiri planet, raged. His adult self knew better. It didn't matter which ancestor gave him which set of fucked-up genes. He was what he was.

"Or the daughter of a fuerrus wandered into the bad part of town." He said it mainly to see what sort of reaction he'd get. She laughed.

He growled and tried to take his hand back. Jossa pinned it between her knees. It actually sort of hurt. He hadn't realized how bony she was until just now.

"Oh stop," she told him when he growled again. The humor was back, for real now, bubbling against his skin and popping in little ticklish bursts. "We'd all be dead on the floor of that room if you didn't have *some* pride in where you came from.

"The fact that you're in line for the Imperial Throne." She looked up at him and shrugged. "Well, you'll get used to that eventually. Maybe, when the Fleet makes it to the Core, you can even use that to legitimize your rule. Who knows?"

The look in Quinn's eyes, sometimes. Iira and Oona's reaction when Kizen mentioned the redacted parts of his personnel file.

"I do suggest you get to work on it, though. Del and I won't be there to help."

"What?"

"Now who's asking questions?" She half smiled at him. Smug satisfaction oozed up his hand to join the humor. "We're not going back to the Fleet, and you can't make us." She picked up the torn scrap of his shirt from the console where she'd laid it, waggling it gently in front of his face. "They took our clothes with the rag covered in your semen. So this will have to do. There's a whole hangar of abandoned ships out there. We'll take one and leave. You fit with the Fleet like you're born to it. If you try to make us go back, we'll fight until it kills us."

He stared at her. She grinned. If she wasn't still in contact with him, he wouldn't have picked up on the fear and uncertainty still lurking behind those huge brown eyes.

He looked at his trapped hand and the knobby knees that pinned it. They were both of them bruised and bleeding. He'd heal soon. She'd look like this for days. Weeks, maybe. "Where will you go? Whole system's crawling with Fleet. Both Barbs are guarded. You make it through the shadow Barbican, there's a battlegroup sitting on the other side, waiting to come through and pound this place to bits. Or implode the Barb. Surprised they haven't done it already."

She wavered. He saw it. Felt it too. Then she set her jaw and glared at him. "What part of kill ourselves trying didn't you understand? Any chance is better than going back to that odavek adifek of a ship and spreading our legs for you."

He pulled his hand free of her knees and took her by the wrist. The fear in her surged. "Doesn't tell me why. Or how you plan to survive in the long run. You come back with me, I could keep you safe." He could try, at least. Like he had with his last batch of women. "You could have standing in the Fleet. Quinn pulls his head out, even he'd agree. Wouldn't need to be concubines." So they'd be what? Wives? Like Iira and Oona for Quinn?

At least they wouldn't be running loose in a universe they didn't belong to.

She tried to take her hand back and failed. He held her, sucked in as much of his sai as he could, and waited to see what she'd do when she wasn't being pushed. He could smell the sweat and dried blood. Could taste it, even. One heartbeat. Two deep breaths. She stared at the needles on the console, nails scraping his skin as she curled her fingers and breathed out uncertainty. Then fear. Then calm.

"You told me to think of why Del and I ran the first time. Do you remember?"

"Yes."

"We left to be free. To be ourselves and no one else's. Not whores to a fuerrus. Not the mothers of his children. Not the guards for his tomb. To be us. To find out who we were."

He sat back and stared at her. She followed him. After a moment, he realized that the tugging on fingers came from her, trying to get free. Free. Of him.

Oh go on, the voice in his head muttered. You know you're going to. You've got the worst impulse control of anyone I've ever met. Besides, she said the magic word.

And here I thought you were going to keep your big mouth shut, he snapped back.

No answer. Good enough for him. Before he could ask himself why, he slapped his palm down on the needle array, hissing as the tiny needles sank down past skin and into muscle. "Well, get the data chips then," he told Jossa. "We'll make two copies."

>>><<<

Iira was trying to pull the keypad off the wall when the door to the infirmary opened. She looked up, did a double take when she saw Jossa, and growled. Syrus pushed her back into the room before she could do anything violent. "Oona awake yet?"

"No milord," Iira replied. "The other one—"

A rain of He'la interrupted her and a bundle of joy shaped like Delfi lurched past them both, nearly bowling Jossa over. Syrus shook his head and kept his hand on the small of Iira's back. "Leave'm be."

"Milord." He'd only known a few women who could pack so much meaning into just one word. Iira was a mistress of the art.

"Here." He slapped a data chip into her hand. "Keys to the kingdom. Empire. Whatever the fuck you want to call it. Exactly what I came to get. Tell your husband that. Tell him if he tries to follow me, or sends anyone after me, or goes rooting around in the databanks for anything about me, I'll . . ." He stopped. "Well, I don't know what I'll do, but I'll figure something out. I'll sure as fuck kill anyone he has tailing me. Got that?"

"Milord? I don't understand." She didn't. For once, he had her completely off guard and confused. Too bad he wasn't going to stick around to savor the moment. And good for him he'd had Jossa show him how to lock all his records. At least on this base. If Quinn ever snapped out of his Frenzy, he wouldn't be able to get into any more information related to his warlord. Former warlord.

"I've had enough," he growled. "I let you psychos put the Helm on me. Give me the Fleet. And the minute I stuck my neck out for you, the whole thing fell to shit. I'm done, you hear? Tell your husband; tell your people. Find another warlord. This one's going back to what he likes best."

"And what's that, milord?" She drew herself up and stuck out her chin. She could be as pissy as she wanted to be. The heat she generated couldn't make a dent in his own emotions. He'd already put the call out to the Fleet, broadcasting the base's security vid of how Kizen had died. Along with their new orders to hold fire until someone told them otherwise. He planned to be out of comms range before they realized they'd been played.

"Running around the Galaxy making trouble." He turned on his heel and started back for the door, catching Jossa and Delfi between the shoulder blades with each hand. "C'mon. Before those assholes out there decide a vid recording isn't enough to prove Kizen's dead."

With Jossa squawking in surprise on one side, Delfi shouting in He'la on the other, and something like relief in his soul, he shoved them out the door and towards the hangar.

Epilogue -- Jossa

It's a pity about the temperament of Savages. The old saying about dropping the baby out a window holds true through adulthood. They're too hard to kill, and too hard to keep long term.
    -overheard in Officer's Mess

Jossa stood on the bridge in a scavenged shirt four sizes too big for her and ranted. "You just had to take a damaged boat! Thirty other ships in that hangar and you had to pick the same crippled heap we used in the first place. What were you thinking?" She glared at Syrus where he sat in the pilot's chair of the little ship, elbow deep in the guts of the control console.

He had a strip of dark fabric, shiny with blood, wrapped around one arm. His other arm, bare to the shoulder since the sleeve had been sacrificed for bandage purposes, was covered in tiny scratches and burns.

Another shower of sparks fell from the destroyed instrumentation in the ceiling. They landed in his hair and across his back in a glowing pattern of light. He didn't flinch, although Jossa thought she might have heard a growl.

Well, good. Let him hurt. This whole mess was his fault.

Jossa waited as he shoved the mass of wires back into the console and snapped the control panel in place. In the back of her mind, Delfi turned listlessly. She'd fallen hard after her initial burst of energy leaving the infirmary. Getting her to stay in the spare bunk had almost been too easy, but Jossa was glad Del was able to move at all. For now, she was happy to lay the sudden docility at the feet of such extensive treatment in the medunit.

Hidden motives would come in a day or so, if Del was still moving slow and staying quiet. Assuming they lived that long.

Del turned again. Jossa clamped down on her worry and speculation, shoving them in some dark corner of her brain where it couldn't escape. For now. She'd gotten sloppy while Del was in the coma. If she didn't regain some measure of control, she might get them both hurt. Or worse.

A trickle of wry humor mixed with just a touch of frustration brushed against her. Jossa looked up in surprise, just in time to see the tail end of a smile slip off Syrus's face. The former warlord watched her, arms crossed over his chest as he leaned back against the console.

"Yes?" she asked in the haughtiest voice she could manage. The fact that her words cracked in the middle didn't help things at all.

"So what now?" he asked once he'd gotten a second almost-smile under control.

Jossa stared. He was asking her that? *Now?* When he'd invited himself along to escape and taken over the whole operation? Now he wanted to know what she wanted to do? They were stuck on a ship that could barely hold air. Shot half to bits by the Fleet and further abused by being hopped through three consecutive Barbicans without ever leaving the grav shields. It was a miracle they weren't missing half their hull. And he wanted to know what she wanted to do next?

"Stay alive," she ground out. "Assuming life support keeps working."

One eyebrow crept up his forehead. "Well. Not very detailed, but I guess I can't really call you on that. Assume we live. Since you're not choosing death or freedom, there are options."

Jossa opened her mouth. Shut it. And glared at him.

His lips twitched, but he had enough decency to keep from mocking her outright. For about a minute. Then he broke, and his amusement washed over her like a warm, slightly effervescent wave as he shook his head and laughed. "You know, I've never met anyone who'll jump out an airlock without even *looking* for an eeva suit."

"Me!?" Jossa waved her arms at the bridge and the mess he'd made of it. "You said they wouldn't shoot at us! And they did! And then you—you!" She sputtered. How could he be so complacent? How could he value life, even his own, so little? He kept laughing at her.

"Only half of them were shooting at us. The other half were on our side." His face was serious again, but he hadn't shielded his emotions.

Jossa crossed her arms and glared. "If they were on our side, you'd think they would have made sure we were out of the crossfire."

And just like that, he sucked it all in, slammed the barriers up, and dropped into the chair. "Look," he said. "We can sit here and argue until we're blue in the face. Doesn't change facts. We got away. Three random Barbs I hopped us through. Without leaving the grav shields. Fleet can't know where we are. Neither can the Karukap, assuming they were sitting outside the grav shield of that first Barbican. Life support's working and we've got enough hull integrity to get us to a Customs base. Which, if the readouts on this system are right, should only be a couple days away. That gives us two problems. Food, and what to do next."

Delfi stirred again, coming out of her doze to find out what had her sousi so agitated. Jossa sucked in a breath and blew it out. She would not give Del a reason to worry. She would *not* pick up the piece of metal sitting next to the door and try to hit Syrus over the head with it. She *wouldn't*. She could control herself.

He didn't speak.

Jossa growled. "Fine. I don't have a plan. I've been more than a little preoccupied. I can say this about it though—it doesn't include *you*."

"Then you're a fucking idiot."

He said it in such a calm, conversational tone of voice that she had to stare at him for a second to realize exactly what he'd said.

"Excuse me!"

"Not your fault. You've been a little busy making sure Del stays breathing. But now that you're away from that fucking freak show you should probably—"

"You're the one who put me there to start with! And kept me prisoner! And demanded sex!"

"And you're the one who offered it up to me later!" Jossa never saw him move. One second he was in the pilot's chair, the next he had her by the shirt front, face inches from hers.

Jossa grabbed at Syrus's hands, fingers looking for nerve clusters and tender spots. He didn't move. Didn't even flinch.

"Don't you ever, *ever* blame me for how you handle your problems." Jossa's teeth clacked together as Syrus shook her once, hard. "You hear me?" His voice was a rasping growl in her ears. She could feel the heat of his anger as if he had no shields at all. Maybe he didn't. Maybe he'd lost his grip on them.

"You all but forced me into it," she snarled. "You threatened to kill Delfi!" She found his thumbnail and dug her own nails into its base. Still nothing.

"I just wanted you to stop fighting long enough to get us into the base. You started in with the sex."

Jossa glared at him. The ceiling was too low for him to lift her completely off the floor. Instead, she wobbled on her tiptoes. If she tried to kick him in the knee or stomp his instep, she'd have to give up her precarious hold on her balance.

"Now. You going to calm down and have a civil conversation? Because this time I *will* snap your neck. Delfi's in no shape to get here before that happens."

She glared at him, wondering if she could blast him with her own feelings fast enough to make any sort of difference. Unfortunately, all she had right now was anger. Counterproductive to say the least, considering what they'd just lived through.

"Fine," she said. "Would you *please* set me down?"

And just like that, his anger vanished. Syrus laughed and let go of her shirt. Jossa staggered a little before she caught her balance. "Thank you."

"You're welcome." He flashed a grin at her and sat back down. "See. Perfectly civil."

Jossa sighed. "Well, here I am. You're still in the vicinity; and barring the sudden rupture of the hull or a great and abiding desire on your part to take a walk without a suit . . ."

There a smile pulled at the warlord's lips. "Here you are. With no way to get rid of me."

"For now," Jossa said. "Once we dock, you may leave and find yourself someone else to torment."

His grip on his shields wavered, and something like outright mocking made its way out. He thought she was funny. Funny!

There was scorn in the mix too. He knew she was catching this. The half-smile on his face said that he'd let her feel it on purpose. Just not enough for her to get more than a taste of the emotions. A bare hint of what was going through his head.

Who taught this man to shield? The Uvlaku?

No. Don't ask questions like that. Don't wonder. You are going to land, kick him off the ship for co-opting *your* escape plan, and live your life without ever having to worry about what a Savage turned warlord turned fugitive might be thinking.

Yes. Good plan. There. It was a plan. She drew herself up "I am the one who decided to leave. You simply followed. Therefore, you can go find yourself a different ship."

One eyebrow climbed his forehead. "It's been three hundred years. You think the Barbican network is the same now as then? Assuming you can get this bucket fixed and learn to fly it."

"Delfi knows how to pilot. We can make our own repairs."

Syrus leaned forward. "She won't be in any shape to function on her own for weeks yet. Even if she could, I've got the masker. First time you log your DNA for something, half the system will land on your head.

"'Sides that, how do you plan to pay for repairs? Stock the ship? How will you pay the bills and get off whatever trash-heap satellite we wind up on? Same way you kept yourself and Delfi fed while you were on the run? Same way you found a berth on—"

"I thought we were having a civil conversation here." Jossa knew she shouldn't provoke him, but she didn't care. She took her anger, turned it to ice, and shoved it at him like a planetside cold front. He stiffened. She watched as goosebumps covered his bare arm.

Ha. Might be able to keep things in, but you're not as good at keeping them *out*, are you?

Then he was there again. Right in her face. The heat of his body evaporated the chill of her fury as if it had never been. His bulk pressed her back against the wall, his eyes burning with something she couldn't name. "Here is how this is going to go," he growled. "You won't try to kill me. Delfi won't try to kill me. I will find a ship that's not about to drop out of orbit. You want to leave? Go back to paying your way through life by spreading your legs for anyone with two credits to throw your way? That's fine. Your sousi won't last a day. She's only barely healed. Adrenaline got her out of that medunit and on the ship. You can't earn enough to feed yourselves and protect her too, and you know it.

"So. You can stick with me on the next ship as crew. We'll pick up a cargo and keep moving. The Gatekeepers and the Seps Coalition managed to hold on to independence since you went under. I have a few contacts there. So long as some other Branch of the Fleet doesn't hit that sector in the next year or so, we should be able to get past their Barbicans."

"A year! But—"

He clamped a hand over her mouth. His emotions went from a radiating presence to a searing brand in her mind, anger and frustration so mixed up that she couldn't tell which was which.

Was this the man he'd been *before*? Before everything with the Fleet? Or was this what they'd made him?

"No buts. This is your option. This is the chance I'm giving you."

Jossa tore at the hand over her mouth and stomped at his foot at the same time. He let go of her face. His hip caught hers and pinned her to the wall so she couldn't move.

"I was the one who decided to escape," Jossa snarled. "You weren't even thinking of leaving until you found me in that room!"

He shrugged. She could feel the movement of his body all the way to her toes. "Maybe, maybe not. Doesn't matter now, 'cause I *did* leave. Just remember. I'm the one who knows my way around here. I know what sort of places are safe, and which ones are going down in flaming glory because some fucker decided to make a try for the throne. You think you can make it through all that? Have at it."

"I won't have sex with you again."

Amusement. Real and warm as a blanket by the fire. He threw his head back and laughed. She could feel the length of his usik against her hip as it made its opinion of that declaration known.

"I mean it," she said through gritted teeth. "You can't make me. And you can't make Del either."

He shifted, grinding his pelvic bone into hers. His eyes were wrong though. They'd taken on a distant quality.

"And what about the Fleet? How long can we run before they find us again?" Get the subject off sex. Distract him, quickly!

Syrus refocused on her face and stepped back, hooking his thumbs in his belt loops. His shields were back, as strong as if he'd never dropped them at all. "Net was set out a fair ways in the first place," he said. "They'll take time to clear it first. And pacify the Border planets. Lot of Karukap out here. It'll take a while. Still plenty of systems between them and the center of the Empire. We'll have time, so long as we play things safe."

Safe. As if anything to do with this man would ever be safe.

::Still better than the alternative,:: Del said quietly.

"Alright! Alright." Jossa crossed her arms and glared at the former warlord. "We'll stay. You'll pay us as crew, once you find work. The *minute* you touch either one of us, we pull out your guts and use them to decorate the ship. Got it?"

He bared white teeth in a feral smile, then spat on one palm and held it out for her. Jossa looked at it. Looked at him. Then spat on her own hand and held it out.

As his long fingers engulfed her much smaller ones, she threw a prayer to the universe. Ancestors protect her. What was she agreeing to?

>>><<<<

Thank you for reading! Reviews are an author's lifeblood. Good, bad, or indifferent, I'd love it if you'd leave a review!

If you'd like to read more in the world of Devour the Stars sign up for my newsletter at: https://www.artseklektos.com/ml-landingpage and get a free short story

>Languages

HE'LA GLOSSARY

A NOTE ON HE'LA PRONUNCIATION:

He'la is a syllabic language. Most vowels are short. If they are doubled, in which case they are given the long pronunciation. I, for example. Mostly it is pronounced "ih". If it is seen as "ii", then it is pronounced "ee". Apostrophes have been added here and there, to indicate glottal stops or separate vowels where the form of the word means they'd otherwise be doubled. Go'o, for example, as seen below, would be "Go-oh"

A'lih pa'richo odeh lu kashezs ya'eks ajzs nihba?
    Why is he the only one with clothes on?

Dikoch kezs i'wehricks nih.
    Truth in death.

Gahtsylii a'liksii yahzi'ii neh. Gahtsylii wekkach dikoksii kaeshy nih. Jennia'yj nehkeh kaeshyj neh!
    I am going to get out of these, go up there, and kill him. Stupid barbarian!

I'jekkea'oks ysho'yj ekki uyrru jekkawyjks neh! Jephilli lu no ysho'yj —
    Don't you tell me what to do, Savage! You have no right to —

Jannudyj neh. Tahts aksyi'krys nih. Tsets lo'teks jekkehsaks ska'eks kasheks i'rhithaks nih. Kashyj kessacks o'zo I'kehaoks nih.
    Rape. Liked idea. Wanted to recondition and break and breed us. We fixed him.

R Coots

Jekkawyj neh! A'lih de'o niayj lu kidda'yjo ch zo'yj iya'zaks neh! Uksu lu zo'yj shavih zi we'ryj neh! Go'oyj lu zo'yj iuriweh fennao lu nuh zo'yj neh! Joss! A'apallih zotturyj nihba?

Bastard! May all your children be born with two heads! May your dick wither and fall off! May your seed dry up and poison all your women! Joss! What the hell?

Khe

Yes.

Larachah nih. Lujko'ksii yzo ykspuch esho, o'zo keha'oksii ekka uethga ykspuch esho nih.

Good. [If] we bring them you, we [can make a] deal with them.

Nehkeh

Wild, aggressive.

O'zo iike'ao nih.

We were.

Zhuzhu he'lao wessia'e kashyj. Okshua'e nih.

He knows big words. Imagine that.

Zhuzhuch nehkch kashe'yj i'innaks e'vah o'li neh!

You are the most disgusting man I've ever met!

High Navlad Glossary

A note on Navlad pronunciation:

Like He'la, High Navlad is syllabic. Vowels are sounded out individually, even when they are next to each other. U and O are usually given long sounds. E and A are short. If I is seen at the end of the word, it sounds like "ee", otherwise it is short.

Achek
>Ass; Literally: [morally] unclean anus.

Ajiri
>Agriculture, designation for Earth -like planets where people can live without artificial life support.

Antesab
>name of a solar system outside Hadra's Net

Asjokoj skatbitteogek
>Breeding bitches; Literally: [morally] unclean female dogs used for breeding.

Bajbar
>An animal genetically engineered to serve as underground guard for owners. Created using mostly badger and brown bear DNA.

Bajbarog
>Plural form of bajbar

Bittehek
>Bitch; Literally: [morally] unclean dog.

Chataf Kuchru lis Churus isk Fuerrus
>Formal title of the imperial harem's head concubine; Literally: Guardian concubine of the [worshipful] Emperor's household.

Ejiodiv do trubokoj

My responsibility; Literally: Mine to guide/lead.

Erlkonsab
Name of a solar system outside Hadra's Net

Etaevatoj bekig
Go back

Fikek
Fuck; Literally: [morally] unclean, illegitimate sex (likely to result in unclean child)

Fikeknuog
Fuckers

Fikekoj
Fucking

Fikek veltukov
Fucking hell; Literally: eternal exile to torturous, [morally] unclean, illegitimate sex.

Fuerrus
[worshipful] Emperor; Literally: Throne Keeper.

Fuerrus datevataf
Emperor's heir -apparent; Literally: One who'll be given the throne.

isk Churusimpir lis Kuchrog lis isk Fuerrus
Formal name for the Emperor's harem; Literally: The [unmarried] women belonging to [worshipful] Emperor's household, used for breeding legitimate children.

Isloste
Imperial fleet commander.

Islosteog

Plural of isloste.

Jenmal
Genetically engineered animal.

Jikujoj
Attack.

Jossalyn lis Churus isk Fuerrus
Jossalyn of the household of the [worshipful] Emperor, a formal title.

Karukap
Military; Literally: strong allies.

Kemvate
A military rank, in charge of all the forces in a solar system.

Kizarard
Ruler of a sector.

Kovavek
Commerce, designation for planets requiring life support systems before they can be settled. Usually used for gathering and processing of various resources.

Kuchek
[Morally unclean] concubine.

Kuchru
An [unmarried] woman used to breed legitimate children, e.g., a concubine.

Kuchruog lis isk Fuerrus
formal name for the Emperor's concubines.

Kuchruog
plural of concubine

lis Disen isk Fuerrus
Formal name of the Emperor's family.

Lozo
A kind of fruit.

Ludesab
A solar system on the imperial Border.

Maruste
Marks on back projected by nanites in blood, showing lineage, place of origin, trade, marriage, children, and any other pertinent information; Literally: Blood rank.

Mechute
An imperial military rank, middling high in the chain of command.

Mechute lis Tova af Mitachte
Syrus's full formal name and rank; Mechute of [the House of] Thorn Moon.

Nehkeh
Subhuman, bestial, [untameable] savage.

Odavek
Shit; Literally: [morally unclean] excrement.

Odavek adifek
Shithole; Literally: hole for [morally unclean] excrement.

Oloteoj Azatlvl
Open Blossom; Literally: Opening Blossom.

Oloteoj duparodivek tukavaf kamogek
Open your cursed eyes; Literally: You [morally unclean person], open your cursed, unclean eyes.

Rard
Honorific/title to denote or address nobility

Rardog
Plural of Rard

Sai
Mental ability/talent

Sar
honorific/suffix to denote military or address military personnel

Sousi
Soul sibling, soul bonded

Svis Konanuog
Star Eaters; Literally: Those who consume stars.

Tukovafek
Damned; Literally: exiled/tortured.

Uvlaku

Military black-ops; Literally: Ghosts, undead.

Vamalkul
 Third highest military rank, Literally: Commander of a Quadrant [of the Empire]

Vamalkuog
 Commander of an Imperial quadrant. Third highest rank.

Vundate
 Military rank. Lowest that might command a 'star cluster' of units.

KUCHEN FLEET GLOSSARY

A NOTE ON KUCHEN PRONUNCIATION:

Like the High Navlad, Kuchen is syllabic. If a vowel starts a word, it is likely pronounced with the long sound. Aye, instead of Ah, for example. Otherwise, the vowels are short and pronounced individually if they occur in succession.

Anined
    Planetary governor, strongest on the planet

Ataorl Banso
    Fifth Branch

Edde Belo
    Leading Outgrowth

Har izrumeor
    Star sucking

Icotusorl
    False born, illegitimate.

Kuchen
    War

Letten
    The strongest member of the smallest Kuchen military unit.

Oiyao
    Cunt; Literally: Oyster.

Ralen
    Strongest member of the largest Kuchen military unit.

Ralenen
    Plural of Ralen.

Tech -Ataoch
　　Fifth-rank tech.

Turan
　　Trunk.

ACKNOWLEDGEMENTS

I grew up in a creative household. Music, art, baking (ok, that's chemistry too). I would have never come this far without the encouragement of my parents. Love you! And my husband, who's been there as I cried, occasionally bled, and clawed my way over the finish line of publishing. Love you too, more than you know.

To all the friends who've supported me, here's all the thanks I can give. To everyone in the Holt, the Alder Cave Academy, and the Brain Health Chatz. For all the support and virtual applications of booze, chocolate and afghans, thank you. To the folks in the Indiepreneur group and the WEL Accountability server, all the appreciation.

Thanks to Sheila, for cackling with me as I hammered out the initial ideas. To Rabbit and her mom for answering my awkward questions. Mom, for medical answers to questions that made you go "Whut?" And to Blair, who so generously offered to look over my fight scenes (I kept adding more, whoops!) and make sure I didn't have feet flying up near the ceiling and that the people who should be dead actually died.

And most of all, God. I'm not sure why I've got the imagination I do, but all thanks and praise.

About the Author

R Coots has been telling stories since the days of imaginary friends. Not serious until a two-week power outage meant that a pencil and paper were the only forms of entertainment, there have been several detours along the roads of comics, animation, and finally the written word. Aided by two neurotic dogs, a murderous cat, and a very down-to-earth husband, she exorcises the imaginary people in her head by means of art and writing, getting them out on paper so she can share them with the world.

Feel free to stop by my site for more on this universe, including art, blog posts, and the occasional bit of character silliness:

https://www.artseklektos.com